WHAT I SAW ON
THE HIBISCUS AIRSHIP

WHAT I SAW ON THE HIBISCUS AIRSHIP

C. L. HENG

PARTRIDGE

To order additional copies of this book, contact
Toll Free 800 101 2657 (Singapore)
Toll Free 1 800 81 7340 (Malaysia)
orders.singapore@partridgepublishing.com

www.partridgepublishing.com/singapore

Contents

Chapter 1

Paradise

Big and bulky, with the strength of a thousand men, the red airship flies. As it drags itself through the skies of Bumi, the ship's eight huge, rusty propellers rotate, and white steam sputters behind it. The airship hovers through windless nights with the determination of a human spirit, boundless and passionate, in search of children who misbehave. As children slumber, long, chilling claws snag their tiny bodies up to the airship's hulls, where they will never see their parents ever again. Thus, the tale of the *Hibiscus Airship* was sung. Every child of Bumi listened to that fable with awe and fear. Some thought of it as a monster, while some with curious minds expected an adventure of pirates, free from the mundane plodding of a normal life.

The tale of the *Hibiscus Airship* covered the entire breadth of history. It gave me a resolve to write my own tale for the times. I was an irrational man who had lost his innocence to the deathly hollow of reality and adulthood. A passionate life had been foregone to satisfy the drudges of society, and I allowed myself to mingle in a discoloured hope of worship. It was a precious mission to preserve my innocence and let it continue to burn like Roman candles far into the twilight of our eternal youth.

My tale began with the birth of Arla, a girl who was one of the curious ones.

Far across the distance through the glimmering lights of Bumi's regal concrete jungle rests nature's untouched, exotic beauty. Respect for the tall, curvy trees bent in ridiculous shapes had been the tradition and culture of the local populace. This was a religious dedication for the preservation of inanimate life, for the lives of generations to come, and for the flurry of lively imaginations that would dominate its playful fields before evenfall. And it was in the starry heavens of a midsummer's night after the celebration of a birthday that pain orchestrated a symphony of melody through the burning and ready body of Mrs Jala Hibby. Permission to bring a deserving life into a deserving world brought her will and tears that only mothers could understand. Her long, soft screams echoed through halls until the songful cries of youth emerged from her womb. Her will gave her the courage to hold her child for the first time, and her will allowed her weak lips to utter the most beautiful words she had ever known: "My dear, dear child, Arla."

"What a beauty she will be, my love," said Mr Dara Hibby. "Strong expectations will be entrusted upon her. Just look at her eyes. She will grow to be my inspiration. I have never been more sure in my life."

Mrs Hibby struggled to move her hand to touch the delicate cheeks of her child. Mr Dara Hibby constantly wiped her wet, sweaty brow. It was the only thing he could do to ensure her comfort.

Mrs Hibby whispered, "She has your nose, my dear. And she has my lips." Then she addressed her child, "What a fortunate life you will live, my dear, dear, sweet Arla. I am sorry for crying. You are the most beautiful thing I have ever seen. You shall know of our world and our customs. You will know of the loving care people will show and the loving embrace of our Holy Heavenly Flower." She turned to her husband. "Come now, my love. Let us pray for our seed to blossom with a future."

"All right, just this once," Dara said. He knelt, opened his palms to face the sky, and begged for a wish he needed to fulfil. They recited together the words they had come to know: "Light of my life, darkness of my doom, shelter us. We give praise for Your red petals to lay over us. We give thanks for the eternal blessing You have endowed upon us. Hear my yearnings for a tomorrow of wilful delight, and guide us and bring us more fortune for tomorrow. Bring us more, and we shall love You with all our hearts and desires. Help us to live our lives like You envisioned and bring—"

"My dear, why did you stop?" said Mrs Hibby when Mr Hibby suddenly could not continue.

Dara was hesitant to utter the words he did not believe. He thought of himself as a person of a different kind: a man of curiosity and dedication. He would not accept words that would place his destiny in the hands of another being, especially one nobody could see. He coughed and silently pleaded to his wife, looking down upon his rough and wearied hands to relieve himself of melancholy. Under the hope of light radiated from Arla's eyes did he find solace to mutter the last words his wife wanted to hear: "All right, please proceed."

The midwife demanded that Jala must rest and recover after her long ordeal. The warm, woolly cotton covers of the birthing chamber gave a warm comfort to Dara when he slept on a couch next to Jala, who was still awake and staring with motherly love at her little darling. Dara stood up and paced through the blue-hued room to reach for a glass of water. He poured himself a pint of what was believed to have been blessed by the Heavenly Flower herself: a gift sent by Jala's friends at her party. "You will feel Her run through your veins, Jala," her friend said. "You will be protected by Her embrace, as our world depends on Her."

And with that thought, Dara poured another for himself. With a wholesome swig, he woke to the bright lights of Paradise.

He saw a whole new generation mingling and roaming the lively streets below and thought how much Bumi had changed after the era of Enlightenment. Neon lights had replaced oil lamps, horses of iron had replaced horses of flesh, concrete walls had replaced wooden walls – all the while the crime rate had dropped to almost nothing.

Dara remembered his youth when struggling was a daily necessity; he remembered how he had scrambled and fought with other children for firewood; he remembered the dangerous times and how fear had held him. Yet, somehow, he knew hope would remain. So he turned back to see his wife staring at Arla, knowing his daughter would have the hope Dara always wanted. He walked surely and said, "I will be outside. Fresh air will help me think. Don't stay up for me. Not to worry. I won't be long."

He put on his moccasins and marched out with vigour.

I am a father now were the words that ran through his head. He wasn't a boy anymore, and he could not afford to be. He lifted his umbrella higher as he stared up into the dark skies and the dripping rain tip-tapped upon his skin. "The season has arrived. The gardens will flourish, and food will be plenty. I must work harder now."

Dara continued walking on the same cobbled street. Iron horses galloped next to him, towing a carriage of privileged women who, in their gallant frocks, were sipping tea and discussing their latest gossip. The driver leaned over to listen and maybe strike up a conversation that might lead to more. The horses galloped on, lifeless and stubborn.

"How do you do, sir? How can I help with cleaning your shoes?" said the cobbler. "I will polish them and make them the best shoes you ever wore. Please help me, sir. Nobody wants to have shoes polished anymore."

"I am sorry, old man. But I do not need my shoes polished."

"Please, sir. I have children to feed."

"Do not worry. Tomorrow will be a new day for harvesting. The government will authorize the new Equality Act that shall make all of us equals. You won't have to polish shoes anymore."

"If I can survive until tomorrow … we'll see."

Dara smiled at the old man and tossed him a white piece of paper covered with red markings. "Here. Use this to get some food for your family. It should be enough until tomorrow comes."

"Bless the Heavenly Flower! Thank you!" said the old man in a joyous tone. His aging expression turned happy, and for a moment, he remembered the kindness people still possessed.

Down the road, Dara came across a builder. Her strong stature, merged with years of experience, haunted her eyes as she turned to Dara. "Sorry, gent. This area is closed for a while. We are moving in some heavy equipment."

"No worries," said Dara as he tipped his head in a gentleman's bow. "How is work progressing?"

"Great! New ideas and new machines make our work easier. We will live a better life, I guarantee. I am happy, and my family are happy."

Dara smiled and nodded. "Please proceed. I will use another way around. Be careful."

The yellow lines restricting access into the work area led Dara into a small alleyway behind a grocer's store. The bins were filled with rubbish and many unmentionables. The alleyway reeked of decay, and flowing sewage seeped up from the ground. Filthy rats scattered about proclaiming their right to own that particular alleyway, and Dara was intruding upon their home.

As Dara hop scotched his way to the other side, he realized the rats were not the only occupants of the alley. A young woman, dishevelled through hardship and tragedy, held on to her infant, which was wrapped in white cloth. The woman was terrified as Dara asked, "Are you all right, young lady?"

"Get away from me. Do not touch me!"

"Calm down. I am here to help. What is the matter?" Dara reached out with his hands and pulled down the cloth covering the infant's face. "Is your child all right?"

Before he could check on the infant, the mother pulled away and screamed. "I said get away from me! I don't know who you are and—"

"Over here! She is over here!"

From around the corner came two men wearing uniforms bearing the seal of the government. They ran and violently arrested the young woman. She lost her grip, and her child fell to the ground. She struggled to reach for her babe. "Wait! My child! Please help him!"

"Bova Trala, You are guilty of thievery and malevolence. You are to be sent to the dungeon at once. Your sentence shall be known tomorrow," said a third officer of the law, who had followed the first two. His bulky exterior suggested a man of immense strength. "Put her into the back, boys, and off you go."

Dara was shocked at the whole scene of sudden drama. He quickly bent down and picked up her child from the filthy ground. As he pulled back the white cloth covering the babe's face, Dara was sullen. He expected movement or at the least crying. The child was as calm as the monsoon winds of the Pasir Lands. Dara knew Death had claimed a life that night, and he was afraid it wouldn't be the last. "*You! Officer!* This child needs help!" commanded Dara as he held on to the man's monstrous arm. "This baby needs to get to the Healing Chamber."

The guard turned and stared at Dara intensively as if he was being interrogated. "What is your name? What relationship do you have with this particular woman?"

"Nothing! She was in need of help, and I was just coming around the corner to offer her assistance! Look at her child. Please take him to the Healing Chamber." Dara begged as much as he possibly could with the man who wore a huge tag pinned across his chest that proclaimed that his name was Rizal.

"Bun! Come over here! Get the tot out of here, and quick," commanded Rizal with a sadistic malicious grin while he stared at Dara. Dara felt his whole heart and soul sink into a dark pit. Rizal was the embodiment of evil, he thought.

Rizal turned back onto Dara once again and said, "Go home, fellow Paradisian. It is a night on which you should not be out and about. Return to your family. Changes are happening all around Paradise. Be safe."

"Wait! What changes?" asked Dara, but it was too late for an answer. Rizal had left as fast as he had come in, efficient and merciless. Dara walked on and returned to the main street. He blissfully ignored the chaos that exploded around him. People covered in slime and dirt ran away from the guards while children cried and became homeless. Dara knew of it but chose to stay on his walk. He was a father, and there was no need to put himself in danger. He needed to think of Arla's welfare. Who was going to support his newborn if he ended up in the dungeon? Arla must come first; there was so much compassion and goodness in their world he wanted to show her.

"Well, well, well!" a black-haired man greeted Dara.

"Oh ... my, Penn? Is it really you?" said a surprised Dara, who had been looking down on the cobblestones as he walked. He had not noticed his friend, Penn, in front of him until they were literally chest to chest. Dara's stature was short compared to his friend's. But, as they say in Paradise, whatever was short makes up for it in width.

"How long has it been, Dara? Still working at the Garden?"

"Yes, Penn. I am still working at the Garden. Making ends meet you see, with everything happening around us. I have a daughter now."

"Splendid news! We obviously need to have a chat. Come! I'll buy you a drink, if you have the time to spare."

Dara was hesitant to go with Penn, for his mind was focused on his family. He wanted to return to their embrace, but somehow an unknown blood bond he'd once had with Penn pulled him towards the Iron Mare. He knew he needed to talk with Penn, and wondered if maybe Penn could understand the dilemma he faced. With a renewed belief that Arla and Jala were safe in the Birthing Chamber, Dara joined Penn.

The Iron Mare was unusually filled with customers. Chatter and banter crammed the room like firecrackers bustling during a New Year's celebration. With Penn leading the way, Dara squeezed and dodged through walls of human mass as if he was just swimming through. Dara's wider body, however, required him to gently push people away to create a path, apologetically. As they sat in a small corner of the room, away from the rumblings at the bar, Penn took off his jacket and officially reached out his hand to shake Dara's. "It has been a while."

They nodded in acknowledgement, and Penn raised his hand for the waitress. Dara felt awkward when meeting an old friend he had not seen for ages. He did not know where he had left Penn in his life. Was he the same boy, or had he changed? Dara avoided making eye contact as he turned to observe the comings and goings of the Iron Mare. The place was lit with a warm tinge of orange yellow that gave off a comfortable ambience. Scratches and spills on the wooden floor divulged a long history of many generations. Peculiar mementoes cluttered the walls in no organized theme, but were displayed in a relatively organized grid. The more Dara looked at them, the more they resonated with him. No words were needed, just the feeling. At the bar, joyous laughter drowned the room with happiness. People talked about possibilities and opportunities with equal rights, and about upcoming better lives for their families while swigging entire pints of lager down their throats. The more Dara looked at them, they more he saw them as hogs – big, gluttonous hogs. He turned back to Penn who had been staring at him since they sat down, which made Dara felt even more awkward.

"What is it?" asked Dara as his eyes darted up and down to find anything amiss. "Do I have something in my hair?"

"Still the insecure sort, hmm? My, you haven't change one bit, have you?" said Penn. "Last time I saw you we were at the Garden at a young age, remember?"

"Oh yes. I remember yes … the Garden," replied Dara in a meek sort of way. He did not remember one bit at all. After realizing his lie, Dara apologetically said, "I am sorry, Penn. I don't exactly remember."

"Well, what do you remember then?"

"Besides the fact that we used to be best friends, I don't really remember anything else. This is odd, even for me. I don't usually forget these sorts of things."

"I see," uttered Penn as he looked up at the sky through the window. It was raining cats and dogs. "Doesn't matter, Dara. People hardly remember their childhood, and they remember even less as they grow up. Everybody is so much in a hurry nowadays they don't really know what's essential. Don't worry. It does not matter. We need to be in the present, so tell me! Tell me your story! How did you end up with a daughter?"

Dara began relating a long, laid-out script of what he had done and what he had achieved. He praised the fortunes bestowed on him because the government had given him an opportunity to lead a fortunate life. He thanked the Heavenly Flower for giving him a daughter, and he eventually raised his glass in a toast. He even began to talk about how the world would be a better place the next day.

"Is that what you believe, Dara?"

"Err … Yes, Penn. What made you ask?"

"Then this conversation is going to be boring indeed."

"Excuse me?"

"You heard me, Dara. I was your best friend. This is not how you used to think. You are better than this. I know you are just putting on an act. I am different, Dara. Tell me your real story."

Dara was overwhelmed by a sudden need to come clean with his old friend. The dreaded awkwardness he experienced dissipated into smoke. Dara gathered his thoughts in brief meditation and spoke with a voice of certainty and sincerity. "It was a warm day in the afternoon, Penn. The sun was high, and I was ploughing the lands of the Garden. It was eight years after I last saw you. I worked hard, and my hands were tired. I had a purpose, and it made me happy. Growing the food for the people of Bumi was a purpose I was most happy to have been given. Anyway, so there I was, working my way through the day, when I saw the most beautiful lady I had ever seen. She was clad in her work attire but covered with a clear, white silk cloth to protect her against the sun. She did not see me that time. But the encounter bewitched me in so many ways. It was a memory I cherish to this day."

"Yes, yes I see. You are blushing by the way."

"What? Really?"

"Joking, Dara. Please proceed. How did you two eventually meet?"

"The Harvest Festival. Bright decorative lights painted the evening with a festive mood. I went at the request of Davi, a work colleague of mine. He and I wore our best attire and tried our luck at the Harvest Dance where we got to charm our future significant others. My, my, was I nervous! The sheer enormity of the dance floor was enough to scare me away. You've experienced that before?"

Penn nodded. He was smiling at sheer delight of a good story.

Dara continued, "I was standing at a corner when I became mesmerized by the beauty of a lone lady. She looked lovely, just like the Heavenly Flower. The girl was waiting to be invited to dance, but no one took notice of her. I knew I had to ask her to be my dance partner. I steeled my resolve and approached her across the grassy floor. 'May I have this dance?' I asked. She looked at me in bewilderment as she stared at my outreached palm. When our eyes met, her slight gentle ripple of a smile struck my heart. 'Yes, but only if you take off your shoes,' she said. We danced barefoot with the wisps of grass tickling between our toes under the starlit night sky. It was the best dance I ever had."

Dara was starting to get restless as he took a sip from the drink the waitress had given him. Neither of the men had realized the waitress had arrived with their drinks. Dara took a deep breath and proceeded. "After the dance, I invited her to a bonfire gathering in the Garden. We listened to melodies sung by a fiery songstress of bygone days and tough days to come. Some danced on while some watched, lying on the grassy lands of the Garden smoking colitas. She had gone to get drinks, and when she returned, I noticed more. Her silk-black hair was loose on her shoulders, and it lit up under the sparks of a nearby fire. Her white gown swayed under the breath of the night, meticulously suggesting her womanly curves. 'Hi,' she said.

"We sat and spoke from our hearts. Flirtatious suggestions pounded each sentence into my heart, and never before had I understood the definitions of romance and desire. They were manifested in Jala. As they say, one thing led to another, and I invited her for a stroll to the edge of the Garden. Nervousness crept through my bones like a slithering snake as I stuttered. Under the starry constellations of the night sky, I showed her the secrets the Garden hid. At the jagged trees and ferns where the fireflies nested against the evening winds, Jala grabbed my hand. 'What is the matter, Dara? You look nervous,' she said. She knew I was turning mad with her hands on mine. I swore she could feel the sweat of my shame drenching my palms. Then, with her other hand, she lifted my chin and stared at me, asking again. 'I hope you don't find this weird.'

Her puppy-brown eyes conveyed signs of worry and intense curiosity as she wanted to know what my next move would be. My resistance to those soulful eyes had completely drowned. I grabbed her waist and pulled her soft body against mine until our heartbeats were as one as they sorely yearned for one another. Her body and mine melted together as I encased her completely within my firm embrace, and with her lips so close to mine, I felt every breath she made. With her palms flat against my chest, I whispered to her as I grinned, 'Not weird at all.'

"With clenched fists, Jala raised her feet like a dancer to give me a quick peck on my lips. By that time, I knew we could not settle for a peck. I lifted her, and we finally kissed under a thunderous excitement that bewildered all my senses. We were like Roman candles burning madly through the milky way of the Universe, knowing for sure in our lives that we were truly living."

Dara was looking at his own reflection in the window. The rain fell silently as he took another sip of lager. "And so, the rest is history. We got married, and we have lived together ever since. Our new adventure begins now with the birth of our daughter, Arla."

"Splendid story, Dara! I am amazed. It was probably the best I have heard in years!" said Penn as he clapped with excited splendour. "You captivated my curiosity, and you told your story with conviction. A hard quality to find nowadays."

"Thank you, Penn. You haven't touched your lager, by the way."

"Hahaha. My apologies, Dara. I was so intrigued by your story I lost sight of my lager. But no matter! It will now taste all the better!"

"What about your story, Penn? I have to apologize. I drifted off with my own story and never gave you the opportunity to tell yours."

"No need to apologize, my friend. Just a curious question though, Dara. What Milky Way of the Universe were you talking about anyway? I mean, what is that?"

Dara looked stunned as he wondered why he said those particular words. They meant nothing to him, but he had used them to describe a wonderful memory he had.

"It was just an expression, Penn. Nothing to be curious about."

"Well, look around, Dara. Do you know of anyone who knows those words you used a moment ago? Do you remember your fellow scholars or your teachers mentioning those words?"

"No, Penn. It was something I made up. It sounded nice; that's all."

"Oh no, Dara. It was not something you made up. It was a memory of something you once knew. Tell me, do you remember why we were at the Garden on the day we last met?"

"As I said, Penn, I do not remember."

"Is it because you don't remember, or is it something you chose to ignore? Think, my friend."

"Penn, this is getting a little annoying. I just wanted to have a chat, and now I think I should be leaving and heading back to my family." Dara rose from his seat and headed to pay at the bar. Before he could reach to his pocket, Penn raised his arm and stopped him.

"Wait. I will pay. It is the least I can do." Dara nodded.

As Penn and Dara walked out to the open street in the cold wet night, Dara reached out his hand to Penn for a handshake. They shook like acquaintances who would never meet again. When Dara walked off in the opposite direction, Penn murmured. "Hey, Dara!"

Dara turned to look back at Penn, who crossed his arm behind his back. "What is it?"

"Do you remember the story of the *Hibiscus Airship*?"

Dara stood still.

Chapter 2

A Clockwork Life

The rising sun brought a glorious morning. The clock ticked away on its own, measuring the passage of time. Curtains fluttered as the morning breeze made its way through the window, allowing light and tender shadows to dance across the wooden floor. Dara was in bed waking to the most beautiful woman he had ever known. He woke on his side of the bed with the precision of a sneaky thief, trying not to wake Jala. The smooth rays of the rising sun reflected from her glowing complexion and mesmerised Dara's heart, and he felt nothing but love and admiration. He decided to lie back down to watch her until she, too, opened her eyes. It wasn't long before she woke. Jala knew the day had started, and her lover was eager to begin the day. But both of them remained still, staring each other with amorous eyes as they had done on the first day of their romantic story. They said nothing, but knew what was meant.

"Morning," whispered Dara in a quiet, jovial tone, the loveliest whisper of them all. "You look absolutely beautiful."

Jala smiled in return, revealing her innocent dimples that melted Dara's spirit. It was a subtle sign that all fears were thrown aside, so great passionate love could be made again.

They came close to each other, skimming closer and closer until they felt each other's heartbeats. Their hearts danced at an unusual rate, which startled them both. They wondered if it was Death they felt. But with each touch they gave, they knew each beat the heart skipped was a royal call that they were alive. They were present in their room, and they felt each other's presence. The future held nothing, and the past haunted no more. It was the two of them against the world. "I love you so much. The father of my child, the man of my life, and the gentleman of my soul. I love you so …" thus sang Jala and they kissed.

"Mommy! Wake up!"

Dara and Jala were in another chapter of their lives together. And as all great lovers eventually experience, there was another to share that love. With a burst of energy and vigour, Arla came storming in and jumped on the bed, demanding the attention she deserved for the day. Dara lifted Arla and tickled her. "Daddy!" Laughter burst out of her adorable cheeks, and she snuggled against her father's hand. "Daddy! Daddy! I dreamt of finding treasure last night. I almost had it, but it was too late. I woke up!" Arla pouted with a sad face, crossing her arms like a typical child having a playful tantrum.

"Sorry to hear about that, my child," said Jala as she squeezed the child's cherry-pink cheeks. Arla burst into smiles all over again. She was a cheerful bundle of joy, and that joy was infectious.

Dara couldn't stop smiling himself. "Tell me, young explorer, how did your journey begin? I am absolutely curious and craving to know!" begged Dara light-heartedly. Arla beamed with more delight as she began telling her story, pausing occasionally as she tried to catch her breath. For her, it was as if time itself had stolen away her moment to tell an epic tale, while Jala made humorous faces of excitement and gasps at every moment of suspense. Dara wanted nothing more than to ask time to slow down so he could cherish a magical minute.

"And that was how I defeated a monster!" Arla took a deep breath and let it all out in one fell swoop. She bowed to her only two proud audience members and crashed to the bed.

"Oh no little one!" said Jala. "You are not going to bed. You are going to head to the bathroom and get ready for school."

"Oh no. Mooooommmmyyyy! Just a little while longggggeeeerrrr."

"Oh no, darling. Not any longer. You are already late. Now get into the bathroom and brush your teeth!"

"Erghhhhh … Okay!" whined Arla, and she dragged her feet with every step she took.

Dara and Jala shook their heads as they acknowledged the tough challenge they would face together when Arla became a teenager. They shuddered at the thought.

"All right, dear. Let's start the day, shall we?" Dara smiled.

The radio played the uplifting tune of Bumi's patriotic song. Dara put on his white coverall. It had a collar and it zipped from his neck to his groin. It was fairly comfortable attire. He, Jala, and Arla walked to their door and wished each other a wonderful day. "Come back to me tonight and tell me stories," whispered Jala into Dara's sensitive ears. "Of course I will, my love," he replied, staring dreamily into her eyes. Jala picked up Arla and headed out of their apartment. After locking the apartment door, she walked to the elevator as Dara followed. The corridor they walked on was made entirely of glass – a strong glass invented during the Era of Enlightenment. In fact, most buildings in Paradise were made of that fascinating glass. It was the discovery of this material that had propelled the people of Bumi into a new standard of living. Brand new concepts of architecture emulated the Paradisians' spirit and courage. Paradisians no longer lived in shanty shacks made of second-grade wood. They lived in luxury and style, all grateful to the Forlorn's political policies that united scientific discovery and social altruism. Everybody in Paradise was free from poverty and travail. It was the grandest achievement in Bumi's history.

Their elevators were also a peculiar sort. They did not just take occupants from their homes to the ground floor. The elevators were actually a form of transportation that carried people from one part of Paradise to the other. Thanks to a scientific discovery of an infinite energy source called the Ketuhanan, transportation was free of charge. "All right, Arla, say bye-bye to Daddy."

"Bye Daddyyyy. I will miss you."

"Goodbye, my little angel. See you tonight. Mommy will cook us something nice, won't she?"

Arla winked and gave her dad a thumbs up.

"All right, here comes my ride. Have a great day, my darlings."

"Daddy! Wait!"

"What is it, Arla?" Dara knelt down as his daughter grabbed his head to mutter a secret into his ear: "Remember to buy her flowers, Daddy."

Dara nodded in agreement to a secret that was not quite a secret. Jala smiled and played along with their whole innocent scheme. Dara stood up and waved as he entered another elevator in which other occupants on their way to work. The elevator shot down while Jala and Arla continued to wave downwards at an endless arrangement of transport tubes stacked on top one another. In a second or two, Dara was lost in a heap of other elevators that contained workers wearing the same attire he wore.

Paradise had turned into a thriving city where everyone led a satisfying life. The streets were painted silvery white, and residents could see their own reflections as they walked. The buildings were painted white, and everything was spotless and clean. Grand motorized horses galloped with more grace than the past horses of flesh had ever displayed. They still carried elegant, posh ladies and gents in their fashionable frocks and suits. There were no hints of Paradise's poor past – no beggars, no desperate street performers, no shoe shiners. Everyone walking in the streets wore coveralls that were colour coded, each colour designating a different profession in Bumi's society. Wearing red meant you were an engineer; blue meant you were a medical worker; white meant you were part of the agricultural work force; yellow meant you were a government official. Red, blue, white and yellow – all were the colours of progress and development. They were the colours of the Forlorn. In Paradise's pristine, clean white image, only the Forlorn's flags coloured the city, and they could be seen almost everywhere.

"Coffee. I need coffee," muttered Dara as he tried to move around subtly with other passengers. He needed more room to breathe due to his claustrophobic tendencies. "Don't we all, Dara my friend." Dara was surprised by the sudden utterance of his name. He'd never heard his name mentioned in an elevator before. It was a place where people were together, but at the same time, it was a vacuum where no human interaction usually took place. Dara looked around to spot the person who had called him "friend". He was greeted only by the sound of silence. All the passengers were connected to their data pads, staring blindly at small screens for their latest dose of Paradise's theatrical and unnecessary melodrama. Dara had never understood how the evolution of Paradisian's desire for living companionship had turned into a desire for self-doubting solitude.

"Did somebody mention my name? Hello?"

"Hello," said the voice in return.

"What is this? Show yourself like a true gentleman."

"I am afraid I cannot."

"Why is that?"

"Because I am not in the elevator with you."

Dara's attention and curiosity began to peak as he knew somebody was manipulating the elevator's speakers. He gave one more look around. "I look like a fool talking to myself."

"Since when do you care of what others think of you, Dara? Besides, those people wouldn't even know if the Heavenly Flower herself was on board."

"Right. That makes the most absolute sense. This seems to be the most impressive joke I have seen so far."

"Joke? You think this is a joke? Why is that?"

"Why? Because things would have been simpler if you could have just faced me and talked and not spoken through some clever trickery."

A minute of silence echoed. Dara became impatient. "What do you want from me, trickster?"

"Very simple. I want you to not go to work today. I want you to meet me at the Temple of the Red Flower."

"What? No. I can't just not work today. I am needed to finish replanting seeds for the next Harvesting Season. I can't just leave my work like that."

"Tell me, Dara. Why do you want to work today?"

"I really do not know how to reply. I am not living in some fantasy world as you seem to be doing. I have responsibilities, and I do love what I do. And who says I am blindly following? My life is the definition of my own actions. I work because I enjoy it, and I have a purpose to ensure the people of Bumi have food," stressed Dara as he emphasized his point on his right palm, using his left-hand finger. Dara was a supervisor at the cabbage department of the Gardens. He was to coordinate replanting efforts for the next Harvesting Season. He was important to people, according to what people often told him.

"You don't remember anything at all, do you? I guess I'll have to wake you from the fear that consumes you."

"What are you babbling about? What fear? Do you see any fear in Paradise? The place is the definition of peace. War is over!"

"Fear comes in many forms, Dara. Your fear comes in the form of ignorance and stubbornness. Just come," said the voice as the speakers went offline. Dara heard nothing again except the chewing sounds of a fellow worker next to him. She was completely unaware of the event that had just transpired. Dara thought the voice he'd heard was rude, but familiar. He was furious that someone was playing him like a fiddly fool.

The bell of the elevator rang when the car reached its destination. The other passengers all lifted to life as they shuffled their way out of the elevator for another day at work. Dara stayed back and pondered helplessly on whether he should or should not attend work. But with his loyal conviction of a righteous life, he fulfilled his obligation by stepping forward into the known.

"Must be a joke among my colleagues. Who else would do such a trick?"

Dara shuffled through multiple halls of the same architectural design. The roofs were coloured to represent the Forlorn's flag. The side walls were white, while the floors reflected whatever was above them. The archways were grand and contained spiritual murals of the hibiscus flower.

The hibiscus flower was the only flower to exist in the world of Bumi. It was a symbol of dreams to come, and the hopes of many. As Dara rode along the escalator to the Gardens, he watched holographic animations that depicted the history of the Great War and the hero who had ended it. As he rode higher on the escalator, he looked at the murals that displayed a time in history that was closer to the present.

"Welcome to the Gardens," announced the computer-generated voice when Dara stepped off the escalator at the entrance to the Gardens. That seductive voice could be heard everywhere on Paradise. It deserved the attention of the people when it was heard. "Try the tomato soup," it said, and people would be eager to be first in line. "Wear Para's newest Harvest Festival collection," it said, and people would wait for shops to open so they could be the first to purchase. It was the voice of every person's wants and needs, and Paradise listened.

"Hi, Dara. Another day?"

"Another day, Guan. How are the children?" asked Dara in return according to social customs. It was the same question he'd been asking since Dara began working in the Gardens.

"Fine as always. We are very happy," said Guan in return with a smile. Guan was a Garden security guard. He had a cheery attitude, as all Paradisians had. Dara remembered how Guan had told him of a time when he was living on the streets, begging for food. With the Equality Act, Guan now had a job and a beautiful family. He was fit and tough as well. "All right, Dara. You are cleared. Have a nice day."

"Thanks, Guan. Send my regards to the family."

"And mine to yours."

The Gardens were a place of grand significance to Bumi's economy and society. It was a place where food was grown to sustain life on Bumi. Livestock roamed free on the land under the watchful eyes of caretakers. Planters walked about organizing land into grids, managed by supervisors from an observatory not far away, while supervisors planned and coordinated resources on their data pads, which were linked to the main network of the Gardens. Up-to-date information was sent for immediate decisions. Operators of equipment could directly link to Engineering if there were any malfunctions. The Gardens ran like a well-oiled machine; efficiency was its name, and longevity was its goal. Everyone in the Gardens had a purpose, and each employee executed his or her role flawlessly. Dara was a busy bee with his data pad linked up to the network. His earphones were ringing non-stop, asking for his instructions. His messages were always straightforward. Nobody asked the same question twice when Dara was in charge.

"Beul, get the generators up and running in Sector 8. The planters will be needing power to run their pumps. Rose, Sectors 4 and 5 are ready to receive their seedlings to be planted. Have the Nursery send a batch as soon as possible. Jev, get Engineering to send some technicians to get that bloody tractor back online."

Dara's experience and leadership were tantamount to the powers of a respected general. He did his work with such natural dynamism and vitality that everyone assumed he had held the position since he was born. Dara was a natural at what he did, and he was not afraid to show it. He knew his purpose, and he was a man on a mission. His bright smile was ever present to a purpose fulfilled. All seemed well on that day until his data pad became corrupted with a sort of electrical interference. "What is going on?" whispered Dara to himself. "Are you all having the same problem with your data pads?" he asked those nearby.

"Hmm. Ours are working as usual. Maybe you didn't connect it to the server in the proper sequence?" answered a co-worker.

"No, impossible. I've checked it twice." Dara restarted his data pad in a furious attempt to regain control of his work at the most decisive moment. "To hell with this!" he said when his attempt failed. "I am heading down to Maintenance to retrieve a new one. Tell everyone to mind their duties."

Dara stormed out of the room and down the winding stairs to a corridor that led to Maintenance. His earpiece came alive with a loud crackle. "Come in, Dara. Come in. Are you receiving this broadcast?"

"You again? Who are you, and why do you keep harassing me?"

"I am very disappointed in you, Dara, my friend. You chose the common path and went to work. Such an obedient slave. You really have forgotten, haven't you?"

"Stop with your stupid riddles. I have work to do. If I see you, I will deliver you my fist! You hear me?"

"I have some information that might be relevant to you. It is about your daughter."

Dara's blood boiled with the wrath of a vengeful behemoth. "What about my daughter? If you hurt my daughter or my family, I will personally hunt you down with everything I have, and you shall know no peace! Do you *hear* me?"

Dara's anger was met with a loud, dull, insistent laughter. The person with the voice lost his patience and muttered indiscriminately, "I do not intend to hurt you or your family, my friend. Have I not told you I am your friend? I am here to warn you that somebody else might intend to take your daughter away tonight. You see, it was not I who meant any harm. Somebody else intended that evil thought, and I am your guardian angel. I am here to warn you. Alas, I was mistreated with soulless clarity. This is an age in which good men will be rewarded with ungrateful anger."

"How am I to believe your foul lies? You played me like a fool, and you mentioned my daughter being taken away tonight. How am I to trust you?"

"To be honest. You can't ... at the moment. Listen, I am going through a lot of trouble trying to get you to meet me. If you want to know what threat will fall on your daughter, meet me at the Temple. It is the only way you can keep your daughter safe."

Dara stood in the corridor with his head lowered, brooding up an unspeakable hatred towards a situation he could not control. He helplessly decided to weigh the options he'd been presented with. Then he remembered of a warning he'd received quite a few years ago from his friend, Penn, on a cold evening – the day Arla was born. The story of the *Hibiscus Airship* waved through his mind. "This happened before. I don't remember … so familiar but so far in the past," he thought. Dara tossed his data pad aside and headed out of the Garden. "This is it. I will get to the bottom of this."

The quest of a desperate, lone father to protect his daughter began with a quick and urgent journey. His steps were fuelled by a raging desire; his mind clogged up with different scenarios and their eventual solution. At the gates of the Temple, he allowed fear to take his heart. He wasn't sure what awaited him beyond those golden gates. He knew of a beautiful garden that grew hibiscus flowers; he knew of the countless, young, and pretty priestesses tending to the flowers like graceful mothers providing wonderful care of winter nights to their children. And he knew of awe-inspiring stone statues of men that inspired the people of Paradise. With a desperate huff that choked his breath, Dara opened the gate and jumped into a dangerous mystery.

The chirps of morning birds echoed through the long, ancient hall of the Temple. The brown, shiny marble that made up the foundation of the Temple's structure gave the building the strength and ambience that made a hot day seem comfortably cool. Marble pillars were arranged on opposite sides of the walkway to the end of the hall. The open roof design of the garden allowed natural sunlight to shine through at mid-morning, giving life to many lovely red hibiscus flowers. The flowers were tended by priestesses covered in red garb from top to toe. They were not aware of Dara's presence. His bare feet absorbed the coolness of the stone floor, relieving the heat he had carried along with him. He felt light, and a heavy burden seemed to lift from his shoulders. Dara walked to the end of the hall where the holy red hibiscus flower rested on a pedestal, and within the petals of the red hibiscus bloomed the beautiful image of a naked young woman, bearing forth a round seed. She was the Holy Heavenly Flower herself, the purest maiden and the fairest. Dara stood before the pedestal staring, wondering about his intentions of meeting Her in person. But he knew his love for the superstitious was a flawed concept. He bowed his head down a little as a sign of respect, and left the way he had arrived. Then, a sweet voice spoke from behind him. "How may I help you, Dara?"

Dara jerked back to life in a sudden fright that reminded him of the reason he was in the Temple. He turned to face his potential foe, but was stunned to see a friend he knew. "Lady Malla. I did not expect to see you here."

"What are you talking about? Of course I'm here. I am the Matron of the Temple. I should be asking you that question Dara," said Lady Malla with a knowing smile that reminded him of a mother stumbling upon her child who was in the midst of committing an innocent crime. "I don't usually see you pray in the Temple. The last time I saw you here with your head bowed down was during your wedding ceremony."

"I apologize, Lady Malla. It was rude of me to barge in so suddenly."

"Nonsense! You are in the house of the Heavenly Flower. As long as the blood of Bumi runs in you, you are always welcomed with open arms – faithless or not."

Dara smirked with a judgemental disdain for the faithful righteous. He spoke with Lady Malla of his comings and goings while looking at her facial expressions that publicly acknowledged how clockwork his life was, and the drudgery it represented. The more bile he spewed out, the more he realized he was staring at a mirror and was self-criticising with ruthless shrewdness that made his eyes avoid the kind and patient gaze of Lady Malla.

"What is the matter, Dara? You are not at ease. I can see it, Dara."

Dara turned his head left and right in hopes of finding the reason he had come to the Temple.

C. L. Heng

Dara's anger emerged again with renewed purpose as he desperately asked Lady Malla, "Where is the world going to, my lady? Where is the world heading when foul threats go freely mentioned to an innocent man? A man's child is his life, and he vows to protect her. I am here to meet a dangerous man, and I am here to stop him."

"What are you raging on about, Dara?" uttered a startled Lady Malla.

"Are there any suspiciously vile men walking about in these holy halls, my lady? My daughter's life depends on it."

"No, of course not. Who threatened you? Should you not report this to the Guards? Do Jala and Arla know about this?"

"No. They don't know about this. And I intend to keep it that way. I do not want to create panic before I can meet him first. Please, have you seen anyone coming in here besides me?"

Lady Malla became nervous and restless. She was adamant to call the Guards while Dara pleaded her to keep a secret between them. They threw whispers back and forth about what action they should take until another tall man came barging in upon their argument. "I believe you both can calm down now," he said

It was Penn, the one man who had not been part of Dara's suspicions. He stood between Dara and Lady Malla, bowing first to the Heavenly Flower before pulling both aside where privacy was a little more forthcoming. Penn set a tone of seriousness when he began to speak in rough authority. "Lady Malla, I apologize for this sudden debacle. I hope the Matron of the Temple can forgive the foibles of my playful nature. I was just having a little fun with my innocent and serious friend here."

Lady Malla was drenched in confusion. She did not know whether to laugh or to be furiously mad at a cruel joke. She shook her head in utter disapproval, and walked away. Dara noticed she was terribly disappointed in him, and he hoped Lady Malla could find it in her heart to forgive an innocent man.

"Well, at least she seems to be all right about it," mocked Penn as he gazed back to Dara. "I am glad you came. I knew you would come."

Dara mentioned nothing as his fringe covered his eyes from Penn. He stared down on the cold, hard floor, tightening his fist, as he figured it would be best to punch Penn in the face. At the right moment, Dara's fist smashed right into Penn's chin. Penn fell to the ground. Dara stood above Penn with his chest pumping in and out, his shoulders arched forward, and his fists tucked in for another round. But their fight was rudely interrupted as priestesses gathered round them. The situation became awkward enough to diffuse a tense scenario. Dara gave up the fight. Penn stayed where he was.

"What are you all watching?" Dara bellowed. "Get back to your flowers. They need more tending." Penn wiped the blood from his lips and slowly stood up, using a pillar for support. The poor man twisted and turned in his head.

"Are you satisfied? Have you completely unleashed your anger?" said Penn as he wiped the blood off his lips. "Because if you have, we can now proceed with the purpose of this meeting."

Dara shook his head.

"Your daughter has come of age, Dara. And she possess a certain quality that would catch the Navigator's interest."

"What nonsense is this? Who is this Navigator, and what have I done to anger him?"

Penn and Dara were sitting on a garden bench in the Temple grounds, sipping warm tea that quenched their thirst. Lady Malla had brought the tea along with an ice pack for Penn's swelling chin and cheeks. Under the rays of the afternoon sun, the birds continued to sing their eternal song as they danced on branches of an old oak tree. Both men were relaxed to the point of melancholy, each of them reaching to the recesses of his dusty memory, thinking of a time when he was a brother of the other on a grand adventure.

"You really don't remember do you?" asked Penn. "I am not surprised. Few people remember their childhood memories. It requires a certain courage and willpower no ordinary man can muster. I am sad that you are not one of them. I always thought you were. Even on that day, at the Iron Mare."

"The Iron Mare?"

"Look at you, Dara. You can't recall such a simple memory as the day your child was born? Very sad indeed."

"What makes you think I don't remember? Maybe I chose to ignore the part when I stumbled upon you."

"I see. So you do remember that day then?"

Dara did not utter a reply; rather, he stared back at the old oak tree. He wondered about the many fond childhood memories people had long forgotten. "These are the fundamental intelligent thoughts that help fire our future and dreams," he thought, "but are destroyed when we succumb to the temptations of cowardice – fashioned by the forlorn rags of growing old: 'You are crazy', 'You should look for a better line of work', 'You should give up' – those are the words muttered in the schools of Paradise. Children are guided and educated to lead clockwork lives."

"Dara. Please. You do remember the story of the *Hibiscus Airship*, don't you?

"Vaguely, Penn. I remember my parents telling it to me when I was very young."

"Do you remember that night outside the Iron Mare when I mentioned to you this story?"

"Yes, I do."

"Then you know who the Navigator is. You know it, and I know it. It is a menace, and we need to destroy it for the sake of your daughter."

Dara stood up in disagreement. "How are we going to stop a fairy tale? By climbing on a magical airship, eh? This conversation has become absurd. I am going to report to the Guards. They will at least help me."

"The Guards will not do anything."

"Does this mean my daughter will be taken by this man no matter what?"

"Unless we stop it."

"Penn! How?"

"By … No, don't worry about the how. You just need to help me locate it before the Forlorn do."

Dara realized that Penn was withholding information about his plan. He knew he could not trust Penn in his endeavour. Dara knew more about the airship than he had led Penn to think. He just wanted to know of Penn's intentions. Dara played along, pleading ignorance as his main weapon. "By helping, you mean you want me to let you use my daughter to find the airship?"

"You see? Not so hard, is it? You caught on pretty fast there."

"Yes, I caught on pretty fast. Sorry, Penn. But you have gone mad with all your fantasy. I am reporting to the Guards. Stop harassing my family and me. If I see you anywhere close to my family, I will put you down like a dog, Penn. I really will."

Dara turned his back on Penn and trudged on, ignoring the hours he felt he'd wasted listening to a mad man preaching his perverted ambitions of mass destruction. He wanted to go home for the party he promised Arla that morning.

"Running away again, Dara? You always run away, don't you? I know you still remember everything, Dara. You need to choose which side to stand on. There is no middle ground! The day of the Red Flower Revolution is approaching!"

Dara walked on, out of the Temple and back to the streets. He walked with his collar raised, hurrying to the nearest shop to purchase the flowers he'd promised. Dara was happy. On this night, Arla would be taken on an adventure.

Dara slowly remembered.

Chapter 3

Paradise Lost

It was going to be a wonderful celebration, and a comfortable evening with his two favourite people on Bumi. "I would like to purchase a dozen of these, please," claimed Dara as he pointed at a bunch of plastic hibiscus flowers standing still in a vase.

Dara had tinges of regret for not stealing a real posy back at the Temple, but the consequences of theft were not desirable. The florist packed up his flowers in a decorative box that sealed for freshness – as if plastic flowers needed to be fresh. Dara scanned his payment chip to be granted access to make the purchase. It was a straightforward payment plan. The more luxury goods residents bought, the less food they would have at their tables. In terms of food rations, Dara and his family were well fed, and it seemed the rest of Paradise residents were as well. Bumi's resources were well managed by the government. Loyalty to the Forlorn had strengthened to considerable heights ever since the day Arla was born, and loyalty continued to rise.

At the door to his apartment, he knocked gently to a home he had missed all day. He had forgotten his keys as usual, and was feeling that age was catching up with him. He was weary but eager to see his daughter's joyful face.

A reply came through the door. "Daddy? Is that you? What's the password?"

"Mr Hibby went to the market and bought a donut."

"What type of donut, Daddy?"

"Arla, dear. You already know it's me. Can you open the door so we can have dinner? I am starving."

"Nope. Not until you give me the whole password."

Dara was amused, and he knew he had to dig deep into his head to find the eternal answer for a pragmatic gatekeeper, who was bound to her gatekeeper's oath. It was remember or plead for the assistance of the gatekeeper's mother. Either way, mercy was rarely given by her scatty mind. Fortunately, Dara came well prepared as he always wrote down his daughter's password, each time she came up with a new one.

"All right, little gatekeeper! The password is 'Mr Hibby went to the market and bought a rainbow donut with chocolate sprinkles!' Is that it, oh little gatekeeper?"

The door unlocked and opened gently. Arla stood there looking like a little angel in her pyjamas. "I am not little," she said. Dara grabbed her and placed her on his shoulders. He ran her around the apartment like a giggling flying airship. Jala was in the kitchen cooking up a feast. Dara went to her and gave her a peck on her forehead, to which Arla reacted in playful disgust. The clouds outside were dark and gloomy, but the warm stove and a well-prepared meal encouraged an appreciation of comfort and gladness in the soul of Dara. They feasted together as a family and sang songs of joyous delight. It was a night of celebration for the birthday of Jala – a gratifying party.

Once they had feasted, the cool droplets of rain began to shower down from the heavens, gliding and dancing down the exterior wall of Dara's apartment, creating a small symphony of spotty splatters that soothed the body to a rhythm of intoxicating relaxation. Jala decided to unwind on her favourite chair with a good book to read; she was probably the only soul left on Bumi who still read from a book. Dara and Arla, on the other hand, were both restless and eager to fill their time with fun. With their imagination, they turned the rest of their day into a rainy evening of chocolate ice cream, which soon smudged lips and cheeks, of crazy rocket adventures, and tiny toy soldiers. It all ended under the cover of a starry night, the rain having finished and the wind having blown the storm clouds away. A father and his daughter rested soundly under a warm duvet, waiting for the arrival of a better day.

"Go to sleep, my dear child," Dara told Arla. "You have had an adventurous day. Go to sleep, my child, for tomorrow is another day." He caressed Arla's tiny head, making her yawn stoutly, eager to sleep and dream of more. "Tomorrow will definitely be a day you will always remember. Do not fear, and remember I will always be there in your heart, cheering you on." And with that, Arla descended into a deep slumber fit for a princess. Dara gently lifted Arla into his embrace and slowly snuggled her into her own comfortable and fluffy bed. Dara kissed her forehead and left to join Jala in the living room. There was a story he was eager to tell.

"There she is," thought Dara. He worshipped his beautiful wife of magnificent grace. It had come to the time of day when they would sit down together and talk. The moon appeared in the heavens, and stars guided and protected their motherly matron. Staring out beyond the confines of their apartment, they watched the tame moonlit glow and drape the city in a reflective radiance that made Dara worship Paradise. For the rest of the night, he was to worship his wife, giving her the comfort and love she deserved.

Dara subsided on to the carpeted floor, crossed his legs, and rested his head on Jala's soft lap. She placed her finger between the pages of her book to mark her place and said, "My dear, how was your day?"

"It did not lack in amusement, that's for sure."

"What happened?" asked Jala as she carefully closed her book and placed it on her lap. She was fully focused on Dara. "Tell me from the beginning."

Dara began with beguiling eagerness, and in the telling, he left nothing out. He was expressive as he explained the emotions he'd felt, embellishing certain parts from time to time. Jala listened with care and devotion.

"Did you report to the Guards? Why did you not report? We should be grateful nothing happened to Arla!"

Dara rolled his eyes. "Don't worry, Jala. It was just an old friend playing a prank on me. Let's go to bed."

Dara rose and extended his hand as a gentle gesture of permission to lead Jala into their bedroom. Jala, with her fervid acceptance of his hand, lighted up with rosy red cheeks, letting Dara know that she permitted him to explore further possibilities. Dara grabbed her waist, and they went into a calm and temperate dance. Dara danced in a soothing swaying motion that invigorated their sensual desire. Romance struck stubbornly into their hearts as the moon became brighter and more and more domineering.

"How was your day then, my dear?" queried Dara.

"Sad. The children of Paradise deserve more. We tell 'truths' that lie and we do things that disgust. Hope does not reside in my heart anymore. If we do not change the way we teach, we are going to go down in a downward spiral. But what is to be done? I am but a mere educator, teaching the young to recite the Charter of the Forlorn over and over again with mindless integrity." She sighed. "If we taught differently, we would be questioned. Wait ... *questioned* would not be the right word. *Interrogation* would be more like it."

"Interrogation? Have you been interrogated before?" asked Dara.

"My darling, it's nothing to worry about. Nothing happened ... they just asked a few questions. I was reported to the Guards for teaching in a different way than seemed right."

"But that's unacceptable. A teacher should be respected and allowed to dictate his or her own style of teaching, as long as it allows the children to explore knowledge independently. We should not be breeding husks that care only for passing grades in exams. How can parents allow this?"

"Darling, please. Do not make any more fuss with this. If you continue to pursue this, I might be dismissed from my job. There is nothing I love more than to teach."

"Then continue to defy them by teaching! Who cares about what parents think of us or their children? We are there to guide Paradise's future. I fought for something long ago, but along the way, I lost my way. I forgot why I fought and why I gave up. But after meeting a friend of mine, I now remember what happened long ago," said Dara with a triumphant declaration. "Do you remember the story of the *Hibiscus Airship*, my dear?"

"Yes, I do remember," said Jala. Dara was surprised. He'd never known that Jala had heard of that story. "Look at this." She handed him the book she had been reading a moment ago.

Dara took the book. It was rather light and thin and contained barely thirty pages. The cover was red and thick, giving it a sturdy feel. Dara flipped over the hard cover and read the title of the book: *The Adventurous Tale of the Hibiscus Airship*. "This … this is … How did you get this?"

"A man gave it to me at school. He looked familiar to me, but I do not remember him. I felt that perhaps we had known each other long ago."

"What was his name? What was his name!" demanded Dara. "Was it Penn?"

"No. He introduced himself as Mr Hamzee. He passed the book to me and smiled. He told me to tell this story to my class. That was how I got into trouble. My students did not want to listen to stories. By luck, I managed to quickly hide the book somewhere before the guards arrived."

"This book had been banned by the Forlorn. Because you have it in your possession, we are all headed to the dungeon! We need to destroy it!"

"What? No, Dara. We are not going to destroy this book. The Forlorn banned all storybooks except the ones about their greatness. This book has brought out a passion I once had. It makes me want to understand more. This is something I want to show to my students!"

Dara was stuck. He knew he needed to hide that book from the Guards. The family life he had worked hard to build and protect would crumble if the Guards knew about it. "But, my dear, do you care for this book more than you care for our family?"

"You know that is not fair! How can you do that? You know how important this book is for the future of Bumi. You are despicable."

"This book is no more important than the Heavenly Flower herself. Both are just creations from our imagination. You cannot possibly expect to sacrifice what we have now for made-up fantasies!"

Jala said nothing. She turned away from Dara and walked over to the window to gaze upon the moon, looking for solace away from her husband's flawed convictions. Dara stood on the carpet with his eyes looking straight down at his feet. He was in a dilemma that tore his heart apart. He had known of the book's existence, and he remembered reading it long ago. He understood its power, but he could not risk the comfortable life he had built for his family. He could not risk his life being destroyed by revolutionary idealism that would only bring the wrath of tyranny down upon them. Arla deserved more, and unnecessary violence and hardship was not what Dara intended for her.

"Jala, my dear. Are you willing to risk the life of our daughter for this ridiculous book?"

"A life in which we do not fight for our freedom to think and imagine is the same as Death, Dara. I have seen the children of today. They are dead in their minds and their souls. They care only for the gossip of the day, and the more hurtful it is, the better. There is no future. I do not want Arla to have that."

"But dear …"

"Stop it, Dara. I did not marry a man who was afraid to imagine. When I met you, you were so passionate about life and the possibilities

C. L. Heng

of adventure. You told me of the story of the *Hibiscus Airship*. You told me of the adventures you had on it. I was mesmerized. I fell in love—"

"I told you that? I told you I was on the airship before?" said Dara who could not recall any of it and felt incredibly guilty.

"You don't remember many things that happened when we were young. I appreciate all you sacrificed to make sure Arla and I are free from harm. But we cannot ignore this anymore."

Dara slumped onto the couch, gasping in disbelieve at the many questions that swam in his head. "Why, Jala? Why can't I remember I told you this before?" Dara knew he had drowned in waves of his own ecstasy, in a tower where his ego resided. He was consumed by a wondrous lust for self-satisfaction until his desire for wanderlust died. Dara plunged deeply into his own abyss as he grew. The creative spark he once possessed fizzled under the temptations of dreariness.

"Because you told me not to," whispered Jala.

Dara was ever more confused. He suffered in a ghastly rage. He heaved over a glass table and shattered it. "I don't understand. Why did I tell you that?"

"You wanted to forget. You said it was not right. Something was happening, and you wanted no part of it." Dara sat down on the carpeted floor with his mind numb, but refreshingly light and relaxed. He did not fight that feeling; rather, he allowed it to take over. On that day, Dara felt a burden lifted.

"Mommy? Daddy? What happened?"

Jala and Dara were surprised Arla had been standing in the doorway to her room. Now she was looking sheepishly at them. They had not meant to wake their child, and they felt pangs of bad parenting. Jala made the first move to walk over to Arla, but Dara stopped her. "No, my love. Let me." He picked up the storybook and went in to the room with Arla. Jala understood and nodded. She knew it was to be a cherished moment that would be shared between a father and his daughter.

"Daddy? Why were you and Mommy fighting?"

"We were not fighting, my dear. Daddy was angry with himself."

Arla was a little confused about the wonders of being an adult and the troubles associated with it. She thought maybe it would be best to stay young forever. It was a possible dream, and she thought that somebody might help her stay that way one day.

"Daddy, what is that?" She was pointing at the book Dara was holding tightly against his chest.

"Oh, this? This, my child, is a storybook."

"Wow. Does it tell a story? Is it the same as the stories you told me?" asked Arla with her beaming eyes. "Show me! Show me!"

Dara had never told a story through a book before. It was the first time Arla had laid her eyes on one. Jala had books that she hid under her bed, but none of them had the magic of a storybook. Even Dara was excited to read a book. It was sort of a key to nostalgia that would take him back his childhood days. He shared his past with his beautiful future – Arla.

"Haha, all right. Let me tuck you nice and comfy into your bed first."

Arla was elated and restless as she abided with Dara's request. "Hurry, Daddy! I am already comfy as it is."

"Haha, patience. A good story is always worth the wait. All right, let's begin shall we? 'Big and bulky with the strength of a thousand men, the red airship flies …'"

Awe and wonder filled the room as Dara recited words from the book. He enacted wonderful memories of his past beyond his adult expectations. He was innocent again, and free from the shackles of dread. He joined Arla on the high seas of another world, where they slew monsters for treasures of great wealth. They met people of different shapes and sizes, all of whom opened the world to possibilities and the unknown. They were pirates and they were saints, living fully under a banner of conviction so few had in their own world. To them, nobody was a stranger anymore. When the final pages were put to rest, Dara and Arla spoke for a while about ideas that were not hindered by the respect of age or how ridiculous they sounded. They bonded ever more, tirelessly connecting the dots of their existence.

"Daddy, so you were on the airship when you were young?"

"Yes, yes I was," replied Dara with a confident smile. "It was one of the best days of my life."

"I want to go on the airship, Daddy. Can you take me there one day?"

Dara gently placed Arla's duvet up to her chin and gave her a peck on her tiny forehead, whispering into her ear, "Don't worry, my child. The *Hibiscus Airship* will come and find you one day. Be patient and the Navigator will come."

"Promise me you will come with me, Daddy? I want to go on adventures with you."

"Of course I will go with you," Dara declared as he switched off the lights and opened the window so a gust of night wind could sway the curtains and the rays of the moon could commit themselves to a dance that would that illuminate Arla's room in sweet ambience.

"Good night."

"Night, Daddy."

The night was a restless night for Dara, as there was work to be done and notes to write. Dara sat in his study skimming through pages of the storybook. He had so much to catch up on, and it was best to bring out his old dust-filled notes and the records he had made before Arla's birth. When he had read the last page of the book, he'd noticed there was an unusual bulge in the cover – a sort of bulge that made him think that another page was hidden, struggling to erupt for the attention of a reader.

"This is … by the Heavenly Flower, it is!" Dara took out his desk knife and sliced the cover open to reveal a letter. It was from the Navigator. He was speechless and breathless at the same time when he realized it was addressed to him. He knew the letter was a message from the Navigator. It was a message to the reader that he or she was ready for an adventure. Upon the back of the letter, a note read: "Sail the stardust – MH."

The words caused tears to stream down Dara's cheeks. It was a moment to cherish and a moment in which to be grateful. Jala walked towards Dara and kissed his forehead. She stood by him with loving attention as Dara was finally liberated from his past. The doors to his future could finally be opened. "I love you, Dara."

"I love you too."

There were several sharp knocks on the door.

It was an ungodly hour to expect visitors. Dara and Jala were curious as to who it might be. Dara proceeded to the door cautiously. As he approached, the sharp knocking was repeated. "Who is it?"

"A friend. I have come for you."

Dara was ecstatic at the arrival of a long-lost friend. He was elated at the questions he wanted to ask. He opened the door without hesitation, but his celebration was short lived as the person he greeted was not the person he had expected. Jala followed behind him, and she too was shocked at the sudden appearance of five young adults wearing the yellow coveralls of government workers. They carried bottles of liquor in their hands. They were unkempt and their stares were blank.

"Hi!" said one of the men. "Oh, my apologies. I thought I was at my friend's place. What are you doing here?"

"I should be asking the questions," said Dara. "Please leave the premises at once before I call the Guards." He remained courteous while still showing intimidating defiance at strangers he did not know. Jala was afraid, as she noticed the others were staring at her like lustful vultures. Dara knew they were using drugs, which were quite easily accessible down on the streets.

"Are you threatening me? Can't you not see what we are wearing? My work keeps Paradise in motion. Where you live is where I live. So be a little more grateful," said the man, who at that moment was looking behind Dara. "You have a nice, place by the way. Just you two?"

"Look, I do not want any trouble. You were right. I was a little ungrateful. Please, we just want to go to bed."

"You look like you are hiding something. We are living in a dangerous place. The net of peace won't hold forever with threats from terrorists. Are you a terrorist?"

"No, of course not. I am an honest citizen. I have been working at the Gardens for a long time now. I am an upstanding individual like yourself."

"Haha. Calm down. I was just making sure. I have seen you before. You make sure our citizens have enough food. I am grateful."

"All right," replied Dara, heaving a sigh of relief. "I bid a good night to you and your friends. I must wake early tomorrow for work."

"Wait a moment!" The man placed his hands on the door as Dara politely tried to close it. He said, "But I am not sure about your wife. She may be related to the terrorists I speak of. I may need to inspect your home."

"What is this? You have no right to barge into my home and accuse my wife! Get out!"

"Gents, seize him."

The man's accomplices grabbed Dara in a binding hold, rendering him defenceless. He shouted with all his might, but it was a fruitless endeavour as they punched Dara in his throat. The assault almost knocked him out.

"That should keep him quiet. Quick! Grab the wife before she locks herself inside the room."

While the assailants were busy with Dara, Jala had run into Arla's room to keep safe the one thing that was most precious to her. She locked the door, but volleys of banging and kicking were not going to stop an onslaught of violent men. Arla was shaking in her bed, fearful for the first time as she saw the empty, hopeless stare of her mother. "Where is Daddy?" she thought.

Jala was shivering as she tried to look for the best place to hide Arla. "Arla, get up and clear your toy box. Mommy needs the bed now."

Arla complied like an anxious rabbit with her two ears standing straight. Arla opened the toy box and emptied everything in a savage flurry, tossing Mr Brown the bear and Smuffletoe under her bed. Jala pushed the bed to block the door.

"Mommy, the toy box is empty now."

Jala hurried over to her daughter and grabbed her gently by her arms, caressing her daughter in a warm rub. "Arla, my dear. Look at me and listen."

Arla began to cry softly.

"Listen, my dear, and look me in the eyes," whispered Jala as she used her hands to wipe Arla's tears away. "Don't cry, my child. Everything is going to be all right. I am here. But I need you to listen to me."

Arla looked up at her mother, who smiled tenderly. It was with a tender smile that Jala had always proved everything was going to be all right.

"My child, do you remember the time when your daddy and I talked about hiding when the monsters come? Do you remember?"

Arla nodded.

"Well today is the day *you* are going to hide. I need you to be the sweet precious girl Mommy loves, who is brave and strong. Do you understand me?" Jala shook, as her words slid through her lips. The door began to crack; the fiendish screams of the intruders turned louder.

Arla nodded.

"All right then. Come, let's put you in the box now. Make sure you don't come out until I say so. All right! Your feet in first, Arla."

Arla did not move.

"Arla, please don't do this now. Please get into the box now!"

Arla shook her head.

"*Arla!* Stop playing games and get in! Or I will not let you have any chocolates!"

Arla was conflicted.

"*Arla!* This is it! I am carrying you inside now!"

Jala picked up Arla's little body and placed her forcefully into a dark cage with no place to move. Jala placed all the child's stuffed toys on top of her, concealing her tiny body. Arla stared blankly at Jala as the closing darkness fell upon her. She felt her mother's cold tears drip on her cheeks. The door to the room crashed open, and the predators of a moonlit night came into the room to claim their victim. Arla heard only footsteps, screams, and the hurtful onslaught of abuse. It was her imagination in a lonely darkness that gave her a vision she never wanted to see. She tried to shut it out, but the danger was all too real. Her imagination, once her friend, betrayed her. It turned into her worst nightmare. She stayed still, fighting on to fulfil her mother's wishes.

"Get her next to him! Tie them up!"

Dara and Jala were both on the couch, bruises on their faces and bodies. Dara felt helpless and guilty. He was desperately furious that he could not protect the woman he loved. The men in yellow had made Dara worthless. He stared at them as they moved about, turning his home upside down as if they were searching for something.

"What are you looking for?" asked Dara. "If it is something valuable you want, I can assure you, we don't have anything."

Their leader, who had a notable scar on his left cheek in the shape of a star, turned and sat next to Jala. His arms curled around her shoulders, tempting Dara's anger. "You have a beautiful wife, Dara. It is a shame indeed."

"You had better not harm her," said Dara as he spat blood on the evil one's foot. Their leader continued to molest Jala, who was too weak and vulnerable to do anything but cry.

"You coward! Stop it!"

The star-scarred leader got up and paced in dainty steps as he danced to an imaginary partner, smashing and crashing any fragile objects along his way. He sang a song, a song unheard of.

Guardians of the lame and the hollow,
Wearing the same woes through a hole,
Give me something to quench this dread,
For my life is wreathed in sorrow and pain,
Bring me a gun to shoot myself;
For I shall not complain.
I was mauled by the monster of boredom anyway.

He sang it repeatedly in a monotonous tone. He was a maniac; he was a psychopath. He sang a ballad for suicide.

"Dear Dara. Imagine now my life. Just imagine, all right? Can you do that for me? Can you just give a bit of your time to listen to me? Are you listening to me, you worthless scum? I am your saviour and your tormentor. I can kill you and your wife right here, right now. Please listen to me? *I say, please listen to me!*"

Dara raised his head and looked upon the yellow man's maniacal expression. He nodded. "Tell me, and I will imagine it for you."

"Wise, Dara. You may live to see another day. All right, listen. This place pales in comparison to what my place has. I am a servant of the government, and I sacrificed for the greater good."

"What did you sacrifice? What did you do? I would like to know, oh hero of Paradise," interrupted Dara. A swift, powerful slap met his face.

"Did I say you could interrupt? Did I say you could question me? I am wearing yellow aren't I? Nobody should be questioning me!"

"Then why are you bored? Why are you doing this to people? You have everything, but you still do such things? Why?"

"You stupid shit! What you are asking is the ending of my story! Dara ruined it! Completely ruined it! Nobody would listen! *Nobody!* All of you are the same!"

"You are the boring one!" Dara said. "Nobody on Bumi deserves to listen to the rant of a boring man. You live for no purpose and you complain with no reason. You deserve to kill yourself."

"How dare you!" shrieked the man in yellow.

"Jobb! Come here! Look what I found!" shouted another man who was in Dara's study. He was waving with great energy to get the attention of his leader. Jobb retreated and left Dara to suffer his own.

"You'd better have something good to show," said Jobb as he marched into the room. Dara took this opportunity to move closer to Jala, trying to give her hope and keep her safe. He looked around for broken glass he could use to free their hands. He stretched his back towards the ground, and with his fingers, he picked up a glass shard. He sliced away as fast as he could and felt his binds loosen.

"All right, Jala, your turn. Come now. Let me cut those."

It wasn't long before Jala's hands were freed as well. The first thought that came through his mind was Arla. "Jala, my dear. Where is Arla? Where did you hide her?"

"In … the … room … in the … toy—"

"Jala. Please stay awake. I need you to tell me where our daughter is."

"Toy … box."

Dara crawled on all fours and raced to Arla's room. He reached the toy box and began calling upon his daughter. There was no reply. "Arla, darling … this is your daddy. Come on out." Dara opened the box and moved her toys away. He did not notice that another member of Jobb's gang was sitting in a dark corner observing. That man, with his balding head weaving from left to right, slowly crept forward in a slumped position, letting Dara continue his futile attempt to save his daughter. "Arla, dear … look at Daddy. Mommy is safe, and we need to go, all right? Look at Daddy."

"No, Daddy. It is not safe. The monster is still in the room," whispered Arla.

"What monster?"

Dara felt a sudden chill creep and crawl up his spine, promiscuously travelling from his lower back to the base of his neck. He had made a mistake – a terrible mistake. He knew he had just revealed his daughter to Jobb. Now his whole family was in danger. He felt fear, with a terrible realization that his hope for salvation had turned completely into hellish despair. He felt a bony but demonic hand, icy and shivering, touch his lower back. He felt the man's presence push his heart out until his breath was at Dara's warm ear. The man huffed and puffed in perverted thirst that made Dara freeze in his place. Dara let out a grieving choke.

"Well, you have been a very, very bad boy haven't you?" said the man as his rancid breath smothered Dara's lungs. "Your daughter is very adorable. I love them adorable …"

Dara felt a sharp blade slide against his neck, forcing him to confront the monster. The man had no eyebrows. His skin was white, pale like the boring walls of Paradise. The monster kept trying to push back his almost non-present hair. "Your daughter is correct. I am a monster, but a necessary one. I keep Paradise safe."

The monster slid his hand into the toy box with a euphoric longing for a prey suited to his appetite. Arla cried and whispered to herself, "Help me … Daddy."

Dara shrieked in anger and pushed the monster back away from Arla. He grabbed a broken chair and began assaulting the man with extreme prejudice. The man turned and kicked, using his leg as defence, but he smiled and laughed with pleasure. Dara stopped when two men grabbed his arms and overpowered him. The monster, who now lay on the floor, was delighted. "Is that it, Dara?"

The monster jumped up and approached Dara.

"Jeella, do not do anything to him. Jobb wants him alive," ordered the man on Dara's left.

"Shut up."

A terrible shock washed through Dara's entire body as Jeella's piercing sharp blade invaded his torso. Jeella twisted his knife and stared deep into Dara's eyes. The violent pain Dara felt burst out of his mouth. He screamed as Jeella pushed his blade further in at a different, twisted angle, causing Dara to jerk upward. Dara was dizzy, and his world slowly faded from reality into darkness.

"Jeella! You stupid fool! What have you done?"

"Oh, do not worry. He will live. Just don't take the knife out," whispered Jeella to Dara. "I will have your daughter now."

"No … no … no," begged Dara. "Please leave my daughter alone. Please!"

The two men dragged Dara away from the room. He caught a last glimpse of the despicable monster turning his attention to the toy box. It was the last time he saw Arla.

The men dragged Dara back into the living room and tossed him back onto the couch. He grimaced at the cold pain caused by the blade that was stuck into his body.

The big man who had been in study was holding down Jala. He held a knife to her throat. Next to Jala, Jobb was reading the red book, all the while letting out a sly smirk.

"Dara, oh Dara. You are a bad boy. Look! What do we have here? It seems you two have been dabbling in something illegal!"

"That is not ours …" muttered Dara weakly.

"I know you both are with the Party! We should promptly execute you all right now! *Don't lie to me!*"

"Wait … wait … no we are not with the Party. We are innocent. Please … let my wife and daughter go."

"What? What daughter?" asked Jobb as he stared at the man who guarded Dara.

"His daughter, sir. We found her in the room. Jeella is with her at the moment."

"Ah … I see. Never mind about the little girl. Kill her mother."

The tall big man holding Jala turned into an executioner at the snap of a finger. With the efficiency of a butcher, the big man tore his blade through the entire breadth of Jala's neck. Blood gushed out like a red fountain. She had no time to respond. Her eyes turned upwards as she crashed to the floor, shuddering in a pool of her own blood. If only Dara had been able to hear her last words: "It … is all right."

And silence.

Staring upon the lifeless body of his wife, Dara died but continued to breathe. There was an invisible pain aching in his heart. His soul was butchered until there was nothing left. Dara had lost it, and nothing could ever bring him back. His last rites were Jala's last words. Jobb and his men laughed and celebrated, joking at the hilarity of how Jala had died without a fight.

"All right, next. Bring Dara over. It is his turn now. Let's give him the reunion he wants."

The two men lifted their prisoner and took him to Jobb and his executioner.

"I see Jeella had done some damage already. No matter, this book will justify today's actions, and we will emerge as heroes," said Jobb proudly. "You and your wife, however, will go down through the annals of history as criminals. At least you will be remembered, yes?"

With the snap of his finger, the executioner approached and grabbed the top of Dara's head and pushed it backward, revealing his neck. "Another one without a fight huh? This is so boring," said Jobb.

But Jobb was wrong. Dara manoeuvred his hands and pulled the death knife from his torso. He knew he had a few more minutes before he lost too much blood. Realizing Death was at the door, he thought he might as well take a few along to meet her. Dara used the blade to slice the crotch of the big man, making him stumble backward with a bleeding artery. The big man screamed in horrid pain. The other two tried to defend themselves, but Dara's violent rage was no match. Dara stabbed one of them in the throat, killing him instantly. The other crawled behind a table to cower in fear, but he later died from blood loss. Jobb was awestruck.

"You can still fight! Oh my! The Heavenly Flower has granted me a wonderful night!"

Dara pulled Jobb by his neck. His bloodied hands gave him trouble in establishing a solid grip, which Jobb easily swatted away. "You fascinating man! I'm impressed. Unfortunately, you are going to die soon. Do you feel tired? Is your consciousness drifting yet? You are losing a lot of blood eh? Come here!"

Jobb slapped Dara hard causing him to drop his weapon. Jobb proceeded to pull Dara's hair, dragging him to the glass window of his home. "If I pushed you hard against this, it will break and you will plunge to your death. Which would you prefer Dara? Death by loss of blood or a fall from this height? Which one? Which one? Which one?"

Jobb then dropped Dara to the floor. Dara was tired and weak. He could not muster much strength. Jobb grabbed a decorative rock, given by Jala's mother as a souvenir, and used it to smash the glass. A huge gust of wind filled the apartment, and Jobb laughed, "Look at Paradise! What a wonderful city! We are kings! I am king!"

Dara was looking at his wife – his lovely wife who had been alive not long ago. He knew he had failed to protect her, and he blamed himself. He knew it was time, and he would meet her again, sailing through the stardust. It was time to jump into the unknown. With all that remained of his strength, he climbed up sluggishly onto his two feet. Jobb was enjoying the view, but as he turned back he found Dara standing, and he smiled. "I'm impressed. You are the one to free me, aren't you?"

Dara ran towards Jobb, pushing him over the edge. Jobb greeted Dara with open arms, and they both fell off into the abyss together. It was Dara's last courageous move to avenge his wife and his daughter. As he fell, his happiest memories filled his mind. With a strong will, he smiled one last time.

Chapter 4

Life in a Time of Hate

"Hmm … dear, dear girl. You have such lovely hair. I cannot stop admiring it. Come on now, don't be shy. We are beyond strangers now. I know you better than anybody else."

A childish young man who rather resembled a rodent was stroking Arla's long, dark hair. She was looking beyond him, staring at an invisible man, not moving an inch. The dark grey room, covered in patches of wet moss, was not the same place she knew and loved. It was an evil place lighted only by a tiny light bulb that glowed a dull yellow and created shadows on walls that had been sullied by a despicable hand. She felt naked, exposed to the gazes of the wind. She had once felt touches that were warm and loving; now all touch had turned cold and undeserving. She felt as if her skin needed to be peeled, one layer at a time, letting her red, muscled flesh bloom with pain. She had a need to wash; she felt terribly filthy. "Arla, I love you. Please let me be yours. We grew up together in this horrid place, helping each other out and giving each other company. I love you more than anything else. Please?"

Ten years had passed since the day Arla had lost her parents in brutal murder that had never seen justice. She barely remembered what had happened; neither did she have memories of her life before that event. She had forgotten what having a family felt like. She no longer knew how the warmth of the sun could bring happiness, and she hated the touch of another soul. The damp and boring room she lived in brought no solace to her torment. She was an orphan, and all orphans in Bumi were either adopted by childless families or lived in the orphanage until they grew to an age when they were tossed back into the world with nothing. Most people thought it was better to be dead than to be an orphan. However, it was a definitely curious thing that Arla had not given up. She was not like the other orphans who were not accepted. They were usually eventually found hanging in the middle of their room, with their necks strangled in a bed sheet, and nobody gave them a care in the world. Their bodies were cut down and taken to the incinerator where neither a name nor a prayer was ever mentioned. It was something Arla had witnessed too many times. At first she cared, but as her roommates came and went, she felt they were better off choosing to let go.

Arla wondered why she was still alive. Why had the monster not killed her? Why had he only chosen to feast on her from the inside? She remembered its three long tentacles sliming their way all over her body. Goosebumps emerged from her skin; she felt disgusted, and her roommate, Bahl, was not making her feel comfortable. He slowly blew into Arla's ear, thinking it would entice from Arla a sensual desire, but Arla continued to be vacuous, like a puppet to be manipulated.

"Why are you not returning my love? Why? I am lonely! You are lonely! Why not?"

Arla turned her head and said, "I am not interested."

"You don't want to? It is as if you are dead! We are already in this godforsaken place. Don't you want to have whatever fun we can have? I really love you."

Arla was growing impatient with the word *love*. How pathetic it was that men could use such words as if they were at a flea market bargaining for something that never was theirs to claim. If he were to replace the word *love* with *lust*, then his motives would be truthful. But Bahl was just a desperate boy, spewing intentions that caught none of Arla's attention. He was the same as everyone on Bumi. Bahl would not last long.

"You don't care, do you? You would not care if I lived or died! I have heard many things about you – whispers and gossips. They say you are a cruel girl who cares for no one! No wonder nobody wants you!"

"What difference does it make?"

"Difference? Do you not care what others think about you? You are a loner, and I can see it. Nobody wants to be friends with you. I am concerned, Arla. I am a concerned friend. Do you want to be alone forever? Aren't we all the same?"

"I am content with being alone."

"No you are not! Look at you! No friends or anything! I'm afraid you will kill yourself."

Arla stood up from her bed and paced forward to the window, looking down at the other orphans playing ball. There were cheers and jeers, but in their eyes, she saw that they were afraid. None of the orphans knew if they could ever have a normal life again. They didn't want to be cast out into Paradise and be humiliated by the thought of not having a family, and being useless as well.

"Why are you here, really?" asked Arla.

"What? I told you, Arla. I am here to save you."

"But I don't need saving. I am content with what I have now."

"The others are saying horrible things about you. I thought I could make you feel wanted."

"But I don't want to feel wanted. And I do not care what others think of me."

"Everybody in this world needs somebody. Do you want to die alone?"

Arla turned and walked straight to Bahl, who was sitting on her bed buttoning up his shirt. Arla kindly raised his chin with her soft hands. "Bahl, you don't love me, and you are not here to help me. You may not realize this, but you are here because of others. I do not care what others think of me, and if I am to be alone, that is fine. I am not complaining. You want more of me, but you want something I won't give you. Please realize this: I do not need you."

Bahl was mesmerized by the kind smile Arla had given him. For a moment, his loneliness had dissipated like mist, and the wonders of believing returned. He said nothing, but got up and packed his bag. Classes were about to begin.

"Hey, Arla, better get ready or you'll be late for class. I'll head out first."

Arla nodded, and Bahl went out and closed the door behind him. Arla let out a breath of relief as she paced to the washroom to wash her face. She felt filthy, but she decided to skip her bath until she returned from class. There might be more filth to encounter, she thought. She brushed her hair while she looked into the mirror and stared for a moment. "Please let me get through today," she said. The girl in the mirror nodded.

Going to class was a daily routine Arla had become used to. She tried her best to go through a different path every day, but options were limited. Arla needed to get used to people's attempts to bully on her path to class. They wanted to get back at her for being different, for being a loner. She could predict which paths her bullies would choose when they decided to lie in wait for her. If she was uncertain, she would usually take the path with the most people on it. There was one time, however, when her bullies had managed to bully her publicly. She had been slapped in the head. The bullies had called her names that were humiliating. To her surprise, not one pedestrian had stopped to help her, except for her only friend, Bellel Wallee. Bell, for short, was also an orphan. She was older than Arla, and one could say she was like a sister. Bell tried to get the orphanage to let her be Arla's roommate; unfortunately, the orphanage had ridiculous policies that discouraged orphans of different ages from staying together, but allowed Arla a roommate of the opposite sex who had problems controlling his sexual urges. "Nothing to be done. The rules have been set," they said. "If you don't like it, leave," they said. "Dress appropriately then," they said. "It is your fault," they said. So many so-called suggestions and solutions, but none addressed the problem; they were only excuses. Arla hated everyone on Bumi, except for Bell.

On that day, Arla chose the common path everybody used. The rain had begun to drizzle, and she walked along with her coat collar raised. Her shoes were drenched and stained as she walked along the half-repaired muddy roads. She trudged on and on, not knowing where she would end. Rows of similar white buildings were arranged in boring unison on her right while brown and yellow trees rose into the sky on her left. And in between lay the penumbra of her former self. She brooded along.

"Hey, Arla! Hey!" hollered Bell from the corner of a café. "I see you! Come, come!"

Arla was a little embarrassed as everyone looked at her with prying eyes. She felt an awareness of being naked again. She stared down on the ground, picking up pace as she walked towards Bell just so her friend would stop saying her name. Her anxiety built up. At Bell's side, she gasped for air. "Bell, you know I don't like you calling me from afar. You know I hate people looking at me."

"Sorry, Arla. But there were a few guys behind you who were up to no good."

Arla looked back and saw three young yobs staring at her with animosity. They were obviously feeling disappointed in a prank gone to waste. "It's them again. Thanks, Bell."

"It's all right. Come here." Bell grabbed Arla and gave her a warm, welcoming hug. Arla just buried her face in Bell's bosom, allowing her friend to console her in a vicious world. "All right, all right, I love you too. Come on, let's go to class."

"Do I have to?" asked Arla demurely.

"Yes, you do. Who does not want to understand the Forlorn a little better?" said Bell sarcastically. They both smiled.

At the black gates of the school, two golden eagles stared down at the children of Bumi from their perches on the gateposts with their large wings spread wide, ready to pounce on their prey. Bell thought the eagles were the only grand statues in the school, and she believed if any of the students were to stare at the eagles long enough, they would realize the statues were of chickens painted to resemble eagles. It was one of the many things Arla loved about Bell – her ebullience. "Hey, Arla, look! The golden chickens! Haha! I call the left Dom, and the right Pom. They will make fine stew."

The school was designed to look like all the other buildings in Paradise. It manifested a modern and technologically superior theme that made viewers worship importance and feel smart and sophisticated.

Many parents often told their children about how clever and fortunate they were to be able to get a good education. They told their children that their particular intellect was of a higher quality, and they would invest a lot to ensure the children were comfortable enough to pass their exams. They even went so far as to carry their children's bags to class, taking over the children's responsibilities. Parents had no clue about what their children were learning, as long they grew up to contribute substantially to Paradise as important men and women. They wanted them to be groomed to don the infamous yellow coveralls – the garb of the most-sought-after position in society, the government worker. But positions were limited; therefore, competition was high. Every night at the dinner table, parents would drill motivation into their children to be callous and to do whatever it took to win. Children were urged to make friends, but not trust them; to be kind, but not merciful; to help, but only to win. There was no denying the amount of sacrifice and hard work parents had to make for the future of their children. However, it was a sacrifice worth taking for the universal prestige that came when a child donned the yellow coverall. It was a recognition that filled the egos of hard-working parents because it showed how important they'd become. Their vile satisfaction in seeing people glow in jealousy was their reward. A parent's world revolved around his or her child. In the end, the child's life was forfeit.

"So here we are again. I'll see you at lunch, all right? Remember to save me a strawberry." Bell gave Arla another hug, and she turned right into the long corridor where one of the doors would open to her first class of the day. Arla longed to follow in Bell's footsteps, but sometimes there are roads we need to take ourselves along without the guiding hands of a loved one. This was definitely the most terrifying thing for any young Paradisian. Arla looked down the corridor where dozens of students mingled about, hurrying to go through classroom doors. The corridor echoed with so many voices they sounded like white noise. Within a minute, there was silence. The corridor that had been teaming with life turned into a solitary hallway, and Arla stood in the middle of it. She liked it; it wasn't solitude she craved, but the absence of stupid people.

Arla gave a customary knock on a classroom door. The teacher greeted her: "Arla. Again? Why are you always late?"

"She was especially tired this morning, eh?" said Bahl, who was seated at the back of the room. He gave Arla a naughty wink. His entourage, surrounding him, roared to laughter. The others in the room smirked and giggled. Arla and the teacher, Ms Liimm, wondered what sort of prank they were all up to. Arla, again, felt terribly alone.

"Shut it!" shouted Ms Liimm. "Now please turn to page thirty-eight of the Charter of the Forlorn. Today we will be discussing the discovery of the Ketuhanan."

As if the teacher had thrown a switch, the students snapped into obedience and flipped through their data pads in unison. Arla sat at a desk next to the window where she could stare out into the beautiful blue sky and watch little critters chattering up in the trees. She placed her data pad on the table and began flipping to the desired page. Propping the data pad to a vertical position, she hid her head from the teacher. Once she was hidden, Arla took out a small knife and began carving a small hibiscus flower on her desk. It was her morning routine. Her desk already contained numerous carvings of many things she had on her mind. She had been caught a few times, but Ms Liimm eventually gave up and ignored Arla's stubbornness and assumed she was bored. But Arla knew otherwise. She was never bored, because she believed there was more to see and discover than whatever she could get from reading about the superficial achievements of a political entity. She understood that out there somewhere she could be alive. She turned to the window and began dreaming of possibilities. To become a dreamer of the day was the only education and hope she could get. Sometimes, when feeling lonely, the only cure was to be with herself.

"Psst! Arla! Hey, Arla!"

Arla turned around, and saw Bahl waving his tongue from left to right. His entourage were laughing hard. Ms Liimm continued preaching.

At lunch, Arla and Bell retreated to their favourite area of the lawn. An oak tree stood in the middle. Under the guarding branches of the oak, Bell and Arla laid out their lunch for each other to share. They caught up with the happenings of the day, embellishing events that made them laugh.

"So, seriously, what was Bahl doing?" asked Bahl.

"I have no idea. But I know it was mean. I felt like punching him in the face, and to make matters worse, I have to see him every single day."

Arla left out the part about Bahl trying to get "intimate" with her that morning. She felt it was best not to elevate an already-complicated situation into something even more disturbing. But that did not stop Arla from being angry.

"Arla, did he do anything to you?"

"What? What do you mean?"

"You know ... things. Is he making you feel uncomfortable?"

Arla knew Bell suspected something. She was on the verge of bursting into tears, but gained enough courage and willpower to say, "Of course not. I'm fine."

"Look, if that perverted rat did anything to you, tell me. I will help you. I am your friend."

"All right, Bell. Here. Have the strawberry you wanted. I've kept it for you."

Bell's face beamed with delight as she started munching away in tiny bites, savouring each one. Orphans rarely had the opportunity to taste such wonderful delights. The best and tastiest foods were mostly distributed to Paradisians who wore coveralls – to people who had a purpose and could contribute back to their community. Orphans had no families to support them. But Bell and Arla had each other. And that was enough.

"This strawberry sure brings back memories," said Bell as she looked up into the sunny skies. "It brings back memories."

"What do you remember?" asked Arla.

"You know – happy things. I can't really recall specifics, but I know I used to be happy. I remember a warm rock I used to sit on as I stared at the setting sun. I remember how beautiful it was. And that warm hug I received from someone. I can't remember who it was, but I know it gave me happiness."

"Do you remember your family?" asked Arla.

"No … I don't." Bell turned away from Arla and started to hug herself, trying to close up a memory she did not want to remember. "Better not go there. I'd rather not go back."

"I understand, Bell. I'm sorry I asked."

Arla moved closer to Bell, nudging her shoulder with her nose, trying to get Bell's attention. Bell looked at Arla and gave her an adorable smile, and she flipped Arla's nose with her finger. Arla sneezed timidly, her hands flinging desperately as she tried to cover her mouth. Bell had forgotten about the past and smiled.

"Memories are funny things aren't they? One moment they are there, and another moment they hide. Very ethereal."

"Yeah. They are aren't they? I don't remember much, but I know the past was bittersweet. I feel guilty for not remembering everything, I truly do. I just hope I can make it up with madness because I am sick, and I want life to come back."

Bell and Arla placed their heads together, vowing silently that neither would leave the other behind.

Arla was walking down the corridor listening to her music. She noticed students were looking at her and showing a variety of different emotions – shock, disgust, and hilarity. By the time she took her headphones off, everyone was surrounding her, staring straight at her. "Wha … why … why is everyone looking at me?"

"I did not think you were that kind of girl, Arla," said one of them. "You are a slut! The Heavenly Flower looks down upon you!" said the girl with an obvious love bite. "Hey, can I get some?" said another. Arla was overwhelmed with a barrage of accusations she did not understand. She began to shake violently and felt light-headed. She pushed her way out. "Please, please. I need to get to the bathroom."

As she entered the bathroom, everyone was still calling her names. She shut the door behind her and fell to the ground crying her heart out. It was the only thing she could do. "Bell, where are you?"

"She won't be coming. But I don't mind if she does," said Bahl, who had opened the door. "Hey, everyone! Looks like she wants me desperately. I think I have some time before class starts!"

Everyone laughed. His goons came in with him. One of them guarded the door.

"Arla, come and give me a kiss. Don't you want to kiss your lover? Didn't we do it this morning?"

Arla stood up. "What, Bahl? What did we do?"

"Well, you begged me to be your lover. You desperately kissed me and wanted more."

Bahl's goons smirked and nodded to him. They all seemed to be proud of him. "I still can't believe you actually did it, Bahl!" one of them shouted.

"What he told you all were lies!" cried Arla. "I did not do anything with him."

Bahl slapped Arla hard, causing her to fall back into one of his goons. One of the boys held her arms in a locked position, trapping her and preventing her from moving about. "You are a coward," Arla said. "Did you actually think you had a chance? Look at you, doing this for the sake of being famous!"

"Shut it! You slut! You approached me, and this is what I get?"

Bahl looked back at one of his goons. He seemed to be looking for recognition for what he had done. The guy was uninterested; he continued to stare at his fingernails. Bahl became angrier and moved his face close to Arla. "Let me cut a little of your face, you liar. Looks like you can't do anything about it, huh? You see? You need friends."

Arla slammed her head towards Bahl as hard as she could, smashing his nose. Bahl tumbled and fell on his back. Once he was incapacitated, Arla slammed the back of her head to the goon who held her. He fell backwards holding his nose, screaming in pain. In the sudden confusion, Arla took out her carving knife and prepared to defend herself. But the mere sight of a knife did not drive fear into Arla's tormentors. They were offended, in fact, at the sight of a vulnerable girl with a petty knife. They taunted her, challenging her to make her next move, bringing themselves closer and closer, daring her act further. Arla retreated into a corner, quivering and uncertain about her decision to bring out her knife. They had called her bluff.

"Nowhere to go now, huh?" said Bahl as he struggled to get up with his bleeding nose. "You will regret that."

With her back against the wall, Arla remembered a vague and uncertain past. She remembered blurry visions of a woman with her throat sliced, and the mangled bodies of two men down on the street. She remembered a face – a horrible face that was neither man nor beast. She felt touches on her body that screamed humiliation and defilement. Alarms rang in her mind to fight back against a monster with his tentacles and devious laugh. She had sliced and diced with all her might, but nothing daunted him, and he had come back bigger than he'd been before. She had been helpless as she screamed as loud as she could to scare the monster away. Then the blur lifted. Bell was holding her, calling her to wake up.

"Bell, I was so scared. It came back again."

"Don't worry, Arla. I'm here."

Arla hugged Bell with all her might. As she hugged her, Arla saw goons displaying countless terrified expressions standing behind Bell. The goon with the fingernails was on the ground unconscious with multiple bleeding wounds. Bahl and the rest stood in shock, trying to comprehend the madness that had occurred.

"Arla is a monster!"

"Come on, Arla. Let's go home. We have nothing else to do over here. Screw them all! We'll go back to where we belong," said Bell.

Hurrying out from the bathroom was an easy feat, as everyone who was brave enough to taunt was afraid to touch Arla. They were worried of a curse from the witch. "Come on, Arla. You can do it. We'll make it back. Don't worry about what they think."

They hurriedly walked past the black gates and onto the path they had taken in the morning. Arla began to feel the willpower drain out of her body as she struggled to keep up with Bell. Bell had no choice but to lift Arla's arm and lay it across her shoulders. In her mind, Arla entertained the thought of giving up. She was no longer present; in a blink, she did not realize she had already walked up an entire flight of stairs and was lying on her bed staring at an empty ceiling.

"Arla, wake up. Have some water."

"No, I don't think I want to."

"Why not? You need your strength back. You can do it."

"I am tired, Bell. So, so tired. I … don't want to get up anymore," muttered Arla, as a sad tear came rolling down her cheeks. "I am very tired."

"Do you think you are the only one, Arla? I am tired as well. We are better than they are, and we can beat them. Every single one of them, Arla. Every single one of them. And we will one day be free."

Arla dragged herself up into a sitting position. It was an effort no person in the world should notice. Bell insisted with her water, so Arla took a sip and placed the glass down on the floor. "Do you really think we are free? I doubt it."

"Why do you say that? Why so dull?"

"It is because we live in this world on terms that dictate our future – the future of the unwanted," said Arla. "We live with an incredible notion of freedom while knowing we are bound like slaves. Here is the harsh reality. I will spit it out: we are not free. We are fleeting beings living on borrowed time, allowed to live in this world with scraps given to us for charity." Arla stared blankly into the room, trembling. "We were meant to die. Our sole purpose is to die and become fertilizer for our hibiscus."

Bell was devastated; not because Arla's ramblings had a hint of truth, but because of Arla's choice to let go of her responsibility, leaving the world even worse than it had been before.

Bell held Arla's two hands, and she held them close to her chest. "I know you to be many things, Arla. But a coward is not one of them. Yes, what you said may be true, but it is not how it is supposed to end. I believe in us, Arla. I feel strong when we are together. We can move mountains and oceans. All we have to do is believe in ourselves. I cannot imagine a world without you, Arla. You mean everything to me. Please … don't do anything that will break my heart."

Arla had stopped trembling. She wasn't thinking anymore; she was light-headed and clear. She turned to look at Bell, who was now in tears. She had not known her life meant so much to Bell. She realized she had terrorized a loved one's heart. Arla held Bell's hands, feeling every crevice and wrinkle that indicated a desiring presence. Arla noticed that Bell's palpitating lips held the colour of a strawberry, promising hints of sweetness and passion. Arla took a chance and dove deep towards Bell, locking her lips with hers, caring not of the consequence.

Bell did not stop her. The innocent temptation of a young kiss was warm and gentle. They found themselves lying on the bed, staring longingly at each other. "I love you, Bell."

"I love you too, Arla."

"I knew there was something wrong with you two. I had a feeling and I was right!" said Bahl, who stood at the door. "I knew it when you did not return my love!"

Arla and Bell woke up forcefully, trying to comprehend how much time had passed. They struggled awkwardly to get away from each other's embrace.

"Bahl, do not tell anybody about this," said Bell. Arla was too shocked to say anything.

"Well, I don't have to tell anybody about anything. There are guards on their way up right now as we speak."

Then Bell heard the rumbling of heavy boots storming up the wooden stairs. She and Bell were trapped. The only way out was the door where Bahl stood. Bell, with her ability to make a quick decision, grabbed Arla's wrists and pulled her towards the window. Arla had no choice but to abandon her pants. Only her nightclothes covered her skin.

"Bell, what are we going to do? Where are we going?"

"Quick! Out the window! Hug the wall and walk towards the roof!"

Bell opened the window as fast as she could, and helped Arla through it gently, making sure she did not fall.

"Bell, this is too high. We might fall."

"Better than being in the dungeon! Hurry, Arla! Keep going! I'll be right behind you!"

Arla was almost to the roof when she slipped. Bell's hands grabbed Arla's wrists and pulled her back, and they kept moving until they reached to the roof. They noticed there was a crowd of people standing below, hollering for them to give up. Bahl was at the window screaming at the fugitives. "Queers! The queers are running away!"

Orphans and queers. Arla realized that she and Bell were Paradise's most wanted. The crazed populace desired them to be thrown into the dungeon and executed. They were officially shunned by society. On the roof, Bell held on to Arla's hands as they looked down upon an angry mob. "At least we still have each other," she said. And they ran along the rooftops, jumping from one building to the next, the presence of the guards ever so close behind them.

"Stop, Bell. I need to rest. I can't keep up."

"All right, Arla. I think we have covered enough distance. Have a rest."

The rain was falling upon them. Their clothes were stuck to their skin, and the chill in the air caused their bodies to shiver. Bell sat with Arla and sheltered her with her arms, giving any warmth she could give. Upon the horizon, flashes of lightning and echoes of thunder filled the dark clouds. Arla held Bell's arms as tightly as possible.

"There! There they are!" shouted a guard.

"Come on, Arla! Let's go!"

With a heave of breath, Arla got up and ran. Neither of them knew if they would be running forever, and the thought of forever made both of them weary. They had no idea where to run or where to hide. But they knew they must never turn back. They kept running forward clawing for every inch of freedom. It was only ignorance and trepidation that waited behind them.

"Bell! I think we need to get off the roof! This ladder can take us back down!"

The ladder was rusty and creaked at every touch. Nobody had used it for a long time, and it was not safe. With a push, Bell extended the ladder down to the ground, and thus they climbed downward, feeling the rust on their hands. Midway, a guard who was too big for his own good decided to climb down with them. The integrity of the ladder's rungs was insufficient to sustain their combined weight, and the ladder jerked forward. Bell lost her grip and fell all the way down. Arla climbed down as fast as she could, ignoring the ladder's wobble. "Bell! Are you all right? By the Heavenly Flower, your arm!"

"Thanks for the observation, Miss Obvious. Urgh! Lift me up. You see that store up ahead? Let's go there."

Arla gathered her strength and supported Bell as they ran all the way to the store. The keeper was alarmed at the entrance of two young girls, half naked and drenched from head to toe. He asked, "What happened to you two? Where are the rest of your clothes?"

The young girls ignored the keeper and proceeded to the back of the store. Other workers were all stunned at the sight of them as they loaded cargo onto a coach carried by iron horses. Not long afterwards, the girls found themselves in a back alley where they were exposed to the rain. Bell had regained enough strength so she could carry herself again. The guard who had followed them on the ladder caught up. "Halt! Stop running!"

Arla ran ahead of Bell. At the next corner, Arla looked back and could not see Bell. Arla paused and retraced her steps. She found Bell catching her breath, leaning against a wall, holding on to her broken arm. "Keep going, Arla."

Before Arla took a step forward to help her friend, a group of guards approached, moving towards Bell. They surrounded her like a pack of wolves. One of them grabbed her broken arm and pressed hard. Bell screamed in horrible pain. Arla fumed, but Bell had her eyes on Arla, telling her to do nothing. A guard noticed her stare and turned around to see Arla standing in the corner. "Hey! The other one is over there!"

"Run!" screamed Bell.

By instinct, Arla turned and ran as fast as she could, far away from the guards. She ran and ran until her lungs burned fumes. Finding another storehouse, she ran inside and found a good hiding spot among the goods. She huffed and puffed as fast as she could to keep her lungs from failing. When she heard the guards, she fell silent, breathing through her mouth. The heavy boots of the guards thumped loudly. Arla spotted a guard who was walking towards her. She thought she had been discovered, but realized the guard was focused on something else.

"You, boy! Have you seen a young girl pass by around these premises?"

"Oh, I have not. I have been keeping an eye on these products for the keeper. I swear I have not seen anybody suspicious entering this bay."

Arla had been in such a hurry to hide, she had not noticed a young man sitting among crates. She looked up at the young man from her hiding spot, hoping he would not sell her out.

"Please feel free to check about," said the young man to the guard. "I am sure the keeper will oblige."

The guard turned back to his comrades. The young man let out a quick wink at Arla, and she immediately let out a breath of relief.

"That won't be necessary, boy. Keep up the good work. We shall not be bothering you anymore."

"A fine day to you, sir. I hope you catch the criminal you are looking for."

And just like that, the guards left. Arla stood up and faced the young man. "Thank you. I am in your debt. What can I offer you in return?"

"Nothing! You don't have to give me anything. In fact, it looks to me as if you are in a more desperate situation than I am – running about in the rain without much clothing on for cover."

Arla recalled that she was half naked and instantly covered herself from the young man, blushing bright red. She pleaded to him not to harm her. The young man nodded. He walked away and quickly returned with a towel, which he handed to Arla. "Do not worry. I will not hurt you in any way."

"What is your name?"

"My name is Idrisele Eblazeem. You can call me Idris."

"What do you do here?"

"I don't work here. I lied to the guards."

"Then why are you here."

"To help you, Arla."

"How do you know my name? What do you want from me?"

"My mentor told me to find you. He mentioned that you were in trouble, and he wanted me to bring you to safety. Why you specifically, I have no idea. But as long as you are important to him, I will oblige."

"Who is this mentor of yours? What is his name?"

"If I told you, you would not know. It is best if I take you to him. He is waiting."

She felt a tinge of dishonesty in him. She knew he was doubtful of her, and he was secretive. She did not trust him, but he was the only chance Arla had to rely on.

"But my friend, Bell. What about her?"

"My mentor gave no mention of her. He told me about you, and you only."

"She will be tortured! I need to save her! I won't follow you."

Idris scoffed at her feeble attempt to understand her situation. "Do you know that the dungeon is one of the most protected parts of Paradise? If you and I go to save your friend, we will both be executed. Think, Arla. Think logically and strategically. It would be suicide."

"I can't leave her behind!"

Idris stared at her. "I understand you want to save your friend. But can we please go to a safe house before we make any rash decisions? I mean, you don't have proper clothing on. How do you expect to rescue your friend in your undies?"

Arla considered her situation and calmed down. She nodded to Idris and followed him down to the basement. There he moved a cupboard to one side to reveal a hidden underground tunnel that looked crude but reliable. Arla knew that tunnels were used for subversive reasons. They had not been created for mere games of hide and seek. Something felt wrong.

"Who built this tunnel? It can't be just you."

Idris lit an oil lamp and gazed at Arla. "Well, I might as well tell you now rather than later I guess," he muttered. He led her into the tunnel and closed up the entrance behind them. They then proceeded to crawl through, with Idris leading.

"Well? Are you going to tell me?"

Idris let out a sigh and said, "The Hibiscus Party built this tunnel. We dug it."

Chapter 5

Down the Rabbit Hole

After he had told Arla he was part of the Hibiscus Party in that damp tunnel, which countless men and women had dug, he became nervous about whether she was a person to trust. He knew their leader wanted to meet her with utmost urgency, but helping a fugitive to escape from authorities and then bringing her in was all too dodgy. However, even then, he knew Arla was ... different.

"All right, Idris. You are with the Party. Where are you taking me?"

He did not want to start a conversation with her. Hence, he remained the quiet mysterious man he had hoped to be.

"Why should I trust you?" she asked. "I do not even know you, and you are suddenly leading me into a tunnel nobody knows? What would you do if you were me?"

"I would shut up and just follow," he said. It was the longest crawl he'd ever had to endure. The dirt stained his shirt as he crawled further, holding aloft a fragile oil lamp. The lamp acted as their silent guide through a dark path. To his surprise, never did she complain, and for that, he did not understand why he hated her. He gave her a gaudy smile and continued forward.

"So, I heard you were an orphan," he said.

"Yes, I am."

"What does it feel like?" He gave a sudden grunt while he removed a huge worm blocking his way.

"It feels like ... dragging oneself through the dirt."

"Was that a joke or was it serious?"

"A little of both. Everything is a little of both, to be fair."

He heard voices echoing from the end – they were close. She told Idris in a whisper, "I like it in here."

"You can stay here if you like."

"But it would be lonely here."

"Then come with me and meet the others."

"But I do not know which choice is lonelier: being alone in the dark or being with a circle of strangers I do not know or trust. You included."

He felt sorry for Arla. She was right, in a cynical sort of way. If he had been in her shoes, he would have thought the same way. She was definitely the braver one, and he hated her for it, making him angrier. "Look! You do not have any choice here. Come with me or I will leave you behind and bury you in this place. Have you ever thought that maybe you are the one who can't be trusted?"

Arla stayed quiet. He hated the silence and began to crawl faster, leaving behind a person he considered unnecessary baggage who was not worthy of his cause. He desired to leave the tunnel as soon as possible. He hated being in a small, tight spot. He hated everything.

"Idris! There you are! Glad the tunnel did not fall on you."

"Hi, Livi. Glad to see you are not sleeping on watch."

"Hah! How could I fall asleep if a new recruit is coming in today! Anyway, where is she?" Idris dusted his attire and snuffed out the fire of the oil lamp. He never looked back into that hole, hoping Livi would just let it be.

They were in the basement of a grocery shop. The walls were coloured in a mundane colour of grey; peelings of paint had been left dangling freely, revealing a hint of the wall's original yellow. Idris placed his gloves on a white musky desk where a small radio lay crackling inaudible noises. Livi was a recent recruit. He'd been with the group no longer than six months, and he was glad to be a guard of a tunnel for the rest of his life, as he'd reported that he wasn't suited for decision making. Hence, he lazed through life with his fat belly. If only he would mind his own business and not ask too many questions. Arla was not a concern of his.

"I am supposed to radio in if you come back with Arla, Idris. Where is she?" He looked into the tunnel one more time.

"I guess she decided not to come. Radio back to whoever asked you."

"*She* asked me, Idris!"

"Why do you care? As long as your belly is full, nothing matters, right?"

Idris sat on the ground to clean his boots. His back faced Livi, but he sensed his companion's disgruntled expression. Livi turned around in circles panicking, plotting to evade punishment for a small duty gone wrong.

"Just radio in and tell her it was Arla's decision. Isn't that enough?"

"I … don't know."

"Well, it is for the better. We don't need another fresh face around here."

After he scrubbed the last crevice of his boots, Idris turned to Livi and suggested they cover the entrance of the tunnel with a wooden board. Before they could hammer in the final nail to seal the coffin, they could hear the dragging sound of a scratch from the other side. Livi and Idris reopened the tunnel and found Arla crawling out. Idris offered her his hand, but in an act of defiance and dignity, she stood up on her own, wiping the remnants of sadness from her face and from her past. The darkness had been a cruel teacher and taught her something only the silence of loneliness could teach, for she now knew the only way out was to save herself. There she stood before Idris, confident and proud. He could only look aside and introduce Livi to Arla.

"Nice to meet you, Livi."

"Err … nice to meet you too. There are changes of clothing upstairs, all ready for you both. Go on ahead, and I will radio in to Jasmine about your arrival."

"Thank you, Livi. I look forward to seeing you again."

They nodded to each other as if there existed a profound respect between them. Livi must have taken fancy to the girl to behave in such a way. Never had he done the same to Jasmine or any of the others. It was as if Arla had brought out a faint hint of nobility within Livi's manners. Idris admitted in his mind that the green horns of his dark jealousy were growing with the presence of Arla, for Livi was under his guidance and supervision, and he had never once shown Idris the same respect he gave to Arla.

"All right, Livi. I leave it to you to close the tunnel. Arla and I will go upstairs to change."

"Yes, do not worry. I will get it done."

Arla was ahead of Idris as they climbed creaky old stairs. Every step they made was a chilling announcement of their arrival. It was made worse when he tried his best to silence his steps. He was afraid Arla would judge him. For a young man, Idris was embarrassed by his childish nature. Either way, he thought it best to remain a mystery to Arla. It was his only defence against the magnetic aura she seemed to exude.

"Hey. Do you mind if I change first?" she asked.

"Yes, of course, Arla. I will wait outside."

Idris walked towards a window down the hall. He dilly-dallied on his way, appreciating various paintings of the old Paradise that hung on decrepit walls. His arms were crossed behind his back, which made him look wise beyond his years. He was patient and unhurried as he enjoyed watching the shadows through the windowpane reveal a wooden floor. The morning sun was up, and another day had begun. He walked closer to the window to feel the light of the sun warm on his hands. Through the window, he caught a view that would make any young man aspire to a great future. Paradise had awakened, and its high buildings towered the smallest of men. Airships were flying about carrying large amounts of cargo to the Southern Lands as they glistened in the light of dawn. Their immense strength and defiance towards Bumi's gravity was physical proof of the fact that, if one was to dream and work hard, anything was possible. He was proud to be part of it. He knew that not many appreciated such aspirations. He knew his dreams were his alone, because he knew there was a sickness growing, a sickness he could not define, that ate the roots of a hibiscus flower. On a halcyon day, he stood by the window staring out, hoping to be the man who would change the world.

Bright and *white*, *clean* and *posh* – those were the words that described the interrogation room of Paradise's dungeon. Bell was free to move anywhere within it, but decided to have a rest on the only chair available. There was no other furniture. She had been left half naked with an untreated broken arm. Bell placed her arm at a certain angle to encourage a numbness that dulled her pain to a tolerable level. A bluish bruise had emerged on her skin, bringing no comfort to Bell. Still, she waited patiently, holding back her tears; being alone in that room was torture enough. The only noise she listened to was the scream of her own illusion.

"Belle Wallee, please stand up and face the wall," blared the speakers of the room. "Place your hands behind your head."

"But my arm ... it's broken."

There was no reply. Bell tried her best to lift her hands to her head, but to no avail. She trembled in pain and fear, as there were cruel rumours about the guards. The acted as they pleased when their prisoner was an orphan; nobody cared if they disappeared. Within the walls of the dungeon, Bell's fate was not for her to decide. The white mechanical door opened, and in came a big man. Behind him, two others stormed towards Bell. They shouted, "Put your hands on your head!"

"My arm … it's broken …"

A barrage of punches and kicks flew into Bell, giving her no quarter for breathing. She threw up everything she had in her belly. Mercifully, the big man waved his underlings to halt. They obeyed like vicious dogs and left the room.

"Belle. Please have a seat," said the man with a coarse voice. He held his hairy arms to his side; they shone under the light. He sifted through screens in his data pad, studying information sent to him about Bell. He nodded, moving his lips as if he was talking to himself. Bell was on the ground, desperate to rest on her chair.

"Come on. We don't have all day," he growled.

"My arm, sir … it is broken."

The big man walked over to Bell who wriggled like a worm. He glared at her and gave a disappointed, smug look. "And do you see it to be my problem? You ran away from the guards, miss. You reap what you sow, miss."

"I'm sorry. I'm really sorry. Please—"

The big man squatted next to her, patting her. "Oh, you. An orphan with nowhere to go. Why did you have to slice up an innocent boy, huh? You know your evil doings will not go unchallenged by the law. And it seems that this time, you hurt the wrong victim. His family are protective of him, and they are important. They care about him so much they are willing to exact revenge deemed 'appropriate'. You see what parents do for their children? So enduring … I guess it is something an orphan like you will never understand."

Bell was tired, and her pain had turned her numb. She looked at the big man to find him gentle on her eyes. His hair was combed backwards, revealing a strong forehead. His chin was chiseled and gruff with hints of stubble. Because of the way he carried himself, he emanated an air of fine upbringing. Bell could smell a distinct scent that was alluring to her nose. Clean and flawless, he was the perfect example of a gentleman.

"My name is Rizal, by the way," he said as he picked her up and carried her in his arms with no effort. In his arms, Bell was dwarfed in comparison to his stature. He placed her on her chair and arranged her hair to a palatable state. "Now there you go. Pretty."

Bell did not care about her arm anymore. She knew no treatment would be given to her.

"Shall we make ourselves comfortable?" said Rizal as he keyed an instruction into his data pad. The room came alive in minor rumbles as the walls moved in closer. Mirrors, each the size of a wall, slide down from above, surrounding Rizal and Bell.

Bell looked around, seeing rows upon rows of herself in every single direction. Everywhere she looked, she saw herself staring back. Rizal had disappeared, leaving Bell with the company of her own reflections. It felt as if the room had only her in it, and she was the main attraction of a show.

"Look around, little girl. Look around. There is only you in a room of mirrors. I don't exist anymore. You are talking to nobody but yourself."

Bell drifted into a chaotic slumber in which she dreamt she was awake, speaking to Rizal. He was her, and she was him; she was not sure if she was staring straight out or straight in. Rizal's voice chuckled from a Bell to her left, while the Bell on her right asked, "Are you comfortable yet?"

"What is this? What is going on?"

"I am in you, Bell. In your mind."

"No, this is … not real."

"Yes it is. You are looking at yourself now. Staring into a limitless abyss of your mind. Stare longer, and the abyss will stare right back at you. Go try it."

Bell complied and stared. The longer she waited, the more her fear grew at what she might see. The darkness moved and it consumed Bell, bit by bit. She felt the darkness touching her, molesting her naked skin. It was alive, in her mouth, her lungs, and her brain. She opened and closed her eyes to disrupt the illusion, but she saw only pitch black. Bell paced slowly to touch the dark, and she felt it went on forever.

"What is this?" she asked.

"You."

Bell was pulled into the dark. She could not see anything but the white chair she sat on. In a sudden bright flash, she was surrounded by countless vacant bodies of herself, staring with big eyes. "Let me out! Please!"

"I can't. I don't know how to," a vacant voice replied.

"Please … stop … please."

From the fringes of dark ashes where Bell lay, Arla emerged. She walked with such grace and sultriness that Bell felt warmed. "Come to me …" Arla said.

"Arla? No … What are you doing here? Get out! Get out!"

"Come to me, Bell."

"What? No! You don't understand! Get out!"

Bell stood up and ran towards Arla. She embraced Arla with a hug that showed how much she missed her friend, but what Bell held in her arms was not flesh and blood. Arla had turned into a wooden puppet that gave Bell a creepy vibe of horror. It looked at Bell and cried out with the voice of a baby. Her wooden skin soon decomposed to reveal a muscled interior; her veins splashed pints of blood that stained Bell's entire body. Bell felt her mind intertwined with fearful confusion, churning her head to ache. She beat herself, while all the other Bells mutilated themselves in their own creative fashion, tearing at limbs or gouging a lung. Each Bell died in horrid suicide. Bell's vision blurred as she lay on a battlefield riddled with bodies that had suffered violent death. A crack of thunder danced through a red moon sky. In her soul, Bell no longer lived.

"All right then. Now, can you hear what I am saying?" Rizal asked. "Nod your head if you understand me."

Bell nodded.

"Good. Where is your friend?"

"I don't know," said Bell as she winced at a growing pain.

"Why did you and your friend harm an innocent boy?"

"It was he who wanted to hurt Arla. She defended herself."

"But eyewitnesses claimed that it was Arla and you who attacked."

Bell sighed. "The most despicable accusation comes from the poison of intentions. Believe in what you may. I have told the truth. Would you believe an orphan?"

Rizal walked towards Bell, who still had her eyes closed. She was elegantly beautiful and calm. No harm had been done to her physically. Rizal touched her cheeks and caressed her hair, saying: "You are telling the truth. Interesting. Guards!"

"Sir?" asked his youngling who came in with eager haste.

"Get her back to her cell. And help me inform the inspector general. I will be meeting him later in the evening to discuss a few matters."

The young guard saluted and proceeded with his instructions. Rizal, strutting gently with his arms behind his back, walked across the white corridor, passing by staff and fellow guards. He was on his way to his desk to touch more upon Bell's story. He was silent throughout, but excited as he looked around. One of Rizal's young guard recruits who stumbled upon him turned curious, asking his friend, "Who is that?"

"You do not know who that is? He was at your graduating ceremony of the guards. He is *the* Captain Rizal!"

"Are you kidding me? Please tell me you are kidding me? The Hero of Paradise?"

Arla was at the window staring at her reflection in the glass. The weight of slumber loomed in her body, as thoughts of her best friend kept her awake. The dusty windows blocked what she could see outside. They were closed shut, leaving behind a stuffy room that suffocated her. Her hands trembled to imagine her friend trapped in the dungeon. She wished they were together instead of one being free and the other caged. Arla left the windows closed. She saw an old, solid antique dresser standing against the wall. It had been left there to collect dust and melancholy.

She found a bathroom and decided to clean herself up a bit. Turning on a faucet, she let the water flow into the white sink. She stared as the water swirled in a circle and plunged deep into a dark hole. The water was cold to her trembling hands as she scrubbed her hands clean. It was a tempting relief from a sadness that never left. Then she decided that she needed to wash her entire body. So there she was, standing in the middle of the bathroom, removing her filthy clothes one by one until she was naked. She filled the tub to the brim. She got into the water head first, and stayed below. She held her breath and blew a few bubbles, which distorted her view of the world above. Under the surface, the world was quiet; time had stopped. She could hear herself and the demons that haunted her. Then she wondered if she could cry under water. Frustrated and alone, she screamed with her last breath, letting in water to flood her lungs as she gasped for air. The tremble of drowning went through her entire body. Her hands on the side of the tub were desperate to save her. But she felt it was better to endure the pain one last time and drift into nothing. She closed her eyes and released her grip.

"Wake up! What are you doing!"

Arla woke on a cold damp floor covered only by a towel. Idris was on his knees next to her, holding her head while gently tapping on her cheeks. He was about to give her another breath of life. She saw his face and realized her lungs were filled. She rolled onto her side and threw up pints of clear water.

"Are you all right? Why did you do that? Nobody should be doing that."

Arla coughed deeply, making sure every remnant of her mistake was gone. She looked at Idris, who had the pale face of a frightened boy, but had the true caring eyes of a gentleman. She knew she was not all right. She was broken, and her soul could not be mended. She held on to her towel and cried over the broken truth of her lowly life.

"Hey ... it is all right. Really. I don't seem like much, but you can cry as much as you want. I will stay."

She continued to cry, but she was not crying alone; someone had listened. Idris came close and gave her a hug. "Well, I won't say I am not comfortable being with a naked woman, but do you mind?"

Arla smiled a little and allowed Idris to put his hands around her shoulders so she could lay her head against him. Idris did nothing but listen. It was the afternoon. Arla began to tire, and her tears were dry. Idris stood up and gave her his hands. Arla nodded, and they both went out of the bathroom. Idris passed her dry towels and fresh clothes. As she dressed, Idris looked out beyond the dusty window. He wiped the glass with his sleeve and stared out a little. "I did not know there was a nice view here," he said. And he continued to unlock the window and open it. Fresh winds blew in a sudden gust that made Idris fall back a little, and the white curtains fluttered. "This feels much better. The winds from the lake should clean everything up in this room. You will feel better."

Idris turned around to find Arla dressed in simple attire. Her khaki pants fitted well from her waist to her thighs. And they went well with the dark grey shirt that hugged her figure. They both looked at each other in acknowledgement of what had happened. She was tired, and she slowly crept onto the bed. Idris placed an extra pillow under her head and gave her another to hug. He stayed next to her until she was deeply asleep, hoping she would not wake to a bad dream. He later took his own clothes and changed before he went downstairs to find Livi.

"Livi, we will meet Jasmine tomorrow."

Livi was cleaning his shop floor with a trusty broom, while two young helpers arranged new food products on his shelves. A few customers were browsing at the other end of the shop. Upon hearing Idris, Livi became stressed out as he had promised Jasmine they would meet with her as soon as possible. He became flustered and started to blame everything on Idris. His bad manners were crude. Customers caught a whiff of his rudeness and left as uninterested as they had entered.

"Shout as much as you want, Livi. But we are leaving tomorrow."

Livi grew tired of his own pointless rage. He knew he had to obey whatever Idris ordered, as he was his captain. With a troubled mind, Livi went down into the basement to radio in a change of plans. Idris strutted out of the store to bask under a midday sun. He scuffed the soles of his feet on the green grass of a summer season. He sat down and felt the tips of the grass caress his hands while he lay his head on the earth. He thought of many things, but most of his thoughts were about Arla. He wondered ….

He shook his head and searched beyond the blue skies for more dreams of the day. At the same time, another soul dreamt in the dark, experiencing dreams she never wanted.

Chapter 6

The Old Prince

A black bleeding heart stood on a huge mahogany desk in his room. It was where he hid his key to a cabinet where he stored his precious possessions. He was eager and desperate for the rough times that come and go. Curtains were draped over the windows, allowing only a dim shimmer of candlelight to dance across his posh study. It was regal and traditional, a place old books could call home. There were no shelves for these books; rather, they were stacked upon one another to create buildings of books – a city of knowledge as he called it. Among the city's nooks and crannies, his throne was hidden.

Hunched on his throne, he gazed upon a piece of paper on which he wrote carefully. Three candles melted together to form a large common candle that provided the right light for his academic interest and enjoyment. He had compiled note upon note of his thoughts with a long dance of his pen across endless white empty planes. His occasional pause to refer to his books demonstrated his interest in details. A mighty mind in his solitude, he was a constant wave that hit the cliffs of fortitude. He was known as the Prince.

"Morning, morning, morning," screamed his wooden clock hanging from the wall. It ticked and tocked as annoyingly as it did when the sun had set. For the Prince, the sun rose when the shadow of dusk came creeping. It was his moment – his moment to rise from his throne and to mingle among his subjects. He rose in an unhurried fashion. The cloak he wore fell upon the marble floor as natural as silk. His muscle memory was his guide as he moved among his books like a dancer – light and graceful. At a huge door made of ancient wood carved with little golden hibiscus flowers, lay waiting two pretty young maids who had prepared his toiletries for his washing ritual. "Please, sir. Your warm water is ready."

"Thank you, Mae," greeted the Prince, and he drowned his face in his washing pan. He raised his head in gratification and let out a short laugh. "Quick, Tae! Give me my towel!"

Both Mae and Tae were so used to his routine, they knew exactly where the Prince would step after he dried his face and hands. It was a mechanical memory ingrained after years of serving the Prince. Mae and Tae had never left his side since they were children. The Prince became their guardian when their parents were killed in a mysterious incident. It was an unsolved murder. Mae and Tae, as orphans, had been tossed into the streets to fend for themselves. Fortunately, his royal highness the Prince had taken pity on them and raised them to his liking. They were his most loyal subjects. As usual, Mae brought his mirror to him while Tae brought a candle close to shine upon the Prince's reflection.

"Another day, another wrinkle. What do you think, ladies?"

"Quite refreshing," said Mae. "You still look absolutely dashing." But it was the way Mae made her comment that made the Prince feel insecure. He knew everyone was noticing that his age was showing. But it meant the world to him to hear Mae say he looked good. A few more praises, he thought. Maybe then he could die in peace – hopefully soon before more of his youth was taken away.

"Open the door, Tae. Let out the old Prince!" Tae unlocked the huge door, and in came a gust of wind that flowed through his long, white hair. His dry, wrinkled skin hid a youthful bone structure as he went forth eager to meet his evening's chore. Patches of pale grey dots covered his entire body; he was glad no one had to see him in the nude. The Prince did not mind; at his age, he knew his wisdom came first.

The door opened to an old alley. People clothed in heavy drapery sat along the sides, selling wares and junk that seemed useless to the naïve. They were chanting and singing to their customers to encourage business. When a song or a chant caught a passer-by's interest, both customer and seller would lock in battle to haggle over the price. Residents of the alley liked to be as loud as they could, for the world above did not care for those who were below. The old Prince walked with grace through a long alleyway, and everyone gave way to his passage. There were some who touched and kissed his hands, and the old Prince gave them his love in return, as Mae and Tae followed in his shadow. There hid a history of the life of the people within the alley's walls. Mae and Tae had once studied these walls and discovered many carvings and engravings of ancient words. They had asked the old Prince before, but he'd only smiled with a sad face and had nothing to tell. But Mae and Tae knew the alley had once been part of a huge labyrinth of an old city. Due to the bashings of time, the old city had been reduced to a marketplace for poor barter traders and vagabonds. It was not a Paradise many wanted to see.

"Come! Let's dance and cheer on another day, shall we? I believe I am already late,"

"You are about an hour late, sir," replied one of his maids. "You are unbelievably late."

"Haha! So un-princely of me, but also very innocent of you both. On some occasions, being a little late can provide us with power. Let the impatience of others play with their own self-control. I will always have the last say, and probably the last laugh," gushed the Prince as he turned forward and walked on. "Come! Let's not waste any more time now, shall we?"

Mae and Tae nodded to each other and placed cowls over their heads, like priestesses. The Prince, with his shaggy attire, never displayed royalty, but strutted on as the most graceful royal there was. They passed through to a canal where a little wooden boat lay anchored. The boatman tipped his hat and began pulling and untying the knots of a rope, preparing the boat to leave port. The rickety boat began to shake and roll as all three stepped into it. The boatman tried his best to balance it as much as he could. The stench that came from the water of the canal was vile. The sewage from the living quarters of makeshift huts all around flowed into it. The Prince had learned to love that stench. Like his books, the makeshift huts found their way to coexist upon one another without the fatal danger of falling. They were homes for many, and a refuge for the unwanted. Families lived together with a code; they shared their food, and they shared their love. All those who lived down below were part of a big family, and the Prince was their patriarch. Lined up on the sides of the canal, the huts went up all the way to the ceiling, where the moonlight had managed to shine through the cracks. The cracks also allowed the night air from the outside world to slip in. The Prince stared down upon the dark waters of the canal, imagining the twinkling stars of the land above that he sorely missed.

"Mae, please give this nice boatman a coin for his efforts," said the Prince.

Mae shifted her hands below her waist to retrieve a coin – a coin that only the city below used. She stood up and extended her hand to the boatman, who accepted his gift with a smile.

"All right now, sit down and tell me the events of the day."

Mae signalled Tae to pass her a list she had made the night before. "Today you will need to proceed with discussing terms of food supplies to the western hall. They are beginning to get fidgety. They are worried they might not be getting their fair share."

"Typical. They will never have enough. Proceed."

"Next, you will be meeting with the priestesses. They urgently request that you help them spread the word of the Heavenly Flower."

"Yes, that's just shit. Heavenly my ass. I do not want to spend my time going through the pointless topic of how important the hibiscus flower is. Religious preaching was so last season."

"Uh huh." Tae nodded.

"So continuing, you will be meeting with ... Ram," Mae said.

The Prince turned and stared at Mae. He nodded.

"All right, and after that you should be free for the day," muttered Mae as she slowly folded her papers and snuck them into her bosom.

At the end of the canal, the boat emerged into a great underground lake that stretched beyond the normal perspective. The air was fresh, and the water was still. The lamp hanging on the front of the boat provided the boatman a clear view of his passengers. They felt as if they were the only star shining brightly in a night sky. It was their only solace, as the darkness reigned on all sides. With a sharp ear, one could only imagine the sort of creatures that lurked. Mae once told Tae that she'd seen a sly shadow on all fours looking at her, and Tae had seen the shadow of a flower burning in a dark flame. It was a great lake, and many princes had rowed upon it, yet it was a journey the Prince never loved. "The cheers and jeers I could get used to," he'd once said. "It's knowing that I am still alone even in a crowd that gets to me." He tried his best to stare ahead to discover a hint of where they were headed, but he failed badly at every try. Only the boatman knew where they were going. Experience was the boatman's sight.

"Just relax," said the boatman. "I am here. Just rest while I row the boat. We are almost there. I apologize for the boat."

"No, that's not a matter really. You are very helpful. You have served us well," uttered the Prince. "How old are you? I never asked you this before, all these times. I have aged, but I noticed ... you remain ... eternal."

"I have a secret."

"What secret is that?"

The boatman bent forward to the Prince and whispered. He said: "I drink the water of this lake."

"How could you? It's cursed! And filthy!"

The boatman stood back up and proceeded rowing. A few strokes later, the boatman again spoke to the Prince. "The other secret …" he paused as he went down to grab a handful of water to drink. "Is not minding it to be anything."

The Prince kept his eyes upon the boatman. He was not sure if he should treat his words as something wise or something spoken just for the sake of being spoken – pointless and common. After the boatman noticed the Prince was looking at him, he gave a smile and a shrug. The Prince smiled in return and took out his small notebook, which he kept hidden in his garb. He jotted down something he could revise later in the morning.

"All right. We are here," uttered the boatman as they came to shore. Mae and Tae, who had fallen asleep as they leaned on one another with their heads together, were jolted back from their dream world. They wiped away their drool.

"Come on, you two. Be presentable. It is time to work!" The Prince and his assistants stepped onto soft, crunchy ground as they helped each other. The boatman mentioned he would wait while they went about their daily duties. They were never late to return.

"Thank you again. We will be back at our usual hour," the Prince told him.

"No rush, Prince. I will entertain myself with a book."

Mae and Tae were already at the bottom of a grand stairway, holding on to their candles as they gawked upward and waited for the Prince to catch up. No matter how many trips they made, the experience was still spellbinding. The masonry was a testament to a long-lost skill in Paradise. Stonemasons had carved strange creatures that curled around the sides of a stairway like serpents; their workmanship was a testament to their passion and attention to detail. Drips of water from that magical cavern made the only sound they could hear. It was a serene place, and they found it inspirational, which enhanced their appreciation of the adventures of discovery. They climbed up a step at a time, turning their heads occasionally to view a tiny boat and its boatman. The boatman was deeply engrossed in his book.

"Tae, if you would please give that door a knock?" asked the Prince as they reached the summit. Describing the huge stone wall as a door was a huge understatement. Through skilled masonry, huge *nagas* had been carved into it. They were elegant serpent-like creatures that dominated Bumi's waters. Two of them crawled downward from the top of the stone wall to the middle, where their heads met. They displayed huge grins with intimidating fangs. Their cold, lifeless eyes stared at their unwelcomed visitors, who were dwarfed in comparison to the grey-shaded giant wall.

Tae walked over to stand next to a hole that was just the right size to fit a hand. She reached within it and pulled a small lever. A huge gong sound, accompanied by the jingle of a bell, echoed through the cavern.

They waited.

The cavern vibrated to a low hum. Small speckles of dust and tiny rocks came falling from the overhead. Mae sneezed, and the Prince took no care. The line where the two heads of the nagas met opened up, revealing a hall that contained a flight of stairs. The stairs were built within stone walls leading to the top. It was a vertical labyrinth where a careless step could lead one to one's doom. It was a deathly way, but only to the unaware. Many adventurers and explorers had fallen to their deaths after they had been trapped for days on their way down. Madness had clawed its way into their minds, causing them to become impatient and miss a step. Once a year, their bodies were taken away by the Prince and given a hero's burial.

"I love this place," whispered the Prince. "It is a wonderful place to test the wits of the adventurous. Sometimes for an adventurer, the key is to be observant, to assess a challenge, and to explore many options. Do not to take a challenge just as it is. That could result in an unnecessary risk." He looked down upon the mossy floor on which many bodies had once rested. "And now, after seeing many fail, the adventurer turns into nothing, revealing the true nature of a Paradisian. It's been years now since I've heard of any who wanted to try. Many from the world above just gave up."

The Prince shook his head. "Hence, that is why we always have to meet them above. They decided this was a useless game."

"Hmm. I still think it was a bit … extreme," said Tae. "I mean, was it really necessary?"

The Prince gave Tae a stare and pretended he heard nothing.

"I mean—" Tae tried to continue, but Mae raised her hands to stop her from continuing to pursue a sensitive subject.

"What did you do with the bodies?" Mae asked.

The Prince turned to Mae and pointed in the direction from where they had come. "I gave them proper funerals. I buried them on the other side of the lake. I erected a memorial in honour of the few who wanted to learn and explore."

"What memorial? I don't remember seeing it anywhere," said Mae.

"Oh you know – that rubble on the left when we came out of the canal and into the lake."

Mae and Tae shook their heads.

"Oh it is there. Next time pay more attention, all right? Now, let's continue."

The Prince and his maids proceeded to a small cave to the left of the stairs. Overgrown flora concealed its presence. Gently pushing aside the vegetation, they entered to look for a wooden ladder that would grant them access directly to the surface. Tae, who sighed at the sight of the ladder, thought about the meaningless purpose of the labyrinth and the wasted lives of those who had been fooled.

"Arla, are you ready?" asked Idris, who was wearing his blue coverall along with a blue cap he wore pulled down to cover his identity as much as possible. "We are going to a safe house not far from where we are at the moment. We will meet with Jasmine over there."

Arla tidied up her equipment and did a final check on her provisions in her backpack. She tied her hair back and put on a cap identical to the one Idris wore. Her long black ponytail dangled down her back. She nodded to Idris, and they were ready.

Under the cover of night, Idris and Arla walked among the street corners as medical officers out on patrol. They moved swiftly but cautiously, avoiding contact with other souls. As on any night in Paradise, Paradisians were letting loose their capacity for revelry. A person with a chosen bottle of poison in one hand and a promiscuous lover in the other was a common sight. Cheers and songs echoed throughout Paradise; and drunkenness and a yearning for more were the lyrics. Flashes of neon light in different colours – like a rainbow – invaded Arla's senses with a full penetrative force that would give any brain a migraine and destroy nervous system synapses, preventing intelligent reasoning. But like all sickness of the mind, this could be happily cured by the introduction of a common addiction that made lights dance. It was famous in Paradise. Nearly everyone had a box of it in his or her pocket. It was a unique grass that filled lungs and minds with an eventual silent high, changing a Paradisian's drink into a more potent enjoyment. Those who carried it between their fingers projected the image of sexiness. The looming sense of being in control of everything as the world fell was an addiction that served a purpose for those who breathed it. It was one of those self-served satisfactions nobody could truly escape.

Arla enjoyed her brisk walk through the city. She'd never had a chance to see it because the orphanage enforced a curfew, never allowing anybody out after sundown. She looked up and down and to the left and to the right. It was not enough to absorb something so new and foreign to her innocent eyes. To her, it was such a beautiful place, but Idris had seen too much in his short lifetime.

"Idris, how long have you been living in Paradise?"

Idris kept looking straight ahead, planning the best route to take. He was cautious to the presence of guards.

"Idris? Did you hear me? How long have you been living in Paradise?"

Idris finally cocked up his head and turned partially to the right, revealing the side of his face. "Quite long enough."

"That's vague."

"Well, what did you expect? I don't really keep count of such trivial matters," he said as he turned to face front once more. Arla sprinted a little until they were walking side by side. She looked at him, but he looked straight on without flinching.

"It's beautiful isn't it?" said Arla.

"Hmm? What is?"

"Paradise of course! The lights and sounds. It is a dramatic show for us to see. Don't you think so?"

He shook his head in disappointment.

"Well, you don't seem to agree with me. Why is that?"

"I hate it. That's all."

The revelry of the city had escalated as they inched closer to their safe house. They observed a higher presence of guards in the area, as more people lost control. Cheers turned to curses and shouts while friendly bumps on shoulders turned into violent confrontations. There were a few who passed out on the ground, and their friends let them be for the night. Medical officers on duty took the initiative to make sure the drunk and injured were cared for.

"Hey, you two! What are you doing? Get over here!"

Idris and Arla tried their best to ignore the call of one of their blue-clad colleagues. It seemed he needed help with a patient. Arla and Idris walked as fast as they could until they noticed a guard staring at them. Idris turned around and replied. "Yeah? Did you call us? What is the matter?"

"What is the matter? The matter is that you are not doing your job! Get over here and help me out with this."

Idris ran over with Arla trailing behind him. Arla knew nothing about treating a sick person; neither was she sure Idris knew anything about it either. She rummaged through her backpack pretending she knew what she was doing. The curious guard turned around to break up a fight in a pub nearby.

"All right," said Idris. "I took her pulse, and she seems to be fine. She just drank too much and decided to take a nap. Get out a foil blanket and wrap her in it to keep her warm. I used up mine with the others."

As Arla went through the items in her backpack, she realized they were not equipped with any medical equipment that would uphold their cover. She only gave a nervous nod to Idris.

"What is the matter? Come on! We don't have all night." Idris then laughed. "Oh what a fool I am. I used up your supply as well. We've already treated three patients."

The medical officer looked at them with seriousness. "Have I seen you guys before? I mean, do we work in the same chamber?"

"Sorry, buddy, I do not recall seeing you anywhere to be honest. We all look the same you see." He laughed weakly.

"Look, 'buddy', which chamber do you work in? Who is your superior?"

Arla was drenched in a cold sweat as she prepared to sprint off or even fight if required. She reached down into her backpack where Livi had stored an electric stun gun. Before they left, Idris had taught her how to use it.

"Hey, Meell! There's another casualty over here!" shouted another blue officer, who had just come out of a pub. He had blood on his coverall from the aftermath of a fight. Before Meell, the man who had been interrogating Arla and Idris, diverted his attention to more pressing issues, he said, "I don't know who you two are, but you'd better stay put!"

Idris and Arla stared at each other with a sigh of relief. Idris, his muscles tense, decided to take a seat on the ground next to the incapacitated woman. Idris patted his chest and said, "Damn, we got out of a tight spot. We were bloody lucky!"

"Should we take this woman out of the way to somewhere safe?" asked Arla. She ruffled her attire as if dust had accumulated on her. During their entire ordeal, she felt an eternity had gone by.

"Yeah, you're right. It would be best to take her over to that pole there. But we'd better do it fast. Meell might be back soon. Grab her legs."

In a swift move, Idris got up and found himself standing over the drunk woman. As he squatted down to lift the woman up with his two hands, Arla imagined Idris tea-bagging a poor and innocent woman. Arla gave out a giggle.

"Err, what's so funny?"

Arla sealed her lips and choked back a hoot. "Nothing. Come on! We don't have all day."

They carried the woman close to a light pole. The drunk woman seemed lonely under a shimmer of light. She had been surrounded by friends before, and yet, at the end of the night, she was alone. Idris and Arla continued walking at a brisk pace, hoping nobody would ask them for help if they looked busy.

"How could her friends leave her on the ground like that?" Arla asked curiously.

"Not sure myself. They probably figured the government could take care of her."

"The Forlorn you mean?"

Idris stopped and looked at Arla. "Yes, Arla. To be specific, the Forlorn."

"I have to admit. Paradise to me is a beautiful place. I've never seen it before at night, but it sure can be more interesting than it is during the day. I am, however, curious about one thing," said Arla, and she paused, contemplating her next words.

"And what is that one thing?" asked Idris curiously. They were standing in front of a signboard showing a woman and a man carrying a baby in a sweet embrace. And over their heads, were the words: "Paradise – a place the Heavenly Flower blesses." At the bottom were the words: "The government will keep you safe."

"The Heavenly Flower," said Arla. "I remember we were taught something about it when I was young in school. We were taught about the necessary need to believe in the Heavenly Flower. It was part of the Charter. We were taught about the bad things we should not be doing, and the good we should be following."

Idris listened.

"Assuming everyone in Paradise embraced that religion, I do not see how they followed its teachings. I mean is hypocrisy the main source of living nowadays?"

Arla wiped her brow and looked around.

"In the Temple of the Red Flower, I remember the matron telling us that the Forlorn had been blessed by the Heavenly Flower to be a beacon of hope in Bumi. They are our salvation and servants of the Heavenly Flower. They care about us, and we should be eternally grateful for what we have. Without them, we are lost," said Arla with a sigh. "And all I see now are the sins we should not commit. But it was the Forlorn who classified the existence of these sins to a believer. I am utterly confused. What was the point then?"

Idris let out a smile. "Are you asking me? Because I am not an authority on this subject. You see, I have never been to school before. I never had the privilege of being 'educated' as you call it. I lived to survive, and survival is all I know. If you are looking for answers, I am not the guy you should ask. It would be better to ask someone else."

"Right. Just for the record, I don't think you are that smart anyway," replied Arla, who returned a smile of her own. "You are honest, however, and that is good enough."

"Hey, being honestly dumb can be something of a liberation. At least I don't carry the weight of trying to be somebody I am not."

"Great. Now I believe we will get along just fine," said Arla. She extended her hand seeking a friendly shake.

"Well don't get too cosy with me. You haven't seen how I chew with my mouth open. It gets to people. You won't believe how unpopular I am at the dining table." Idris smirked, but he returned her handshake. And with a little strength, they moved their hands up and down like flapping jelly. They shared a silly grin, making curious heads turn.

"Well, come on now," said Idris. "I think we have gathered a little too much attention. This way." He led Arla back on a path to their safe house. They walked faster as prying eyes began to follow them. They pulled their hats as low as they could and avoided areas where they might encounter guard patrols. It was not long before they entered a more "civilized" part of town. They were at the Gallery. It was a long silvery street where the neon signs were bearable and less annoying. The people here were different to the people they'd seen at the beginning of the evening. Gentlemen wore black suits and ties that matched their silver sticks, while the ladies wore huge skirts inflated to puff out around them. Apparently, a blow-up skirt defended its wearer against unfavourable gossip. Idris had an irritated look on his face. The high noses of the people there had aggravated him. It was no surprise for Arla to understand that people there aggravated each other with their high-flung notions and noses in the air. She noticed that some held their heads so high, she thought they were looking up at the sky.

"This is … an interesting part of town," commented Arla.

"Yeah, a peachy place indeed," replied Idris in a deep voice that seemed to spew irritation. He was allergic to that place it seemed. Arla smiled again.

"All right – over here," said Idris when they stopped in front of a small, dimly lit backstreet. "A little further this way and we should be in time to meet Jasmine."

"Are you sure?"

Idris proceeded with utmost care and strutted down the alley. His fired-up focus caught every sound and every smell. The path was cobbled. The stones came from a time in the past before changes had been made. Nice as it may have seemed, Arla had trouble accepting the unholy stench of the premises. She was sure many Paradisians were too lazy to use the loo for relief.

"I know the smell is terrible. But, trust me, I have been through worse," said Idris. "Just around that corner and we are there."

Around the corner stood a green metal door with a hibiscus flower painted on it. Arla walked forward while Idris hugged the wall to peep behind them to make sure nobody had tailed them. Arla was fascinated at the painting of the red flower, as it reminded her of her carvings she had made on her school desk during those boring days.

"That's the hibiscus flower. That's the symbol of the Party," said Idris.

"I know that. It's just that it reminded me of something. Anyway, is Jasmine here?"

"Not sure. We will know soon enough. Go ahead. Knock the door."

Mae knocked upon the small green metal door that was just the right size for a child. This door stood between the Prince and his meeting. A small slit slid opened, and two inquisitive eyes appeared. The eyes scanned the Prince along with Mae and Tae. Once the owner of the eyes was satisfied, the door opened, and they were allowed through. Tae was surprised to see it was a dwarf who guarded the door. Michel, the usual guard dog had gone on a holiday. With a goofy look, Tae said hello.

"What the hell are you looking at? Haven't you ever seen a dwarf?" the keeper of the door growled. She stared feverishly at Tae, who still stared with offensive curiosity.

"Actually, you are the first," Tae said. "I have never met such a fine specimen as yourself before."

"Oh you fucking little punk!" cried the dwarf as she raised her gun at Tae.

"Whoa! Hold on! Calm down, you two idiots!" intervened Mae. "Don't start a fight for no reason. Please ma'am. Please do forgive my retarded brother for being ... retarded. I will shoot him myself one day." The Prince had already gone ahead.

"Wait! What?" asked the dwarf, who had the same curious and goofy look. Are you saying this lady here is your brother? He looks like a woman! He is the queerest thing I have ever seen. Is he queer? Hey! Are you queer?"

Mae looked at the dwarf with a tinge of hatred. "Does it matter?"

"Hell yes, it matters! These creatures should be tossed into the Temple of the Red Flower for some teaching! The matron says the Heavenly Flower disapproves of such leanings."

Mae had turned red with anger. "And I am assuming here that you are friends with the Matron? Did she actually say that?"

"You don't go to the Temple often do you?" asked the dwarf. "You should see. Everybody needs to hear the truth of our Heavenly Flower."

Mae had lost her temper and instantly punched the dwarf in her self-righteous, smug face. The dwarf dropped her gun, and lay still on the ground. Tae picked up the gun and pointed it towards the dwarf.

With her nose bleeding, the dwarf begged for her life. "Please … enough. I'm sorry. Don't shoot me."

Tae kneeled down and inched close to the dwarf and asked, "What is your name?"

"Kerdil. My name is Kerdil."

"That is an old name. I will remember it."

Tae gave Kerdil a slap, sending a splatter of blood to the ground. He got up and shoved her gun in one of his pockets. "Stay down, little one."

Mae and Tae proceeded to the meeting room where the Prince had already begun conducting his chores of the day. The meeting with the chief of the Western Hall had been completed, and everyone was satisfied with an agreement made about their food supply. The Eastern Hall dwellers would no longer pose a threat to their Western counterpart. The Prince's domain had been secured. As Tae and Mae walked in, they came across a well-lit ancient hall that seemed to have survived years of severe decay. Five grand arches spread across the ceiling. Between them were murals of hibiscus flowers and nagas. The paintings on the wall, however, were flaking away bit by bit. They were a depiction of a past that seemed to be inspiring and encouraging, showing the people of Paradise gathering together with an enlightened mind, singing a song that bore forth a future. The paintings extended all along the wall to the other end of the room where two priestesses sat. Mae noticed the elegance the priestesses conveyed. She knew it was going to be a short meeting, as she saw the Prince nodding off as the priestesses mumbled on.

"I believe that, with your blessing, my lord, we can help bring enlightenment to your people."

The Prince nodded with his eyes closed.

"It will be a future in which we can finally all live equally for a common cause."

The Prince nodded again.

"No more will your people live in poverty. Just imagine! Paradise finally uniting as one."

As Mae had expected, the Prince dozed off and accidently slammed his head on the negotiating table. He had fallen deeply asleep. A loud thump echoed through the hall. Glances of awkwardness flew around. He got back up as fast as he could and wiped the drool from his lips.

"My dear darlings, I apologize for my sleepiness, but you were all just too boring! I mean it with every drip of honesty left in my body. You are all pathetic."

"Excuse me?" said one of the priestesses, who wore a gold bracelet. She was their leader.

"You heard me. Get the fuck out of this sacred hall. You do not deserve to step into this holy place."

"But, my Prince, there are no holier places than the Temple of the Red Flower."

"Well, my dear, you can believe in anything you wish, but do not for once assume my people or I will accept your teachings. Do you see that man in the painting behind you?"

The priestesses turned around and looked upon a painting of a strong, defiant man. He had long hair and wore black metallic armour. He was beautiful, and in his palm he held a ball of light. The painting was not as vibrant as it had been long ago, but the pride represented in that painting could still be felt.

"That, my dears, is Mazy Hamzees, the true courageous hero who ended the Great War. You don't learn about this anymore, thanks to your government. But we down below still stay true to our roots. The real Paradise exists down there."

The priestesses were agitated. They were restless, and they turned from the painting and faced the Prince. "You are worshipping a false god!" one of them said. "No man can rule the heart of the people."

The Prince rose up from his seat and politely asked, "Who said anything about worshipping him? He was our teacher – a wise teacher. It was his guidance that made us who we are, until of course, a betrayal happened. You don't get it. We are not worshipping anything. We are just inspired to protect the truth and our spirit."

"But, you have no proof!" said another priestess. "The government never mentions such a person. You are ignorant and will bring suffering."

The Prince slammed his fist on to the table. "Get out! Get out! I do not want to see any of you anymore!"

The priestesses were shocked at the harsh treatment the Prince had given them. They scurried out nervously. The Prince breathed in and out, and his sudden burst of anger subsided. "I tell you, I am one day going to shoot those little devils," said the Prince. Mae and Tae, who were the only people left in the hall, acknowledged the Prince by clapping their hands.

With the departure of the religious, came the faithless. A tall, plump, fidgety man shuffled in from the entrance. He was well dressed in fine, silvery-white silk clothes that seemed to be Paradise's latest fashion. A red scarf hung loosely over his shoulders. The scarf served as his serviette when he gorged his food. Mae knew this because of the stains that soiled it. With such a demeanour, Mae and Tae did not like the double-chinned man known as Ram. He arrived at his chair and forced his way down to fit into it. The mere act of sitting was a physical challenge for him. It disgusted Mae.

"Welcome, Ram. It has been a long time. You look fabulous!" greeted the Prince.

"Shut up, Prince. I did not come all the way down here just to have a nice chat. I am here to discuss some troubling accusations. I hear that you and your underground dwellers are up to no good." Ram burped rudely. He'd had a meal before he came.

"I do not know what you mean, Ram. What are you talking about? I thought we had a deal. The Forlorn will not interfere with our lives, and we will not interfere with theirs. How would we benefit by troubling you?"

Ram raised his red scarf and wiped a smudge of gravy from his right cheek. He smiled devilishly. "We have a reliable source. Our security system has noticed some unwanted vandalism spreading throughout Paradise. Vandals have drawn the hibiscus flower in various places. It is illegal to do so. It is sacrilege. These vandals were badly dressed with no coveralls. I say, is it safe to assume these hooligans were part of your entourage?"

The Prince raised his thumb to his chin and started fidgeting. He was deep in thought. "There is no proof, is there?" he asked. "What gives you the right to throw such accusations? I am the Prince and protector of the underworld. You had better be more careful about what you say."

Ram took notice of the Prince's agitation, and he leaned forward, placing his arms on the table. "Haha! Hilarious! Did you think names would give you power? The Forlorn run Bumi. We are its true protectors. We will bring the people into the future. And you cannot stop it. Your people will come over to us and beg for the privileges we provide. It's just a matter of time."

"We will see about that. Tell that to your bosses. If that is all you needed to talk about, please leave."

Ram sat on his chair, making himself more comfortable. He smiled like a fat clown. "One more thing. We have reports of missing children in Paradise. These new reports seem to match all the previous cases of kidnapping in the city. Are you sure you had nothing to do with this?"

The Prince knew about these kidnappings, which had happened over the past few years. It was a strange mystery that baffled everyone. The victims mostly consisted of orphans and runaways – people who never wanted to be part of society. Some had returned to play a part in Bumi society, while some never did. Those who returned possessed a different way of thinking. Fiercely independent and critical in thought, they were mostly shunned by society. They carried a secret they vowed never to reveal.

"Have you heard of the tale?" asked the Prince. "The one about a red airship that comes and takes naughty kids away from their beds at night if they have misbehaved?"

"Haha! Are you saying a children's story has something to do with this? It is time to grow up, Prince!"

"I just wanted to mention it. I loved that story. It seems to be related."

"You did have something to do with it. Where do you keep those kids? Do you have a cellar where you chain them up? Did it satisfy you when you managed to jerk off while feeling their smooth innocent skin?"

The Prince gave a nod to Tae. He walked over to Ram and stood behind him.

"Your lap dog here is ready to show me out of the premises?" asked Ram. "I guess I did hit a nerve. You will hear from me soon, Prince. I will return."

"Ram, what makes you think you will be leaving here?" Ram felt a cold piece of metal touching the back of his neck. He heard the sickening sound of a gun being cocked.

"You do not dare! The Forlorn will hunt you!"

The Prince stood up. "You have disrespected me long enough, Ram. It is time to pay for your mistakes. I know the Forlorn will eventually come for me. Might as well kill you first."

Two shots rang through the hall. Ram choked on his own blood, which soon filled his lungs. He slumped forward on the table with a part of his skull missing. Ram's eyes never closed. The smiling Prince was the last thing he saw.

"Sir? What was that noise?"

Ram's servant and bodyguard ran through the entrance and was shocked to witness the gory presentation of red his painted by his boss's murder. He immediately reached for his weapon, which was holstered on his hip. Before he could arm himself, a shadow lurking behind him emerged with a blade that slit his throat in one fast movement. The bodyguard was paralyzed as he felt his life drain away. His blood and Ram's flowed together. Mae sheathed her blade and walked back to the Prince. Tae welcomed another person into the hall.

"Does this mean we are now part of your organization?" asked the Prince.

A young woman with silver and red hair stood over the dead bodies. She was careful not to tread upon the pool of blood growing around them. She was slender but tough. Her thick brown boots were appealing, especially as they were marked with hibiscus flower symbols. Mae and Tae thought she was a beautiful lady. But her eye shadow seemed to hide something menacing about her.

"Nicely done, Prince. You have my respect. And, yes, you are now one of us. We will need to get you to safety, of course. There will be repercussions from this. I will take you to my father."

The Prince nodded and followed her out of the hall. He was reluctant to leave as he stared at the painting of Mazy.

"We will make this hall great once more, Prince. We will change Bumi back to his true vision – Mazy's vision."

The Prince shed a tear and extended his hand to shake hers. "Tell me. I've met your father many times. But I never had the chance to meet you before. What is your name?"

The young woman beamed with delight and shook the Prince's hand eagerly. "My name is Jasmine. Welcome to the Party."

Chapter 7

White Flower

There was a golden path that covered the dusty recesses of the past underground. It still had a hidden charm left over from a golden age. Arla trotted through debris that had fallen from the damaged ceiling and walls, avoiding as much noise as possible that might echo in a foreign land she had never been to before.

"This used to be the place where all the heroes of the past would gather. They would discuss important matters and make decisions that charted the course of our future," said Idris. He was walking in front, clearing any obstacles blocking their way. Specks of dust floated under the fiery glow of the lamp Idris carried. "When we get this place up and running again, we can bring the glory of old back into our history."

"This is amazing. How can this be hidden away from us? And why?" asked Arla.

"The Forlorn does not like to show the diversity of our past. The strength and pride we had were not in the interest of their clan."

"Shame!" Arla bellowed as she picked up a small, lion-like statue covered in grime. She rubbed it a little and blew on it to remove the dirt, revealing polished green stone. She placed it back on its pedestal respectfully. She did not know how such inanimate objects would or could demand the immense respect that only old things deserved. Nostalgia and memories were the ingredients that created such mellow and powerful feelings.

"When I was little, I used to play in these ancient halls," said Idris. "My guardian brought us here to tell us grand stories of heroes and explorers. He taught us about many things, and we listened. We felt proud and discovered a purpose.

Arla was engrossed with the details of the walls, which she saw had been carved with intricate care. She forced herself to stop and observe such curiosities. From a distance, Idris hollered, and she realized she had lagged behind. She picked up her pace and tried to catch up with her guide. As she moved forward as fast as she could, she noticed the air had become crisp. She found herself under an arch leading to the opening of a grand hall that had once housed the bustle of the original Paradise. The crown of the hall was a high dome made of white marble. Statues spaced evenly under the dome depicted golden-winged creatures, Idris told her that they were the legendary hornbills who had once flown through the skies of Bumi. Arla counted. There were supposed to be eight of them, but one was missing. A crack in the dome revealed the night sky to Arla. Idris stood in the centre where the glimmer of a lunar beam graced his presence. Arla raised her hands and spun around to the glory of the night. They experienced a happy and comforting silence that provided a contrast to a livelier past. Idris found it amusing the way Arla could find such happiness in a beautiful, desolate place.

"Do you like it?" Idris laughed.

"Of course! What a curious place this is! So much life!"

Idris looked around. "I don't know about you, but I do not see any life."

"Idris! Don't you know? You can see life only when there is death. The place may be dead, but what I see is a place that once had so much life. And it is precious."

"Where did you learn to see it that way?" asked Idris.

"A dear friend taught me. She is all alone now."

"It was that girl, wasn't it? The one who was caught. What was her name?"

Arla walked over to Idris, and they stood under the gaze of a moon. "Her name was Bell."

"I'm sorry about what happened. I never thought—"

"Don't. You don't have to say anything. She was caught, and I do not want to know anymore."

Idris placed his lamp down and moved close to Arla, placing his hands on her shoulders. "Do not worry. We will get her back. Jasmine will know where she is."

"Jasmine? Who is she?" asked Arla.

"Where do I begin?" said Idris as he turned. "She is a good friend of mine. She was there when I was in trouble. She once rescued me from the guards. If it had not been for her, I would be dead. So, yeah, she is a nice girl."

"And what does she want from me?"

"Not sure. I never did know why she wanted you. She was all mysterious about it when I asked."

"And you just followed orders? Like a dog?" quizzed Arla. "I never thought of you as the obedient type."

"Well I'm not, so don't you be getting any ideas. It's just hard to resist following someone who saved your life before. I feel that I owe her."

Arla gave out a huge grin, annoying Idris.

"What's up?" he asked

"Admit it," coaxed Arla. "I can see it."

"Admit what?"

"Admit you actually like her!"

It was a generalized statement many had made about Idris and Jasmine. He was so weary of such triviality that he'd even decided to undertake an unusual experiment. He'd tried to create a difficult situation by confessing his interest towards the individual who asked, be it a man or a woman. If he did so to a woman, he mostly got slapped in return, which he somehow gladly accepted. But if he did it to a man, he received a tremendous exhibition of awkward resistance. So much so that Idris felt they were trying to hide something carnal. This was typical but understandable, considering the amount of odd looks he had received, festered by rumours about him boggling his orientation in many unpredictable ways. He was proud of it. And hence, in that particular situation, Idris decided to test his experiment upon Arla. He suddenly moved in closer and grabbed her voluptuous waist, pulling her in towards his chest. It was an impulsive move that caught Arla with her guard down.

"Wait … w–what are you doing?"

Idris knew she was resisting, but he insisted on moving his lips closer to hers, his gaze redolent with intent. "What if I told you that the only girl who has ever caught my attention is actually you, Arla?" He waited for a reply.

They both stood in the middle of a great hall, each anticipating the other to react first. Arla did not move; neither did Idris want to test her limits. It was an impasse that sort of ended with wincing eyes that showed neither disdain nor acceptance. The only suitable word that might describe the experience was *gauche*.

"What the fuck are you two doing?"

Idris and Arla, bewildered by the sudden appearance of a third party into their peculiar foreplay, detached themselves from each other like gawky turtles.

"Well nothing, of course," Idris grumbled. "Nothing of the sort you're thinking about. Just getting to know each other a little better."

"I really had no idea what you were doing! It was so confusing," said Arla, as she grabbed her hair in utter frustration. "What were you doing?"

The girl with silver and red hair tittered as she snapped her fingers. "Don't worry about it, Arla. It was just his way of saying hello. Idris, can't you just say 'hi' normally for once?"

Idris ambled his way towards Jasmine. "I was just testing her."

"Well, what was the result of your test then? A slap I hope."

"Weirdness," retorted Idris. Jasmine then raised her arms and gave Idris a heartfelt hug. He returned her affection and proceeded to lead her towards the awkward black-haired girl who was still standing in the middle of the room. "Jasmine, this is Arla."

"Well met, Arla! I never thought you would be taller than I."

"Well, I never thought you were as pretty as you are!"

"Oh my, Arla. A pleasure. Hey, Idris, I think she is a better flirt than you ever will be."

Jasmine held out her hand for Arla to accept, and with grace guided Arla towards the door through which she had entered, leaving Idris to tail behind with their bags.

"I can carry those—" Arla began.

"Nonsense, Arla. Idris can handle them. He likes to do that sort of thing."

"I heard that," murmured Idris.

"Good morning, love."

Bell woke to the lingering shadow of a giant. She knew who it was and what his presence meant. She grunted from her spotlessly white single bed. No pillows cushioned her head, which no longer held the hair she once had. Going bald was nothing; at least her broken arm was now mending.

"Come on. Wake up. You've got a bright day ahead."

She knew what the events of the day were. It was a routine that forced a person to accept the idea of obedience in a cage. It was a sort of routine that demonstrated the futility of escape. The main highlight of every day? A drowning session meant to refresh. Also, it was the only moment of the day during which water was available for consumption.

Bell rose to her feet in half slumber. The "activities" of the previous day were already taxing her mental and physical state. She was at the edge of her limit, thinking of the endless nature of not being alive any longer. But the path to suicide was limited to the gruesome choice of slamming her head as hard as possible against her cage, for a guard she came to know as White Beast made sure it was the only way to kill herself. She actually had tried one day. But she lacked strength, and her weakness made it an unsuccessful endeavour. The whole ordeal ended with Bell having a bruised forehead. She wallowed in self-pity as her freedom to take her own life was taken as well.

Bell, with a hand on the whitewashed walls of her new home, dragged herself out of her prison and into a hall that was similarly whitewashed. The lights flickered like candles in the night, falsifying a reality Bell thought was a dream. It was a nonsensical fantasy in which nothing existed but the futility of accepting sanity over insanity. It was a mirage made more confusing because White Beast wore a mask that transformed his voice, causing it to sound strangely robotic and catchy.

The bathroom was as silent as a grave, and its decor was not anything that could be considered art of the century. It was, fundamentally, a four-walled room with only a bathtub filled to the brim in the middle. Bell sauntered over to the tub. White Beast forcefully tore off her robe. "Get in," it said.

Bell hesitated, but resistance was met with a furious slap to the back of her head, sending her crashing forward into the water. She managed to raise her head back up to catch her breath, but only to be carried and forcefully pushed under the water. Panic and chaos forcefully fed her with pints of fluid that sloshed and sunk into her tummy. Her lungs burst in desperation for fresh air; indeed, every sip of air she had a chance to take, she cherished as another second to live. "Please! Please! Let me be!" Bell screamed. No answer. White Beast was a merciless creature, trained in the fine art of torture. Its emotions were clouded by its lust for vengeance and suffering – hopefully to find retribution in its pointless life. Bell tried to judge it with all she could so she could gather hate and impose a verdict to free her from the guilt of killing the creature when she had a chance. In the meantime, it was best to cooperate with White Beast.

Time passed by within a wink of White Beast's eyes. The bath was over, and Bell hurled the excess water from her belly. "Get out!" it said. Bell got out struggling because of her weak legs. She was barely able to stand on the slippery white marble floor. "Walk!" it said. Bell slowly took one step forward at a time, refusing to black out. Unfortunately, she had tasted the sore consequence of blacking out. She had felt nothing at the time, of course, but upon waking up the next day she felt everything. She was not sure what had happened. But the numerous love bites that inched across her whole body were a sure sign her body had been taken as well.

They both returned to a white passageway as they walked towards her next sentence. Bell's bare skin glistened with moisture as she felt White Beast stare at her from behind. The path they were walking on turned grey and damp. She turned back to ensure she had not gone the wrong way, but a violent shove by White Beast indicated she was heading the right way. Bell went with it. Their footsteps echoed in the tight path, sounding as if they were marching towards an execution chamber. They heard the clambering of chains beyond. Finally, there they were, standing in a gigantic chamber where the insane were kept. Bell believed the word *huge* would not be sufficient to demonstrate the immensity of that black chasm. There were countless birdcages hung by thin yet strong metal chains, and within those cages, she saw only the sad shadows of what looked like birds.

"Where are we?" Bell asked. It was the first time Bell had set foot into that chamber, and it contained the paraphernalia of nightmares. "Why—"

White Guard took her hand and pointed in the direction of a nearby cage. "They wanted to be free like the birds, so I made them into birds," declared White Beast as it leisurely moved its hand across the chamber to point out countless naked prisoners gawking and shouting, flapping their hands as if trying to fly. They wore nothing but their skin, and most of them were eager to shed it by scratching and biting. They thought their skin was merely a catalyst for their feathers to grow. Hopelessly muddled, they smiled and grinned with a hope of flying away one day.

"Futility at its best," stated White Beast. It seemed to be proud of its work. "Come. There is more to see."

"Why are you showing me this?" begged Bell. Instead of giving her a reply, White Beast showed its solitary side. It gave a cold blank stare.

The anomalous couple continued their journey down to a nearby elevator. In the elevator, the hum of a broken tune signified the dying breath of a child; it sang through Bell's ears. "I love this song," said White Beast. "It was the cry of an orphan child I played with yesterday. You should have been there. I would like you to have seen it."

Bell had her hands pressed on her ears as hard as she could. White Beast began to hum louder and louder. "Would you like to know what happened to him?"

Bell curled up in a corner, rocking forward and backward, trying to alleviate the discomfort of horror in her head. Her eyes were wide open as she tried to avoid the vision of a dying child that appeared when her eyes were closed. Sometimes, one's worst enemy disguises itself as one's imagination.

The elevator came to an abrupt halt, and the doors slid open. White Beast pulled Bell up onto her feet and shoved her forward. They continued to walk down a lonely passage slightly different to the one they'd travelled before. There definitely was a change in colour. Here there were no peelings of shedding paint. These walls had been painted a fresh red. "I thought this place could use a little bit of a makeover. But red seems to be in short supply around here. So I decided to be creative," declared White Guard. "Go ahead. Touch it."

Bell placed her hands as close as she could to her chest, avoiding the paint she knew was not paint. But White Beast insisted, and with great strength, it forcefully threw her entire body against the wall. The left side of Bell's face was smudged completely in red, and the mild taste and smell of iron was ubiquitous. Bell knew what the main ingredient for the paint was. She writhed in fear as she guessed the purpose of the next chamber.

"Don't be afraid," said White Beast. "Don't be afraid. It is just blood, you see."

With the stub of its big finger, White Beast then flicked a blotch of blood from Bell's nose and moved its finger to a small opening in its mask where the mouth should be. A small pink bit of slithering pith emerged from the opening and licked its finger. "Mmm … That's the taste I like. Come try some more."

White Beast, with its handful of bloody paint, stuffed Bell's face against the wall, suffocating her. She swallowed and breathed as much as she could of the blood that filled her throat with a sickening aftertaste. Bell coughed and yelped at the happiness of White Beast. It was soft, but Bell could hear the sick gurgle of a towering monster.

"You will get used to the taste. I mean this chamber will require you to like it," said White Beast.

They continued on straight until they reached a cold room. It was a huge refrigerator. Bell saw people who were dressed in clean white attire. "They are butchers," thought Bell as she noticed they were sharpening their knives as if for a feast. She was led to a swivelling door that led to a decent kitchen where many chefs looked to be preparing delicate ingredients. Bell could identify some of the ingredients – vegetables and something that smelled like chicken stock. Bell was hungry, and her stomach began to growl as, in her mind, she cooked various dishes that tantalized her palate. She remembered a pot of warm chicken soup the kitchen lady at her orphanage once cooked for her. The kitchen lady was the only kind lady she knew back at the orphanage. Bell had been devastated when the old lady died. The feeling she felt of losing someone she held dear had been too much to bear. That night, Bell had tried to kill herself. She decided to climb the stairs to the roof of her orphanage. But on her way she heard the cries of a little girl who sounded almost as young as Bell was. She followed the soft cries, which led her to a closet at the end of a hall. Bell sat with that girl in the darkness of the closet. The girl grabbed Bell and gave her a hug. She said "Thank you." But Bell knew she was the one who should be thanking the other girl. The thunder of a rainy night echoed until morning. Both of them felt safe together and had been like peas in a pod ever since.

"Hey, wake up!" said White Beast, bring Bell back from her memories. "Put this red dress on. You are going to have a proper dinner tonight. There will be guests, so you need to be dressed in your best."

Bell accepted a simple, straight, red dress and proceeded to the kitchen latrine. She cleaned herself up and put on the frock; it was a perfect fit. She turned around in front of a mirror to find the fabric hugging at all the right places; she was impressed. However, she noticed she had aged beyond her years. She tried to find peace, but in her heart she knew she was broken. The memory of the girl she had met in the closet was the only thing left that brought a smile to the red-clad woman in the mirror.

White Beast hollered at her to hasten, as dinner was about to be served. She splashed a bit of water into her hands and ran them over her hairless scalp. She opened the door. White Beast stood ready to guide her to the venue. In bare feet, she skipped along the kitchen floor and did a twirl for it to see. "What do you think?" she asked.

White Beast raised its huge hands and gave a booming clap. "Yes, I was correct. The colour red suits you," said White Beast. "You look absolutely beautiful. Perfection. I apologize for the lack of shoes to go with the dress. I am not good at shopping."

"Do not worry. I am glad as it is. Should we be heading into the dining room now?"

White Beast nodded and led the way to a mahogany door with a golden knob. It turned the knob as gently as it could and swung the door open to the most radiant and posh dining room Bell had ever seen. Crystal chandeliers emitted wonderful colours of the rainbow that made the room glow, while gold plates and cutlery twinkled in the light. At the massive dining table sat guests White Beast had mentioned. Bell estimated there were about a dozen guests as she was hurriedly led to her seat where a waiter shook out her napkin and placed it on her lap.

"Hello, dear. My name is Wlak. And I will be your headwaiter for the day. Your dinner will be served shortly, but in the meantime, shall I get you something to drink?"

"Hi there, Wlak. May I have a glass of wine?"

"Fine choice. Would you prefer the red or the white, ma'am?"

"What would you recommend?"

"I would go for the red, as it will match well with our deliciously grilled main course. Besides, it is also the colour of your lovely dress."

"Thank you. But I don't think I am as well dressed as you think."

"Nonsense! You are the attraction of the day!" said Wlak as he came in closer to Bell. "Don't tell anyone, but I believe you have been the talk of the day ever since you walked in that door." Wlak winked at Bell and proceeded to the kitchen to pour her wine.

She noticed that White Beast was standing at the ready behind her, quietly observing the events that transpired. Bell then took notice of the arrangement of the dining table. The guests were not seated close enough to have a conversation. In fact, the guest closest to her did not seem to be aware of her when she hollered at him. Some of the guests stared at their plates, while some stared at the chandeliers. Then she noticed someone waving a hand at her from the far end. It was a young man. She awkwardly answered with a wave of her own, but no other guests seemed to be aware of it. The young man tried to indicate something through gestures. He pointed at the plate furiously. Bell tried to make sense the signs of what seemed to be a madman, but the dinner chimes had rung. Like clockwork, the guests sat straight and stared forward, and the young man was last seen being led into the kitchen.

"Ladies and gentlemen, without further ado, may I present – dinner."

Musical melodies fit for fine dining floated across the dining hall. Waiters pranced around guests, presenting them with dish after dish. Bell was famished, and she stared at the succulent, steaming meat in front of her. She grabbed her knife and her fork and hesitated no more to satisfy the pangs of starvation that clawed inside her. With a stab and a slice, dear old Bell chomped down upon the tender, rare meat that oozed with a flavourful magic she had never tasted before.

"I do apologize, Wlak, for her eagerness. She has not tasted a good meal for a long while," said White Beast.

"Not a problem. I will let the chef know how pleased she is with his main course."

As she sliced and gobbled up her last bite, she saw that the other guests had finished their meals. They grinned at everything except the empty plates. Bell found it a little hilarious, and she smiled a small smile. She figured maybe it was their way of talking to each other, since most of them were like her, trapped in a godforsaken prison with nothing more than their minds. She laughed.

"I see you are enjoying your time here. I am glad, because not many people do," hummed White Beast.

"It is amazing. The food was great, and the company is delightful! I remember watching these sorts of dinner parties on television, out on the streets of Paradise. It was mostly when I was out under the rain, in fact. And mostly alone—"

"Well you don't have to be alone anymore. You have friends now. They love what you love, and they love being here. Maybe you should consider being here forever," murmured White Beast.

Bell hesitated at this suggestion of White Beast. She felt its request was a personal demand. There was a flair in how it had spoken, as if a little humanity had seeped through its mask. She wondered if it was human, or if it had a gender. It was too hard to tell she decided. She turned and asked, "Do you want me here?"

White Beast said nothing.

Wlak came back to her side and was glad to announce a special dessert of the day. "Bell, I have wonderful news! The chef was happy you liked his food; therefore, he wanted to make you something special."

"Oh my, what is it?"

"Red pie! The sweetness of a moulded crust blended with a soothing sauce will bring more cheer to today's event, making you deliciously more desirable."

"Err … thank you. I am not desirable," said Bell timidly.

The pies came, each one set in front of a diner to feast his or her eyes upon. Bell was captivated by the pie and was excited beyond her own comprehension. "This looks amazing! Can I have a bite of it?"

"Why of course! Everyone can dig in!" exclaimed Wlak as he danced along the side of the room to the embrace of another waiter.

Without any qualms, Bell used her hands to dig into a deep part of the pie. With a chunk of the pie in her palm, she stuffed it into her mouth. As she chewed, she felt something rubbery – something uncooked. She slowly pulled it out of her mouth and found a piece of pale looking … something. It looked like pig's skin, and it immediately demanded Wlak's attention. The man was as fast as a squirrel to apologize about the carelessness of the chef, and begged her forgiveness. "It is all right. I loved it. I was just curious as to what that is."

"Oh that? It is part of an ear."

Bell nodded and was quite delighted with the responsiveness of the staff. Wlak disappeared in a second, and she could hear his screams through the door. Bell suddenly felt guilty for causing what seemed to her a bad day for the chef.

"I must go and apologize to the chef for making such a ruckus. He did a great job with the food, and getting scolded for such a mistake seems unnecessary," expressed Bell. White Beast listened.

"You do not need to do so. Let Wlak do his job, and you stay here. You are our special guest."

Bell thought for a while. "No. I must meet the chef to tell him how I appreciated his work. A silly mistake with a pig's ear should not be a problem."

White Beast stayed silent.

Bell rose from her seat. Off she walked towards the kitchen door. A heated argument between the chef and Wlak slowly died down as she heard Wlak passing on words of encouragement. She was glad matters had settled, but she felt she needed to personally apologize to the chef for creating such unnecessary drama.

As the door inched open to the sound of creaking rusted hinges, Bell was filled with bouncing desire to meet the chef. As she walked in, she noticed no one but Wlak. He was standing next to a grotesque pile of meat. She could see hints of skin, but it all seemed too big for a pig. "Hello, Wlak, where is the chef? I would like to thank him."

"Yes! Hello, young miss! I am glad to make your acquaintance!"

Bell was baffled by the sudden change in Wlak as he walked towards her with a raised hand. In the other hand he held a cleaver. "Wlak, are you all right? Where is the chef?"

"What do you mean, young miss? I am the chef. Wlak is over there." The chef looked over his shoulder indicating that Wlak was behind him. Bell trembled as she quickly grabbed the side of a chopping table. The damp, stickiness of the table stained her hands in the colour red again. "Apologies, but I think I should go back to my seat now."

The chef stepped backwards and placed his knife on the table. "Ma'am? Are you all right? The chef is right here. You can say whatever you want to say. I apologize for the argument, but he won't be making any more mistakes! Now, as compensation, what would you like to have?"

Bell was at the door, prepared to run or scream for White Beast to come and help. Wlak took a step forward and held up his knife again. "Yeah, young miss. Let me show you what I can cook! Look at the table. The meat is very fresh! Would you like to try a thigh? Or would you like the ankle? The toes would make a great sorbet. But I would prefer to cook them in a spicy soup."

Bell became perplexed as to the type of meat he referred to. With a curious mind that already held an answer to the mystery of that meat, Bell walked along the other end of the table. It was not clear, but she saw hints of an organ here and there. Actually, there were plenty. Bell's legs began to weaken as she came closer to the end where she expected the head would be. Looking down, she saw dripping red drops of blood trickling into to a disfigured ball with a gaping hole that resembled a mouth. It was a mess, but Bell knew the head belonged to the young man who had tried to warn her. Bell fell a step backwards, holding her hand tightly over her mouth. The air in the slaughter room began to suffocate her. She found herself on the ground trying to cough up whatever vile contents were trapped in her body. She was haunted by the guilt of liking the taste of it.

"Wlak, it seems the young miss will not be going back to her seat again. What should we do?"

"I don't know, chef. But the madam here seems to know our secret ingredient now. I believe it would be best to cook her. I can see our guests find her deliciously desirable!"

"You think so? She has beautiful, smooth skin. Maybe I could fry it!"

"Nonsense! That would spoil the texture! Steaming it would be a better choice."

"Are you sure? I am the chef. What makes you think you have the right to contradict me?"

"Chef? Ha! You can't survive out there with your skills. I am the one who made you who you are. Now, don't go trying to be all superior. Besides, whether you steam it or fry it, there will be lots of skin to spare. Bring her up and place her on the table. We can slowly skin her alive. That would make the meat fresher."

"I have to agree with you, Wlak. You do think what's best for us."

The chef closed in on Bell with all his might. Bell was stunned for a moment, but had managed to regain her composure enough to smack the chef straight on his nose. The chef dropped his knife, and out came Wlak who shrieked in a hollow and sickly yelp. "Fucking bitch! I will fuck you up!"

Bell turned around and ran through the door, calling for White Beast. It was nowhere to be seen. She felt alone in a nightmarish land. She hated White Beast, though it was the only being she could trust. She grabbed a table knife as soon as she could, knocking down a wine glass. It created a loud commotion that attracted the attention of Wlak's guests. They stared at her with bloodshot eyes. As she retreated into a corner, Wlak crashed through the door with a bloody nose. He demanded that his guests grab her so he could cook her and serve her at the table. His guests gave no hesitation. They rose in unison to lure Bell further into her corner. They craved for her flesh. Their hands trembled with the greed and lust of animals.

Hands caressed Bell's skin as the guests tried to feel the tenderness of her flesh. Bell flinched as Wlak's guests decided to take a whiff of her scent, pushing her further back into her corner. Their grip turned rough as they lifted her onto the dining table. Wlak stood at her side, and the chef sharpened his knife. She breathed heavily under the gaze of crazed cannibals, pushing those away who tried to get an early bite. She kicked and threw herself around to find an opportunity to break free from a feast.

"Move away! Let me chop her up for you guys so you might digest her more easily! Move away!"

With flawless obedience, the guests all moved to the side. The chef raised his blade up high and chopped downward, but with defiance, Bell gathered her fear, and off she rolled to the side. The edge of Wlak's blade met with solid wood.

"Still have that fight in you, I see? Try dodging many more attacks!"

With a thundering clap of Wlak's skull, Bell saw the chef grab his wounded head. He turned to see who it was, but before he could move, another blow was dealt. It was White Beast. Its monstrous palm was so huge he could grasp a man's head with one hand. Bell felt sorry for Wlak and the chef, for that impact would have destroyed anything that stood in its way.

"Feed the guests yourself, Wlak," said White Beast, who was holding the head waiter close to its face.

"But … I am the best chef you ever had—"

"Vanity. You think you're so great? Let me remind you are still a prisoner in my domain. And as it eventually will be for all prisoners, your time of execution has arrived."

Without showing an effort, White Beast threw Wlak and the chef into a corner of the room. Bell saw Wlak's mangled body breathing, his eyes stared at her while his guests circled him like vultures. As they all knelt before him to pay homage to his sacrifice, each one of them took a bite, regardless of Wlak and the chef's muffled screams.

"Come on. Let us leave them to their meal. We need to proceed to the next chamber," ordered White Beast as it grabbed Bell's wrist.

"Why are you doing this? Why are you taking me to these chambers? Why do you show me this?"

"I am trying to figure out which sentence suits you best."

"Sentence? On what crime?"

"The crime of indecent behaviour banned by the Heavenly Flower, and a threat to the government."

"Threat? What sort of a threat are you referring to?"

"Terrorism and civil unrest."

Bell tried to grasp the severity of the words that had come from its mouth. She had thought her sentence would be a short one – so they could get more information about Arla's location. But the truth had sunk in. She was being held without trial, and she knew she had been tossed into a hell where the unwanted go – terrorists and orphans alike.

"How many chambers are there? How much more do I need to go through before you make up your mind?"

"Do not worry. There is only one left."

They walked through yet another dark passageway, grey and dreary. She thought hard about being a bird, but it would be a slow and painful death. Maybe allowing them to feast upon the flesh would at least be faster. However, to obey the temptations of desire and to be turned into a mindless ghoul was, in itself, a personal torment. She would prefer to die with her mind still her own.

The door to the final chamber was decayed. White Beast unlocked it, and a rumble shook the ground. They moved in with little care of the dangers that lurked. As Bell strutted along the edges of the chamber, she saw a glowing pond in the middle. The pond was sunk low into the ground and was divided accurately into multiple squares.

As Bell looked at the steps that led to the middle of the pond, she decided it looked like an upside down pyramid.

"Am I to drown in this pond? Is that it?"

"No," replied White Beast. "You are to go to the middle and drink the water."

"What? Why?"

"Because I will not repeat myself, and I will force it on you if I need to," replied White Beast, obviously delirious in its intentions. "I believe this is the place for you. Freedom. That's what you want and need."

"Freedom?"

White Beast spoke no more. He pointed at the middle of the pond. Bell waded through hesitantly until she was waist deep in the water. With her palms clasped together, she gathered a hand full of bluish water and brought it close to her mouth. She sniffed it and then drank; nothing felt out of the ordinary. "This seems to taste good."

Bell turned around to find she was alone, wading in the rippling water. A booming sound echoed through her head, and she found herself on a familiar grassy knoll. She was standing near an oak tree. A familiar gust of wind touched her cheeks, unravelling a past, which she desperately wanted to be a gift. There was a girl under that tree. She was staring at the sky; it seemed as if she was looking beyond a blue sea. Bell sat next to her; the girl felt familiar. Bell greeted her, but there was no answer. She kept staring into the sky, until a gust blew down a few leaves that floated and danced towards her lap. She smiled, and Bell loved.

"Wake up!"

A shocking thrill went through Bell's veins like an invasive force that pushed her out of her dream. Electrocution was a first for her, and her body jolted and convulsed at the wandering fingers of White Beast. The intensity of the current fluctuated with the measure of White Beast's benevolence. Bell choked on her own spit as her muscles tensed. At the brink, White Beast released his trigger, and Bell gasped for air. Without the paralyzing shocks running through her, Bell slipped back into her dream.

Bell stood in the kitchen she remembered from the orphanage. The smiling girl who had been under the oak tree was there again, looking through all the utensils, searching for the perfect one. "Did you see where she put that cutting knife?"

Bell thought she heard a voice. "What?"

"I said, did you see where she placed that knife?"

"Err, no."

"Then, how are we going to cut this cake of yours?"

Bell remembered why she was in the kitchen. It was her birthday, and the girl had managed to smuggle in a huge chocolate fudge cake. It was Bell's favourite. A wave of nostalgia washed over her.

"I guess we'll just have to use our hands then!" said Bell. "Come, you! Let's eat before they come back!"

They started with a dip of a finger, but they slowly turned their attack on the cake into a massacre. They laughed at each other for how messy they had become. The girl snorted so loudly, a piece of chocolate managed to go up her nose. Bell lost control as she took a huge chunk and tossed it at the face of the jester. Their huge commotion did not go unnoticed, as they heard from above the clambering march of a pair boots. Bell was desperate to run but reluctant to leave their cake. She tried her best to gather all of it within the confines of her arms. The girl did not help, but ridiculously laughed at Bell's greedy antics. Unfortunately, for both of them, they did not escape detention and punishment. Although they had been made to clean the kitchen, they smiled all day.

"Happy birthday, Bell."

"Thank you, Ar—"

A surge of current went through Bell's body suddenly and violently. She woke to a depressing notion that everything she had recently seen was from her past. It was a taste of sweet nostalgia, but it turned sour when she realized it was made of nothing more substantial than a fluffy cloud.

"How … long … more …"

White Beast stopped.

"Please … how … long … more …"

White Beast moved in closer. "What did you say?"

"Please … no more … I don't … remember …"

White Beast stood straight and sent another jolt of electricity that made Bell scream out through her lungs. To White Beast, it was an orchestral delight of pain and suffering – a symphony made by a blind man. White Beast swung its arms to left and right. With a bursting, eager heart, White Beast yelled, "Bell! Stay with me forever!"

Chapter 8

To Meet a Prince

Along the murky water and into the winding maze of Kampung, residents gazed upon a new stranger who came from above. They were curious about her – not so much of her appearance, but of her personality. They wanted to witness if the new stranger had the will to live a life as they did.

"How does this place exist?"

"It has always been here, Arla. This place was part of the grander Paradise long ago," explained Jasmine. "It was only after the Great War that Paradise was split into two."

"But how is this not known to me, or anybody?"

"You were not looking for it," replied Idris. "The Forlorn invested a lot to divert the attention of the people away from here. But mostly, people wanted to hear only what they wanted. They had a hidden hatred for anything they could not grasp.

"It is a pity," Jasmine said. "It's so easy to get people to eagerly become willing to divert their attention away from the truth – *if* you give them everything they need." They were standing on a patio that overlooked the whole settlement. It was a shady place, but flickering candles illuminated the settlement like stars in the night. To Arla, who was used to the invasive nature of neon lights, the settlement exuded a ray of calm with the lingering energy of a living spirit. Existence burned a fervid curiosity within her to discover more.

"Beautiful, isn't it?"

"Yes, Jasmine, it is," Arla replied.

"Idris, I will be heading off to check on our supplies. Take Arla around and show her more. When you're done, the Prince will be waiting."

Idris waved his hand insouciantly, and Jasmine walked away into the shadows of one of the houses; her glistening silver hair was the last they saw of her for now.

"Come, let's go," said Idris

"I have a lot of questions that need answering."

"We will talk as we walk. Come on then."

The settlement burst with the energy of daily trade as everyone screamed for Arla's attention. "Young lady, would you like to buy this beautiful jewellery?" "Miss, how 'bout a nice dress to go with that beautiful skin of yours?"

"Thank you. No, I don't need that. What is this? Does it come smaller?" Arla asked to the barrage of proposals for trade. Her countenance was fired with joy at beautiful little things she wanted to buy. But Idris noticed that she was particularly fascinated with a glimmering pair of earrings.

"Do you like that? They are moon-drops," he said.

"Moon-drops? What is that?"

"It is a rare stone found in the sands of the Pasir Lands. The settlement and the ancient hall used to have dozens of these, but they were plundered as Paradise was rebuilt to the image of the Forlorn. I used to wear one in my ear as well, but … people did not like guys to be wearing an earring." He laughed quietly.

"Idris, I think you would look great with an earring!"

"Heh? Are you commenting on my looks, Arla? I believe my irresistible good looks are starting to interest you."

Arla looked at Idris with an insipid stare before she turned back to a mirror and dangled the earrings next to her face. Idris shrugged.

"Anyway, why is it called a moon-drop?" Arla asked.

"It is because of the way it glows under a moonlit night. It is rare, and the only way to search for it is to wait for the right night. The gatherers wait patiently as the winds blow the sands away layer by layer, until they can see a white glow. When they find it, they just pick it up. Some believe it is the patience of a gatherer that makes the stone."

"There used to be plenty of these a long time ago?"

"Yes, they were priceless. They bear meaning for those who carry them."

"What meaning?" asked Arla, as she stared deeply at the pair of round, milky stones in the ornaments. Her ears twitched for more. Idris obliged.

"It means that, even on the darkest of days, a light can always shine. Courage and patience are all that's needed."

Arla gawped at Idris.

"Cheesy? I know—"

"What? No! That was beautiful. But why doesn't anybody wear them?"

"The Temple of the Heavenly Flower preached that the stones are evil. Besides, they just weren't fashionably desirable anymore."

Arla turned away from the mirror and asked the seller the cost of such priceless jewels. The old lady shook her head and came up with a huge sum that Arla could not afford. Defeated, and with a glum smile, Arla said goodbye to her moon-drops. The old lady noticed her sadness, and probably regretted trying to place such a high price for someone who deserved to bear the gems. The old lady hollered to Arla, but she walked on dreaming of a day when she could buy anything she wanted. She felt a tug, pulling her back towards the old lady. Idris's strong clench seemed harsh to Arla. "What are you doing, Idris?"

"You like the stones, don't you?"

Arla nodded.

"Well you have to convince her."

"Convince her of what?"

"Your honesty."

The old lady and Arla faced each other. They were two souls of different generations, both bludgeoned by the passing affairs of time. They searched for mutual understanding. Arla wanted the stones, but the old lady wanted to understand why she wanted them. It was in the old lady's interest to comprehend the selfish nature Arla retained, as nothing could be given free for something of significant value.

"May I have the stones?" said Arla, unsurely.

"Why, dear child? Why should I give them to you for free?"

"I think they are the most beautiful things I had ever seen."

The old lady closed her hand into a fist and retreated back into the rambling crowd. Arla stood perplexed by the consequence of her statement. Self-judging and self-loathing, she stood among the people in the crowd aware of her unworthiness.

"Hey, you all right?" Idris asked.

"I don't know what I should say."

"It is all right. They are just stones anyway," Idris replied. Arla walked along with Idris, but she felt she had left a heavy heart among the crowd. There was something magical lying within those moon-drops, and Arla wanted to own it. Idris saw an unwavering desire in her and recognized it as familiar. In a sense, he saw himself in her.

They travelled through alleys of the settlement. Instead of finding it dark and filled with sewage, Arla was surprised to witness immaculate sanitation throughout. Children ran back and forth through the alleys, chasing fireflies that flashed their yellow-green light. Idris and Arla did not exist to them; they were wholly engrossed in their quest to catch mythical creatures.

"These are fireflies! It is … They are fireflies!"

"You *have* seen them before, right? They exist above land as well," mocked Idris.

"Yes I have seen them a few times. It is just that I never expected to find them down here. They look more beautiful."

"I have to agree with you. They look like they belong here, don't they?" said Idris. With a swift movement of his hand, he captured one of them. "Do you know the story about the Fireflies of Paradise?"

Arla nodded. "Yes, I can recall it. Bell used to tell me about it."

Idris passed his firefly to Arla. She took a peek at it, and a glow of yellow and green painted her face. She smiled brightly and allowed the firefly to return to where it belonged.

"You and Bell. You were close?"

Arla watched her firefly swirl around its company of friends. "She was my only friend, Idris."

"I'm really sorry that we could not save her."

Arla turned back to him with a smile of cheer. "You did save *me*, Idris. I thank you for that," she uttered. "I look forward to getting her out of there."

Idris knew Arla's background. He knew of her tragic and violent past. But it was all on sheets of paper that told an inert history that cultivated no sympathy. He knew of suffering and despair, but it was almost impossible to understand it without having walked in her shoes. Idris was torn to understand Arla better, for it was tragedy to carry the burden of others. He hesitated to ask for more. To him, it was best to not get intertwined with thorny tangles of strange vines that grew in the backyard of someone's dysfunctional home. He was stuck in his own, praying hard every day to burn it all away in an epic bonfire that would enable him to turn to ash within.

The tour peaked Arla's curiosity as she found herself being drenched in dull red luminescence. There were more rowdy drunk men stalking about and touching and seducing women who stood in front of flimsy doors. The women were scantily clad and provocative. Arla noticed Idris was walking at a faster pace, efficiently dodging the attention of those around them.

"Hey! Why are you walking fast? Are you in a hurry or something?"

"Yeah, Arla. We need to get to the Prince. Jasmine ordered it."

"Well, hold it. I remember Jasmine saying I could see this place. So, let me see it."

"This is not really a place you want to see."

"I know what this place is. So stop acting as if I am innocent or something," muttered Arla with a twinkle. "Do you come here?"

"Of course not."

Arla could not fathom how to respond to a straight answer given by Idris. It seemed to be a touchy subject for Idris to tackle. Hence, Arla dropped it, but continued to observe the liveliness of a different market with a different trade. She noted the attractiveness of the women who were there. She admired their presence and their sultry ways, which made her blush. Even under the glimmer of red light, the women's rouge was unmistakably obvious. To the workingwomen of the alley, Arla exuded an innocent, alluring charm.

"You seem to be getting a lot of attention. More than the men, I see—"

"Are you jealous, Idris?"

"What? No! Why should I be?"

Arla shrugged.

"Well, they are your type. You like women, don't you?" he asked.

Arla turned. Idris wasn't sure if she was furious or serious. Either way, she was not pleased with the way Idris had phrased his sentence. "It is not that simple."

"But you and Bell. You had—"

"Yes, I love her, if that's what you mean."

"I mean … you guys did it, didn't you?"

"You mean sex?"

"So, you like women then. You don't like men. Hey, I understand," Idris boasted.

Arla stared at Idris. "You really do not understand. It is not about sex. I love Bell. That's it."

"Hey, it is all right to be a different, Arla. You're now in a safe place. The guards won't come for you. It's all right to be different here."

124

"What is wrong with you? You seem to emphasize the fact that you think I'm different. Do you want a confession? Isn't it normal for a person to lust? I don't think gender matters. And it *is* different. Bell is not here. That is the only difference."

Idris caught himself trying to explain what he thought he understood, but he failed to comprehend the sorrow Arla was feeling. He had always thought she had kept that part of her to herself. "Of course it matters – sexual preference, right? I like women, not men."

"How would you know, if that is all you think about?" Arla stormed off away from Idris. He was caught by surprise and picked up his pace to catch up to her. But the presence of a group of horny old men haggling for the best price blocked his path. With all its mystery and roots, the underground city devoured Arla. Idris became passive and strangely decided not to follow or find her. Letting her get lost in a strange place was probably a better choice.

As he stared into the crowd where he had lost Arla, a familiar voice crept up from behind Idris. "Typical, Idris. Always caring about yourself. You might end up alone—"

"Everybody ends up alone, Setia."

"That's what you say, Idris. Do you want to come up?"

Idris hesitated, but eventually conceded to his basic instincts. The lady held his hand and leisurely guided him to her quarters upstairs. Without any tangles to hold him down, Idris forgot about Arla. In his mind, he repeated words he wanted to hear the most: "She will be safe. She won't go anywhere. I will find her later."

And thus, like Arla, Idris was consumed by the roots of the city, satisfied with his impious addiction for a sort of temporary love men desperately find, flooded with waves of boredom and loneliness.

"What is this place?" Arla thought. She had come upon a huge cavern that extended beyond the echoes of her voice. Stubborn and strong vegetation grew steadfastly among the cracks of its walls. She could hear whispers of life in little trees that grew from the soil. They were exposed to the elements, and their roots were deep within Bumi. Arla wandered through little creeks that crept among debris of grey bricks fallen from above. She made tiny splashes in the creek, getting her feet wet. It was a joyous moment, just to witness a beautiful garden. As she came close to a shrub, a flock of birds flew out, chirping a melody for Arla. She smiled in gratitude for the garden she had found. She had shared her smiles and laughs with a dear friend once. But the joy within her smile was haunted by the emptiness of solitude and the pain of losing a love she had thought was forever.

"You can't kill me!"

Arla was surprised when she heard the giggles of children in the garden. She had thought she was the only one there. With curiosity, she watched a boy and a girl running in circles trying to fend off one another with sticks. They were playing war she presumed. It was the entertaining play of a brother and his sister, each trying to defeat the other for dominion in the garden. "I will kill you, Dom! For the garden is mine to rule! Haha!"

"Oh yeah? I have the sword of might that you can never stop, Pom! Let's end this!"

They clashed again one last time, and eventually their tired little bodies fell to the ground in the laughter of playful youth. They huffed and puffed, finally giving up and deciding there was enough space for the both of them. The little girl, Pom, took notice of Arla's presence where she was hidden among the leaves.

"I know how you feel, Arla. It is you, isn't it? Arla?"

Arla wiped away a tear that rolled down her cheek as she walked towards Dom and Pom. "How do you know my name?"

"Don't wipe it away. Some tears are meant to stay," said Dom as he stretched. "Where is Idris?"

"Back in the settlement. I ran away and left him back there."

"You rightfully deserve to do so. He can be a bit mean sometimes. Always up above in Paradise as they say!" said Dom as he picked up a stone and threw it far. "Idris is boring."

"He is not that bad," said Arla. "I guess nobody is perfect."

"Is that so? So why are you here, Arla? Are you lost?" queried Pom while she held on to Dom's hand.

"I was just exploring. I've never seen anything like this before. But, yes, I am lost actually. I need to find the Prince."

Dom and Pom looked at each other. "Pom, nobody can get lost here. You can always find a way. All you have to do is step forward!"

Pom nodded. "Yes, Dom, you are right. Come on now, I think we should head back home."

"Wait! Do you know where the Prince is?"

"Follow the butterfly," said Dom.

"Wait! What butterfly?"

In a wisp of smoke, Dom and Pom disappeared into the humid air. Arla turned around and around, spinning in all directions trying to find the slightest hint of the existence of a butterfly. She crossed the creek and ran down the slope of a demolished steel structure. The vegetation grew thicker and denser as she went deeper into the cavern. The light from the night disappeared, and it was replaced by the collective shine of fireflies. In sheer randomness, a voice came like a flicker from somewhere in front of her. "Are you lost, my dear?"

"Yes, I am. I can't seem to find my way back."

"Certainly! Nobody can go back when one is going forward."

"Who are you? And where are you?"

"Will you care for me or love me for who I am?"

"I don't know. I don't know you well enough."

"Then ... does it matter who ... I ... am?" The voice was cold but she thought there was a slight hint of cheer in its tone. She knew it was coming from the foliage in the shadows. The speaker was shy and reluctant to emerge and break the mystery. It stalked silently.

"Do you know where I can find the Prince?"

"Why? Do you know why you are looking for him?"

"I don't. I was told I was supposed to find him."

"Whoo? Whoo told you?"

"Idris and Jasmine. Do you know them?"

"No, certainly not. I do not know them, but they do sound interesting. Where are they?"

"They are back in the settlement doing their own thing I assume."

"And here you are alone without a clue about where to go. Why did you follow their order? Do you trust them?"

Arla looked down at her feet, finally answering a question she had often asked herself. "I'm not sure—"

"Follow my voice then, Arla."

Arla obeyed with natural instinct to a new world she promised to not offend. The voice was distinct and mellow in its delivery. It floated deeper into a dense jungle, and Arla trailed it. At the entrance of a cave, she stopped. "Who are you?" she asked.

"I am nobody, and it does not matter."

"Why should I follow you into this cave then?"

"Because you wanted to find the Prince. I am here to show you the way."

"What does he look like? The Prince—"

"An old man, Arla. He has seen many things. He has even seen Paradise before the Forlorn took over. Certainly, if you have questions, he is the man you should be looking for. Come in."

"Show yourself first!"

"I can show you ... but please have the courtesy of not hitting or screaming!"

Arla was at the ready as she prepared to encounter a threat. She turned around timidly, hoping not to find her nightmare come true. Every ruffle was a danger to her. In her head, the creature was a huge monstrosity ready to devour her in an instant. She even imagined a giant rabbit. It was cute and cuddly, but its imagined fangs sank deep into Arla's neck, causing her to bleed a slow and terrible death. Arla thought, "Dammit."

She heard the echo of footsteps coming from the cave. She turned to face her ghost, but was met with nothing but a tiny gust of wind. Arla felt relieved.

"Hi, Arla. You can turn around and see me."

The voice startled Arla. She hyperventilated at the sudden unexpectedness of actually meeting the voice. She, of course, did not turn around.

"Arla, I'm behind you. I thought you wanted to see me."

"You know what? I think I changed my mind. You can go back from where you came."

"Fine. I'm gone."

Arla felt the presence of the creature disappear. She turned cautiously, but to her surprise, the "creature" was standing there, and it looked exactly like her. "I thought you said you were gone?"

"Haha. So did I. But I can't really go unless you really want me to," said Imposter Arla.

"What are you? And why do you look like me?"

"Because I am what you think I am. It's a very curious choice – what you think I am. Never thought I would be you!"

Arla staggered back as she tried to regain the composure she had lost at the sight of herself. But before she could fall, Imposter Arla was there to catch her. She basically swept herself off her feet. The real Arla, helpless in deciding the course of events that had taken her, did what any normal person would do – she blacked out. Imposter Arla stood looking perplexed. Not knowing what to do next, Imposter Arla carried Arla into the cave.

He was on her bed lying in the dampness of his own sweat. He stared at the ceiling, reminiscing about the tragic day on which his parents were killed in a massive accident. That morning, his eyes were bloodshot from a night of no sleep. His thoughts wandered to a barren wasteland that sought a solution for his life. Pain was what followed. And for many years, even in his adolescent years, a bottle of liquor had been his best companion. Not many people knew of his silent addiction. Because for many, judgement was their crowning purpose. Hence, Idris came back to her room every night, seeking shelter from invisible troubles that pursued him, and to satisfy his desire for lustful adventures.

"Still thinking about things?"

Idris moved his left hand, which held a bottle. There was still a drink left in it, and he turned it up and drank every last drop in a single gulp. Stiff with the effects of drunkenness, he cracked the hint of a smile on his dried-out face.

"Hey, drink some water, will you? You've been drinking too much of that shit."

To Idris, there were mostly two types of Paradisians in Paradise – those who pursued a nightly secret with the Nightingales, and those who did not. The Nightingales were an enterprising group of young individuals, both men and women. Their income came from the lonely and loveless nights of Paradisians. The Nightingales posed a question to the concept of love. Idris believed the word *love* had been thrown around too often in his world. So much so, it seemed like waste paper being thrown into a beggar's hands, knowing the person who threw it, was a beggar as well. It was a careless search to feel the need of belonging, to feel a sense of purpose in a perplexing society. Idris had never truly felt what love meant. To him, love was like that drink in a bottle – intoxicating, but the giver of a bad hangover. It was so good to feel, however, that he came back again and again for more. He scratched his crotch.

"Hey, did you hear me?"

Idris pulled himself up and leaned against the wall. He sensed his bottle was empty and tossed it aside. "Yes … I heard you."

The curves of her body, visible through the thin veil of her flowery gown, had caught the attention of many. She was the golden maiden everyone knew best, or so they thought. She wanted to be many things. For her trade, she was anything her clients wanted her to be. She was a woman Idris dreamt of in his restless sleep. At the fair price of the day, she was his to love.

Her short dark hair, spiked by a night of roughing it out with Idris's love, made her look absolutely tarnished. She had met Idris long ago while they were growing up down below. She had seen everything that had made Idris the way he was, but there was still a closed chapter he never revealed. On her bed, the naked man who stared at his hands was, to her, a close friend who never learned how to smile again. And so was she. Her lifestyle had taken her spirit. She knew she was long gone from her world and into the fray; never could she return to the innocence she had once known. She knew that the naked man in her bed could still be taken in by the arms of the world. She gave everything to him that she could afford to give; she was bound to be a saviour until the end, singing a song of redemption.

"Idris, who was that girl?" asked Setia as she lay next to him, her head resting upon a pillow.

Idris dreaded that sort of question posed by his loving companion. They both knew what they had was a simple business transaction of human desire, and there were no strings attached. But there were times when they did quarrel like lovers. Maybe they did love each other in another sort of way. "She is that new girl. Jasmine has become obsessed with her."

"Where is she from?"

"From above. From Paradise." Idris held back his breath and let it out with a sigh. He knew a barrage of questions he could not answer was approaching. He raised his chin and prepared to face an onslaught.

"Aren't you supposed to be with her at this moment?" she replied with a curious twitch of her eyebrow. "You know? To show her around?"

Idris tumbled off her bed and embraced Setia, wrapping his hands around her waist. "Well, I wanted to see you."

Setia blushed bright red and tried to push him away gently. But his determined glare was too much, and he caught her off guard as he delivered a kiss on her lips. She returned it in kind but only as a teaser, for she then whispered a price for another bout of lovemaking. Idris cheekily requested free service for old time's sake. Setia blinked and suggested that Idris come back another time. For now, she was satisfied with just having a chat with an old friend.

Idris put on his pants and sat on her bed while she lay next to him, stroking his back with the gentle touch of her fingers. "How are you? You seem less chatty."

"Don't treat me like I'm dumb. I noticed that bruise on your hand. Who did that to you?"

Setia hid her abused hand away and stayed quiet.

"Did you hear me? Who was the son of a bitch who did that to you?"

She got up and opened the curtains. The night had turned to day. She knew it was midday because the rays of the sun had managed to sneak in through the cracks above, and the light cast no shadow on the ground. She stared outside.

"Hey, I'm talking to you. Who did that to you?" said Idris impatiently as he walked up to her. Setia held herself close. Idris knew it was something uncomfortable she did not want to explain. With both his arms, he gave her a sweet embrace. She knew it was false security, but she was grateful to have someone close who was attempting to give her comfort. Setia relaxed. "I'm fine, Idris. Let it be."

"I cannot protect you if I do not know who it was."

"You don't need to protect me! Why are you so dense? It comes with the job. Please don't repeat what you did last time," she insisted. "You were lucky you were part of the Party."

"I understand. But at least tell me who it was so I can at least keep an eye out. It's the fat guy isn't it? That rich Paradisian fuck … Mr Fook, right?"

Setia choked, "Yes …"

Idris fumed and punched the thin wall, opening a hole that surprised their neighbours. Setia's friend, who was in the same profession, was midway through attending to her client, and his pants were down. The surprise seemed to give Setia's friend a scare that caused her jaw to clench a little too hard. The poor man silently bawled, but remained brave as he maintained his composure in such a situation. Idris was impressed.

"Sorry, Kam! I'm so sorry! And to you sir!"

"Get out!" shrieked Kam.

Idris patched up the hole with paper while Setia lay again upon her bed. "Please leave. Another client is coming up later."

"Is it him?"

"No. And it's none of your business. So please leave."

"Fine. Take care of yourself. I won't be able to protect you all the time."

Setia stood up and slapped Idris. "Do not think I need your protection because you think you are stronger than I am. I can take care of myself. Go play with your friends."

Idris was disappointed that Setia did not feel she needed him as she used to. He was afraid of the bitterness he felt at being useless. He raised his eyes and saw her standing with such boldness. Dejected, but proud at the same time, Idris put on his clothes and headed to the door. He tried to turn back and give her a smile, but he felt that was not the right thing to do; the timing was not perfect. He stormed through the door and violently slammed it shut, angry at his indecision and merely saying "See you soon" to his friend. He did not know, however, that the feeling was mutual. Setia stood in her room holding on to herself, regretted that she had raised her voice. She waited for another man to take the pain away.

The stone slab was cold. Her neck began to ache as she realized she was somewhere new. Her body was stiff, and she looked up towards a huge rocky ceiling lit up by glowing dots of bluish lights, making it seem as if the stars had come to stay. She slowly turned her head to see what was around her.

There was a clear pond that bloomed in pink water lilies. From its depth glowed the same bluish colour that was above. Into the pond, a clear flow of water came splashing down gently and calmly. Arla got onto her two feet and ambled her way to the pond. She sat next to it and leaned down to scoop a handful of water into her palm. She took a sip, and its freshness provided a strange tinge of energy that brought her back to life. Feeling the surge of happiness she had gathered, Arla dunked her whole head into the pond to greedily possess more of its elixir. As she lifted her head and took in a deep breath, she felt her skin turn smooth and subtle, as if she was four years old again. Her hair seemed to have grown longer and darker, and felt fuller than usual. Whatever the water contained, Arla enjoyed it.

"Ahem."

Surprised, Arla awkwardly stood up, which caused one of her legs to slip into the pond. She awkwardly pulled it out of the water and stood still.

"Are you enjoying that drink? You should know that you are drinking shit from glow-worms."

Arla looked confused. "Shit? Glow-worms?"

It took a while for Arla to realize the stars she had seen on the ceiling were actually glow-worms. Even the bluish glow emitted from the bottom of the pond was caused by those fat, sluggish blue creatures. As with all living creatures, they had to defecate. Arla puked a little in her mouth but managed to control herself.

"Hahaha. Don't worry. It's not that disgusting. You tasted it yourself. Amazing effects, yes?"

Arla nodded.

"Great! I was about to give you a glass of that water. Since you made yourself at home, I shall just introduce myself. My name is Mae, and this is Tae."

Arla was a little wobbly from the effects of her drink, but could see they were smiling and holding on to a bag, which they proceeded to set down on the green mossy ground. Arla sat back on a flat rock, trying to keep her world from falling apart.

"Yes, if it's your first time, the drink will knock the spirit out of you," said Tae. "I told you, Mae. She won't be able to take it."

"Shut it! The Prince wants her to drink it. She just took too much of it, that's all."

Mae sauntered towards Arla and gently guided her to their bag. "Don't worry. You will be fine. We have a change of clothes for you."

Tae opened the bag and carefully unfolded a white satin dress for Arla. "All right, you, put this on."

"Why do I need to change into this dress?" asked Arla.

"You will be meeting with the Prince. He wants to see you in your best," Tae explained.

Arla noticed that Tae and Mae looked very much alike. "Are you twins?"

Mae and Tae looked at each other and nodded.

"Will there be any other questions, or do you just want me to keep holding this dress up in front of you?"

"Not until you answer one more question."

Tae shook his head impatiently. "Fine. Just one."

"Who is the Prince? What does he want with me?"

As Arla was strong enough to stand on her own, Mae released Arla's hands. "Just one question, Arla. We don't have much time," warned Mae.

"The Prince is an old man who likes girls in dresses," said Tae with a serious look on his face. "He likes them clean."

Arla stared at Tae with a quizzical expression, thinking that she had been taken hostage as a sex slave. Her heart skipped a beat as she accepted her fate in the lair of a pervert. She became nervous as she remembered the cases of missing children who had been kidnapped back in Paradise. It was a similar fate she was about to endure.

"Tae was kidding, Arla," said Mae, smirking. "The Prince is a nice man. Old, but nice. He just wants to have a meal with you and get to know you."

Arla took a deep breath, and Tae broke into a laugh. "I had you didn't I? Hahahaha ..."

"Arla, please take off your clothes and put on this dress," asked Mae politely. "Or I will have to take it off for you."

"What? Wait, you haven't answered my question!"

"We did. You asked who the Prince was, and we told you he was a nice man."

"I meant *who* he was, not his personality!"

"Well you should have been more specific, Arla" said Mae. "I guess we have to take your clothes off for you then. Tae?"

Mae and Tae both overpowered Arla and started to forcefully remove her shirt and pants. "Stop squirming, Arla! Tae, get her arms please!"

"Stop!" shouted Arla in a futile attempt as she saw her clothes being ripped apart piece by piece. Tae held her two arms and was silent during the entire duration. Mae's gentle touch seemed to know her way around Arla's body. Arla struggled, but Mae was quick and efficient, leaving Arla naked. Tae let her go.

"Hey! Why did you do that?" Arla blushed, her face bright red. She held her arms over her chest as her long black hair swept over her breasts.

"Listen, we can forcefully put this dress on you or you can do it yourself. Either way, you are getting into this dress and meeting the Prince!" said Mae.

Tae picked up the dress and extended it to her. Arla looked at Tae and took it unwillingly. Arla noticed Tae's cheeks were growing red. Mae walked over and pinched his ears, "Now aren't you cute."

Arla awkwardly slid into the satin dress and adjusted her hair. The dress was a perfect fit; it hugged her body in all the right places, emphasizing the beauty of her figure. She twirled around, impressed by the comfort the dress provided. Mae clapped while Tae kept quiet and continued to avoid eye contact.

"All right. Take me to the Prince."

Tae led the way through a corridor. Torches burned brightly along its entire length, leaving flickering shadows dancing on the dirt floor. Arla walked behind Tae, while Mae was last in line. It was a solemn march. "So, who are you two?"

"Nobody."

"Why are you here?"

"We live here."

"Why do you work for the Prince?"

"We don't work for him," said Mae. "We were raised by him."

"Yeah, he is like a cancer we can't just get rid of," continued Tae. "He is like our father. The one and only."

Arla turned around, and her eyes met Mae's. Mae looked back with cat-like attention, wondering why Arla was asking so many questions. "Have you two ever seen your real father?"

"No. We never did." Mae replied. "He said we were left out in the rain. He found us and took us underground to raise us."

"I am assuming that 'he' was the Prince?"

"Yeah."

"He sounds like a wonderful guy. But why just you two? There were so many orphans out there. Why did he raise only you?"

"You know what, Arla? We have asked ourselves the same fucking thing since the beginning. And it always comes back to a question, not an answer. A question," Tae replied.

"What's the question?"

"Do we really care?" answered Mae in an affable voice. Arla did not follow up with her answer, for she understood dearly. The Prince was a caring man they had known since they were babies. They had somebody who cared for them. They believed in the love the Prince had shown to them. It was best to forget a past they had never known, so they could live and love the present. Arla understood it, but the love she felt had been taken away too many times – until her memories broke her heart. The most terrible punishment a life could give was to have memories torture you from within as you wake up to an unknown tomorrow, carrying the shrapnel of your soul.

"Do you know your parents, Arla? I heard you were an orphan, but we were wondering if you ever had the chance to meet them," asked Mae.

"Yes, I did know them. And I still do. I feel my life would be so much better if I actually didn't know them."

Mae frowned and realized she had stepped on a sensitive subject Arla was trying hard to forget. Tae carried on their march.

They had reached a wooden archway that led to a set of stairs made of the strongest timber from Paradise. The arch had been crafted with beautiful etchings of the hibiscus flower. The arch, made by the hands of skilled craftsmen, was built into the walls of a stone cave. Arla was ordered to remove her shoes as they stepped on a wooden stairwell and into a living room lit up by bright candles. There were many trinkets and paintings created with the fluidity of a dancing hand, picturing many strange venues she had never seen before. There was one painting of a purplish-orange sky that dominated the horizon of a cliff where the strength of the wind pushed hard on a man who had golden hair. At his side grew a strange white flower. There was another picture: white lands spreads across an endless expanse, limited only to the confines of an observer's perspective. And in the middle, a woman covered in her warmest attire was looking into the horizon in a similar way to the way the golden-haired man looked into his own horizon. A dark-red flower bloomed next to her with thorns covering its stem. Arla was fascinated with that flower. "Come on, Arla. The Prince is in the kitchen cooking. You can wait in the dining room," said Mae. "Tae, go help the Prince. You know he can't really cook."

Arla was led into a dining room where a fire was burning in the fireplace. She did not realize she had been cold until she felt the warm sensation of a spitting fire caressing her skin. Shivers spread across her body as she felt mightily relaxed and stretched her feet upon a soft, furry carpet. It was hard to resist the temptation to fall asleep on that carpet next to the fire. Mae requested that she sit at the table.

"Lunch will be out shortly! Food is almost done!" shouted a coarse and unfamiliar voice. "Have a drink first!"

Metal pans clanked on the stove. The cook was busy and seemed in a hurry to have his meal prepared. "Tae! Stop trying to help me and get me that pepper!"

"The Prince has … how shall I put it? A unique character?" said Mae. She had just retrieved a bottle and poured a wonderfully scented wine into a glass. She was careful, and her focus was to amuse Arla. "Here – have some."

Arla extended her hand and unhurriedly sipped a little of the red elixir. It was her first time tasting wine. Its dark-red colour was alluring to her eyes, but its bitter taste was something she needed to get used to.

Regardless, Arla became addicted to that drink. Mae poured another round for her.

"Take it easy," Mae said with a chuckle. "Too much of that and you will probably find yourself a little too happy."

"It's delicious!" said Arla.

"Well try it with this! The buttery taste of this beef will melt your mouth. The wine … mmmhmm … will excite your taste buds."

Arla was only halfway through her glass when an old man walked in gaily. Trailing behind him was Tae carrying a huge, heavy pan fresh from the oven. Arla spilled some wine on her dress, causing an interesting blotch of red to spread across her chest. She was rather embarrassed about it. The Prince laughed to his heart's content. Mae snickered a little while Tae was busy arranging the table for dinner.

"My, my, what a clumsy girl you are!" said the Prince. "And very beautiful as well."

Arla blushed. She grew as red as the fine wine when the Prince grabbed her hand and kissed it. With a gracious bow, he introduced himself as the Prince, Lord of the Underworld and Servant to the Hero. Arla did not know what to say.

"Come, let's dine! I'm absolutely famished! Come and have a meal with me."

Tae pulled out the Prince's chair – or his dining throne as the Prince called it. Mae rolled her eyes while Tae proceeded to cut the meat and place a slice on each plate. The Prince took up his cutlery and elegantly devoured the food on his plate. Mae and Tae ate with such precision and good manners, Arla became reticent about her own barbarity. She remained quiet as much as possible, trying to imitate their customs.

"So, Arla," said the Prince. "What do you think of Kampung? Do you think it is wonderful? Better than Paradise?"

Arla thought about the Prince's question as deeply as she could. She recalled her adventure through a mythical wonderland. She nodded gently. "Yes, I find it very interesting."

"Wonderful! Tell me. I hope Idris was a good guide."

"Yeah, he was," said Arla sheepishly. She tried to avoid mentioning that Idris had ditched her for a romp in the red-light district. She was worried he would be punished. Arla did not know why she was protecting someone she did not know all that well.

"Ah, I see he left you for another woman. That boy! Such an ungentlemanly brute! To leave a guest roaming on her own is out of the question. When he returns, there will be no dinner," said the Prince. "By the way, is he on his way back? Or is he planning to move in with Setia?"

Mae shrugged. Tae focused on devouring his meal. Arla awkwardly played with her steak, gently tucking her hair back behind her ear. Tae noticed. "Prince?" asked Arla, in a somewhat embarrassed way. Everyone at the table gave his or her full attention, even when Mae's fork was halfway towards her mouth. Her eyes were locked on Arla, but her mouth remained wide open. There was an awkward silence as they waited for Arla's question, but soon realized she needed a little push.

"Yes, Arla?"

"Why am I here?"

The Prince picked up his wine, downed it, and wiped his mouth with his serviette. "Shhh, dear Arla. Not yet. Finish your meal and we'll move over to the fireplace and get comfy."

Arla did not ask any more questions. She merely proceeded to finish her meal. There were many questions that haunted her, many questions that challenged her sanity. She was excited, but at the same time doubtful as events unfolded too fast before her. The question she wanted to ask the most was about a strange person she had met at the entrance of the cave. It had looked like her and spoken like her, but obviously was not her.

Who was Arla?

Chapter 9

Crossing the Sand

Two days had passed since Idris had started on a journey through the Pasir Lands. The burning sun scorched every living thing, leaving nothing but the frustration of the heat. Idris took a sip from a canteen he had stored in his sling bag. There was no amount of water capable of quenching his thirst. Everything was dry. He wore only one thin layer of cotton clothing over his skin. It wasn't his first crossing, but every time he touched the sand, the experience was always different, and finding a way was always unpredictable. For this unfortunate journey, he was lost, along with two poor souls: Mae and Jasmine. It was Mae's first journey. She was stubborn and had not heeded Jasmine's advice to wear something more comfortable. But having stayed underground for a little too long, Mae had developed a timid habit of not showing what was underneath her attire. It was the first time Idris had seen Mae without her hood on. Her fair complexion glowed as her sweat glimmered under the rays of a desert sun. Her ginger hair flew in the parched wind.

"Oh boy, guys. I think we are lost," said the girl with a red and silver hair. "I do not see anything. We should be seeing something by now."

"Jasmine. We need to get out of the sun and travel by night," Idris replied. He passed his canteen to Mae, who was moving forward in a dream-like state. Idris had to keep making sure she was talking, so she did not turn delirious. "Mae, have some. You need to keep yourself hydrated."

"Thanks, Idris."

"Mae, I keep telling you to take off that ridiculous thing you're wearing. It's not going to help you!"

"I know how to take care of myself. Just keep moving," muttered Mae as she took a sip from Idris's canteen. Jasmine, irritated by Mae's stubbornness, stormed off a few steps ahead and took out a map. Idris knelt down and checked his inventory: clothes, canned food, medicine, a torch, and a bundle of rope. He took out a piece of white linen clothing and started to tear it apart.

"Mae, stand still," ordered Idris as he stood up and walked towards Mae. His actions took Mae by surprise, and she instinctively raised her arms to protect herself. "Wait, what are you doing?"

"Relax. I'm giving you something."

Idris gently pulled Mae's fringe aside and began to put the white linen cloth over her head. "Why are you tensed up? I'm not going to hurt you. I'm just making you a *tudung* – a headscarf. It will help protect you."

Mae avoided looking at Idris, for she felt his towering strength too intimidating in such close proximity. She ran her fingers across the soft, smooth texture of linen. She nodded shyly to Idris.

"Look, we are in a place really not suited to that thick attire you're wearing. You will overheat and faint. That clothing works well for a cool place like Kampung, but out here it's dangerous. You will need to adapt."

Mae ignored Idris, pushed him aside, and strode towards Jasmine, who was concentrating on studying her map. From where he was standing, Idris knew Jasmine's patience was running low. He knew of the wrath she could inflict if nothing was solved. Mae politely stood next to Jasmine and silently observed her map.

"This is ridiculous! The map is definitely wrong! Somebody changed it!" yelled Jasmine.

"Jas," said Idris, "you have used the same map every time we have crossed the sands. You need to calm down."

"Idris, I do not have time to argue with you. Please shut the fuck up."

"Can I borrow this?" asked Mae.

Jasmine looked at Mae, baffled at where her tudung had come from. "What makes you think you can figure it out?"

"I'll try regardless. May I?"

"Jas, let her try, all right?" said Idris.

Jasmine forcefully pushed her map into Mae's hands. She stared at Mae and declared, "You'd better change into something else. You underground dwellers must learn to adapt!" She then walked away and sat on top of a dune. From there she looked out at countless other dunes that dominated the view. Her mind swam in a desert sea.

Idris chose to sit looking in the other direction. He had known Jasmine long enough to understand that she wanted to be left alone. Whatever Mae intended to do, he decided to let her focus and hope she would have some luck in getting them somewhere safe that day. He sat on the ground looking upon the same desert sea Jasmine was staring at. He felt calm and serene. Despite the life-threatening situation they had been tossed into, Idris nodded off to sleep.

Shaking himself awake, Idris took a moment to assess how they had ended up where they were. It had happened in a blink. He remembered preparing his equipment in the Prince's home before they all climbed out of the underground to a forest path that led them to the Pasir Lands. Everybody was fine as they travelled on their way. Unpredictably, however, a sandstorm had turned everything upside down. He recalled being blown off his feet and landing upon a rocky outcropping. He believed he must have been knocked out. He could still feel the bruise of that impact on the back of his head. When he woke, Mae was next to him bandaging his wound. Jasmine was out looking for the rest of the group, and she returned with a decision to head west. Only the three of them were present; the rest of the group – Arla, Tae, and the Prince – had vanished. In an empty horizon with nothing but sand, it was a miserable reality that the rest might have been buried underneath that sand. But they had pushed on. Mae, being the optimist, believed they would meet the others again. Jasmine did not believe her, and that was a crushing blow to Mae's heart. Idris could see it; he knew her too well.

"Idris! I have found a place where we can take shelter!" hollered Mae.

Idris sprang onto his feet and ran towards Mae. She eagerly pointed at the map, showing him that they were close to a small cavern. She adjusted her compass again and verified her readings. Idris rushed over to Jasmine. "Jas, Mae has found a place to hide! Come on, let's go!"

Idris grabbed Jasmine's shoulder and caught a glimpse of a shy and mysterious wisp of a tear that disappeared into thin air. Jasmine breathed hard and stood up with her back facing Idris. She shook off the sand and turned around with a sarcastic smile. "So, I guess an underground dweller can be helpful after all."

Idris beamed.

"All right, follow me!" said Mae as she led the way. As they crossed the dunes, they occasionally fell and rolled. After every fall, they picked themselves up and climbed up and over the next dune. It was physically demanding work, and they all were breathing hard with every step they took. They were dehydrated, and they needed to ration the water as much as they could. They silently hoped the Heavenly Flower would answer their hushed prayers that they would soon find water. They desperately needed it. And in a hellish place like that, any help would be lifesaving.

"All right. It should be here somewhere," uttered Mae.

"Well, I don't see it. I don't know … Maybe you read the map wrong?" asked Jasmine, condescendingly. "And now you have brought us along on a wild goose chase. Good job! You have wasted our energy."

"Jas, calm down," suggested Idris.

"Shut it, Idris. We cannot afford to keep exerting ourselves pointlessly!"

"Well, I guess you must have a better solution than to sit in the open?" asked Mae. She re-examined her map, tracing her steps.

Jasmine fumed with rage as she approached Mae. "Give that map back!"

Mae backed away, but Jasmine immediately subdued her in a swift physical exchange than left Mae on the ground, her head down against the sand. Idris stepped in, however, when Jasmine unsheathed her blade. He grabbed Mae and pulled her away, standing between both of them. Jasmine was still angry as she held her blade, ready to fight.

"Jas! Fuck! Put that knife away!" shouted Idris. "Don't do something you will regret! Focus!"

Jasmine gradually gathered her composure and finally withdrew from her combat stance. She apologized and politely requested her map. Mae kindly passed it back to Jasmine, who studied her map and nodded a few times before she had a revelation. "You were right, Mae. This is the place. The question is not whether we are in the right place; rather, we should ask where is the cavern hiding?" Jasmine scanned her surroundings. "It is here. The sand must have covered it. Be careful where you step."

Idris and Mae both started to glance over the area. Each of them placed one leg forward and stepped hard, hoping to find a hidden hole. Idris climbed up the side of the dune and carefully slid downwards. And as he did, the sand consumed him. Mae saw what had happened and screamed in disbelieve. "Idris had just been eaten!"

"Right! He found it!" said Jasmine as she laughed with excitement. "We are saved!"

Mae and Jasmine tried to follow where Idris had gone through, but were confused when they couldn't find the entrance. Suddenly, two arms came out of the sand and pulled both of them into the sand, where they landed in the embrace of Idris.

"Comfy?" he asked.

Jasmine wanted to come up with a witty remark, but soon found many spectacular old markings on the cavern walls. Previously, this cavern had been inhabited by mercenaries, traders, and refugees during the Great War. Valuable water pouring down from a fissure provided a sense of relief for the explorers. It was testament to a day in which they had narrowly escaped death. Jasmine studied the writings and began taking notes in her pocket notebook, gnashing and scratching on the paper with her pencil as if she was recording the most important discovery of her life. Mae and Idris went straight for the water where they refreshed themselves and refilled their canteens.

"This is amazing!" yelled Jasmine. Her voice echoed through the small cavern, which amplified its resonance, much to Mae's annoyance.

"Is she always like that?" Mae asked Idris, who was removing his upper clothing and hanging on a rock. He took out a cotton rag and drenched it in water.

"Yeah, you need to get used to it. She loves these sorts of things. My mentor taught her about it when she was young." He started to clean himself up with his wet rag, and Mae noticed his badly scarred chest. There were few people who knew about it. Mae was shocked to see it, and for the sake of courtesy, decided not to ask him directly.

"You do know you are staring, right?" said Idris as he soaked his rag again.

"I'm sorry. It's rude. I'll let you be," uttered Mae as she placed her canteen back into her pack and found a comfortable corner in the cavern where she found some privacy in a slightly crowded place. Jasmine was still studying the walls, laughing, and celebrating by herself. Idris and Mae stared upon a mad person.

"Jas, what are you doing?" asked Idris.

"What you see here is art!"

"I don't get it. It's just gibberish," said Mae. "You know, you surprise me, Jasmine. One minute you're mean, and the other you're insane."

"To the likes of you two, these images mean nothing. But to me, they reveal the amazing history of our people – the vibrancy and the passion of countless adventurers who took refuge in this very cave."

Fairly insulted, Mae ignored what Jasmine had meant by "the likes of you". She walked in closer to the wall and touched its dry, rough surface. As she swiped her fingers across it, she felt a lingering sensation of history playing through her fingertips. The flow of an old story hid within, and Mae felt it. It was the same with the walls in the underworld where she lived. Bare, precious secrets of the past were never obvious to the eyes of Paradise residents; to them, the gossip of people's private lives was tantamount to a discovery of treasure. To observe and preserve precious relics of history the way Jasmine did was a skill most of the residents of Paradise did not possess.

"What does it say?" asked Mae.

Jasmine, with a smile, invited Mae to come closer.

In the shelter of an ancient ruined temple, Arla, along with Tae and the Prince, huddled around a small fire. The storm had emerged out of nowhere, and it had been taunting them ever since their party had broken apart. Tae was worried for Mae, while the Prince was worried for everyone. Arla did not worry about anything. She knew that, through life or death, everyone leaves. Her attachments to other souls had been severed long ago. She had made the mistake of inviting another into her heart, and by force, that person had been taken away.

"You two look miserable. Come, let's share this shall we?" said the Prince. He ransacked his pouch to retrieve the familiar bottle he had introduced back in his dining hall. Arla had the impression that she was living under the will of others, but freedom to her was overrated.

"Here you go," said the Prince as he gently offered Arla a bottle of wine. Arla desperately accepted. "Hold on, my dear. Let's have a toast first."

Arla was eager to chug the wine, but, embarrassed, she stopped and raised her bottle to the Prince's imaginary glass. "Now, we can drink!" he said.

Arla had the honour of the first taste. She had never appreciated such drinks, but the alcohol provided a chance to take her mind off the hurt she felt. It was an opportunistic addiction no one resisted. She downed a large dose in a display of impatience and a joyful appreciation of the little things. Usually, the Prince would frown upon such vulgarity, but he understood the circumstance Arla had been thrown into, and he allowed her behaviour to slide. The old Prince knew about such desperation, for it reminded him that time was often wasted on miserable things. It was important to truly live one's short life, despite being afraid of Death. Indeed, happiness was necessary no matter its source, and some pain could not be healed in conventional ways. At his age, he delicately sipped his drink, for each taste was precious.

"How was it?" the Prince asked Arla. "It was made by my ancestors before the Great War."

"It's lovely. Sorry, I did not—"

"What are you apologizing for, girl? Come! Drink! Rejoice! The bottle is yours for the night. Drink as much as you need."

Tae switched on his radio, and a crackling sound spread across the halls of the temple. He adjusted a dial to find the right frequency. Finally, the whisper of a person's voice resonated from its speakers. It came like a purr; it was the soothing voice of a young woman. Her voice was like a lullaby, a hushed prayer given by a mother to her child. Tae got up and sauntered towards one of the pillars, trying to find personal space for contemplation. Arla sat with the old Prince for company. The woman on the radio sang a sad song; her words were a mystery because she sang in a language of old. With good music, the wine tasted sweeter and fresher. The Prince and Arla stared into the fire, hoping the rest of their friends were safe. They could still hear the haunting rush of the storm outside. It seemed that the night had come earlier than usual.

"Don't worry about the others, Arla. I know Mae will guide them to the right path."

"I'm not worried."

The Prince looked at her with a smile. But under the fire's flickering rays, Arla appeared to be devoid of any emotion. She had turned into a shadow of her former self. The Prince gave up his smile. "Arla, do you know why you are here?"

Arla wasn't paying attention to the Prince. The young woman on the radio reminded her too much of Bell. She hoped it was her singing across the radio waves, from her cell in the dungeon. It was the only solace she found.

The Prince gave a light touch on her shoulders. "Arla, you've gone through too much."

A tear streamed down her cheek. "I don't know what to do."

"Nobody does. Follow me. Let me show you where you are instead."

The Prince fumbled through his bag and retrieved a lamp. It was the lamp Idris had carried before. He lit it with a branch from the fire and walked off, hoping Arla would follow. Reluctantly, Arla did.

"Tae, make sure the fire stays alive. We will be back," said the Prince.

Leaving the main court of the temple, the Prince led Arla into an old, dark hallway that led them into the interior of the temple compound. The sullen gleam of his lamp lighted up the path. Dust floated through the murky air of the temple. The Prince brought up his scarf and covered his face. The corridor was starting to narrow, and soon only one person could pass through at a time. "This place is getting tighter. How much further do we need to go?" asked Arla as she held her hand over her mouth.

"Patience, Arla. We are almost there."

Arla's claustrophobic tendencies were taking over, reminding her of a night trapped in a toy box. She twitched in nervousness as each step forward was a crippling burden on her legs. She was about to falter and give up, but just as she was about to fall, the Prince grabbed her hand and pulled her close to his lamp. He stared into her eyes, and she looked back. "The dark scares you doesn't it?" he said.

Arla could not reply.

"Every dark path leads somewhere," whispered the Prince. "Just follow me and the light."

With his hand holding on to hers, the Prince unhurriedly guided Arla forward. It was an assuring touch that made Arla believe the Prince trusted her, and this encouraged her to place her own trust in him. In the dark, she remembered a small, dark toy box. She remembered being left alone with nothing but voices. It was a suffocating memory, and it was destructive, pulling down rock foundations she had built up over the years since that tragic day. It had been a soul-breaking process to move on when nobody she loved had survived. After she had been alone for a long time, Bell had been the fresh air she needed – the light at the end of the tunnel. Bell had encouraged Arla to reclaim her strength; hence, it was her determination to keep the hard work she had committed from crumbling.

The further they went, the more the smothering air turned salubrious. As Arla breathed deeply, her stifled mind began to open. The yellow rays from the lamp began to fade as a glow with a bluish tinge emerged. "Careful now. We are here," said the Prince.

Their claustrophobic path turned into a huge chamber from which a grey stone stairway, strong and proud, guided any pilgrim to a shrine below. At the end of the steps, long stone benches were aligned parallel to each other on both sides of the chamber, leaving a path in the middle that led to a pedestal decorated with an emblem of a hibiscus flower. It was an arrangement that would give any preacher an unspoken authority over his sheep. Behind the pedestal was a painted mural of a hero Arla did not recognize. He was dressed silver armour, and a curved blade hung at his side. His hands were clasped together holding what seemed to be a hibiscus flower, which he was protecting from harm. In the background, there was a setting sun, which glowed upon his long, dark hair and bushy beard. To Arla, his beard made him seem like a combination of a regal king and a vagrant. It gave Arla an impression of a fair and just king – a people's king. Her head pounded with questions about his existence, and she began to entertain an idea of a different history of Paradise than the one she'd been taught. Or, maybe this was all an elaborate hoax to trick an untrained mind. Either way, it was by far the most inspiring painting she had ever seen; it had left her speechless.

"Welcome, Arla, to the Temple of the Hero, where passion lies and the glory of the past lies buried."

"The temple of what?"

"The Temple of the Hero."

"Who is this hero?"

"He is the man who ended the Great War."

"Well, I haven't heard of him before. Was he real?"

"Well, you *now* have heard of him. And yes, he was real."

"How do you know he was real?"

"I knew him. I was there when he was alive."

"But the history books mentioned nothing about him."

"It is the Forlorn. Don't trust the books they use in their schools."

There was a pause. Arla looked at the Prince suspiciously. "And I'm supposed to believe you just like that?"

"Well, no ... I mean ... all right, look," explained the Prince. "I do not have proof that I was there when this man existed. But I *was* there, and he lives on in the memories of a few. This temple is the only remaining vague evidence of his existence from a time when Bumi was at war with itself."

"Well, in books I've seen, a guy called Rizal was the hero. He saved the world from utter destruction with his wisdom and compassion."

"Hah! Rizal! With wisdom and compassion? The traitor knew nothing!" said the Prince, while pounding his chest with his fist. "That idiot knew nothing!"

Arla was amused at how riled up the Prince got get about his hero. She had never taken anything seriously during her school classes. Her carvings of the hibiscus flower that bloomed all over her desk were a testament to the lack of her attention to lessons.

"You don't have to get all excited about the hero, old man. I was just teasing you," Arla said with a smile.

The Prince noticed that smile. He beamed in return. "Old man?"

They laughed and they strutted down the aisle like old kings and queens of the past, gloriously swaying their hips from left to right. The antediluvian walls, which had been dead to the ages, were now roused back to existence with the colours of life painted by the jovial prattle of Arla and the Prince.

"Wonderful place, isn't it?" asked the Prince. "It is so sad that it has been erased from the memories and hearts of the people of Bumi."

"Yes, it is sad," said Arla, admiring the painting on the wall.

The Prince stared at Arla. He found it pleasing to observe a person admiring a lost work of art. He wondered about the thoughts that were swimming in her mind. At his age, observing a member of the younger generation admiring work forged through skill and passion was a trumpet call to the glory days of his youth. The Prince found a seat on one of the long stone benches and relieved his old knees of his body weight. He returned to his memories, recalling when hymns of joy floated among the walls of this chamber. He was young again. He was singing with joy. The beautiful girl next to him was clapping her hands and tapping her feet to the beat of the music. People were spinning, holding onto each other's waists, swaying from side to side, perspiring with the passion of a dance. There was a festival, he remembered; it was the Harvest Festival. It was the only festival the people of Bumi knew. And it was truly a party. A visitor to Bumi would never be able to understand the complexities of a small world without joining them in their happiest of times. The Prince was euphoric. He was glad he had never forgotten how beautiful that girl looked. His heart skipped a beat.

"Hey! You look like you're sleeping. Do you need to rest or something?"

The Prince opened his eyes. "I was meditating. And it was rude to disturb me."

"Well, I thought you had more to show me. I did not know we would end up meditating."

"Patience, Arla. We are not going anywhere. I just needed to remember something."

"What was it?"

"What was what?"

"That thing you wanted to remember."

The Prince patted the seat next to him. Like a curious child, Arla sat down with an eagerness to listen an old man's tale. But the Prince said nothing at all. Awkwardness filled the temple.

"Hey! I thought you were about to tell me something."

"Calm down. Let me collect my thoughts."

Arla sighed. "Fine. Just don't take too long."

The Prince scratched his palms, took a deep breath, opened his eyes, and exhaled. "Arla, do you know why you are here?"

She nodded. "You led me here."

"No. But nice try," said the Prince. "You're here because of what that man did. He was the Hero – the protagonist of a story that was created for the night skies and the stars." The Prince breathed to calm his stormy memories of good times and bad. He thought back to a year when he still had the pride of youth and no broken dignity from growing up. Arla looked at him and noticed a powerful glow of enlightenment reclaim his old façade. His spine jumped upright, and his voice turned young. Arla stared in silence, admiring the power of memories.

"That man was the true Hero of Paradise. The real Hero who ended the Great War," said the Prince. "I was there, Arla. I was called by another name then, and I was there."

Arla saw a tear stream down his cheek. She did not know what was to say other than to ask the obvious. "You were there? What was it like?"

"The war you mean?"

"Everything," said Arla.

The Prince knew she was ignorant of Bumi's past, but he was also aware of the lies she had been fed. Those lies were like a taste of poison that slowly killed a hopeful future. She knew of those mornings where she stared upon "bright minds" fed with ridiculous notions of ignorance and satire, allowing themselves to be indoctrinated with the dogma of unity, but not seeing the differences that separated them. Every morning, Arla waged a war of hypocrisy in silence. She did not know the truth, but she knew it was wrong to accept a judgemental ideal that further divided a ravine that had never been there in the first place. The people of the underground were lazy and traditional, while the people above were productive but greedy. The Prince, coming from both worlds, knew the threat was worse than she understood.

"Fires of hate and cruelty burned. We were fighting among ourselves. There were different *kaums* that dominated Bumi. We waged countless battles for food," said the Prince. "Many died. I remember endless battlefields covered in the bodies of my friends and family members. I still mourn that day."

"Sounds like it was necessary."

The Prince nodded. "Yes, it was. It was better to die fighting than to die watching your loved ones die of hunger. It was a gamble we all made. If we won, we could survive another day. If we lost, we died. But at least we maintained a sense of dignity by not giving up. I cried myself to sleep every night. One night I watched my eight-year-old brother preparing for a battle at dawn that he did not survive."

Arla dared not to look at the Prince. The tragedy he felt was a burden she could not afford to carry. She gazed ahead, choking in her words. "How did it come to that? What happened?"

"Nobody knew. It just came like a hammer hitting an anvil. We found ourselves without enough space for everyone. We thought we had enough food, but it was not enough for everyone. Our kaum leaders managed to settle a deal for sharing our food, but it was only a matter of time before some people decided they should have everything. Overnight, Bumi was consumed in rage," said the Prince, "separated and divided ever more."

"How long did it last?" asked Arla.

"It lasted for many years. I did not count; every day was the same to me. The bodies kept piling up until, at a certain point, we realized there was enough food to feed the mouths that remained."

"But it did not stop, did it?"

"No. We continued to murder."

"Why?"

"The hate was too great. Seeing my dead family in my dreams killed all my tomorrows," the Prince said. "We did not want to live alone. The Great War turned into a massive suicide event because no one dared to take his or her own life, fearing the consequences in the afterlife."

Arla swept dust that had accumulated on her lap. "If you ask me, allowing someone to kill you is the same as committing suicide."

"The book only mentioned death by our own hand. Getting others to kill you was not the same."

Arla sighed but maintained her interest in and respect for the Prince. "I'm assuming this is where the hero comes in? You're still alive, obviously."

"Yes, this was where he came in. He was from one of our rival kaums. Our kaums were locked in fighting, each for the extermination of the other. My Kaum won," said the Prince with a tinge of regret. "The others were wiped out. Everyone – even women and children – lay on the ground. I was looking for survivors. As I walked to the edge of the valley where the tall trees of the jungle grew, I saw a shadow limping, and I gave chase."

As Arla understood it, the Prince had been a savage warrior for his kaum – merciless, violent, and suicidal. The person he gave chase to was a man named Mazy Hamzees. Injured, and running away from a mad man, Mazy did his best. The Prince took pride in the chase, but was disappointed at Mazy's cowardly antics. The Prince said to Arla, "It was time for his death, but he kept running. Why?"

The chase ended at the edge of a waterfall where the defiant current of a river surged into a caldera. Mazy stared into a dark hole, waiting for the blow that would take his life. The Prince was a few steps away from Mazy. "Nowhere to run now. Give up."

"Why do you want to kill me? What will this bring?" asked the young man with long, silky, dark hair.

"An end ..." said the young Prince. With an explosive lunge, he charged with his bloodied axe raised.

Mazy grabbed the Prince and started to struggle with the crazed man. Mazy pulled the Prince in as close as possible to avoid giving the Prince a chance to deliver a deadly blow. It was a struggle for survival for Mazy, but then he found an opportunity. He felt the Prince was losing strength, and his will had waned. He pushed the Prince away to ready his fist, but then he saw it.

"He saw it. Mazy saw my face. He saw something that made him pity a murderer like me," said the Prince to Arla. "He charged forward."

Mazy disarmed the Prince, taking the axe from his hand. He started to push the Prince towards the edge. The Prince still struggled, hissing and grunting at Mazy, trying to grab hold of his throat. Mazy whispered into the Prince's ear, "Let's die together then, shall we?"

"We fell into the dark gulch. I remember hearing the gushing sounds of the waterfall as we fell. It felt like ... an eternity," said the Prince. Arla rested her head upon her arms. "Then, I felt a sudden crash. I felt a staggering weight on my chest that almost knocked me out. The water choked my nose and my lungs. I was drowning. It was the scariest moment of my life, but I let it be. I allowed the air to escape me so I could finally die."

But Death had not been merciful to the young Prince. Mazy, who also survived the fall, pulled the Prince out of the water and dragged his body onto the wet rocks. The Prince coughed and panted, bawling at a lost opportunity to finally meet his maker ... and his family. Mazy was the evil that had saved his life.

"We said nothing. I stared up at the edge of rock from which we had fallen. It was a miracle we even survived. We each had a few broken ribs, yes, but we were alive. Mazy also had broken his leg."

The young Prince stood up and strutted toward Mazy, who had perched himself upon a boulder and was holding on to his swollen leg. The Prince picked up a stone the size of his fist and towered over a weakened Mazy.

"You were about to kill an unarmed man?" asked Arla.

"I wasn't a sane man, Arla. I was just doing what I thought I had to do."

"But he saved your life!"

"Do you mind? Can you let me finish this?"

"Pig."

The young Prince, in all his victory, stood aimlessly, staring upon a man he did not know. Mazy's blue eyes showed a fear of death. He still wanted to live in a hopeless and cruel world. the Prince had forgotten that eyes could look like that because other victims of his cruelty had invited Death into their lives. This victim's eyes did not show that he had given up. Mazy's fear was, to the young Prince, the sign of hope the world desperately needed. The young Prince dropped his stone.

"Why did you save me?" asked the Prince. "Why did you spare me? Didn't you see I wanted to die?"

"Because nobody has to die anymore."

The Prince threw a raging fit and told Mazy that he had taken away his precious chance for death. He blamed it all on an injured man who had tried to save his life, and accused Mazy of not understanding the pain of losing everyone he cared for. "And you think I don't understand?" Mazy had asked. "The people you killed a moment ago were my family members!" Mazy had laid his head against a boulder. He was exhausted.

"Then you must hate me. You must want to kill me," said the Prince.

"Yes, if I had met you before today, I would have wanted to bash your skull in."

"Then what changed?"

"I was afraid," said Mazy. "I wanted to live."

"What were you afraid of? Don't you know you can finally meet the Heavenly Flower and your family again?"

"And where will that happen, my friend?" asked Mazy. "Where is that magical place you speak of?"

The young Prince was stunned by the words *my friend*. It had been a while since he had heard those words, especially from a member of another kaum. He ignored it and pointed his finger at the red-orange sky where the sun was setting. Mazy stared up together with him. "That's where we will go when we end," the young Prince said.

"You are looking at the right place, but I see it as a place where we could live again," responded Mazy.

The old Prince, Arla, and Tae were trudging through the hot sands of the Pasir Lands. The storm had dispersed, and it was safe to continue their journey. Tae was displaying a melancholic expression that was bugging the Prince, who was still optimistic that Mae was still alive. Arla tried to talk to Tae as often as she could, but mostly got simple one-word answers. Arla pitied Tae. She knew Mae meant everything to him.

"They have never been apart from each other since I found them," said the Prince. "Without the other, each loses true potential."

Arla understood.

The Prince led the way using nothing but his memories of a direction to their destination. They were behind schedule, and they had to keep up their pace. The tremendous heat, however, weighed on their strength. They drained their meagre supply of water faster than expected. The Prince, with his experience and tolerance for suffering, offered most of his precious water to the rest of the group. Arla and Tae gobbled it up uncontrollably, leaving almost nothing for the Prince. He pushed on, ignoring the recklessness of his young followers.

"Prince! We are running out of water. We cannot go on without it," complained Arla.

The Prince continued walking forward in the vast empty horizon, waving his hands as acknowledgement.

"Are we lost, Prince?"

"No, we are not."

"Well we seem lost!"

"Shut up, Arla," said Tae. "The Prince has been to the place before. Just trust him."

As the light diminished, the night emerged looking as if a painter had dotted her canvas with stars. The brightest star gazed upon them from above, overseeing their deeds of the night. The Prince searched for the right star and followed it forward when he found it. Arla and Tae followed.

Arla covered her mouth with her scarf as the subtle wind of the night blew a few specks of sand into her face. The temperature started to cool, and she developed the chills. She stopped and retrieved another layer of clothing from her bag. Tae, who walked behind her, helped her put on an extra shirt. "Are you all right?" said Tae.

"Yes, I'm good."

Tae then ran forward to catch up with the Prince. Arla assured that everything was in order and proceeded to catch up with the others. For an hour or two, they walked in complete silence. The Prince turned back once in a while to make sure nobody had decided to follow them along the unbeaten path. The silence of the day left them, but the tranquil howls of the night managed to keep reminding Arla of the beauty of the Pasir Lands. She listened to musical cries of animals in the distance as she walked through lands of a different reality to what she was used to. The story she had heard from the Prince back in the old temple gave her necessary purpose for completing her trek to the Hibiscus Party. Upon a distant dune, Arla saw a tiger staring curiously upon three strangers trekking upon its holy land. "That's a tiger – long thought to be extinct from Bumi, yet it still survives," said Tae. "It's a lucky night for all of us."

The travelling band of curious wanderers later came across dusty, derelict columns that had once carried a structure that welcomed visitors. It still had the same effect of awe-inspiring radiance under the peaceful rays of the moon. They trudged in between the remnants of the mammoth structure, their fragile bodies dwarfed in comparison. Arla had had the same awe-struck reaction when Idris brought her underground to meet Jasmine. The painting in the temple and the columns all had that quiet hint of a story that was ready to be told. It was one of those stories that had vanished into the carelessness of history, turning into a mysterious beauty that only Arla's sentiments could muster.

The tiger's spirit could be felt curling gently upon the pillars. Its ghostly shadow emerged from under her feet, smiling graciously with its striking blue eyes. The tiger came with another – it was its mate. Arla saw them fly onto the path Tae had walked upon, and they jested at the Prince's lumbering movements in the sand. The tigers sniffed Tae's hair, and the tigers danced away.

Arla spoke to them. "Who are you?" she asked.

The tigers took notice upon hearing Arla's question. "Did she speak to us?" asked one of the tigers. Arla was confused because she couldn't tell them apart, even though she knew one was male and the other female. "Yes. I think she did."

"Isn't it obvious that I spoke to you?" Arla queried.

"Oh my. She sees us! This is a first," said the tiger with a soft voice.

"Oh, silly! This is not a first! We have met her before!" said the other tiger with a coarse voice. "She asked us where to find the Prince underground, remember?"

"Oh! Now I remember. The girl who was lost. Why are you here, Arla?"

"I'm here for the Hibiscus Party," said Arla.

The tiger with a soft voice pranced around her with excitement. "Oh my! Oh my! A party? I love parties!"

"It's not that type of party, you idiot. It's *the* party – the red one," said the coarse-voiced tiger.

The soft-voiced Tiger calmed down, her whiskers bent downwards. "Oh that party. Interesting."

"Why? What is wrong with the Hibiscus Party?" asked Arla.

"Oh, nothing. You are heading into an adventure, do you know that?" muttered the coarse-voiced Tiger. "Open your eyes, Arla! Open them and go mad!"

"Wait! Wait!" screamed Arla as the tigers were flying into the moon. "What are you?"

"Hahahaha! Such a question! What are you, Arla?"

"I'm Arla."

"Yes, yes you are aren't you!" The tigers laughed. "Tell us. Have you wondered who is it who is aware when you have a thought?"

"What the fuck?"

The tigers giggled and vanished, leaving nothing but their striking blue eyes, which merged together with the stars of the night sky.

"Hey, Arla! Can you catch up? You are lagging behind!" shouted Tae from a distance. Arla was running as fast as she could when she found something glowing gently in the sand. She ran up to it and carefully brushed the sand away. There was a stone – a beautiful, pearl-white stone. She had seen one of these before. It was a moon-drop, she remembered. She placed it in her pocket and ran back towards Tae.

The Prince halted his march. He squatted down and ruffled his fingers in the sand. He smelled the air and got up again. He hunched and stalked something that caught his attention. "Deeza! Are you still alive? Deeza!"

From under a fallen ruin, they witnessed a sudden disturbance as the sands started to move, revealing a carefully hidden home. They watched an old lady emerge. "Who is it? Who is it that disturbs me?"

"It is me, you old hag! Don't you remember?" said the Prince, who was apparently annoyed.

"Oh, Ali! Is that you?" shouted Deeza. "Are you still alive? Come in!"

The Prince walked in and hugged the old lady as if she was his mother. They mumbled swiftly to each other as if catching up for lost time. Arla and Tae thought they were blood relatives – perhaps a mother and her son reuniting after a long period of separation. They entered her dwelling and cosied up in front of a fireplace. Deeza stoked the fire and prepared a meal. As they munched away, Deeza, who sat next to the fire, stared upon her visitors, Arla and Tae in particular. It was a humble home made by the careful burrowing of a skilled hand. It was warm enough to keep the cold desert night away. The sweet smell of the hibiscus flower filled each nook and cranny, making it a lovely sanctuary. A vase of fresh hibiscus flowers displayed over the fireplace concealed a portrait of a young woman and her family.

"Deeza, stop it. It's creepy," said the Prince.

"Ali, I'm an old woman who hasn't seen a living soul for almost … err … I don't know how long anymore," mumbled Deeza. "I'm glad I don't remember."

Arla and Tae continued their meal.

"Deeza, it is time you followed me back to Paradise. There are very few travellers nowadays. Times have changed."

"I have been doing this my whole life," said the old lady. "There are only few travellers, but there will be one or two left, like these two."

"You are old, Deeza. It is time to retire. When I return, I will take you with me," said the Prince.

"It does not matter. To see these two was worth the wait. And I can sense something magical that one of you is carrying, is that not so?"

Deeza stood up and found something glowing in Arla's pocket. "My dear, I see you have something of importance in your pocket. May I see it?"

The Prince nodded to Arla, and she passed on her moon-drop to Deeza. Tae was transfixed by the beauty of the stone; even the Prince admired it.

"Ah! You have found a moon-drop! That is rare. My dear girl, you are meant for great things in the future," said Deeza.

Deeza looked at it in the reflection of the fire. "May I borrow it for a while?"

"Yes, you may," said Arla.

Deeza went to a cabinet next to her bed and searched for a few trinkets. She retrieved some things and combined them together with Arla's stone to form necklace. Deeza said a few words, and the glow of the stone subsided.

"Come here, dear. Stand up and move your hair to the side."

Arla obeyed, and Deeza softly placed the necklace around her neck. "The power and magic of the moon-drop hides within you now. This necklace is now a testament of your destiny. Remember to keep it safe."

"I will, Deeza. Thank you so very much," said Arla.

"Wait! But the glow has disappeared. It's not a moon-drop anymore?" asked the Prince.

"Oh, you old fool! The moon-drop has been tamed, and it is part of Arla now. You only see things as objects. You need to feel the spirit of things!"

Arla kissed her moon-drop and placed it within her shirt.

On that night, Arla slept soundly.

Chapter 10

A Secret Oasis

"**Y**ou're lucky, you know that? Too lucky."

Idris was walking on the metal grill that formed the platform of an airship hangar. He had disembarked from a trading airship that carried goods to be traded in the markets of the Southern Lands. The captain of that flying beauty walked beside Idris. The captain had found him, along with Mae and Jasmine, desperately screaming, dancing, and cursing in the middle of nowhere on the Pasir Lands. All three of them had been burned to a crisp, and Mae had been half dead on a stretcher. It was sheer dumb luck that the captain had decided to try a scenic route, flying over lost majestic ruins. Most airship captains did so occasionally, flying off illegally to places not many had seen.

"If it wasn't for me, the *Naga*, and her crew, you would be dead," said the captain as he adjusted the tip of his cigar so he could light it with a match. His high black boots were painted with the brown dusty remnants of a rough road. His black leather jacket fitted firmly upon his shoulders, giving him the notoriety of a rogue. But the way he carried himself was a tribute to his past in the military.

"Thank you, sir. You saved our lives," said Idris. Idris insisted on helping the captain and his ragtag crew unload their goods. "You really run a tight ship."

"I do, don't I? My mates don't seem like much, but they are the best for a guy like me," said the captain as he puffed on his precious cigar. "Would you like to try?"

"I would under normal circumstances, but I need to get somewhere immediately. Maybe some other time perhaps? At a pub?"

"Hahaha. Yeah, sure. The drinks are on you!" The captain smiled. "My mates will get your friend to the clinic, then you and your pretty girlfriend here can go wherever you need to go."

"I am not his girlfriend," said Jasmine.

"Righhhttt ..." said the captain with a wink.

As promised, Mae was sent to a clinic not far from the hangar. The healer was fast in his craft, and Mae woke in a weakened state. "How did we get here?" she asked.

"On an airship. We are safe now," said Jasmine. "When you are all right, just tell the healer, and he will see that you are returned to us."

Mae nodded and whispered to Jasmine, "I always wanted to be on an airship." And she fell into deep sleep.

Mae had lived her life underground mostly, except for a few rare occasions when she had been sent by the Prince to purchase a few groceries he needed. She always took a detour with Tae that led them straight to the airship hangars of the Gardens. Usually they entered illegally through small gaps in the fence. They had witnessed many dedicated men and women who bustled back and forth as they conducted maintenance upon their airships, while another group loaded and unloaded their airships with supplies and goods for the next mission. The sheer size of the airships was enough to hold them both in awe. Many young children dreamed of the grand possibilities of commandeering any of these beasts. But there was only one they wanted to ride on, and it was the *Hibiscus Airship*. Parents would sing of this airship in tales of the night as they snuggled their children into bed. It was a scary story intended to make sure toddlers would go to sleep, and to encourage them to fear the consequences of misbehaving. However, the twins had always just wanted to be snagged away by the airship. They wanted to fly it to many places they hadn't seen before, and to explore the boundaries of what an adventure could mean. But it was just a tale many knew. The twins had almost allowed their dream to die, until one day they had been caught sneaking.

They were taken to the supervisor of the Gardens. He was a tall man with a slightly built frame. He was working on his data pad, typing furiously and giving instructions. He was a busy man. When the twins were presented to him, they expected to be yelled at. But it was a smile they received. "What were you two doing down there?"

"Sir, they were trespassing upon—" began the guard who had brought them to him.

"I did not ask you, kind sir. I asked these two," said the supervisor.

The guard gave a salute and left the room, disgruntled. Mae and Tae were pretty delighted.

"Now, who are you?"

"I am Mae and this is Tae. We just wanted to see the airships."

"The airships? It's pretty common to see them flying around in Paradise."

"Yes, but we wanted to see them up close. We don't get to see them as often as many people do."

The supervisor placed his data pad on his desk and walked towards his window. "It's almost sunset. Where do you two live? Your parents will be worried."

"We don't have any parents. We live underground, in Kampung."

The supervisor was unfazed, and he knew what happened to orphans caught by the guards. He was amazed, however, at the honesty the two seemed to possess. "Why did you tell me you were orphans?"

"You seem like a good guy, sir. Our guardian always told us to tell the truth."

"Does your guardian know that both of you are in Paradise?"

"Yes, he does. He wanted us to learn more about Paradise by coming up once in a while to get purchase his supplies."

"Your guardian is rather careless. He should not do that."

"It does not matter, sir," said Mae. "The thing is, we were caught because of our own mistake, not his."

The supervisor turned to them and requested that the twins follow him. He waved the guards away and informed his assistant that he would personally send the twins back to their guardian. And right after that, they went on a tour of the facility. The supervisor introduced the twins to the airships and explained how they flew. He showed them the mechanical parts that made it possible. He was patient, and the twins understood everything he said. Mae asked if she could try to fly an airship, but the supervisor kindly rejected her request because he did not want to take the risk of revealing the identity of the twins. Mae and Tae were disappointed.

"Sorry, guys. I don't own the airship. The captains do," said the supervisor. "Look. There is a spot I know where you can see them launch up close. Would you like to see that? Not many people get to do it."

Mae and Tae's eyes lit up with sparkles as they nodded eagerly. The supervisor smiled and led them upward to the roof. It was a perfect moment that defined Mae and Tae as they grew up. The clear orange skies, coloured in splashes of maroon, reminded the twins of beautiful paintings they had found in the world below. But it was the roaring engines of an airship and the fierce wind produced by its propellers that gave them a new perspective on what they thought was impossible. They cheered and clapped, and they wondered if there was a chance they would fly in it one day – perhaps in the infamous red airship. Mae hummed the tune of the song about the red airship.

"That's the song of the *Hibiscus Airship*, isn't it?"

"Yes. That is the one. My brother loves it."

"But it should be a scary tale right? You like scary tales?"

"How can it be scary? It's an exciting story about being kidnapped and being taken to places you've never seen before!" said Mae.

The supervisor laughed and patted Mae on her back. "Both of you are just interesting. I wish I had a chance to get to know you a little better," said the supervisor. "I need to go back and play with my daughter and have the dinner my wife has cooked. And both of you have to go back to your guardian before some other guards get suspicious."

The supervisor took the twins to an alley behind the hangar where there was a passage to an underground sewage system. The twins thanked him profusely and asked for his name. "My name is Dara. Don't get caught again, all right?"

The twins said another thank you and proceeded into the bowels of Paradise. It was a day that was etched in their memories for the rest of their lives – a day when children of the underworld were able to see a future in the skies. Mae dreamt of it almost every day. In that clinic, it she had the same dream she'd had as a child.

Idris and Jasmine thanked the healer and continued their journey to find the Hibiscus Party in the industrial cesspit of the Southern Lands.

Tae woke in his groggiest state. He'd had a dream – a dream in which Mae was flying in an airship. She was cheerful, and it worried him. Tae had never lived his life without the company of his sister. It was a dream that haunted him consistently in those lonely days when his depression ate his soul in the most delectable way. He breathed in deeply and shallowly exhaled. The Prince was sleeping to his left, while Arla slept to his right.

"Where am I?" said Tae. He turned his head around cautiously as a headache thumped to the beating of his heart. He remembered it was the tea he had drunk the night before. It contained an added ingredient thanks to Deeza. It had been almost three days since they had stumbled upon Deeza's den. All they had been doing was chatting and drinking tea. Sleeping on the ground with only a blanket was not doing any favours for his back. He could only imagine how the

Prince felt. But the Prince never complained. "We are still at Deeza's place. Shit."

Tae rose from the floor and trudged towards the kitchen. The water came from the ground, fresh from an unknown natural source. He took a pan and dunked it into a little basin. He freshened up with a wash to his face and was surprised to see Mae in the mirror. They were the most identical twins anybody had stumbled upon, even though they were fraternal twins. There were occasions when people could not even identify their gender. In their usual garb, the fine lines of their figures were concealed. If they tried hard to imitate each other's voices, each could live the life of the other.

Tae did not like Deeza. She was old, and her stubbornness was annoying. She never listened to the Prince when he suggested she would be better off living somewhere other than her desolate wasteland. He could not grasp the reason that a fragile woman like her would want to live alone, away from everyone. He hated her for giving people a reason to worry. The attention she desired was, to him, a selfish choice. But he adored her cooking.

The stone door opened to a sudden flash of daylight into her den. Tae's eyes were stunned, and he woke up more abruptly than he would after drinking any sort of coffee.

"Good morning, boy! What would you like to have for lunch?"

"Lunch? What time is it?"

"It's almost midday. You had a rough night."

Tae scratched his head and sluggishly recalled the humiliating acts he had engaged in the night before. He remembered there had been a party – a celebration of Deeza's birthday. The Prince had insisted they celebrate since it had been ages since she had celebrated her birthday with anyone. She deserved that at least. And so, the desert night had been filled with a joyous mood. He had become a bit drunk, and they had danced without care for their reputations. It was a mistake he would regret the next day, especially in front of Arla. Tae hoped she would sleep a little longer.

"Let me cook you something. Here have a seat on the chair."

Deeza did not go easy on her lunch supplies. She made a feast fit for a king. The fragrance tantalized everybody's palate. It was a miracle the Prince and Arla were still sound asleep. Tae, at the end of his meal, was filled to the brim, giving a reason for Deeza to smile. After clearing his dishes, Deeza put on her goggles and her desert wear, which covered her from the raging afternoon sun.

"Where are you going?" asked Tae.

"I'm going to work."

"Work? What do you do out here? Dig sand?"

Despite her hunched back and weak knees, Deeza still managed to pick up a backpack of tools that was twice her size. "Curious, boy? Why don't you come with me?" said Deeza. Tae got up from his seat and followed her out the door. He took one last look back at Arla, who was still soundly asleep.

The scorching sun was exactly above them as they trudged through the soft sand. Even under the cover of his clothes, Tae still felt his skin burn. The clothes he was wearing weighed down upon him, taking his energy away a step at a time. Deeza paid no attention, but lumbered forward without saying a word.

"Where are we going?" questioned Tae. It was probably the fifth time he had asked Deeza, and a cold silence was her only reply. Tae had lost patience and thought it would be best to go back.

As he was about to turn, Deeza stopped and raised her arm like a soldier. Her gesture caught Tae by surprise. A gust of air flew through his ears, humming a song of the Pasir Lands. Deeza heard it and pointed to the left. Tae looked from the edge of an empty wasteland and saw desert winds twirl a heap of sand into the sky, transforming it into something recognizable. The desert winds had taken life of their own, and they danced in pairs with each other. Tae gaped at a miracle. His heart mellowed down to the chilling realization that he was no longer the most special creature out in a wasteland.

Deeza waved her hand, and they both continued their journey to Deeza's secret.

The furnaces of the Southern Lands were running full blast, burning with the power of the Ketuhanan. Their industrial machine was running at maximum capacity. Workers joined in a dedicated effort to ensure Paradise had the necessary infrastructure to flourish. Jasmine had grown up in that land. She had awakened every morning to rising pillars of black smoke no Paradisians would see. Ketuhanan's metal walls and copper steam engines, held together by bolts and nuts, were her playground. She knew every nook and cranny in the place. There was never a day when Jasmine and her friends did not go home uncovered by the grime and dirt of Bumi's industrial soul.

Jasmine's father was a man who worked with the steam turbines of the power plants. He translated managerial orders from the engineers of Paradise into realistic technical applications. He was as good at his job as Dara was in the Gardens. The sweat and blood he gave were the reason Paradise ran well. In return, the grateful people of Paradise showered him with second-grade farm goods from the Gardens. Paradisians were truly grateful. As long as they didn't have to touch the grime of hard work, Paradisians were satisfied.

As Jasmine traversed through the Southern Lands, Idris tagged closely behind her. Big men wearing yellow work hats laughed and shouted rudely as they blocked many passages to their destination. Jasmine knew a few of them, and she felt right at home. Idris had lived in the Southern Lands before, but it was the call of the North that resonated with him the most. Bumi was not a huge world. A person on an airship could fly from the South to the North within seven days. Hence, even if there was work to be done, he would prefer to travel back and forth, never staying in the Southern Lands more than necessary.

"Hey, Idris, what are you going to say when you meet my father?" asked Jasmine.

"I am not sure, Jas. I will mostly tell him the truth," said Idris. "No point in lying to him."

"But he can be a bit impatient."

"I know, but it happened. Nobody could have known a storm was going to happen."

They looked at the time. Idris and Jasmine picked up their pace.

"Do you think they are still alive?"

"I don't know, Jas. But I would like to believe they are."

The horns of power plants sounded in unison, informing tough and hungry workers it was time to fill their bellies. The foreman shouted at the top of her lungs, and everyone walked off in the direction of the main gate. Idris and Jasmine continued on until they reached the mark of a hibiscus on a green metal door. "We're here," said Jasmine.

Idris knocked on the door. It creaked open to reveal a short man wearing a green hard hat. His bushy facial hair shook, and specks of dirt dropped as he spoke. "Ah, Jasmine! Welcome back! Your father is waiting for you."

"Halo, Adi! It's been a while now, hasn't it? You still have that wonderful beer belly I see."

"You know I don't go anywhere without it! Haha. Fancy a drink with me later?"

"I would love to, Adi. But first, I must be off to see Father. I hate it when he gets moody," said Jasmine.

"Well? Come on in. Oh, hey, Idris."

It was not a long walk. There were a few young men standing by her father's door, and Jasmine told them to move away. The young men said nothing but obeyed. Idris recognized them.

"Hey, get that out of my face," shouted Jasmine's father from his study. He was with a huge muscular guard with a tight moustache who was gorging himself on a big sandwich, which annoyed her father. One of the young men gently knocked on his door and whispered and announcement of the arrival of his daughter.

"Bloody hell. Why did you not say so? Let them in! Let them in!"

Jasmine entered first and rushed over to hug her father. It was a joyous reunion as Jasmine started jabbering about her time in Paradise, under Kampung, and her adventure through the Pasir Lands. Idris shut the door behind him, stood in the corner, and remained silent until he was spoken to. His mentor paid no attention to his young apprentice. Eventually, it was Jasmine who explained what had happened to the others. Her father said nothing, but listened. His face showed no sentiment as he only nodded occasionally to express his full attention to his daughter's story. When she finished, he sat back in his armchair and started to reflect. In a few seconds, he summoned one of his trusted men. Idris understood a search-and-rescue operation was to be launched. Without hesitation, he left the room and followed the man who was going to lead the operation.

"Let me come with you," said Idris to the stout man with the white beard. "I can help, and I know them."

He stared at Idris with his doubtful eyes. "It's been a while. Do you still remember your training?"

"I was away on a mission, not taking a holiday, Raf. I know what I'm doing."

"Good. Now go get my airship ready. I will go get more help and supplies."

Idris saluted the old man and ran down the corridor to a door that opened to an outdoor platform. A small airship was anchored on the platform. There were propellers to the rear, and over it was suspended a huge yellow helium balloon drifting in a light breeze. After a brief inspection, Idris began to initiate standard operating procedures for launch. He checked oil levels and ensured the engine was running at the right temperature. As he completed his preparations, Raf returned in the company of a boy. They brought with them food supplies to last almost two weeks.

"Your ship is ready to sail, Raf," said Idris. "Who is this? I was expecting someone ... bigger."

"This is my grandson. Don't let his size fool you. I have taught him all there is to know about sailing an airship. In fact, he is better than you."

Idris smiled at the little boy and extended his arms to shake. "And what might your name be?"

The boy shyly moved behind his grandfather, and timidly peeked from the side of his grandfather's legs. "I'm Taf."

"Well nice to meet you, Taf. What do you think? Did I do a good job preparing the ship?"

The boy looked around with the eyes of a hawk. He emerged from behind his grandfather and started his inspections. "Hey, Raf, don't you think this team is a little too small to conduct a rescue operation?" asked Idris. "Two and a half men really won't be able to cover a lot of ground."

Idris helped Raf load the supplies into the airship. Even at his age, Raf was still the heavy-duty, no-nonsense soldier he used to be when he was young. His arms and his back were covered with various tattoos, and each of them had a meaning and a story. He was an experienced sailor with countless tales to tell. If one had the time, the local tavern would be the best place to seek his advice. His joyous storytelling and courageous cheer showed him to be an adventurous soul for everyone to experience. Nobody doubted his tales, for many had experienced his adventures with him. Most of them owed him their lives. Under the orders of his mentor, Idris had trained under Raf since he was a boy.

"Idris, you underestimate me," said Raf. "I was the one who taught you many things, and this is how you repay me?"

Idris shook his head and smiled. "Still the cocky man you always were."

Raf scoffed and waved him off. Taf was already at the helm. He started the engines and was ready for take-off. Raf gave Taf a salute, and the airship began to rise. Idris made a final visual check of the propellers and jumped on. As the engines puttered away, Idris witnessed the immensity of the Southern Lands. The higher they went, the smaller its people looked, until they resembled ants. And off they flew across borders and into a desert wasteland to find Arla, Tae, and the Prince.

"I don't believe this," said Tae.

Deeza unpacked her backpack and laid out her tools in an organized manner. Tae's jaw dropped at the sight before him. They had trekked only a short distance and had arrived at the grave of a lost civilization. Huge monuments that once stood tall now lay in ruins, some partly buried under the sands of time. As he passed along those ruins, Tae felt the pain of loss. A sense of melancholy echoed through the walls, briefly relieved by solace in the form of warm rays of sunshine. Tae followed Deeza all the way, and he wondered how many times she had followed that same path. Had she been there when that world still existed?

"Believe it, young man," said Deeza.

"How is this possible? I thought no plants lived out here."

"There is always a way. The problem is believing you are the only way."

The path Deeza had taken all her life led Tae into a world unseen by many who closed their eyes. Deeza and Tae entered into what seemed to be a coliseum where people had gathered to witness a show or a speech. The place was different from anything he'd ever seen, and it teamed with the rhymes of life. At its centre was a mound from which sprouted a small fountain. Water trickled down on all sides and gathered around the base of the fountain. Green plants coiled out of the cracks of pillars and verandas while birds chirped; these days they were the coliseum's main entertainers. Covering the mound, countless hibiscus flowers emitted a wonderful red glow. Tae realized the place was not just an oasis; rather, it was a garden carefully cultivated and taken care of by one person. It was the old woman who had recently been taking care of him, along with his friends in their time of need – the old lady he had thought to be annoying and unreasonable.

"Come on now, boy. Come and help me do some gardening," said Deeza. "We don't have all day. And we need to get back before dinner."

Tae walked towards Deeza and looked at her tools. "What do you want me to do?"

"You can start by helping me pluck out the weeds."

"That's it?"

175

"Yes. It is the most important part of gardening. If you do not pluck out the weeds and have the patience to keep doing so, the weeds will suffocate the hibiscus and stop the flowers from developing. Yes, it is important. It may seem insignificant now, but the results will be truly prominent in the future, even if you do not see it."

Tae nodded and started the tough and backbreaking work. He imagined Deeza's countless years of hard labour, and decided it had been the cause of her hunched back. The hard work she had committed for a wonderful place was a secret that defied all odds.

"Deeza, is this the reason you never wanted to leave here and stay in Paradise?"

"Hmm? More working and less talking, Tae."

"This place is a miracle, but nobody sees it. Why do you even bother to keep it alive? Don't you see? Everything else is dead out here. This is a waste of time."

Deeza gently stood up from her kneeling position and strutted back down towards her bag. She rummaged through it and took out a small bundle. She placed the bundle on the ground and carefully opened it, revealing a crock of butter and slices of fresh bread. She washed her hands in a moat where clean water gathered and said, "Come, Tae. Let's take a break and have tea."

Tae was irritated that she had not answered his question, but the smell of fresh bread and the hot fragrance of boiled tea was enough to attract him to join in the little picnic Deeza had prepared. Tae sat on the dark brown soil with Deeza and politely accepted buttered bread and tea. As they sipped their drink, Deeza said, "Beautiful place for a picnic, no? There's nothing like having tea in a hibiscus garden – a garden no one thought was possible, in a place torn apart by differences."

"What happened?"

Deeza took a bite of her bread. "It was during the Great War. The Pasir Lands never existed before. Bumi was never separated into the North and the South. It was always one. Do you know where we are now? We are in the place where the Hero of Paradise ended the war – the place where Mazy reunited the world." Deeza looked upon the blue skies of the day, which were dotted with cottony clouds. She pointed upward and moved her hand to draw something for Tae to see in his imagination. "There was an airship. A big, red airship."

A blinding bolt of lightning flashed in an instant upon a cold night. Deeza was a young girl hiding with her mother from ravaging bands of marauders from other kaums. On their weapons, fresh blood flowed freely. Her kaum had lost a battle, and she was one of the few remaining survivors. Her mother held her tight, quietly praying for a miracle. "It's going to be all right, Deeza. We are going to be all right."

Marauders ransacked and burned down homes, and they pulled down monuments and pillars of stone. Deeza hoped they would not be found. Another blinding bolt of lightning flared through the night, revealing shadows that hid the innocent. Another scream echoed throughout the area. Deeza could identify two different screams of pain. The first one was short, and she felt death had come fast for the victim. Usually it was a young boy or a disabled man who had the privilege of a quick death. But the screams that haunted her most were the screams that lasted a long time. They came in intervals and were usually made by the female survivors of her kaum. Bouts of sadistic laughter by marauders were thrown into the mix. Deeza knew what was happening, and the realization that she could be next crippled her. Unfortunately, her nightmare turned into a cold, hard blow of reality. Men in their hard leather boots walked about the ruins where they were hiding. As they roamed, they carefully removed stone after stone. When the savage eyes of a marauder spotted them, Deeza's mother shouted, "Run, Deeza! *Run!*"

Deeza thought her mother was behind her as she ran, not realizing her mother had charged at the soldiers armed only with a rock, providing her daughter time to escape. When Deeza turned to find her mother was not following, she stopped right in her tracks and collapsed. She heard her mother's screams and prayed for her death to be quick. As she lay in the dirt, her prayers were never answered. Her mother begged for them to kill her. It was a desperate situation.

Finally, her mother's fear consumed her, and she pleaded for Deeza to come back. Dying alone was all too much for her mother to bear. Fear then consumed Deeza, and cowardice was her whispering demon. She could express her anger and her hate only through tears that flowed. When the screams were over, Deeza gave up. She lay motionless upon the land. Marauders came for her next.

"She wants it," said one of them. "She is just lying there for me! Move away boys! It's my turn!"

As his bloodstained hands grabbed hold of Deeza's legs, she stared up into the sky where dawn had broken. Birds and pillars of smoke rose into the sky endlessly. She closed her eyes and begged it to end, but a crackling boom from an explosion not far away startled the marauders. Then another came, and another. The explosion was so close it blew away any marauder who had been standing near her, leaving Deeza alone on the ground. All of them were killed. Then she heard the whirring sound of an airship. It was the first time she'd actually seen – the big, red airship. The name of the craft – *Hibiscus Airship* – was imprinted onto the side of the ship. Its eight propellers defiantly kept everything afloat. At the base, multiple artillery cannons were aimed downward. Soldiers on the ship showed no mercy and pounded everything dead. It was the most glorious spectacle Deeza had ever seen. And then she saw it – a wide blue beam came striking down, landing upon the land all around her. Deeza passed out.

"What happened?" asked Tae. "What was that blue thing?"

"I don't know. It destroyed everything. Nothing grew anymore, and the land turned arid," said Deeza. "It became the Pasir Lands you see now."

"Then how did this garden happen?"

Deeza poured another cup of tea and sipped a bit of it. "Do you know why I stayed?"

"Why?"

"The body of my mother was never found after that blue beam. I don't know how I survived. Please do not ask me. The *Hibiscus Airship* saved my life, but it also took everything from me. I stayed behind because I had to. This was my home, and it was the only place where I could cherish her. I blame myself for being a coward that night."

"No! You should not blame yourself, Deeza! You did not know what to do."

"You are right – I did not know what to do. But now I know. I should have stayed. I should have stayed and hoped that one day things might grow again in my land. I owe her."

Deeza continued to enjoy her tea, and she stared upon individual hibiscus flowers that blushed under the blue heavens. Tae poured another cup for himself, and together with Deeza, enjoyed every drop of tea he had.

Arla walked along the base of a dune that was not far from Deeza's home. She simmered under the heat, wondering where Tae had gone. She sat on one of the fallen pillars and played with a few small stones, throwing them into the air and seeing them land upon the sand with quiet thuds. The sun began to set, and the colours of the day's last hours spread across the skies. Arla gazed at a beautiful spectacle while she thought about the path she had recently trudged along. Flying red airships and secret organizations? Arla remembered the times when her father played with her. She remembered the stories he told. She wondered if her father had walked on the same path. Did he know of adventures beyond the borders of Paradise? And there Arla sat, imagining adventures she looked forward to. She never knew a part of her had begun to forget parts of her life – parts that seemed irrelevant to her present. She had even started to forget a love she thought would be forever. She was oblivious.

In the sky, in the direction of the sunset, Arla spotted a rather curious-looking black dot. It seemed to be getting larger by the moment. She thought it was a bird, but upon a more careful observation, she realized it was a Guard airship. Arla sprinted towards nearby cover that provided her concealment from detection. The airship droned above and slowed down. Arla knew it wasn't a routine patrol. The guards were there to find somebody.

The big jet propulsion engines emitted so much power that Arla was forced to dig herself into the sand. This airship was different to the airships she had seen in Paradise. The ones she knew were graceful but had the pride of discovery and innocence. The one that hovered above Arla seemed menacing and cruel. It was there to impose and not to foster. Arla hoped she was not the target. Fortunately for her, the airship flew in another direction. Something must have caught the attention of the guards onboard.

Arla rose from her hideout and dusted off. Carefully, she crawled on her belly to get a bird's eye view of the events that unfolded.

"Fuck. It's Tae and Deeza," whispered Arla.

The searchlights of the airship had caught them. Under its blaring white beam, Tae and Deeza covered their faces from the sand kicked up by the airship's exhaust. They were trapped, and there was no cover to run to. The only choice they had was to wait for their fate to be decided by the captain of the airship.

As it hovered over the two souls, Arla saw the cargo doors at the back of the airship open up, letting out two trained guards wearing black tactical gear. Quickly, they began to rappel towards their targets. Their identities were concealed by masks decorated with the faces of dead men's skulls. Not knowing much about firearms, Arla still knew they came prepared to use deadly force. She felt a cold sweat when she thought about another friend being taken away. Arla had no choice but to scream at the top of her lungs, waving frantically to catch the attention of the black guards.

"No, Arla! Run!" shouted Tae as he pushed forward against his captor, bringing him down to the ground. A quick scuffle broke and ended with Tae trying to tackle the other guard. But it was mostly luck that had sustained Tae for a short time in his fight. With superior skill and technique, the guards neutralized the threat efficiently. Deeza and Tae were back in the hands of the guards. And the guards in the airship turned their attention towards Arla.

Arla ran away, hiding behind the cover of ruins.

"What do you want with us?" yelled Tae.

"Sir, you are trespassing in a restricted area. For your safety, you are to be detained and sent back for questioning."

Tae ignored the black guard. He turned his attention towards Deeza. She looked intently into the sand; it seemed as if she was praying.

"Deeza, are you all right?" muttered Tae.

"Hmm? Yes, dear. I am fine."

"Hey! You! Let go a little, will you? She is just an old lady!"

The black guard holding on to Deeza ignored Tae's request and pulled on Deeza's arm as hard as he could, giving Deeza a hellish sort of pain. She screamed with all the energy her lungs could muster. Arla heard it.

"Fucker! Why did you do that?"

"Worthless vagrants!" said the black guard, speaking to himself. Acknowledging a conversation with his captives was below him. People who had no place to go were worthless to him. People who had no use in Bumi were worthless and should be weeded out from the world. To the guards, Tae and Deeza, along with Arla, were like weeds – weeds that choked out the hibiscus flower, weeds that needed to be plucked out before they consumed their whole world.

The guards in the airship had lost contact with Arla and were actively searching the area. Two more guards dropped onto the ground. They searched the area like hounds on the scent of a fox. Arla stalked among the ruins as close as possible to Tae and Deeza, plotting to save them. But to her dismay, she knew she could not do anything but hide from her hunters. Arla felt hopeless all over again.

Arla heard the crackle of a radio. The guards were close. She peeked through a small opening in a fallen wall and observed her hunters as they prowled with assault rifles. They were poised and ready to fire upon anything that made a sudden move. Arla compared the guards in Paradise to these men who hunted her. Her instincts told her these were different – a breed solely bred for war. They hunted with the expectation to murder. Arla feared for her life.

The airship that hovered above her turned away and moved towards Deeza and Tae again. Arla hoped to buy some time. She knew she could not do anything for Deeza and Tae; they were doomed. Arla decided to run and warn the Prince. It was a decision she took no pride in; she just wanted to save what she could.

"Please ..." She heard Deeza begging.

Arla took a breath or two and gazed upon her two helpless friends as they were taken into the airship. She forgave herself, and with strength left in her legs, Arla dashed back towards Deeza's home. The black guards detected her and they immediately fired upon her. Violent waves of copper bullets whizzed by her head and crashed dramatically upon the decrepit stone walls of an ancient city. Gunfire inflicted a psychological damage to Arla's will, causing her to fall a few times. It provided the guards ample opportunity to catch up and take better aim. "Run, Arla. Run!" her head screamed.

Back in Deeza's home, the Prince woke to the distant crackle of gunfire. He jumped up and ran for the pistol he had secretly stashed in his bag. Half naked, the Prince ran out of the building in the presence of twilight. As he ran as fast as he could, he was reminded of the restrictions imposed by his physical age. It was a painful reminder. He pulled out his magazine and blew into the chamber, clearing it of any sand before he reloaded. He pushed his fragile body to its limits. "I hope I am not too late!"

Arla's fear had finally crippled her legs, giving way to her final crumble into the sands. The black guards were upon her, taking their time. They knew that fear was a good tactic to use against those who were inexperienced. The guards saw her give up, and they laughed. "Go ahead. Finish her. I'll radio in," said one of the guards.

The guard with the radio turned his back and walked a few steps away from the execution. He spoke in codes Arla did not understand. She tried to crawl away, but was stopped by the stomping weight of a heavy boot. Arla choked and coughed. The guard stood over her; she was positioned between his legs. Up close, Arla saw his intimidating stare through the dark goggles he wore. The pouches on his webbing contained the rest of his magazines, and the dark emblem etched on the side of his arm represented his authority to enslave and punish. The guard aimed his rifle at Arla, and she saw the dark abyss that one sees in the barrel of a gun.

She refused to close her eyes as a splatter of blood spread across her face.

Raf was singing the old songs of bygone sailors in the skies. His focus was fully committed towards a path they had chosen. Taf was at his side, studying maps and relaying information on the speed and direction of the winds while Idris monitored the temperature and pressure gauges, occasionally turning a few valves to balance the power from the generator. Raf's airship was old, but it was definitely resilient.

The day had turned to night, and the silence of the dark was broken only by the putter of Raf's airship. Raf had tossed open every window on his ship, letting in the wind to caress their skin. "I don't want my ship to feel like a coffin," he said, and Idris approved because there was nothing better than to sail wholeheartedly into the wind and to feel it resist your desire to push forward into the unknown where its reward was to witness nature's majesty.

"How long have you known the Prince?" asked Raf, holding on to his steering wheel. "I've heard of him before. That guy used to be someone, but I heard he has been forgotten."

"Quite some time, I guess. He was one of those people who were secretive. He never said much when I told him about us. He just listened," said Idris. "I was treated well, and then one day, he suddenly decided to join us."

"I know who he was," said Taf. "He was one of Mazy's captains!"

"Hush, Taf! Mind the winds!"

Taf pouted and returned his attention to his papers.

"It was an old tale. If he really was one of the captains, people should know" said Raf. "It's impossible for people to forget so easily, isn't it?"

"I don't know, Raf. You tell me. You have been living way longer than I. You were born not long after the Great War ended, yes? You should have at least seen Mazy before?"

"No I haven't. Nothing … even in school. Reality was different. How I came to know of the Navigator was through a storybook I had when I was a child. What was it called again? It was about this huge red *Hibiscus Airship* that flew around kidnapping children and going on wild adventures."

"It's called *The Adventurous Tale of the Hibiscus Airship*!" said Taf.

"Ah, yes, that was the name. It's illegal, but I managed to hide one from the guards – you know, for telling a good story or two. I always told it to Taf when he was about to go to bed."

"It's the best! I wanted to fly it! To go beyond the stars! And to fight monsters!" exclaimed Taf as he flung his hand wildly and pointed to the skies.

"Yes, yes, Taf. You will one day. Just mind our coordinates."

Idris said nothing. When he was not looking at his gauges, he monitored a cold tingle that came with the wind. They could hear thunder and see lighting striking upon the lands not far from them. "Another storm?" he asked himself.

"Sir! I see something on the horizon!" shouted Taf.

Raf and Idris immediately positioned themselves at the helm and observed through their binoculars. There was an airship.

"Oh no, it's a dragon," muttered Raf in a doomed voice. "What is it doing out here?"

"Patrolling maybe?" said Idris.

"Impossible. Our intel provided us with good information on their patrol routes so we can evade them. That dragon was not supposed to be there."

"Could it be?" whispered Idris. "Raf, can you get us closer?"

"I will try."

Raf's airship flew as close as it could to the airship and gently landed upon the nearby stone roof of a buried building. Idris disembarked and lay on his belly to get a tactical view of the dragon. Raf was just behind him. "Is it them?" he asked.

"Oh boy. Yeah, it's them," Idris replied. "Tae and an old lady are about to be taken aboard the dragon. We need to save them. Do you have a plan, Raf?"

Raf silently contemplated their situation. He had orders to search and rescue, but nobody had mentioned suicide. He was more worried about the life of his grandson than of his own life. Nobody had expected combat. But orders were orders. He was to rescue them.

"A diversion. Taf, you stay here. Do not go anywhere. We will come back for you once this is done," ordered Raf.

"But, sir—"

Raf dragged Taf out of his airship and commanded Idris to board. He gave Taf a pair of binoculars and hugged him, reassuring him that they would return. As the airship took off, Taf stayed low and observed the area. Raf's airship was a hunk of junk, and he wondered what his grandfather's plan was. Not far from the dragon, Taf watched another situation developing. He saw a young girl running away from the Black Guards They were firing on her, and he watched her fall. Taf thought she had been hit, and he saw one of them was about to finish her at point blank range. But, in an instant, the Black Guard who was standing above Arla fell backwards into the sand. The other one on the radio thought his partner had done his job. The dragon was still on the ground, waiting for the rest of its shore party to board.

The Black Guard on the radio turned to find his partner dead, his blood splattered on Arla. Arla had experienced a traumatic shock and was now staring at a dead man. "You! What did you—?"

"I did it," whispered the Prince into the ear of the dead man's partner. In a swift movement, the Prince grabbed the Black Guard in a chokehold, pulled him backwards, and unleashed a barrage of rounds into his back. The man's blank stare was his final expression. The other Guards heard gunshots, and they were ready. The Prince scurried and scavenged the rifle the dead Guard had carried. He retrieved a fresh magazine, tapped it on his knee, and loaded it into the weapon. The

Prince was focused. He kept his body low, out of their line of sight. He occasionally rose up to sneak a peek at the enemy for tactical assessment. The other two Guards were in assault formation, poised to strike and avenge their dead comrades. The Prince moved over to Arla and inspected her condition. "Are you injured? Can you walk?"

Arla nodded with her eyes still wide open.

The Prince carefully lifted Arla's arm, draped it over his shoulder, and perched her closer to the wall. It was the best place to take cover once a gunfight started. "No matter what happens, Arla, keep fighting."

And off he ran into the fire.

The dragon airship was in the air again, providing aerial support. It was armed with an automated spitfire cannon. Engineers had designed it to spew around five hundred rounds of lead towards any determined enemy assault. It was perfect for keeping the heads of your enemies under cover while you positioned your team for the kill. The Prince knew they were doomed, but he tried his best, providing precise pot shots upon an intruding enemy to slow them down. It was a one-sided fight, and the Prince had been lucky so far.

As the pilot of the dragon focused upon providing support, Idris and Raf came from the back. They were stumped at how to take down the dragon. "Raf, do you have any weapons on board?"

"In the back! It's a LRR-01 long range. You know how to use it, right?"

"It's been a while, but we have no other choice," said Idris. "Land me over that mound over there. I'm going to provide cover for the Prince."

Idris pulled out the LRR-01 and a magazine from the cabinet. Raf flew close to his destination, and Idris jumped out. "Hey! What about the dragon?"

"I'll leave it up to you!" shouted Idris.

As time dwindled by the second, Idris ran as fast as possible to a high vantage point. His heart beat with excitement from imminent danger. At the highest vantage point he could find, Idris lay flat upon his belly and perched the barrel of his long range upon a rock. He adjusted his shoulders and his legs, loaded in a magazine, and cocked his rifle. He estimated the distance between himself and the guards, and tuned his scope to the right precision.

His first target was in sight. The crosshair in his scope was red, and it pinpointed a Guard's heart as a target. Idris was not picky at the accuracy of his shots, as he knew that distracting his target was a priority. He hoped that, if he injured his target, the distraction would give the Prince ample opportunity to position himself for a finishing kill. And considering the amount of crosswind in play, Idris would have trouble getting an accurate shot.

Idris counted to himself. The slow whisper of numbers controlled his heart rate as he breathed in and exhaled in a meditative state. Once his mind had calmed and his hands were still, Idris moved his crosshair slightly to the right of his target's shoulder. With a deep breath, Idris squeezed the trigger.

The gunpowder burst with a loud report, and the gun recoiled suddenly. Through his scope, Idris could observe the trail of his bullet. It required an experienced eye to do so. He saw that the round had crashed upon its intended target and struck in the abdomen. Without hesitating, Idris switched his focus on his next target and squeezed the trigger.

Another round hit its target. It was a bloody spectacle, but it sent joy and pride to Idris's heart.

The guards in the dragon immediately turned their attention away from the Prince and fixed their weapons upon Idris's position. It was a barrage of hellfire. Idris had nowhere to run as he saw the sands around him kick up like raindrops falling into a puddle. He heard whizzing sounds as bullets flew close to his ear, as ricocheted bits of rock injured his arms and face. All Idris could do was to stay as low as possible and scream out to drown the furious thunder that came from the mouth of the dragon.

Fortunately for Idris, Raf had come to his rescue to quell a dragon's wrath. On his airship, Raf had installed a homemade harpoon launcher designed for anchoring his airship at hard-to-reach places. He planned to use it as a weapon to control the dragon airship. With his first and only shot, the harpoon penetrated the web that made up the hull of the dragon; the harpoon was anchored within. The guards in the dragon were taken by surprise, and they flew wildly to release Raf's grip.

In their struggle, Raf's high-tension rope had connected the two airships together, causing them to approach each other in dangerous proximity. The dragon, in this desperate moment, fired its last fiery breath upon Raf, destroying the balloons that kept him afloat. To his dismay, Raf was mortally wounded in the process. As an act of final bravery, Raf clutched his wound to delay his bleeding and plunged his ship forward into the dragon, bringing it down into the ravine where Deeza's secret garden lay, causing a loud crash as a pillar of smoke rose.

"Hey! Idris! Are you all right?" shouted the Prince. He was dragging Arla over his shoulders. There was a young child helping the Prince. "Do you know this boy?"

Idris nodded. "We need to get to the crash site. Taf, you don't have to come."

Taf shook his head. There was gloom in his expression. To Idris, Taf was not a boy anymore. Idris carried Arla upon his back and passed his rifle to the Prince. At a marching pace, they went to the crash site, hoping for survivors.

"If the guard pilot survived, I will kill him," said the Prince. He grasped the MAR-02 rifle he carried. "I will show him the old ways of dying."

At the crash site, a small fire burned in the cockpit of the dragon. Fortunately for the pilot, he was dead. But that did not stop the Prince from unleashing his rage by pumping the pilot's dead body with bullets. It was the unwilling passengers of the dragon that worried Idris. At the back of the dragon, where the cargo door was located, billows of smoke forced itself out, blinding and suffocating Idris as he tried to find signs of life. Using only his senses of hearing and touch, Idris crawled as low as he could. He felt someone's foot and guided himself towards the harness that held the person on his seat. Idris carried Tae out into the Hibiscus garden and placed him upon a batch of Hibiscus. Tae regained consciousness as Idris stormed back into the smoke.

"Deeza … she is still …" Tae murmured.

The Prince dropped his gun and fumbled along the soft grass that grew in Deeza's garden. He discovered a beautiful miracle, and he gathered fresh water for Tae. The Prince sat next to him and gently poured cool water upon his head, slowly bringing him back to life. "It's all right, Tae. You are going to be all right."

Tae sat up and stared at a shadowy figure emerging from the airship. Idris had found her. He sat Deeza down to rest next to Tae, while the Prince immediately started to resuscitate her. She was as motionless as a log. Her chest did not move. "Please, you need to save her," said Tae weakly.

Idris ran back to find Raf.

Arla, with the help of Taf, was on her feet again. They both sat with Tae, and she placed her hand upon his shoulder. Tae struggled weakly and grabbed Deeza's hand.

"Raf! Can you hear me?" shouted Idris. His airship was a complete wreck. Taf walked towards his grandfather's airship. He saw Idris riffling through the debris, pulling part by part away from his side until he stopped. Idris stood looking down with his two hands upon his head. Taf could not see, but he knew what Idris saw. Taf said nothing as he looked down upon a dead hibiscus.

The Prince confirmed Deeza's death, as he had found a massive wound on the back of her head. The Prince hoped it had been a swift end for her. He was grateful for the serene countenance she exuded in death. It gave him a certain clarity to the fragility of life.

"Arla, can you pass me a piece of cloth or something?"

Arla tore off a long piece of her clothing and passed it to the Prince. In a solemn ritual to honour Deeza, he placed the brown, tainted cloth with much care and respect on her face. It was the passing of a dear friend. The Prince said no words, for they had been surrounded by evil. Arla held on to Tae's hand, and Tae grabbed it back with as much strength as he could, never letting go. Love was the most painful hurt, and it lasted a lifetime.

"I'm sorry, Taf. Your grandfather is ..." said Idris.

"I know," responded Taf. Idris saw that Taf was familiar with loss. His demeanour was not a display of courage, but a declaration that he was afraid of living without his grandfather. He held on to Idris, and Idris held back.

"Let's go home."

The Prince's past had returned to haunt him. He, Idris, and Arla placed the dead parallel with one another among surviving hibiscus flowers. They retrieved any wood that could be found in the garden, and stacked it in a pile around and above the bodies. With only a few words that only the Prince knew, he tossed in a burning torch, and the garden lit up in flames.

The survivors stood a distance away, staring upon a fiery destruction that consumed an oasis. In the dark of night, the light of the fire reflected in their eyes. Their love for those who died had manifested into a form of revenge.

The last hibiscus flower that grew in the desert dropped its last petal and disappeared into the flame.

Chapter 11

Being Virtuous

Physical training was Mae's most hated endeavour. She wasn't keen on pushing herself for the sake of improved fitness. "Why are we doing this? Aren't we here to find a way to stand up against the Forlorn?"

"Are you dumb?" replied her comrades. Mae had been placed in a team of random individuals. The only friend she had there was Arla. She had no problem with physical fitness. In fact, she excelled. She saw the others as a group of misfits who wanted to play war. Mae had a problem working with people she did not know.

After training, Mae would sit by herself in a corner segregating herself away from her team. But Arla sat with them. They joked and they laughed together in an underground training facility during break. When they took punishment, Arla was there with them. When they were about to give up, Arla was there to push them ahead. Wherever they were, she was there. Nobody who looked her way could not notice her short black hair. To see her was to finish what they had started, while Mae was always in front, silent and steadfast, never stopping for any obstacle that could prove too hard for a friend to overcome. She was determined to destroy the Forlorn. Training was wasting her time.

Arla noticed. She said nothing.

Each team was pushed to its limits, and each team was trained to work upon its members' merits and their weaknesses. Based on Idris and Jasmine's recommendations, trainers knew well how to organize their training and bring out the best in their recruits. They did this to ensure they thought alike so they could foresee what would be needed to stay alive and accomplish their mission. Jasmine's father stood behind a one-way looking glass, silently monitoring each recruit's progress for signs of leadership potential.

During weapons training, Mae had trouble trying to dismantle and reassemble a rifle. Her team ignored her, and some went on to emphasize the fact that Mae was slowing their team's progress. But Arla was always there to catch her. She smiled and patiently taught Mae from step one.

"Thanks, Arla," said Mae.

"It's all right, Mae. Remember, it's just a gun." Arla smiled.

Using a knife during hand-to-hand combat was Mae's forte. Trainers devised a competitive sport to determine the best unit. They had three days to train among themselves. Using her skills and renewed faith, Mae taught her team well. She began to smile again. She began to enjoy the company of others – people other than the Prince and her brother. She almost felt she had a new family – a family as close as blood.

Competition was tough, but Arla and Mae's team had managed to reach the finals. The winner of the grand finale depended upon Arla and Tae's performance. They stood in the middle of a cage, staring at each other with gazes of grit, while their hands clutched the cold, lifeless blades. They walked closer to each other as the lights dimmed, leaving only a beam of light to shine upon two souls on fire. As the speaker announced their names, both fighters immediately engaged in combat.

Others were in awe with the speed they showed. It was a fighting dance that included a display of elegant techniques. For the uninitiated, reflections made as the light flashed on their blades were all they saw. It was an acrobatic show that turned the light into their striking weapon, blinding an opponent with every move. Mae followed their every step, and she knew Tae's movements. But Mae was caught by surprise to witness how fast Arla had picked up techniques from her training. In a swift move, Tae swiped Arla from her feet, and she fell on her back. Tae stood over her, resting the tip of his blade on her throat.

Everyone thought the fight was over, but Mae saw a part of Tae she had never seen. He looked upon Arla with a kind glare. Noticing mercy, Arla countered, rolling over him sideways and mounting him. Arla sweltered on top. It was her turn to place her blade upon Tae's throat. They both breathed heavily. When she went in close to Tae, she said: "I've won."

Arla moved her knife towards Tae's eyes and gave him a small cut next to his right eye. Mae knew it was going to scar, and she was worried that Tae would be incensed that his opponent had turned a sparring session into a real fight. But to her surprise, Tae gave Arla a sly, crooked smile. Mae and Tae did not look the same anymore. The scar clearly defined the difference between them, and that definition broke a piece of Mae's heart; no one stayed the same forever.

Afterwards, they all had their first shower after a long period of four weeks. Trainers had established a sort of showering tent within the confines of their training grounds. It was located at their assembly area. Forgetting the embarrassment of nudity, each man and woman stripped as they ran towards the tent, looking forward to a chance to take in the first drops of warm water. Skins touched, and laughter filled the grounds. Mae, along with Arla and the rest of her unit, enjoyed a little splash of cheeky fun. It was the first time Mae had seen Arla in the nude. Mae's eyes wandered to find her brother. At the opposite end of the tent, Tae was with his mates. The colour of his slender body mimicked her pale complexion, and his face was as feminine as hers. She admired her brother's beauty. As she saw him laugh with joy, a rift started to establish itself between them. They used to be inseparable, but after receiving that scar and surviving his experience out in the Pasir Lands, Tae was no longer the brother she knew. He no longer needed her. It was a torture that stabbed the love she had for Tae. She was proud, and thus she endured. She returned to the company of her newfound family.

At the end of the day, recruits settled on their bunks in their barracks. Some were awake, chatting about possibilities of a future and how the Hibiscus Party would one day bring out the true potential of Bumi. The leader of the Hibiscus Party had once been a part of a crew on the red airship. In a speech, he shared his opinion that the Forlorn Government had poisoned the roots of their beloved hibiscus flower, and explained how it garnered the loyalty of their subjects through blessings from the Heavenly Flower. With Her blessings, it wasn't hard for the Forlorn leader to be made a divine king.

Mae was about to fall into a deep sleep when she felt her bunk gently shake. To her surprise, it was Arla sneaking around in her bare feet. Mae waited and then carefully tailed her. They dodged the sharp eyes of sentries patrolling the training grounds. The grounds were built in the form of a maze, designed to train recruits on the confusing nature of urban warfare. It closely replicated Paradise's nooks and crannies. There was a notorious "kill house" on the training grounds where recruits worked in teams to fight in a room. Nobody had entered the kill house without receiving an injury in return. It was baptism by fire.

At the armoury, Mae huddled behind a few crates containing ammunition. She peeked through narrow gaps and saw Arla standing at the weapons counter waiting for someone. Mae realized there was another person behind that counter. It was Tae. "Are you ready?" he said as he wiped grease from his hands. Mae had forgotten that Tae was apprentice quartermaster for the armoury. Mae often forgot that her brother was as talented as she.

"Always am. What are we going to do today?" said Arla with a cheeky smile.

"Well, it looks like my sister has taught you well in the art of hand-to-hand combat. I do not have anything else to teach you about that. You learn pretty fast."

"There must be something else. How about weapons handling? Show me how to hold a rifle through a tight space!"

Tae nodded and went back behind the counter to retrieve a standard issue MAR-02 rifle. It was the same rifle the Black Guards had been carrying. Still intimidated by them, Arla mustered enough courage to master its use for combat. She trained hard with it until it was instilled within her psyche that a rifle was part of her. Without it, a phantom pain surged through her body.

"Here. Show me how you hold it," demanded Tae as he placed his rifle on her hands.

"My pleasure."

Arla positioned herself in a firing stance. She held her weapon close to her chest and applied marksmanship principles. She took a step forward and tactically manoeuvred herself through an imaginary battlefield, checking her corners and dead spaces.

"Not bad. That was really good," said Tae. "But when you are trying to clear a room, make sure you don't go in alone. Have another set of eyes to cover your back. If you have to do it alone, do it this way."

Tae grabbed Arla by her waist and pulled her in closer. He guided her hands to her rifle, while his legs positioned Arla in a more stable stance. "Before going into a room, remember to check your corners. Instead of going in straight, try tilting your rifle to the side like this. Yes. And take baby steps until you clear your area."

"This applies for both directions?" asked Arla.

"Yes, to the right and later to the left. The method is the same. Just don't rush and get yourself killed."

Arla nodded in understanding. She passed Tae's rifle back to him and stretched, letting out a yawn. "I'm really tired! Did you ever wonder why we are learning all this? I mean, we want to bring down the Forlorn, yes? But are we going to war to do so?" she questioned.

"War? Yes, in a way we are going to go to war, but I do not believe we will be using the skills we learned for that kind of war. As our commander says, it will be a war to wake the people of Bumi. It will be a war to bring back our passion and live once again."

"Aren't we living now?"

"You saw how they treated us – we are the unwanted. You saw with your own eyes what they did to Deeza! Can you imagine what would happen to me if I was taken to their dungeon?" said Tae. "Nobody like us comes back from the dungeon."

Arla touched her head as a phantom pain developed in her skull. She felt that part of a memory was missing. She couldn't recall, and she couldn't remember. She felt the haunting presence of nostalgia and the melancholy of knowing an important person she promised herself not to forget had disappeared from her memories. It was a guilt-ridden pain that chewed at her night and day.

"Are you all right? I'm sorry, I should not have—"

"No it's all right. I just wanted to make sure we are doing this for a reason, you know?" said Arla. "I do not want everything to go back to the Great War. I believe in the *Hibiscus Airship*. There is so much more we could do."

Arla hugged Tae and whispered, "Thank you."

Tae blushed as he felt her warm body press itself against his. He wanted more.

"Arla, I have something to say."

"Hmm? Can it wait for tomorrow? I'm tired."

Tae grabbed her hands and pulled her closer. Arla drowned herself in his eyes. She felt Tae's hands tremble as she smiled. "What is this?" she asked. Tae, without hesitation, moved in and pressed his lips upon hers. Tae prayed her rosy lips would accept his. Arla's lips never left. She relaxed, and her hands moved around his shoulders, pulling him ever closer. Mae saw Tae beam in reaction.

"I have been lonelier in real life than I am out here. I'm glad you're here," said Arla.

Mae quietly snuck out and returned to her barracks. Arla and Tae continued their affair in secret.

"Have you known moments like that?" asked the Prince. "The moments when you imagine what happens? I have. Once when I was walking down a street I saw a girl. I don't know why she caught my attention, she just did. I liked how her nose gently curled. There I was, standing and waiting for something, and then I noticed her reading a book I loved. I walked to her and said, 'How do you do? I love that book you're reading.' She replied with a sceptical look of a stranger, 'Oh, yeah?' We flew into a conversation we never thought possible. We laughed, and we choked, only because we laughed too hard. Eventually we became friends, and the future held possibilities for us to be more. But it was one of those moments of regretted imagination. If only I had actually said, 'How do you do'."

Idris was in his kitchen pouring two glasses of whiskey. The Prince had been paying him visits ever since the Pasir Lands incident in which Idris had saved his life. Idris had finished his report on the progress of his training programme when a knock had come the door came. The Prince was in a jolly mood, and he wanted to find a drinking partner. Idris, a young man who never turned down a good drink, had invited him in. They talked about everything, but mostly about their personal lives.

"Yes, I know of those moments. You won't believe how many of those I have encountered."

"Hahaha! With that many at your age, I must be a walking wreck!"

Idris was in his socks as he shuffled towards the Prince and passed him his drink. "You are not a wreck. The way you handled yourself out there was awesome. You need to teach me a few of your moves."

"In due time, Idris. In due time," said the Prince as he took a sip. "Right now I'm content with just drinking this wonderful miracle."

"I agree with you there. I cannot believe you kept it away from me for so long."

"Good things come at the right time," said the Prince as he took in another sip. "Hey … I know I may not have seemed grateful, but I really want to thank you for your help."

Idris raised his glass in a salute. Their glasses touched and they downed it in one gulp. It was a silent acknowledgement. Idris poured another round.

"How did you end up here, Idris? Paradise would definitely clamour for the attention of a man with your skills."

Idris downed another round. "I'm an orphan. Nobody wants to tangle themselves with a person who has no future."

"I understand. Is that the reason you are against the Forlorn?"

Idris gawked through the window at the horizon beyond which the Pasir Lands lay. The desert was a remarkable place. It was menacing and peaceful at the same time. Treat it with disrespect, and your doom shall be soon, but treat it with respect, and it will show itself as the cleanest place in the world – a place that could purge your soul from the calamities of filth.

"I'm just here trying to find a purpose for myself. I just want to believe that one day I will get to see more."

"And what more is that?"

Idris downed another round. "I don't know."

"Your family … I am really sorry to hear about them."

"Nothing you could have been done, Prince. They died in an accident when I was six. A construction accident, they said."

"At six? That was a very young age. Where did you go?"

"I was playing with my toys at home when suddenly the guards took me to the orphanage. They told me my parents were dead. I never did see their bodies. I never did."

The Prince poured himself another round. He gently shook his bottle, asking if Idris would like another. Idris covered the top of his glass with his palm. "I ran away from the orphanage when I realized it was a prison where they kept unwanted kids until they grew up. Most orphans who grew up ended up in the Southern Lands or Kampung doing things that were important but which other people did not want to do. I was segregated there when I was young. The orphanage was a place where dreams were meant to die."

The Prince sat up and downed another round; he was feeling light and tipsy. Idris poured himself another. He thought, "Might as well."

"When you left, how did you end up with the Party?" asked the Prince.

"There was no Party at first. I wandered everywhere trying to survive. I'd heard of you – the Lord of the Underworld. I tried to find you, but I guess circumstances did not present themselves. I found a friend during that time. Her name was Setia."

"Setia … I know her. Kind young woman. She is one of the Nightingales."

"Yep, that's her. Kind and beautiful. She is one of those moments."

"You love her, don't you?"

"I love her as much as I can. But for a Nightingale, love was an unselfish thing."

In the bottom of his soul – his deep, deep tragic soul – lay the fire of his love for Setia. Like all unfortunate tragedies, secrets of love lay between the darkness and the light. One day, he hoped, under a mirror reflection of moonlight, he would see her again. There was no turning back from the journey on which he was about to embark. Idris would return to Paradise with a future to fight for. He would have no time to make amends with his devotion. There would be time afterwards, if he survived.

"Remember, she is your friend. Talk to her again."

"I will. I will. I will."

The bottle had turned dry. Both men struggled to sit upright. The Prince retrieved another fresh bottle from his pouch. He popped it open and inhaled the fresh aroma of a flowery fragrance. It was not a scent with which Idris was familiar. "What is that smell?"

"Oh? It's rose wine – a rare gift given to me by my best friend. This bottle is the only one in Bumi."

"And you opened it now? And what is rose?"

"It's a flower – a flower you and I have never seen before."

"Where did your friend get it?"

"From another world."

"Are you joking? You're saying your friend has gone to another world?"

"I'm not lying. This drink you're drinking is testament to the truth," said the Prince. "I'm surprised because, as you are one of the captains of the Virtuous, I thought you would believe the red airship had brought young children to other worlds. What they saw is supposed to have changed their lives forever."

"Nope, that's not true. Not for me. The *Hibiscus Airship* did not come and take me when I was a kid. It is a myth. It is a myth we used to inspire a cause for the Hibiscus Party – something to stand up with," said Idris. "The *Hibiscus Airship* may have existed, but to believe it is still flying is childish. It is just a story we aspire to. We make our own destiny."

"I see," muttered the Prince as he rubbed his beard. "So those recruits are living a lie?"

"Jas's father does not think so. He sees the red airship as an entity that exists within our imagination. If it lives within, it must be real? It's like love once you come to think of it."

"Interesting. A metaphor. A symbol. Its existence is in the imagination of a believer. That's a strong power to tap – the mind of a believer."

"If I told them the *Hibiscus Airship* does not exist, I would be condemned. A belief is a ball that keeps rolling on, and nobody can stop it. Fantasy turns into reality," said Idris as he sipped upon his wine. "The only thing you can do is let it roll by."

The Prince was rubbing his beard again, finding breadcrumbs from dinner. "Come! Come! Have more! Have more!"

"Urgh. I think I'm a bit drunk now," cried Idris.

"That's why I'm here!"

"Wait. You said a moment ago that your friend went to another world on the *Hibiscus Airship*?"

"In fact, my friend *is* the *Hibiscus Airship*. He made it!"

Idris rubbed his eyes. "Your friend was Mazy Hamzees? The Hero of the Great War?"

"Yes, Mazy was my friend."

"Are you saying the story of the *Hibiscus Airship* is true?"

"I can't flat out say it is, as all great stories deserves a few embellishments. What I'm saying is that it does exist and it is still flying somewhere out there."

"I'm assuming you have no way of contacting him?"

"If I did know how to, I would share this lovely rose wine with him instead of with you."

Idris laughed and passed the bottle to the Prince. "It is a lovely drink. Thanks for sharing it with me."

"No problem, Idris. No problem."

Arla was inspecting her equipment, which she'd laid out on her bunk in a systematic order, including a rag and other cleaning gear. It was a rest day for everyone. All recruits were free to roam the Southern Land's entertainment district. Booze, women, and sheer debauchery were allowed, as long as they did not reveal their identity, as the guards patrolled the outer borders of the Southern Lands. Arla decided to stay back. She had expected Tae to accompany her, but his teammates had other plans for him. Either way, Arla finally had time for herself. She spent her time cleaning her rifle. With meticulous precision, Arla took it apart piece by piece, laying the pieces down upon a rag. Some parts she drenched in oil and scrubbed to perfection. It was a form of meditation Arla had learned to appreciate. Nothing was more addictive than to focus on a task and finish it with flair.

"Arla? Are you here?"

Arla stopped her work and paid attention to the young lady at the door. "Hi, Jas. I'm here. Do you need anything?"

"You should be hanging out and having fun, not spending time cleaning your rifle."

"I like it, Jas. Besides, why aren't you out there yourself?"

"I have things to do. I'm an errand girl for my father," said Jasmine with a frown. "By the way, he wants to see you."

"To see me? Why me?"

Jasmine stomped her way to Arla and grabbed her. "Will you just come with me? Stop thinking I know the reasons for all his orders."

"Wai ... wait!"

Jasmine was not the patient sort. Pieces of Arla's rifle had scattered on the ground, and she almost fell face first on the floor. Jasmine insisted on holding her arm and dragging her away from her bunk. If Jasmine was involved, her impatience was utmost. Arla shrugged.

"Hey! Where are you taking me? Are we going to the commander's office?"

"Of course not. We are going somewhere else."

Arla fumed. Being dragged around because of Jasmine's eccentricities had been adorable and interesting at the beginning. But Jasmine was being inconsiderate of her feeling about being left out of a secret, and this was not boding well with Arla's patience. She stood her ground and pulled back away from Jasmine, getting her arm back in the process, despite the fact that Jasmine's grip was tight. Arla had witnessed Jasmine's skills in the art of grappling. Nobody had ever beaten her.

"Enough of this! Where are you taking me? Is this some prank?"

Jasmine was shocked to see her friend turn emotional over a little jest. "No, Arla. I *am* taking you to see my father. We must hurry."

"All right, stop it. Just lead the way. I'll follow you."

"Okay. Sorry," said Jasmine. "It's this way."

The furnaces of the Southern Lands remained stoked; the flames never faded. Above the fiery glow that lighted their path, the shadows of the night shift men pranced upon walls. Jasmine and Arla walked faster towards their meeting point. The winds had started to howl, and the stars were as bright as they had ever been. The iron stairs leading up to the roof shook a little under the marching footsteps of Arla and Jasmine. Under a purple moon, they saw a man wearing a uniform with a hibiscus flower insignia etched on his shoulders. He was their commander and their mentor.

"Father, Arla is here."

"Sir," said Arla, "did you want to see me?"

The tall, middle-aged man turned. His stature signified compassion and justice as he addressed them. "Well, hello. Beautiful night isn't it?"

"Yes it is, sir."

"How are you, Arla? I've not been formally introduced to you, I guess."

"No, sir. It is unfortunate."

"My apologies. My name is Pennele Wakezeem. Besides being known as the commander, I am Jas's father. Your father, Dara, who was a good friend of mine, called me Penn."

Arla was caught by surprise. She had almost forgotten her father's name. It was a name nobody had mentioned for a long time. She felt a sudden surge of joy when she understood that somebody else had memories of him. Curiosity was her reigning thought. Who was the commander?

"Your father and I knew each other since we were six if I am correct. We had many adventures together. I miss him terribly. If he were still alive, he would be standing right here, running the Party by my side."

"I did not know my father well. But it is good to know somebody still remembers him."

"He was a good man. Did you know most of this would not have been possible without him?"

Arla beamed with delight. "No I didn't. How and why?"

Penn smiled in return. Jasmine stood in silence and carefully listened.

"Come have a seat with me over here," he said as he guided her towards a clean cloth carefully laid out on the floor. "This is where I usually come to think. Today we have a lot to catch up on."

Arla nodded.

"Do you know what is important for a person growing up, Arla?"

"A dream? A purpose?"

"Yes! That is right – purpose. But a purpose cannot be forged without looking back at one's past to build a foundation. Without a good foundation, a purpose can crumble with terrible ease."

Arla became curious. "You are going to tell me about my father?"

"I see great potential in you, Arla. In fact, when you were six, the *Hibiscus Airship* was supposed to come and take you. Unfortunately, you lost your parents. The *Hibiscus Airship* decided not to come for you."

"What does that have to do with my parents' death? I mean, what was the difference? Without them I'm hopeless. To be honest, that was a time I needed the red airship the most! My life would have been different."

An awkward silence resonated. Arla wiped a tear away. "I'm sorry," she said.

"Arla, you have great potential. On that day, the Navigator saw that you had lost something precious."

"What did I lose?"

"Your passion. Your passion died along with your father. Therefore, the Navigator forsook you," said Penn with a deep breath. "Fortunately, I have not forsaken you. I believe in you."

"I don't care. Why tell me this?" The old wound Arla had tried so hard to heal was torn to tatters. Her pent-up memories of her past resurfaced in a desperate attempt to drown her again.

"I believed in your father as well, even though he and I did not see eye to eye about everything. He remained loyal to his beliefs and his family. I regretted not being able to save him in time."

"Do you know who ..." asked Arla. Her anger boiled to a vehement zeal. "Do you know who killed my family?"

"Yes, I do. It was them – the Forlorn. To be specific, a man named Jeella."

Flashes of light ignited in Arla's head. A minor pain flourished into a full-blown headache, causing her to fall to the ground. Jasmine ran to her, catching her before her head thumped on the floor. Arla drifted, and she could not speak. And when she came up out of the darkness, the light revealed the smirking smile of a monster. Arla went into a terrible shock that took Jasmine by surprise. "Arla! Arla! Wake up!"

"Bell … Where are you …?"

Arla fainted. Penn ordered his security detail to take Arla to the clinic. Jasmine stayed with her the entire time, holding on to Arla's hands.

"How is she?" questioned Idris.

"She will be fine. The sedatives will calm her down," said the healer. "You can visit her now."

Idris and Jasmine were waiting outside the emergency room. Countless stacks of old magazines and health pamphlets about the latest STDs were familiar to Idris. He thought about the times he had visited the same clinic. Mae had been taken there when they were rescued back in the Pasir Lands.

"Come on, Jas. The smell of this place … I hate it."

Idris and Jasmine walked in together and stood at opposite sides of the bed. Arla sat propped up by two comfortable pillows. She greeted them with cheerful optimism. "I see the inseparable two are here. How are you?"

Jasmine grinned and gave Arla a big hug. "Arla! You frightened me! Don't you ever do that again! You hear?"

Arla nodded. "I won't, Jas. Thank you."

Idris felt a little awkward standing at her side. He was not sure whether to proceed with a hug or to start off with a verbal greeting. He shifted his feet. Arla noticed, and she revelled in Idris's discomfort. Arla extended her hand, inviting a big group hug. Idris hesitated, as he never liked being hugged, or perhaps he had never been offered one before. But Arla's puppy-dog eyes disarmed his stiff resistance. He smiled, and in he went.

"Don't you go crazy again," he said.

They laughed, and the mundane tune of the clinic's sounds turned into a melody. It was a precious moment nobody could undo.

"Hey, Jas, did you know your father knew mine?" asked Arla.

"No, I did not. I was as shocked as you were when I heard it," said Jasmine, with regret. "I'm sorry."

"Don't be. It was not your fault. You were just following orders."

"But it was a stupid thing to do, wasn't it?" uttered Idris. "He knew what had happened, and he inconsiderately brought it back up. He could have been subtler."

The door to the emergency room swung open, and the commander entered wearing a black leather jacket. "Yes, I must agree. I came on a little too harsh."

Idris, Jasmine, and Arla broke their bonding session and saluted the arrival of Penn. He was chewing on an ice cream stick, enjoying its cold sweetness. He was confident but a tad arrogant in the way he presented himself. No one, however, questioned his authority.

"I have to admit, I thought you were ready," said Penn. "I thought you were ready to talk about your father again."

Idris and Jasmine nodded to each other in agreement and left them to have their conversation in private.

"So, tell me. What do you want to know?" asked Penn.

"How did you know him?"

Penn walked to the side of Arla's bed and dragged a chair closer to her. He sat down and placed his arms on her bed, smiling gently. "I knew your father when we were young. We met under peculiar circumstances," said Penn as he chuckled at the impossible nature of their meeting. "We met on the bridge of the *Hibiscus Airship*."

Arla slowly pushed herself to sit up straighter. "You both were onboard the airship?"

"*The* airship, Arla. Yes. We were among the children who followed the Navigator."

"I ... I don't know what to say. Those stories he told ... could they have been true?"

"Probably so," said Penn with a chuckle. "Dara always liked to tell stories of his adventures. And he did it with flair as well."

"How was it? Being on the airship with my father?"

"Epic. We hated each other in the beginning. But when the Navigator exposed us to different worlds out there, and the dangers they posed, we turned into blood brothers. We chased creatures we had not seen before and explored forests that were magical in their own way. But it was the people we met that gave us the best moments. They were different but so similar to us. They spoke in different tongues but believed in the values we had. It was a case of different perspectives in the same context. We were welcomed, and sometimes we were shunned. Nevertheless, we discovered. We charted worlds beyond ours. We were infinite."

Arla stared up at the ceiling fan, imagining a vast open space floating out there, waiting to be discovered. The sights and sounds she wanted to experience were out there, but she was bound to the chains of her own world. She wanted to free herself, but everything held her back. She felt hope, but she knew how hope could bring out the biggest misery if discovered without love. She tilted her head back to Penn. "What happened? I mean why are we not travelling among the stars?"

"Frailty and the fear of the unknown. The loss of control and the triumph of greed. We were trumped by the fallacies of our condition."

"What do you mean?" questioned Arla.

"When we returned, the Navigator presented his findings to his council. It was a different world after the Great War. When the council members saw the report, a fracture within the group emerged. Some were excited, and some were afraid. That was how the Forlorn came to be. They betrayed Mazy and dominated our world through their ideology. Mazy and his *Hibiscus Airship* were banished, and soon, with a few rumours and changes in history books, Mazy was completely erased from the memories of Paradisians. The *Hibiscus Airship* became a tale."

"History was changed to the benefit of the Forlorn?"

"We posed a threat to their power. They sought to maintain control and eradicate a fear of the unknown for themselves. A travelling vessel like the *Hibiscus Airship* would expand Bumi's understanding. The reason the Great War happened no longer lingered in our minds. We were an obstacle to their means of control. Those who stood beside the *Hibiscus Airship* were pushed underground or were silenced forever."

"Was that what happened to my father? He was silenced?"

"Dara and I continued to struggle. Mazy and his airship had gone into hiding. We never knew how to contact it. But we carried on his idea. We planned and we recruited. Until of course, she happened."

"What? She?"

"Your mother."

Arla experienced a sudden flood of memories of a beautiful and kind woman. Her words and her embrace were the warmest she had ever felt. It was an awakening for Arla. That woman touched her heart, and Arla remembered the joy and love she gave. It had been Arla's first experience with love, and it had been the sweetest. Arla remembered she had a mother. She remembered she had a family. She remembered the fun, imaginary adventures they had in the mornings as they were waking up. She finally remembered the dreams her mother had told her. Arla's tears flowed down upon her cheeks as she smiled, and she laughed to her heart's content. Arla became the little girl she remembered having been when she was six. She was a little girl who had boundless hope for the future and a boundless capacity to love. She remembered who she was, and she cried with joy, letting go of a burden she had carried for far too long. She was Arla Hibby.

"Yes, you remember now. Growing up alone can do that to you. Loneliness can make you forget. I'm glad you still have those memories. They never left, Arla. They were always there."

Arla wiped her tears away with her sleeves. "Thank you. It means so much to me."

"I know. Your mother, Jala, was a wonderful woman. She and Dara were meant to be together. I believe your father chose the right path. He gave up on the Party, but he never gave up on you. Both he and your mother had you."

Jasmine came in when she heard Arla crying, thinking she was in trouble again. But what Jasmine saw was an image of happiness. "Arla!"

"Jas! I know now!"

Jasmine came in and hugged Arla. It was the warmest hug Jasmine had experienced in such a long time. Idris stood by the door, gleefully looking at them with a happy smile.

"My apologies. But I believe we shall leave it as it is. I can continue the next time we meet," said Penn.

"No, wait! Please tell me the rest. We should finish it. I am ready," replied Arla as she grabbed Penn's hand.

Penn nodded and he sat back on his chair. "Your father decided to leave the Party to pursue a life with your mother. I tried to convince him to stay, but your mother was his true passion. I could not argue with that. So eventually, we grew apart from each other, but the bond was true. He gradually forgot about our time with the *Hibiscus Airship*, and he tried his best to make the world a better place in his own way by living an honest life with his family," said Penn. He smiled as he remembered. "On the day you were born, I paid him a visit. We had a couple of beers in the Iron Mare, and he told me the most beautiful story of how he met your mother. It was too beautiful to be retold. Only he could do it. Only your father could do it."

"When I grew up, he did not need to tell me his story. He showed it every single day," said Arla. Jasmine gave Arla another embrace.

"That he truly did. On your sixth birthday, I met him again. We caught up, and we talked about the past and the airship. He tried to remember as best as he could, but he recalled only fractions of our story. Anyway, we parted ways, and that was the last time I saw him. Come to think of it, I never really did come to terms with that day being the last I will ever see him. We did not end our meeting on good terms actually."

Arla held on tight to Penn's hand. "It's all right," Arla said.

"Why did it not end on good terms with Dara?" Jasmine asked.

"I met him to warn him that the *Hibiscus Airship* was going to pay Arla a visit. I had found a message on my desk that told me Arla was to be part of its crew, the way Dara and I had been chosen. I wanted to locate it, and to meet the Navigator again. So I thought of using you to meet him. But your father accused me of being crazy and refused to help. On that terrible night, a group of young tortured individuals, led by a cruel man, whom I found out had been hired by the Forlorn, destroyed your home. You were immediately taken under the care of the orphanage. The *Hibiscus Airship* had no way of getting close to you without getting the attention of the guards. In the end, the Navigator never showed up."

Arla understood. She nodded and waited patiently for Penn to tell the rest of his story.

"I kept a close watch upon you as well. However, my resources were limited, and I was hunted by the Black Guards. I wanted to save you, but chances were dim. I am very sorry," muttered Penn. Jasmine could see that he was disappointed with himself. "I sent Idris to observe you and to plan an escape. It was the least I could do as your father's friend."

"That same day you were running away from the guards was the day I had planned to take you away in the night," said Idris. "But a situation developed, and I had to adapt. I never considered your friend, Bell. My plan involved only you." He too showed regret for his actions. Bell had meant a lot to Arla, and he had left her to be captured by the guards. "If I had known then how much she meant to you, I would have stopped them from taking her."

Arla put her hands up. "No, do not think yourselves at fault. Nothing could have been done. What had happened … happened. Now, we need to see this through – this revolution. I still intend to save Bell, and I hope I am not too late. We will fulfil the dream Mazy had for our world, and we will save it from the Forlorn. Do you think Mazy will come and help us?"

"I do not know, Arla," Penn declared as he held his fists together. "I haven't seen that man for years. Wherever he is, I hope he will show up one day and finally end the fight – for a better tomorrow."

"With or without him, we will finish what he started," said Arla. Jasmine and Idris nodded; Penn looked on with pride.

"I was right when I said you had great potential," uttered Penn. "I can see it. It's in all of you. Arla, your family would be proud to see the woman you've become. Soon, the Virtuous will be deployed to Paradise, and you will rally the people to our cause. Slowly but surely, we will win. The Red Flower Revolution is finally here."

The stage was set, and a play was about to begin. It was the day when the Virtuous were ready to stand and fight for the Hibiscus Party and for the Navigator. They were ready, and their hard work had paid off. In the next few weeks, they carefully smuggled themselves across the Pasir Lands and into Paradise. They established a propaganda campaign that changed the hearts and minds of the people. They incited protests against the establishment to muster the courage of the people. It was a momentous day for Bumi.

"Recruits, you have seen it," said Penn. "You have gone through it, and now you are ready. You will use the training the Party has endowed you with to defend against the Forlorn and also for standing up for yourselves. You and your team are standing proud, holding the red beret of the hibiscus. You are the true glory of Bumi! The true children of the red flower!"

Cheers of pride resonated through the halls of the training ground. Arla, Tae, Mae, Idris, and Jasmine stood together in a line among a hundred of recruits. Their heads held high, they clutched in their hands the red berets.

"I am proud," continued Penn. "I sincerely am. Proud to see you grow to stand up against tyranny. The Forlorn turned Bumi into a corrupted land. They separate us by the colours we wear and the tones in which we speak. In their eyes we are not their equals. They see knowledge and exploration as a doom that condemns them!" Penn stood on a pedestal and spoke through a microphone. The Prince had been given a seat of honour next to Penn. The Prince still wore the same style of clothing he had worn when Arla first met him. He was stubborn that way.

"Remember, we do not train for violence. We are fighting against the Forlorn by being the exact opposite. We are just! And we are merciful. I understand your grief as you all have lost your families during the Great War or through purges they secretly conducted. You were forced to be orphans, and thus you were cast aside."

The crowd nodded.

"You are not alone in this. The old city that lies under Paradise is against the Forlorn as well. They have sheltered us and helped us stand up against them! We are grateful!"

Another round of applause echoed.

"Even the Southern Lands are with us! The industrial heartland! The backbone of Bumi is standing with us!"

A thunderous applause roared to life, causing the walls to shake.

"We are grateful. We are grateful. We are. We are. We are …" stated Penn. He walked around his stage, looking at each recruit with the caring eyes of a father. He was, to many of them, a father figure they had never had. "Will you fight the good fight?"

"*Yes!*" they shouted.

"Good! From this day onwards, each of you is now a Virtuous. You are the guardians of the Hibiscus Party!" Penn screamed as he reached for the sky and saluted. "Go now! And make the Navigator proud! Proudly don the red beret!"

In unison, the soldiers of the Virtuous placed the red berets upon their heads. They cheered and they celebrated. A big buffet of food and drinks was served in the canteen. They danced to the beat of stirring music and revelled like champions, moving their bodies in the most peculiar ways, as if the end of the world was upon them. The Virtuous allowed madness to dominate their gaiety. Arla and Tae danced together, slowly swaying in their own style, which was different to the style of the rest of the crowd. Theirs was a different kind of madness. It was a soft kind, a loving kind that only two could know. They melted into each other.

"Hey, Arla," said Tae softly. "I wish this moment would never end."

"I wish for it …" said Arla. "For as long as I can."

Tae gently swept back the fringes of Arla's dark hair, revealing her beautiful, tender eyes, which had been bludgeoned by fate. As Tae immersed himself deeply into her eyes, he was dragged into a powerful force his heart had yearned for. It was an addiction to a mysterious revelation he truly believed. "When we go to Paradise," he whispered, "stay with me. Stay as close to me as possible."

Arla looked down. "I'm sorry, Tae. I don't think that will be possible. I have a feeling this will turn into something we cannot control. But don't worry, we will win."

"Then I will be there if you can't."

They kissed among a raging crowd, signifying that nothing else mattered.

Chapter 12

The Red Rebels

The Red Flower Revolution carefully bloomed into a real struggle. Months of careful preparation and dedication had turned the opinion of many toward their cause. Sacrifices were aplenty, since the Hibiscus Party was labelled as a criminal organization. Many of the Virtuous were tossed into the dungeon and were never seen again. But they still pushed on. More and more young recruits took up their cause. The Virtuous were succeeding in waging their propaganda war. The hibiscus symbol was painted everywhere, and the Forlorn were getting desperate. They knew a political uprising was imminent. They would be thrown out of government, and a new group would take over. Penn's strategy of a "peaceful war" was working well. The Hibiscus Party would win the hearts and minds of the people, and the people would decide upon the fate of Bumi.

"All right, you lot," commanded Mae as she walked in a straight line, inspecting the stature of their new recruits. "Listen carefully! We are thankful for your decision to join us. But we are no ordinary riffraff as our enemy portrays us to be. We are an efficient military organization made to bring down the Forlorn in a peaceful way. We are the Red Flower Revolution! You are here to train in the art of subversive strategy and tactics. You will learn how to handle a gun, but only for self-defence. Our true goal is to win by winning the people's support."

Ever since the Forlorn had cracked down hard upon civil unrest, the Black Guards had been ordered to carry out covert operations all around Bumi. They were there to eliminate the command structure of the Virtuous. The Forlorn knew they had to rely solely on keeping operations within the shadows. If evidence broke out to the public about kill orders and secret purges, the Forlorn would completely lose the fight. "Youth's desire for the truth and for the future can never be dampened," declared Penn. "They do it with their own prerogative. They are expressing themselves. It is up to the people to decide who will govern Bumi!"

Mae had been appointed to a new position: trainer of new recruits. She and her platoon were designated to launch a recruiting campaign to fill the ranks of those who were lost. It was a tough struggle, and it was painful to witness the murder of her comrades by the Black Guards. Those who had family ties were spared and tossed in the dungeon, and their families begged for their release. They could still put up a fight politically. However, orphans were prone to end up victims of bullets. They had no value because nobody from the public cared for them. They were dispensable. Mae had the toughest time finding the best way to give them a proper burial – a proper burial fit for someone who mattered to the world. She searched for the best place to honour their memory. She found an answer at the underground lake the Prince, Tae, and she had used all the time to get to meetings. The Prince had once mentioned that a monument for brave souls who had dared to explore existed there – a monument for heroes. She and her platoon found and rebuilt it to perfection, turning it into a grand memorial for the fallen Virtuous. The body of each fallen soul was placed on a wooden barge built to the size of the warrior, who slept, arms across his or chest, surrounded by firewood. A hibiscus flower was laid on the warrior's chest. As the dead were pushed out into the lake, a carefully timed fuse ignited, setting the barge on fire. The captain of the fallen Virtuous would mention his or her name and the role the warrior had played in life. This was a fitting tribute for those who had grown up alone. Their Virtuous family had made their lives whole. Mae had seen too many funeral barges go up in flames. She dreamt that one day it would be her turn. And she hoped to die among the stars.

Idris and Jasmine were in charge of overall tactical planning. They were acting commanders at the absence of the Prince and Penn. Since the start of their campaign, Penn and the Prince had often been hard to find. They were on the most-wanted list – dead or alive. The only form of communication they had with Idris and Jasmine was through written letters. Idris and Jasmine had no choice but to act on their own and they were doing well. They had a simple command structure in place. The Virtuous were divided into eight platoons of 10 men each. Each platoon was led by a captain. The platoons were further separated into three sections, and each section was led by a scribe. The captains were given a freedom to choose their strategies to accomplish certain objectives. Idris believed that, instead of relying on one brain to overcome an obstacle, it was best to put the brains of an entire company to good use. Great decisions were best achieved on the ground where the action took place. Their structure saved time, and resources were well spent. When they were not out working, Idris and Jasmine tirelessly trained their companies. Idris improved the specific skill set of each soldier while Mae and Jasmine kept notes on every soldier's strengths and weaknesses. This gave them necessary information to use when deciding which soldier would be best for each task.

Tae, on the other hand, was placed in charge of a special task force of eight soldiers. Their unit was specially formed to counter the Black Guards covert operations. They were a shadow unit of the Virtuous, created to hunt down any threats the Black Guards posed. They were the only Virtuous who were allowed to conduct full-fledged military combat missions against the enemy. Sabotage or protection – their job was to stop the Black Guards from interfering with the grand strategy of the Virtuous. It was due to the actions of Tae and his unit that many lives were saved from harm. Only Idris, Jasmine, and Arla, along with Penn, knew about the Hunter-Killers, or HKs for short. Since the HKs had the most contact with the enemy hiding in the shadows, they were best used to gather intelligence about the Forlorn's military movements and tactics. The HKs provided many creative ideas, which were implemented by command to make better decisions. The HKs were vital to the Virtuous.

Arla was in charge of her own platoon. She led from the front. Wearing civilian clothing, Arla and her platoon would infiltrate the sparkling city of Paradise to talk and spread word about the Hibiscus Party. Through her own social media campaign, Arla crafted an efficient information war that influenced public perception. Her platoon stirred mischief around the city through graffiti and public unrest. The HKs protected them as they stalked within the shadows to identify Black Guard operatives. In a way, Arla and her platoon were bait, but she felt relieved knowing that Tae was somewhere out there making sure she stayed safe. Arla rotated members of her platoon in different shifts to carry out operations. They had planned what sort of identity to assume and what sort of disguise to wear when they were in Paradise. Therefore, the guards had a hard time pinpointing the real culprits. The guards often mistakenly captured innocent civilians thought to be with the Virtuous, and every time they made a mistake, it was a well-earned victory for the Virtuous. News channels announced the carelessness of the guards, thus diverting people's confidence away from them.

In a nutshell, Arla and her platoon were doing well – until, of course, the Forlorn released the leash on their most vicious dog – Rizal, the so-called Hero of Paradise. A cruel, dedicated monster with the civility of a gentleman, Rizal was the scourge that could single-handedly put out the fires of rebellion. He was known to supporters of the Forlorn as their antidote to the Virtuous disease. Judgement and persecution! These were the two tenets Rizal promised to the public. His rough voice was enough to raise fear within the hearts of Paradisians. Hence, Rizal was placed at the top of the HKs top-priority hit list. Idris and Jasmine had trouble sleeping soundly at night. Jasmine had even begun to sleep with a gun under her pillow. "You never know, Idris. He might even know where we are. Just in case."

The bogeyman was out to get them.

Arla woke in their safe house located in the suburbs of Paradise in the third floor of a building overlooking a posh garden where members of the community spent their evenings strolling around. It was the best place to hide from the guards. It was also a place from which they could monitor the effects of the Virtuous campaign upon the rich.

"Another day in suburbia," said Arla as she stared out the window.

A week ago, Arla had been on the streets participating in and inciting protests against the government's refusal to encourage research for more affordable health care. The Equality Act the Forlorn had implemented had turned corrupt. Healing chambers were made available for those who had the funds to pay, and their services were prioritized in favour of those who lived in Paradise. Strangers were required to sit in a long queuing line. The Equality Act had introduced currency, which led to the eventual creation of a banking system. The public approved of such a system, as everyone had the ability to start building his or her own businesses; creating wealth for oneself was no longer a pipe dream. The people were ecstatic. But as time passed, few realized that the population had increased, but the supply of resources was limited, and the banking system turned its ugly head. The wealthy became wealthier as they created trade barriers against newcomers, destroying the conceptual fabric of economic competition. Trade structures meant to maintain competitive pricing of vital goods such as medicine and food were eliminated. The political power of the rich increased to insurmountable levels until the government depended on them to maintain the economy of Bumi. The government managed to control the people's frustration over unfair business practices by launching a secret movement that diverted the attention of the public towards the motivation of success. It was a movement to encourage greed with the prospect of more greed. It was designed to encourage the rise of consumerism and the fall of moral fibre. The movement encouraged the purchasing of unnecessary items for the sake of keeping up with social standards created by corrupted imagination, flamed through an encouragement of selfish desire. As Arla stood looking through a window, she saw husks walking in the coloured coveralls that segregated a community. The imaginative power the citizens possessed when they had been wild and hopeful children had been turned into a dull representation of self-satisfaction and self-loathing. They lived recklessly, and they prayed to the Heavenly Flower every day that they would have a wonderful afterlife after they passed on. They preached selflessness, but their crowning achievement was to have everything. They carried their dreams to the grave, achieving nothing but death in life.

"Morning, Arla," said Livi, as he knocked and entered her room. Livi was part of Arla's platoon. Ever since her recent operations had been foiled by the Guards, Arla and her four-man team had gathered in their safe house. They were to pretend they were part of the priestesses of the Heavenly Flower. Their red garb covered every inch of skin from their head to toe; it was the perfect disguise. Infiltrating the Temple to gather intelligence on the relationship between the Forlorn and the Temple was beneficial. Arla wanted to know to what extent the Forlorn would use the Heavenly Flower as a source of influence.

"Morning, Livi. Did you prepare our disguises yet?"

"All done, ma'am. What else do you need?"

"Can you get me my breakfast?"

Livi nodded and proceeded downstairs to prepare Arla's favourite pancakes and bacon. She craved it after weeks of not tasting proper food. Arla went into her bathroom and prepared her tub for a cold morning bath. This house was her favourite among the other safe houses. It felt like a real posh home. There were times she imagined herself living in that house with a family and going to work in the mornings. She imagined having a domesticated life and having a lover she could cook breakfast for. The water flowed into her white porcelain tub, and Arla poured in some body wash. Fragrance filled the bathroom with the sweetness of honey.

"I wish Bel ... Tae was here," Arla whispered to herself. Waking to the reality of events, Arla removed her clothing and jumped into her tub to escape reality. Her moon-drop necklace dangled from her neck.

"Ma'am, your breakfast. Should I leave it on your desk?"

"Bring it in, Livi. I'll eat it in my bath."

Livi walked in carrying a plate in his right hand and covering his eyes with his left. "Here it is. Your favourite – with ketchup on the side. We will be downstairs preparing our gear."

"Do what you must, Livi. I will be there shortly as well."

She finished her delightful savoury meal in seconds. She got out of the tub, dressed herself, and seated herself at her desk where an old map of Bumi lay. She studied it again and again, looking at the locations of safe houses, weapons, and supply depots, along with escape tunnels. Every morning she would memorize it and brief her men and women on a plan of action. She relayed her plans to a secret Virtuous base as well. The voice on the other side was always a welcome relief. Jasmine's voice was sweet and reassuring. Once she relayed the message, Arla packed her bag and hid it in a hollow wall behind her bed. She closed the door behind her and walked down the stairs to see her people ready.

"Ma'am, here is your robe. We will walk through the back to avoid prying eyes," said Livi.

Arla nodded.

"All right, everyone. We have just received the green light for our mission today. Dressed as we are in the Heavenly Flower robes, we will be infiltrating the Temple and gathering intel about the position the priestesses will take if this conflict escalates. Whatever we learn will be vital for our efforts. Go in light and try to avoid contact with the other priestesses. Just blend in, and you will do fine. They don't talk much anyway."

"What happens if we are compromised?"

"Yes, come on in close guys. Let me show you …"

The morning briefing had been communicated clearly, and all had understood. The mission was considered dangerous, as the risk of getting caught was high. There were not many avenues of escape. If the mission was compromised, everyone was on his or her own to get to a safe location. It was best not to get caught. Arla knew it, and she reminded her team members again and again.

When Arla had taken command of her platoon, she had inherited a group of uncooperative children. Livi was the only one who followed her willingly, but he was still tempted by the conniving influence of his buddies. Fortunately for Arla, Livi secretly divulged to her information about the morale of her platoon whenever they were alone. It afforded her a good opportunity to whip her men into shape. It was not easy obtaining their trust in her skills, especially when they judged her based upon her sex. In her first few weeks, she had been disobeyed on missions, and this had almost led to their capture. Idris did the best he could to instil a disciplined mindset among their troops. But there were some fights that needed to be fought alone, especially if it involved the respect of others. Thus were the demands of leadership.

On a particular mission, when all had turned south, Arla and her men became trapped in the gutters. Dank and reeking of the stench of waste, Arla and her men held on. The guards hunted and raided buildings to find them. Arla kept everything controlled under pressure. She quietly talked to calm nerves, and she kept the wounded bandaged. Arla had all the reasons to choose to desert. But, no, she retrieved and dragged everyone into hiding and stayed with them until the guards were gone. When everything had cleared, Arla pulled everyone out from the gutter and took them back into safety. She stood by them no matter what. Be it a mistake by her team or a mistake on her part, she would never leave. She took upon herself a responsibility that was sacred and heroic. The lives of her men were, to her, the most important treasure she defended. Her dedication inspired her men and stirred in them a desire to do the same. Even when Arla informed them that it would be their own responsibility to get to a safe location if compromised, they knew Arla would be there to get everyone out. Respect was sealed, and trust established; there were no doubts in her ability to lead.

"All right, let's go. Livi, you take point," ordered Arla.

Disguised in Heavenly Flower's robes, they were concealed from the prying eyes of the world. In their robes, they were seen by the public as a group of the religious pious who had decided to close themselves apart from the world, hiding their true colours. It was a religious debate that flew around in the media: to conceal for the Heavenly Flower or not? The public judged and, later, continued their emotional views upon the coffee they drank.

Through the streets of Paradise, through its glistening silver-white beauty, Arla felt an awakening. The drudgery of a clockwork life had changed. Expressions of individuality were profound as the desire for greatness in life brought forth courage to defy a clockwork mentality. Diversity carefully opened its powerful existence, and Arla felt proud. The wheels of change had turned in their favour.

At the gates of the Temple, Arla nodded to signal the beginning of their operation. Livi carefully pushed open the golden gates, and they sauntered into the halls of sacred religiosity. It was a place where one could find solace from the mumbling thunder of one's inner turmoil. It was also a place where one could find the answer to the nature of existence, or remain ignorant to it. Either way, it was a Temple many had come to in order to seek answers to impossible questions. Some sought help, requiring the assistance of divine intervention to receive an easy miracle for the mistakes of their desiccated morality. In the halls of the Temple, everyone was quiet; their demons were asleep.

Arla and her team separated themselves and covered all corners of the Temple. They were to listen and gather information about the Forlorn. Since the priestesses were all female, Arla was the only one who could talk and inquire about the state of political movements.

The priestesses might appear to be the holiest of beings, but they were still subject to the influence of gossip and worldly interests. Was it hypocrisy, or had they lost their way? Arla never understood matters of the religiously pious.

Arla entered a room. It was a typical room made of the strongest wood that grew in the jungles of Bumi. It was the toughest wood one could find, and it lay dormant, polished to a shine by the use of chemicals. Many ornaments and ancient books filled its cupboards. It reminded Arla of a story Mae told about her life underground. She was reminded of the Prince's study. Priestesses sat at a grand table with stacks of papers in front of them. It was an important meeting, and each priestess wrote her own notes. To Arla, it was amazing to witness the use of paper; in fact, they dominated that chamber, proving that an air of intellectual capacity still ran within Paradise. The face of the elderly woman who sat at one end of the table was not covered by her robe. She dictated her orders of the day. Arla knew her – it was Lady Malla.

Rizal sat at his desk looking through the files of those who had been interrogated. He pieced together vague but relevant information about a secret entity that threatened the foundations of his peaceful city. The name *Virtuous* left a bad taste in his mouth. He slept thinking about the ridiculous notions of how the Virtuous contradicted themselves. To stir up unrest was not a virtuous value, he believed. It was a destruction of law and order that had been established from the tenets of the Heavenly Flower. Such disgrace! Such humiliation! Rizal was dedicated to stopping the Virtuous weed from growing further in the minds of the innocent. The innocent needed his dedication to fight back against such corruption. They had been tempted by lies and trickery. Paradise needed a hero to defend them against devious behaviours of the faithless.

Rizal drafted out a note in his book. He described tactics implemented by the Virtuous command. He had returned from a strategy briefing about countering the effects of guerrilla propaganda.

He needed to act with tact. As the immense power of the Forlorn's military grew, he needed a victory of hearts and minds. Full crushing military action would be launched only when the public agreed to it. Rizal knew he needed to win a moral victory.

Rizal closed his book. He was done for the day, and his plans were presented well. They were ready. His counterinsurgency strategy would be implemented the following day. And he would supervise every inch of it. He would spend the rest of the day at home. He turned off the office lights and proceeded to walk down the infinite empty rows of wooden desks with their yellow pencils on top. He hung his jacket over his right arm and carried his briefcase in his left hand.

Rizal swept his hair back as he stepped out onto the streets. Mechanical horses galloped back and forth on black tar roads. He hated those horses. He felt it was a pompous illusion for rich men and women to display. He hated it. The night was chilly, and a light wind blew through his hair. People were out and about enjoying their nightly entertainment. Usually he would drop by his favourite bar and have his favourite steak. He never cooked at home, for he felt the loneliness of home was not a place to spend a relaxing night. He had no family. His only companions were his colleagues and the members of the public who admired him. When he walked the streets, he was but a simple man. He was a figure too small for the shadow he had been granted. That day, he decided to take the shortcut.

The rain had started to fall. Those out for the evening ran and took refuge in bars, disappointed in a fun night ruined. But Rizal found the rain refreshing. He liked it when it rained in Paradise. The bustling commotion would turn quiet so he could cherish the present moment. There was something magical about it. Rizal turned into an alley, cutting straight to his favourite grocery store. He wanted to get some fruit for his morning breakfast.

At a turn, he noticed a dark figure standing with his back on the wall. He looked brooding and seemed dangerous. Rizal was cautious. Working with the guards had attuned his awareness to such dangers. He stepped carefully against the wall, avoiding eye contact, but keeping his potential threat in his peripheral vision. But the man stood in his way.

"Are you Rizal?" said the man, who wore a hood.

"No, I'm not. I'm just going to the store."

The hooded man pulled a gun from a holster that was hidden within his jacket. "Are you Rizal?"

"I said I'm not!"

The hooded man hesitated. He was not sure whether he had chosen the right target. He began to falter, and then another man came up from behind him. "Keep your sights on him, Ruairi. He is definitely Rizal."

Rizal stepped back slowly. He sensed there was yet another individual hiding in the shadows. Rizal reached for a gun in his hidden holster. It was a defensive weapon all guards were issued to use when times were desperate. Rizal was surrounded.

"So, you are a Virtuous assassination squad?" said Rizal with stale breath. "You are what they call the HKs?"

"It's him! Tae, let's take him out now!" screamed Ruairi.

As Ruairi's trigger-happy finger was about to squeeze off a shot, Rizal, using his honed skills in handling a firearm, pulled out his gun and side stepped to the left, laying down fire upon the men who had threatened him. He hit Ruairi right in his forehead; he fell to the ground. Tae immediately dodged behind cover and he shouted, "Alana! Take him out!"

Alana was hiding behind a dumpster. She stalked silently and stood behind Rizal and raised her assault rifle upon his head. As she was about to pull the trigger, a shot rang out in the distance, and the sudden impact of a high-velocity round penetrated her chest, blasting her into the ground. Her dead mangled body was left bleeding in a puddle. Her killer was a great sniper in the distance.

"So, you are Tae. I've heard of you. You have killed many of my men," said Rizal in a soft voice. "Did you think you could kill me tonight?"

Tae withdrew his CSMG-Vector carbine. From the cover of a pile of concrete rubble, he gave Rizal a burst of blind fire that sent him rolling into cover, but Rizal regained control and set his sights upon Tae, hoping Tae would pop his head up and reveal his location. But Tae was experienced; he knew he had to stay under cover or risk getting his head blown. Tae was in a tight spot, but he planned an escape. He cursed himself for having walked straight into a trap.

"That's the plan! You are too dangerous to live!" shouted Tae.

"Does it matter? Either way, if I die tonight, the guards will still come for you. Another will rise, and that person will be far worse," replied Rizal. "But I'm afraid you are the one who is going to die. You are a hard man to find. I guess knowing what you want and letting you come to me was easier than following your scent. I will end you tonight, and you red rebels will have no chance of stopping me."

Tae released another burst of blind fire into Rizal's position, buying time before an inevitable assault. He sent a distress signal to his backup team. They were coming, but he needed to buy even more time. Tae rummaged through his backpack and found a smoke grenade. The rain would disrupt its overall effectiveness, but it could provide an opportunity for him to move in closer to Rizal. Since he was surrounded, he might as well take out his target and die serving the Virtuous. Tae pulled the pin and tossed the grenade into the alley.

The metal body of the grenade hitting the concrete floor alerted Rizal. He turned back, took cover, and waited for a sudden bang to deafen his ears. When he heard nothing, he peeked around the corner to see that yellow smoke had covered the area. "Can you see him?" Rizal asked his sniper.

"Negative."

The rain made short work of the concealing smoke, which disappeared in a matter of seconds. Rizal proceeded to clear the area, but to his dismay, Tae had managed to escape.

"Sir! Behind you!" shouted the sniper.

The sniper spotted Tae charging up behind Rizal. The sniper tried to fire but hesitated due to the close proximity of Tae to Rizal. They locked themselves in hand-to-hand combat. It was the only combat situation Tae could engage in with Rizal without bringing the sniper into play. All he had to do was to ensure the fight lasted long enough for his rescuer to arrive.

Tae was smaller than Rizal, and Rizal's sheer size and weight would give him an advantage over Tae if he managed to take Tae down onto the ground. However, the alley did not provide very much room for Rizal to manoeuvre his longer arms and bigger size. Tae took advantage of this fact, which levelled the battleground to an equal fight.

It was a fierce clash that required constant focus from both sides. Due to fatigue, Tae was losing the battle. Tae turned to dodge an incoming fist, but he was unable to reverse the momentum of his move so he could dodge Rizal's follow-up blow. The impact on Tae's cheek sent him hobbling backwards. He bled severely from a cut on his eyelid. The impact of that punch caused a delay in Tae's physical reaction, and Rizal took the opportunity to land a few more punches to Tae's torso and face. At the end of a vicious barrage, Tae was on the ground kneeling, spitting blood.

Rizal grabbed Tae by his hair and pulled him up, leaving his legs dangling freely, his feet off the ground. Two more of his goons had arrived. They stood at the entrance of the alley, keeping innocent bystanders at bay.

"Come on! I thought you would be more of a challenge!" said Rizal. He pinched his thumb into Tae's injured eyelid, causing a fresh rush of blood to spew out. Tae was numb to the pain. "The Virtuous. What a joke!"

Rizal dragged Tae towards the body of Alana. He shoved Tae's face into hers, squeezing both their heads into the pavement. Alana's eyes were still open. Tae stared into them.

"Your actions will end the lives of your friends. Is that what you want? Is that what you want to achieve with your little struggle? Look at her. Look at her suffering. It will end like this for all your friends – those who listen to your so-called leaders. Do you even know what the consequences are? *Think!*"

Tae choked on a combination of blood and rainwater as he breathed. He tried his best to move his hands and struggle to retrieve something of importance from Alana. She deserved to live well; she did not deserve to lie dead in a wet alley. Tae moved his hands.

"Trying to take something?" said Rizal. He grabbed Tae's arm and crushed it with his foot. The pain was severe enough to wake him. He screamed. His voice ran into the ears of Paradisians. Tae begged for his life.

"Ready to accept the consequences of your actions?" whispered Rizal to Tae.

Tae looked into Rizal's eyes and saw evil looking back. Rizal was the summation of all of his actions. Tae accepted his fate and was ready for the final blow. Alana and Ruairi had not deserved to die. Tae wanted to atone for his sins.

Fortunately for him, a blast came through a wall that saved him from his demise.

The explosion bloomed behind Rizal. Debris of brick and stones crashed upon Rizal's back, knocking him out. Tae was released from his grasp. He dragged himself on the ground, getting as far away from Rizal as possible. A few smoke grenades were dropped around Tae, and a concealing smoke emerged to blind the enemy. Two men wearing gas masks jumped through the wall and carried Tae into the building. Rizal's two men fired blindly into the smoke. One bullet met its mark on Tae's leg.

In the building, Idris and Rau unmasked themselves and carried Tae to the roof. "Rau, take the rifle. I will carry Tae."

The sniper had been taken out of the game before the rescue plan was executed. Idris had attached a high-grade silencer onto his rifle and killed the sniper silently. The taking out of the sniper was a critical factor in his rescue plan. With her still in play, the plan would fail.

On the rooftops, the three-man team crossed over to the other side of the building, hopping and jumping from roof to roof. Eventually, they cleared the area. They went into a basement where a Hibiscus Party tunnel was located. Through it, they successfully evaded the guards and found themselves back in their hideout. The whole of Paradise went into emergency lockdown. Guards were seen on the streets banging on doors and subsequently arresting suspected individuals. Tension escalated to high levels. All on-going operations conducted by the rest of the Virtuous were placed on hold.

Tae remained unconscious.

"Arla, Paradise is under lockdown."

Arla received the message from one of her teammates through her small earpiece. She understood. She was in the room where Lady Malla was still conducting her meeting. Arla was observing the meeting from a silent corner, standing among the other sisters. Lady Malla had touched upon many issues: the people, the environment, and the state of political change. But most of all, she had discussed the religion of the Heavenly Flower: "Our religion is our only true believe. It unites us and gives us a purpose beyond the confines of our world where, we believe, the Heavenly Flower awaits. Our imagination replaced by sheer certainty of a one true entity that binds us and graces us with true freedom and confidence. We are no longer afraid of death. We are no longer afraid of uncertainty. We have a future when we die!"

The Heavenly Flower congregation shared cheers of joy as they held their hands to their hearts in honour of their sacred worship of the Heavenly Flower. They bowed their heads to thank Lady Malla for her efforts in translating Her divine plan to Her followers.

"With this new commitment of uniting the world with a common believe," Lady Malla continued, "we will finally have peace! Just think! A world where the Great War shall never be repeated. The differences we have will be gone, and we will share our lives under a banner of faith!"

Another round of agreement echoed through that holy room as all the listeners applauded. They felt a surge of passion inspire an emotional awakening.

"The Heavenly Flower has called to me to join hands with the government," said Lady Malla. "It is part of Her divine plan! It is the only way to ensure that our message is sent across to everyone! Even the government had accepted Her! They are our family! We are their sisters, and we will guide them forward! Praise the divine plan. Have faith and believe in the impossible. And now, we see the Heavenly Flower bloom ever more!"

Lady Malla had tears in her eyes; they rolled down over her cheeks. Arla could see she had sought that moment for a long time. Lady Malla's faith was inspiring, and Arla became determined to understand the reason for that. She wanted to speak with Lady Malla. After her congregation received Lady Malla's last inspiring speech, the holy room turned empty. Arla felt relieved.

Lady Malla discussed a few points with a young apprentice of hers before she left through another door, which led to her study. Arla followed and gently knocked upon the door.

"Come in," said Lady Malla.

Arla turned the knob and entered the room. Lady Malla was at her desk rummaging through notes she had just made. Her desk lamp glimmered. She wore glasses. Dozens of books were stacked one upon another on the surface of the desk. A small data pad on a terminal was on a table behind her. It was obvious it hasn't been used very much.

"Apologies for the mess," said Lady Malla. She pointed to the data pad. "I am not fond of that contraption. Blame it on nostalgic preferences."

"It's all right. Books have their charms."

Lady Malla raised her head in curious wonder. "Are you new here? I haven't heard your voice before."

"Yes, ma'am, I'm new here," replied Arla with a nervous tone.

"Ah, right. How are you? What can I do for you? Please have a seat."

Arla politely sat on a chair in front of Lady Malla. Lady Malla received her with a smile.

"I'm ... here to ask a few questions."

"A curious one? Go ahead. Ask away. It's been a while. Is it about your faith?"

"In a way, ma'am. I want to understand – how did the Heavenly Flower choose you?"

Lady Malla sat upright and removed her glasses. She stood up and walked to her little pantry where she poured each of them a cup of tea. "She did not just choose me, young one. We are all chosen."

"I'm afraid I do not understand."

"The Heavenly Flower works in mysterious ways. I accepted her teaching, and she chose me. Just exactly the way she chose you."

Arla stayed quiet.

"The hibiscus flower is the only flower that grows on Bumi," said Lady Malla. "Have you ever wondered why? It's a message from the Heavenly Flower to show it created this world. We live in it; hence, we are the chosen ones. Not many people realize it, but soon people will accept it."

"You mentioned you want to save the world from another Great War. How is it possible? Isn't that a little bit ambitious?"

"I've seen the consequence of war – the killings, the brutality. I cannot let the world burn in flames again."

"What did you see? How was it burned?"

"The Pasir Lands, my dear. It wasn't supposed to exist. It used to be a beautiful place where trees grew and a civilization flourished. All of that ended when the horrid red airship came. That cruel man … that cruel man … he burned everyone with his weapon! The Navigator … he was cruel."

Arla knew a story that Tae had told her. It was a story of how the Pasir Lands once existed. The big red airship was a weapon beyond the comprehension of Bumi's engineers. It flew bringing dread, as its countless guns drummed fear into the hearts who saw it. Arla did not believe it. She remembered a peaceful airship, an airship designed for exploration and not for war. Tae told her it was a necessary evil the airship had to bear – an evil to possess a weapon so powerful, it deterred any violent and cruel ambitions. Arla believed the *Hibiscus*

Airship, flown by the Navigator, was meant only for exploration. It was an airship to save Bumi, not to destroy and threaten. "I have a different memory of that," she said. "The airship was used for peace."

"Was that what the stories told you? The little red book. The little red book about adventures and a good time? It was a lie. That was why the government banned it. Some books were never meant to be read."

Arla felt a discomfort. "Were you there? Did you see it with your eyes?"

Lady Malla rose up from her desk and stood next to Arla. She still had her cup of tea in her hand. "This room is rather cramped. Let's head out to the garden."

Arla and Lady Malla sat on a garden bench. They looked upon the hibiscus flowers that grew on its walls and along the ground. They finished their tea, and a pair of young maidens came and collected their cups.

"I was in Paradise that night. I was young and I was looking at the horizon for a red airship to appear. I had the same wonder you once had. On that night, I saw it for what it truly was. A powerful blue light blinded me. It was so powerful, I felt a shock. The night turned into the quietest night I had ever known. Everyone on the streets stopped and ran into their homes. The next day, news came about buildings destroyed and dead bodies turned to dust. The land turned arid and nothing grew. The survivors had no choice but to abandon their land. What I heard from them was even worse."

Arla stared at a hibiscus flower.

"What if the *Hibiscus Airship* was a necessary evil? What if it was necessary to erase a past and make peace?" What if—"

"My dear child, who gives a person the power to take the lives of the innocent? Who decides who lives and who dies? That power should never be appointed to anyone. That power should forever be in the guidance of the Heavenly Flower."

Arla moved about in her seat. She stood up and walked to one of the flowers that blossomed with a deeper colour.

"You, my dear ... this feels awfully familiar. What is your name?" Lady Malla asked. She remembered having a similar conversation with another young man before.

Arla touched the petal of a flower. "My name is Arla."

"That name ... you're Arla Hibby? Daughter of Dara, my friend?"

Arla was stunned. She did not know whether Lady Malla was truly her enemy or not. She had not expected Lady Malla to mention her father's name, and now she was worried, and she was cautious of a trick; she played along. "Did you know my father?"

"Yes, I did, and I remember. He was a young man about your age when I first saw him. He was standing right where you are. He was looking around trying to understand more about the Heavenly Flower. We had a long conversation that night. We did not see eye to eye on some matters, but we ended up as friends. The last time I saw him, he told me he had troubles. But it was a jest made by a friend of his, Penn."

"You know Penn as well?"

"Yes, I do. From what I can recall, they were best friends. Somewhere along the line, they disagreed on a few matters. I'm not sure what it was, but it seemed important. You have the same look in your eyes that your father had when I saw him. He was confused and unsure."

"Are aware that Penn is leading the Red Flower Revolution?" asked Arla. "He wants to get rid of the Forlorn, whom he believes is going to destroy our future. The Forlorn intend to keep Bumi in a tighter grip, taking away our minds and our freedom for any kind of control. And you help them ... why?"

Lady Malla walked over to Arla. She gently removed Arla's veil. "My, my, what a beautiful girl you've grown into!"

"Thank you, but I am not here for pleasantries."

"My dear child, your father asked me the same thing, and I will tell you exactly what I told him. I am here to end the violence. I want to unite the people through a common faith. The Heavenly Flower is the only way to our salvation. If the Forlorn want to help us make it a reality, I will gladly accept their support. Nobody should have the power to choose another person's fate."

"Even if it means letting go of our freedom and passion?"

"Tell me, what are they, Arla – freedom and passion? What are they besides feelings?"

"That's what makes life worth living! It is the reason we hold on to life! Freedom and passion lead to love and the wonderful things that make us whole! To not have these would mean the death of our souls. Don't you see it?"

"To love the Heavenly Flower is the same. Your passion towards Her would also be shown towards your family. The unpredictable nature of freedom and passion will lead to the eventual corruption of our nature. Would you rather let passion and freedom be governed by the selfish desire of our people?"

"To deal in such absolutes will lead to the corruption of our society! There will always be a way to turn the Heavenly Flower into a force for the corrupted. How can you guarantee that the Forlorn will not use it to enforce its power?"

"You are young, my dear child. As long as the Heavenly Flower can prevent any more unnecessary deaths, the world will truly be at peace."

"I apologize, ma'am. But I do not believe my father would have given up and left the Party for that reason. From what I remember of him, I believe that he did not see things as absolutes. Only those who see things that way will never truly understand the nature of our world, or the nature of the worlds beyond ours."

"Do you truly believe there are other worlds out there? Come now, that's just your imagination talking. It is a fragile believe, and unpredictable. It will cloud our minds and lead us to more confusion. We should worry about what happens here and not have our heads in clouds. The Heavenly Flower is what we should believe in. She will ensure peace will remain."

Arla had trouble understanding the linear nature of Lady Malla's thought process, although she understood Lady Malla's good intentions. The woman could be correct in a way, but deep down in her heart, Arla had a feeling that Lady Malla's solution was corruptible. Arla knew the Forlorn were using her religion to meet their own selfish objectives.

Arla put her veil back on and stormed out of the Temple. Her teammates followed. Lady Malla did not report their presence to the guards, as she knew Arla had good intentions as well. Lady Malla allowed the fate of Bumi be placed under the guiding hands of the Heavenly Flower. She prayed in the Temple garden, hoping Arla would find the right path.

Chapter 13

Finding Bell

Candles lit the room, and tattered drapes hung over the windows. The medical base of the Virtuous was made of mud and stones, and it was where their wounded rested. It was hidden in the concealed alleyways of Kampung. Guards still patrolled Kampung, but were limited to areas allowed by the locals. The guards were afraid of stirring up unrest that placed the government in a bad light. Unless assaulted or fired upon, the guards conducted daily activities as usual. It was just a matter of time before the uneasy tension would blow up.

Tae lay on his bed. White linen touched his skin, giving him the added joy of comfort. He had not taken any rest since the whole campaign began. Idris sat next to him, dictating a few necessary letters to his secretary, who tried to keep up with his quick speech.

"Hey, Idris, where is Arla?" asked Tae.

"She is out on a mission as usual. She is pretty busy."

"Who is leading the HKs at the moment? Is Arla being watched? The Black Guards …"

"Tae! Hey! Calm down, you are supposed to be resting. So please, do what the doctor says, and rest. You don't have to worry about her. She can take care of herself."

The skirmish with Rizal had been an important clash. Rizal had to be eliminated before the Virtuous campaign could proceed without complication. After that day, Rizal's counterinsurgency strategy was launched as planned. First, it was the media. Full broadcast authority was placed under the guards' jurisdiction. A special task force was created to monitor, and filter any Virtuous-related headlines. They replaced available televised slots with their own specialized propaganda. Those who viewed their data pads as their natural source of information were tempted and manipulated to a vision of the Forlorn. Conversations and gossip at social waterholes had slowly been filled with doubt on the legitimacy of the Hibiscus Party and the Virtuous. They had surgically attached the Hibiscus Party and the Virtuous together, tying the title of "terrorist" to the Virtuous, while carefully insinuating the idea of the Hibiscus Party as an abetting party.

Second, once the public had been tempted by the possibility of disruption in their way of life and culture, the politicians of the Forlorn worked tirelessly to repeal the Equality Act, replacing it with a draconian legislation known as the World Security Bill. This bill, also known as the WSB, was designed to give ultimate power to the government to build an army to counter a rising threat of terrorism. The WSB allowed guards to arrest anybody they deemed a threat. The public had to think twice about voicing their opinions. With the removal of the Equality Act, people were not equally treated as citizens of Bumi. Special treatment of certain ethnic groups was placed as a priority, while the minority were placed on hold. Hoary sentiments of kaum relations begin to emerge from an old festering wound. With the control of the media, the government painted a vast canvas to show the Hibiscus Party had instigated such a change to a just constitution. And in a miraculous turn of events, the people actually believed the government. The blame was set, and its flames were fanned. Public opinion of the Hibiscus Party was at an all-time low. Penn and the

Prince pointed out that the Forlorn had taken advantage of a lack of political teaching within Bumi's education system. Many took that statement as an insult to the community's ego. Thus, the Hibiscus Party was painted as a pseudo-intellectual group made up of the bourgeoisie, who would never understand the plight of the proletariat.

Finally, in his brilliant plan of public manipulation, Rizal had convinced Lady Malla of the necessity of public peace. Lady Malla had agreed to commit her religious congregation to the government's cause for law and order. She had publicly declared that the Forlorn had been chosen by the Heavenly Flower to run the government and maintain balance within Bumi. Nobody doubted her words; as a matron of the Temple, her words were truth. They believed the Heavenly Flower had chosen her for a reason. She was a voice that represented Her. To question was to doubt the existence of the Heavenly Flower. This was sin that made a person's future in an afterlife bleak.

"Are we winning?" asked Tae.

"Of course we are, Tae," said Idris.

"I've failed you all. Rizal should have been dead. I fell into his trap."

"Well don't blame yourself," muttered Idris. He was checking through a supply requisition that required his approval. "The fight is still going on, and you are still in the game. We can still win!"

"But I do not think Penn's 'peaceful' war will remain peaceful any longer. I feel it – it is not what it seems."

"Stay calm, Tae. Penn has been planning this for a long time. Focus and keep your spirits up. Do not falter."

Tae shook his head. "Aye. Hey, Idris, did Arla ask about me?"

"Mmm?" whispered Idris as he studied a field report. He was distracted. "I'm sorry, Tae. What was it?"

"Did Arla come visit me?"

"Yes, she did. When you were asleep. She did not want to bother you."

"Good to know. Maybe next time she will wake me up."

"I'll remind her, Tae. Get some sleep, buddy."

As Tae closed his eyes and drifted into slumber, Idris carefully collected his documents and packed them into his backpack. He needed to be ready to move to another location. Idris had not been in one place longer than two hours recently. It was a security precaution that kept him in the game as long as possible. As he walked out the door, he saw Arla standing in a corner. Her hair was shorter and still wild, but she maintained the elegant nature of calm. She was waiting.

"You know, standing there will not make any difference. Can't you just go in and see him face to face?"

"I almost lost him, Idris. I cannot ... I do not know how to say hi to him. It reminds me too much of Bell. I do not understand this. I do not know why ... I cannot see him."

Idris nodded. "I feel the same way about seeing Setia again. I do not know how to do it."

"I need to save her, Idris. I cannot live like this anymore."

"The dungeon is a fortress. Do not do anything rash. Jas and I are doing our best to find a way to get Bell and the rest of our people out of there. Just be patient, all right?"

Arla walked away.

Rizal was standing in wait at the reception desk. The secretary of the premier typed and received calls all day long. The ministry's walls were painted in the colours of the Forlorn: it was a patriotic delight. Rizal was there to submit his recent report on the effectiveness of his plan. He decided to sit on a comfy maroon chair. He always had a tendency to fall asleep on such comfortable furniture. Rizal dreaded the boring intensity of waiting for his turn to be granted audience with the premier.

After a few hours of napping, Rizal finally heard the secretary call his name. He jerked himself awake, sat up, and awkwardly wiped away the drool on his cheek. The secretary giggled as he flashed a dashing smile.

Rizal gently knocked on the door and was granted permission to enter. In the grand chamber sat a fat old man with a grey beard and business-like hair. He was the leader of the government, having been chosen one of the Forlorn, and he was called Mr Allorn. He was a private man. He never liked the spotlight and dreaded public attention. He always told Rizal, "Oh, for the sake of the people, I do not want to take all the attention for myself. Oh no, no, no. The people deserve the attention. The Forlorn deserve it. I'm just here to do my duty."

Rizal did not like Mr Allorn. He saw him as a shrewd man with shrewd principals. The only reason he did not want attention for himself was that he did not want responsibility pushed on him if everything went wrong. He wanted to be known as the man who made it possible, but never the man who was to blame. Mr Allorn's laughter was the worst. Rizal detected a sense of selfish pride within his laugh. It was disgusting, and it did not make Rizal happy. Mr Allorn was laughing at the meal he'd had, and the nap he'd just finished. His only movement was the flick of his wrist as he signed papers deemed "crucial" by his assistant.

"Sir, can you sign this? It is due. It is about—"

"No! Don't tell me what it is about! You read it, and you tell me if it is important or not. That is how we do things around here," he said lazily. "Well? Is it important or not?"

"Yes, sir."

"Good! Now give it to me!"

Mr Allorn was hasty in doing things he did not like. He rushed, and his signature was testament to his careless nature. He did not even rule over his own office. His assistant cleaned and arranged everything in order. Mr Allorn's lazy eyes noticed a strongly built man standing with his face frowning over time wasted. "Rizal! My friend! I did not notice you standing there. Come in! Come in!"

"Mr Allorn, a pleasure as always," said Rizal half-heartedly.

"Are you here to ask me for a raise?"

"Of course not. I'm here to submit the monthly report on the Virtuous."

"Oh, yes. The troublemakers. Have they been eradicated yet?" Rizal passed his report over to Mr Allorn's assistant, who immediately placed it on the desk in front of his boss. Mr Allorn ignored it. "Rizal, are we winning?"

"Considerably. Penn and his Party will not prevail. They will slowly disappear." Rizal spoke with authority. "With your help, and the right opportunity of course."

"Loyal as a whistle! We love you, Rizal! What can we do without you? Hmm?" said Mr Allorn.

"Nothing good I assume—"

Mr Allorn sensed insubordination. "You know we love you, Rizal. You are here because we wanted it that way. You are saving Bumi because we want you to. Just remember, the Forlorn love you."

Rizal, as usual, nodded to the same reminder Mr Allorn drilled into him at every meeting. He was tired of it, but like all abiding citizens, he knew he must obey and listen to the wise words of others. Mr Allorn was careful with his words; he was careful to not divert Rizal's responsibility upon himself.

"I serve the government as I have served the people," said Rizal. "If there is another person who has been deemed fit to replace me, do not hesitate to do so."

"No, no, no, Rizal! Do not be offended. You are irreplaceable! I can guarantee there is nobody like you in Paradise."

"Just to confirm, Mr Allorn, if I become unfit for duty, please replace me."

Rizal took a bow and turned back to the door through which he had entered. Before he stepped through it, Mr Allorn called upon him again. "Rizal, there is one more thing. Come back in."

Rizal reluctantly followed his orders. "What is it, sir?"

"The Forlorn council has decided that the rebels might be a violent nuisance in the future. If it comes to that, please do not hesitate to order full military action against them. Take them out as fast as you could."

"I guarantee you, sir, it won't come to that. The war will be won through the hearts and minds of the people. Nobody will have to go through a war like the Great War ever again."

"Just to inform, Rizal. Just to inform."

"Anything else, sir?"

"Mmm? Of course. One more thing. I would like you to meet your supervising partner … Mr … I'm sorry, I cannot remember your name."

In a dark corner of Mr Allorn's office sat a man. He had no hair on his head, and no eyebrows. His skin was pale. His thin body was comparable to that of a man starving man on the streets, but he looked to be as tough as nails. Rizal sensed it – the man was a cold-blooded murderer.

"My name is Mr Jeella. Nice to meet you, Rizal."

Rizal fumed. "Why are you assigning this man to me? I do not need a babysitter!"

"Orders from the top, Rizal. It is best you obey it. Mr Jeella is an expert at what he does. He will advise you," said Mr Allorn, who was munching on a cookie.

"What will he be advising me on?"

"Riot control" said Jeella. "Matters will escalate into terrible conditions. I will be there to assist you when that happens. And to observe the great work you do."

"It won't come to that, my friend."

"You can never be too sure. I will stay out of your way until then."

"Yeah … whatever."

After Rizal left the office, Jeella gave a devilish smile at Mr Allorn. "Thank you for your hospitality. I will take my leave now."

"Mr Jeella, don't you want a cookie?"

Jeella raised his hand. "Careful, Mr Allorn, that sugar will kill you one day."

Mr Allorn let out a hearty laugh and picked up another cookie without hesitation. Jeella left the office and headed to endow his surgical expertise upon Paradise.

Livi rushed into Arla's room where she was taking her rest. She had not slept well for almost a week, and she was teetering upon collapse.

She dragged herself out of bed, annoyed. "What is it, Livi? Can't you just let me sleep?"

"I'm sorry, ma'am, but you have to read this." Livi passed his data pad to Arla. Under its glowing light, she studied the article. To her surprise, it was news she wished she didn't know.

"Is this true? When did it—"

"It happened last night. We were betrayed."

Arla ran out of her room and hurried towards the cupboard where her gear was stored. "Is this still going on?"

"Arla, it's over. All of them have been captured."

Arla slumped into the side of the cupboard. Idris and Jasmine had been captured, along with a good proportion of the Virtuous manpower. She slid down onto the floor as she contemplated the next course of action to take. The situation was dire. The Virtuous command structure had almost been obliterated. She had no access to communications with Penn or the Prince, and she was not sure the rest were safe from harm.

"Who is in charge?"

"At the moment, I am not sure. We stopped sending our messages as soon as it happened. The guards might have successfully intercepted our communication lines."

"Do you know who betrayed us?"

"Haven't got the faintest idea. What should we do, Arla?"

She knew she had a platoon to command. She planned her next course of action until she received further orders from the top. "Livi, gather our scribes."

"Yes, ma'am!"

All three of her section leaders presented themselves immediately. Given the circumstances that brewed around Bumi, they stood at attention with their ears alerted to Arla's command. "Gents, we are in a situation that some would consider as inevitable, and some, impossible. Idris, Jasmine, and most of our captains were captured during a closed-door meeting in one of our safe houses. We are currently not sure who betrayed them and who else out there is able to operate. It is best to assume that we are the last."

"What are we supposed to do now?" asked a scribe.

"We will operate as usual – evade the guards and keep monitoring their movements. Livi, you will be in charge while I am gone. I need to find a way to contact Penn and the remaining captains."

"Roger that," said Livi. "We will limit our movements within Kampung itself. Arla, shall we make ready our weapons? Just in case—"

"Do it. But act only in self-defence of course. We do not want to blow this out of control," said Arla cautiously. "Dismissed."

Arla's scribes immediately prepared themselves for a potential conflict that might escalate to dangerous heights. Arla donned her cloak, disguising herself as a resident making her way through the market area of Kampung. Only during emergencies was Arla allowed to meet the old woman who stood under the clock tower. It was part of a contingency plan to get in touch with top command. Arla thought the situation qualified as an emergency.

At the market, people were bustling about trying to stock up on as many supplies as possible. People pushed about trying to buy up everything they could. A few scuffles had broken out as the guards tried their best to control the situation. There were rumours flying about the drums of war thumping with feverous eagerness. Fear gripped the populace.

Arla stood under the clock tower. It was an old monument dedicated to the only constant in the world: time. Decorated with beautiful, intricate stone carvings crafted by ancient stonemasons, it had stood for many generations. Arla stood patiently as she waited for an old woman.

As the minute hand turned a full circle, Arla still waited for a person who did not seem to exist. She sat on the ground, calming herself so she could figure out her next course of action. Store supplies were running low in the market. Many groups had started to organize themselves to pillage and steal. The guards were overwhelmed, and some had been beaten. Arla stayed where she was, trying to not get involved, until she heard the beating sounds of sticks in the near distance.

Arla stood up. She quickly fled to higher ground, moving as low as possible through a restless crowd. She climbed on top a roof to get a better view of the market.

At one end of the market, she saw a marching line of guards in white riot gear. They moved to the rhythm of battle. They pushed on in a disciplined routine, advancing straight towards an angry mob. The mob held their ground, tossing stones among the guards. The guards blared warnings to disperse but were met with fiercer resistance. Then, all hell broke loose.

The residents of Kampung started it. They tossed Molotov cocktails into the guards' formation, causing significant confusion at first, but the guards' strict training in riot control kicked in. Under chaos, their philosophy was to meet violence with brutality. During the entire battle, the guards relished in unleashing their desire for the suffering of others. They were white fallen angels coming to claim their victims.

The guards went in, and they went in hard. Within a few seconds, they had curtailed the will of the mob to retaliate. They had broken the back of the riot, as leaders were immediately captured and made an example of. Brutal abuse was inflicted on those who were caught, and loud speakers blared to announce that a curfew had taken effect. All citizens went home with their dignity in shatters. Arla stayed where she was.

"Hi, Arla, how are you?"

Arla turned around to the presence of a familiar face. "Prince! Where have you been? I've missed you!" whispered Arla as she hugged a friend whom she treated as the grandfather she never knew.

"Oh your grip has gotten stronger!" said the Prince. "What have they been doing to you?"

"Enough to make me tougher."

"I see! I see! Good to know. I guess they made you tougher here as well," said the Prince, pointing at her temple. "I'm glad you are doing well."

"Thanks to you, Prince. I couldn't have done it without you."

They smiled at each other. Another man emerged from the shadows. It was Penn. "Well, aren't you getting along well," said Penn as he nodded to her.

"Sir! You're here as well?"

"Yes, we're here to find you. There is something that needs to be done. Apologies for being so straightforward."

Arla pointed down, and the three moved from the roof and into a shop. Once inside the building they exchanged hugs again.

"What is it, Commander?" asked Arla. "What should we do next?"

The Prince laid out a drawing – the schematics of the interior of a certain building. Arla studied it thoroughly, referring to various notes peppered over the entire page.

"We need you to break into the dungeon," said Penn.

"What? I don't think I heard that right," said Arla. "You're saying you want me to break into the dungeon?"

"You heard him right, Arla," said the Prince. "It is probably our most risky mission yet."

Arla studied the schematics further. "What do you want me to do in there?"

"You're to break out all Virtuous prisoners and reveal the corrupt and cruel methods the Forlorn have used against those who were locked in there. We need full exposure of the Forlorn deeds. It is our last hope. We are losing the battle, Arla. We need this to wake the people up again," said Penn.

"Prince? You agree to this as well?" asked Arla.

"I agree with the commander. This is the best way. You and your platoon are the only ones left. The rest dispersed once their captains had been taken. We need this for a significant victory to boost our morale," said the Prince. "Besides, this is an opportunity for you to get your friend out."

Arla was reminded of her lost friend, who was now trapped in the dungeon. She remembered the promise she had made to herself to one day save her. It was a moment she had waited for a long time. She knew deep down that she was supposed to feel excited, but as reality sunk in, she knew she would be risking the lives of her men. The endeavour could prove fatal. But it was the only mission left for the Virtuous. She had made an oath, and it was a mission she could not refuse. Deep in her heart, she was troubled by expectations of finding Bell. Arla felt she had betrayed her.

"Do you know who betrayed us? Do you know how the guards found out where our command were meeting?" asked Arla.

"Nobody knows yet. We are working on it and hope to have an answer soon. Those who did this will pay for their disloyalty," said Penn. "We do not have much time, Arla. Go and prepare. The schematic will provide you with the best route to get in and what to do when you're in there. The operation will start in two days. Tae is leading the HKs again. He will escort you and provide cover as you break in."

"Where can I find him?"

"Don't worry. Two days from now, he will find you," said Penn.

"All right. We need to leave now," uttered the Prince. "Arla, please stay safe and get all your friends out in one piece. Everything depends on you now."

"I will get it done." Arla saluted.

They went their separate ways, and Arla returned to her safe house, trying to find the right words to convince her platoon to embark on a suicide mission.

Arla and Tae were in the sewers moving towards their insertion point. Livi and Mae were leading what was left of the Virtuous on the streets to monitor the guards. The remaining HKs were on rooftops keeping their eyes out for Black Guard snipers. Once Arla had managed to free the prisoners, an all-out prison riot would be launched. A peaceful protest was happening at the gates of the dungeon. The situation was a green light.

"All right, once we find the control room, we will release the prisoners and start a prison riot. Once the prison guards have been subdued, we will lead our guys back through the sewers. We will also be recording through our cameras as we head into the dungeon. The footage will be good for our campaign."

Tae gave the thumbs up and readied his silenced Vector carbine, while Arla loaded her silenced handgun.

"All right, let's go!" said Arla. They both went through a hole dug out previously that led them into the kitchen. They crawled through the dirt and found themselves pushing up through a ceramic tile floor. They had timed their insertion according to staff schedules given by Penn. The cooks and assistants had taken a break and would return only for their next shift. Tae and Arla were grateful that the information given by Penn was extremely reliable. They pushed on.

Arla had memorized the schematics. Before long, they were climbing upstairs towards the dungeon's prison cells. Tae had already silently taken out a few guards who had been difficult to evade. They moved tactically as they had been trained. Arla moved forward while Tae stayed behind to cover her approach. Once she had reached her destination, she covered Tae as he moved to another location. At the prison cells, they found all the prisoners forcefully stuffed into cells like sardines into cans.

"Tae, get to the control room and unlock those gates. I will proceed to find where they are holding Idris and Jasmine." Tae gave the thumbs up, and off he went upstairs. Arla proceeded down through a corridor of holding cells. She heard a few quiet cheers as prisoners saw Arla working hard to save them.

Down past the medical bay, Arla stumbled upon a patrol. Her silenced weapon did fast work. Her shots were accurate and precise, leading to instant kills. Time was running out.

"Arla, I'm at the control room. I have all the security tapes along with the control of the gates. Do you want me to release them?" requested Tae, speaking through his portable earpiece.

"Do it, Tae. Let the alarms go wild."

Immediately, red lights flared up along the entire corridor of the dungeon. Emergency alarms deafened everyone there, and all doors were unlocked. Arla could now access the most terrifying parts of the dungeon. She waited for the elevator. The bell on the elevator rang, and the door opened with the creaking noise of a rusty hinge. Arla stepped inside. A lonely light bulb shone down with a yellow tinge. The elevator door closed, and the car moved with a sudden jerk. The music playing was neither smooth nor fully audible. It was just a crackle – a child's voice echoing in the background. Arla felt a chill along her spine.

There were no buttons on the elevator. It led straight towards the deepest part of the dungeon – a place from which echoes never returned. The bell rang again, and the door opened to a vast derelict basement. Dusty pods were connected through a tube suspended from the ceiling. Arla counted hundreds of pods aligned systematically. Each pod was numbered based upon the row and column in which it had been placed. It was a huge grid system. Arla was at the end of it.

Arla ran. She ran to the middle where she saw two shadows painted on the grey floor.

"Hello. I know you – that hair and those eyes. You are as I imagined you to be."

Arla aimed her gun at a towering white man without a face. He was wearing a mask, and he was looking at her.

"Where is she?" asked Arla.

"She? Or they?

"They ..."

"Does 'they' include Bell?"

Arla shot a few rounds into the air. The bullets missed his skull by an inch. He stood taller. He was menacing. "Bell has been waiting for you a long time," he said. "You left her. You abandoned her. I know you, Arla. The wonderful times you spent together. The love you felt for each other. It feels warm. She screams in her sleep, and she wails in the day. You were not there for her. She hollered your name, and I was there to answer. You were not there, Arla. You were not there …"

"Shut up! Where is she!"

"You don't recognize her, do you? You were never there. She has changed. You were never there. You will never know. 'Why, Arla?' she asks. 'Why were you never there?'"

Arla noticed a young lady sitting on the floor with her legs crossed, mumbling a word over and over again. Her hairless head nodded constantly; a shadow concealed her face. Arla stepped closer, keeping her gun aimed at the creature.

"She was my favourite," he said. "She had a certain quality that I liked. I protected her against herself and the others. She was my favourite."

Arla carefully touched the girl's cold, pale hands. Arla's hands trembled as she screamed. She stood back a few steps, and she saw the girl's face. It was her. It was definitely her, she thought. As she feared, Bell had turned into a husk of her former self.

"Why are you scared?" he asked. "Don't you know this is Bell? She has been waiting for you for a long time. Why are you scared?"

Arla stepped backward and fell. Her legs were shaking from a nightmare she hoped was not real. She wanted to remember Bell as she had been when they were young. The husk Arla now saw was a tragic destruction of her memories from a time long ago. The husk screamed at Arla; her hairless body crawled towards Arla.

"And now she becomes your most hated thing. You loved her before, but when you find her changed, you do not hesitate to shun her … in your case, kill her. Such cruelty. Love only worked when she was beautiful."

Arla had turned her gun upon Bell. She whispered, "Stay back. Stay back …" Arla felt sorrow revive an old guilt that had haunted her for years. She did not understand how or why she had reacted the way she did. She could not understand how she could bring herself to aim a gun at Bell. She was scared. She was scared at how much Bell had changed, and her own troubled distaste for a ghoul who was no longer Bell.

"Look at you! So afraid … so afraid of someone you used to love. So predictable. Everyone loves to hate. Everyone. But not me. I will stay with Bell. I will take her in when nobody wants her. I will show her what love really feels like. Leave, Arla. You have no reason to be here anymore," said White Beast.

Arla stopped. She stared deep into Bell's tearful eyes and saw that a glimmering hope of life still existed within the husk. It was a courage she had come to cherish when they had nobody but themselves. Bell never gave up on Arla, and Arla was not going to give up on Bell. The fear of having her best memories of Bell eradicated by White Beast's handiwork no longer remained in her heart. She would remember the best of it forever.

"Bell … Bell … *Bell!*" shouted Arla.

"She can't hear you. Her ears are not working as well as they used to," said White Beast.

"You monster! What did you do? Why?"

"Because the world does not deserve orphans. Orphans do not deserve the world's love. But it is their loss. I will take them in, and I will love them. Arla, would you like to be loved by me?"

Arla raised her gun and shot White Beast. The first round managed to hit his right shoulder. But a weapon malfunction stopped the second round from discharging. White Beast, with his monstrous size, grabbed Arla by her neck and raised her up. Her own weight and his crushing power choked her airway. She barely had a chance to breath. She dropped her gun.

"It's been a while since anybody shot me. I've been lonely … the pain … the pain was too much. But I've learned. I've learned to adapt. I've learned to love … so much love. I give so much love," whispered White Beast as he dug his fingers into his wound and retrieved the bullet. "The pain … I feel so much better."

Arla choked, and her life drained away. White Beast stared at her futile attempts at resistance. He laughed, and Arla saw her end.

"What are you doing, Bell?" said White Beast. Bell was on the ground clinging to White Beast's leg, trying to pull and tug him away from Arla. "Do you want your friend back?"

As White Beast was distracted from his focus, Arla managed to grab a combat knife from her boot. She stabbed White Beast's wrist. An excruciating scream filled the chamber, and Arla cheated death.

Arla struggled onto the ground as she gasped for air. She took in every ounce of air possible, as much as her lungs could bear. She got back up on her feet and stumbled to reach her gun.

"Oh you little cunt! Sneaky little cunt! Just like Bell!" said White Beast as he kicked Bell away like a whimpering dog. "I'm going to love … killing you … inch by inch."

White Beast had grabbed hold of Arla's leg. He tried to pull her back into his embrace. But Arla managed to kick White Beast in his face with her other leg. It was a stunning blow that caused White Beast to fumble. His mask broke, and his nose was bloodied.

"My face! My face!" shouted White Beast.

White Beast had no real face. It was pale and devoid of any eyes. There was only a nose and a mouth stitched at its sides. It was terribly disfigured. Arla took a chance to jump on her feet. She ran to his legs. With precise movements, Arla sliced the tendons of White Beast's thighs, causing him to helplessly fall onto his knees. Arla knew he could not see, so she carefully made no noise.

"Oh you smart little cunt! Where are you? Show yourself!"

Arla watched White Beast flail his arms around as he tried to hit Arla. As he wore himself out, Arla sneaked to his back and whispered, "This is for what you did to Bell!" In a swift and merciless attack, Arla stabbed the knife into White Beast's left ear. Then she stabbed it into his right ear. He screamed and screamed, rolling on the ground in absolute agony. "My ears! My ears! My Ears!"

Arla picked up her gun and cleared the malfunction. She checked her magazine and reloaded. She walked casually to stand in front of a wailing White Beast.

"I will kill you! I will find you, and I will kill you!" shouted White Beast.

Arla stood above him. "No you won't."

Shots rang within the hall. Bullets were forced into White Beast's face, turning it into a bloody paste. His jaw and some parts of his head twitched. White Beast never spoke again. Arla ran towards Bell. "Bell! Are you okay? Please be—"

"Arla!" cried Bell. She was weak. White Beast's powerful kick had delivered a massive injury to her spine.

Arla turned morose as she saw the injury. "Bell, please stay with me. You are going to be all right. We will fix you up."

"I ... missed you ... so much ... I ..." Bell cried. Her tears flowed down into Arla's hands. Arla gently wiped Bell's face. Bell grabbed Arla's hands and kissed them. "I ... am dying."

"No! You're not! Don't say that! Don't you say that!" howled Arla. "You will be fine. We can go back to the way things were! You and I – we can be together again! Just don't die!"

Bell weakly pulled Arla closer. Her voice was soft, and she whispered, "I ... am already dead. I ... cannot ... live with myself ... any longer ... please end it for me ... if you love me ..."

"What are you saying?" cried Arla, as her tears rolled onto Bell.

"I ... loved you ... I truly did," whispered Bell.

Another shot rang in the hall. Bell stared deeply into Arla's eyes, and then she was gone. Bell's lifeless body remained in Arla's arms. Tae, who had just arrived at the scene along with a wounded Idris and Jasmine, looked on without knowing what to say. Only Idris remembered what Bell looked like. Jasmine and Tae had never had the chance to know her before she was captured. Arla held on to Bell, afraid of losing her forever.

Jasmine put her arms around Arla. "Arla, we need to leave. Bell—"

"No! I can't leave her again! This is my fault! It was all my fault!" screamed Arla.

"Arla, she is dead. She is no longer with us—"

"No!" Arla cried louder. "It was my fault!"

Tae and Idris huddled together with Jasmine and Arla. They hugged each other, feeling the warmth of each other's bodies. They tried their best to comfort a grieving Arla, who still cradled Bell in her arms.

"We love you, Arla," said Idris. "We need to get out of here. We do not want to lose you as well."

Gently, Jasmine held on to Arla's hands. Tae slowly moved Bell's body away from her. In a respectful honour to a fallen Virtuous soldier, Bell was laid down gently with her arms placed on her chest. Tae carefully closed her eyelids and whispered a few words. Idris saluted while Jasmine tenderly supported Arla by her side.

"I won't forget you. I promise," said Arla as she tore her moon-drop necklace and placed it in Bell's hands. "I found it ... for you."

With a final salute from Arla, Bell was at peace.

Chapter 14

Sail the Stardust

There it was. The graffiti of chaos painted upon the walls of Paradise. It was the raging crowd on the streets, which thronged with those wearing the green jumpsuits who had just been broken out of prison. Countless people now comprehended what the prisoners had suffered in the sadistic chambers within the dungeon and the fate of those who were supposed to have been kept there forever. The Hibiscus Party had leaked the tapes to the media. Dark secrets emerged, and the people were angry and haunted over the lies and the loneliness of cruelty. Everyone was on the streets protesting against the rule of the Forlorn. The time for reckoning had arrived. Penn and the Prince were on the streets, cheering and encouraging people forward to demand a change in the politics of Bumi. Every word they said was holy, and their statements represented only the truth. Residents of Kampung emerged to join.

The elites had substantial support from the middle class. They were afraid of change. It was a mentality that grew from living under the comforts of conformity. Young Virtuous soldiers who had been freed praised Arla for her dedication to rescue and reveal the secret purges that had been happening within the dungeon. Freed prisoners wasted no time in giving raging speeches at town halls, pubs, and the Temple of the Heavenly Flower. They preached, and the consciousness of the people was awakened.

"Penn and the Prince moved fast. Their plans are coming to fruition," said Tae.

"Something does not feel right," thought Idris. He noticed the guards were not trying to intervene or halt the rallies. They stood along the sidelines, nervously accepting the remarks of rally goers that echoed the disgraceful treatment of the prisoners. Their construed expressions bore the marks of impatience. They were following orders.

"Arla, can you get in touch with your team?" asked Tae.

Arla spoke into her earpiece. "Livi, come in. Do you read me, Livi?"

"Livi here ... we ... are ... can't ... you ..." Signals were being jammed. All radio transmissions had been cut off. Arla sensed that a situation was developing. They needed to get to Penn and the Prince immediately.

The crown was chanting anti-Forlorn sentiments, and there stood the Prince in the middle pouring out his passion to finally bring down the entity he hated so much. He was talking about the true Hero of Bumi, the one man many had heard about in stories – the man known as Mazy Hamzees. Arla stood underneath him listening to the way he spoke. He gave her a sense of wonder, and she felt the inspirational truth bubbling out of him. It was a curious fascination Arla had noticed. She saw how people were captivated by stories of grandeur and excitement. Previously, they had been inclined to see narratives among the dull confines of reality. It was the only way to afford meaning in their lives – a form of existential revelation. And Arla understood. To carry the power of narratives was to clutch upon a great power of influence.

"Prince! You need to get out of here. We believe you are in danger," shouted Idris.

The Prince continued his speech, ignoring his four young apprentices. Jasmine became restless as well. She was worried about her father. "I need to find my father. He could be in danger as well."

"Jas, I will come with you. Idris and Tae will be right here with the Prince," said Arla, and they began their search. Jas and Arla knew Penn would not be far away.

Trailing through the people attending the rally, Arla and Jasmine paid attention to the concentration level of people. The protests had gently transmuted, and now people were in a festive mood. They were cheering and living it up with copious amounts of ale and sausages. Parties were held to celebrate the freedom of those who had been wrongly accused. Revellers passed on a pint each to Arla and Jasmine, who gladly accepted.

"I cannot believe this! People are celebrating?" pointed out Jasmine.

"I guess Penn's plan worked. We can actually fight without dragging ourselves into a Great War again."

Arla and Jasmine cheered with their pints before drinking them down. It had been a long while since they had celebrated anything. The revelries happening now in Paradise reflected a victory they had long dreamt of.

"Arla! There he is!" declared Jasmine. Penn was on a second-floor balcony giving his own speech. It was as rousing as the Prince's. It was the first time Jasmine had seen her father's joy in a long while. He had lived a life struggle since his days on the *Hibiscus Airship*. On that day, Jasmine saw how a dream could be made a reality.

"Come on, Arla! Let's go to him!"

They entered the building, and up they went through a winding stairwell designed in a bygone era. The marble steps and hardwood railings had been preserved to provide the Forlorn elite a source of regal recognition. Penn and his Virtuous had taken the building back to serve as a symbol of liberation and to send a message of a return to a golden era.

Arla and Jasmine nodded to various Virtuous soldiers who had trained with them. They, too, were in a jubilant mood. The wool carpet that covered floor cushioned their steps as they went, inspiring a feeling of privilege. At the red door, a Virtuous man greeted them with open arms and chatted about how proud he was to have served with Jasmine's father. He declared that it was a momentous day – a day that would go down in history as the day a great victory had been won, and greedy money mongers of the Forlorn could be curtailed. They hugged one another before Arla and Jasmine walked in to see Penn.

The afternoon sun sneaked its rays across the balcony, casting the shadow of a proud man. With every word he uttered, his arms flew in all directions. Every pause he made was met with roaring cries from the people beneath him. The glimmer of the afternoon had embraced him with warmth, and he was in the sun's embrace. If a picture were taken from where Arla stood, with only the eternal colours of black and white, an immortal portrait for generations could hang in the annals of history.

Arla walked over to a couch and sat down. Penn's administrative team bustled to relay messages for the residents of Bumi. It was an important speech, and the cameras loved him. Jasmine stood next to the balcony, taking a peek around the wall. She became a little girl who shyly worshipped her father, as all daughters do. Arla remembered a time when she had done that as well. From where she sat, Penn's shadow resembled her own father.

With one final reverberating round of applause from the people, Penn ended his speech, and he waved to the crowd. One of the Virtuous noticed Jasmine, and she pulled her onto the balcony. Her father gladly embraced her and showed the crowd what he cherished the most. The crowd went wild again. Arla smiled and cheered along for her friend. When the afternoon wind blew across the balcony, Penn and Jasmine gave a salute, and then they retreated from the crowd. White silk drapes fluttered about in a dance with the wind.

"My dear! I am glad that you made it out! My trust in Arla and Tae was rightly placed. Where is Idris?" said a jovial Penn.

"He is with Tae, protecting the Prince. Father, we believe you are in danger."

"Nonsense! The people love us. We have won a great victory! We finally have political leverage to change things in Bumi! It is a political revolution that will see nothing like the Great War!"

"Father, we—"

Penn had nothing more to say to his daughter. He was in his moment, and he wanted to remember it the way he'd planned it to be. He picked up a glass of ale and drank it all with his most loyal soldiers. "Thank you all! Today … today has been magical. This day would not have happened without your support and sacrifice. I want to salute those who have given their lives to the shadows. The people who are out there cheering do not know they are, in fact, cheering for the ultimate sacrifice our soldiers had made. We were there through the fire together, and we will remember them. We will carry their passion into this brand new era!"

Dedicated men and women who were in the room saluted in unison. Then they were silent, and there were some who cried silently. Friends and family members who had pledged their lives to the Virtuous did not have mercy for the Black Guards. Penn honoured these faithful in an old tradition of spilling some of his drink onto the floor. The others followed.

"Arla, thank you very much for saving my daughter and Idris. You have no idea how much it means to me."

"I was doing my job, Commander. It was your schematics that made it possible. How did you get that information?"

"The Prince and I had secretly planned another covert operation with our undercover agents in the guards. They managed to collect as much data as possible before they were executed. Many died."

"I understand. They will be remembered."

"Come now, let's go to the Prince now. There's much left to do."

Rizal was on the roof of an apartment, staring down through his binoculars, monitoring crowds. He was surprised at how the situation had developed in such a short amount of time. The sacking of the dungeon and the escape of the prisoners were unfortunate events. His thoughts were filled with the innocent guards who had been killed protecting it. He was angry at the Virtuous for doing such terrible deeds. To Rizal, they were a bunch of murderers. Usually, he would send in his best units to disperse the rally, but he was on orders by Jeella to let it be. Rizal gripped his binoculars hard.

"Rizal. Do you see anything interesting yet?" said Jeella, who was at the air conditioning vent smoking a cigar.

"Nothing, you pale-skin freak. I'm looking so I can avoid looking at your stupid face."

"Why the hate? I always thought you were a gentleman. Don't hate me because of the way I look. Is this about the dungeon?"

Rizal slammed his binoculars on the railing, breaking the lenses into pieces. "We knew they had broken into the dungeon. We had guards prepared for such an incident. But you let them all escape, and now things have gotten out of control. Many innocent guards have died."

"They died honourably serving the Forlorn cause. You should be proud."

"They were fathers and mothers, sons and daughters, brothers and sisters! The criminals who did this are still out there walking free. We should have cordoned off the dungeon, and now we can't control the crowd anymore. My plans of terminating their influence over the people is for nothing! The exploits of the Black Guards have now been painted vile. We cannot control the peace anymore."

"Are you doubting orders from the Forlorn Council? Are you disobeying me?"

"No ... I'm just pointing—"

"You don't have to point out anything, Rizal. You are to follow my orders and nothing more. If I hear anything about this again, I shall report to the Council that you are behaving like a traitorous dog. Do you understand me?"

Rizal turned away. "Yes. I understand ... sir."

"Good. Ask your Black Guards to get into position now. Once they are ready, inform me."

"Alpha and Delta team. You are good to go. I repeat. You are good to go." Jeella spoke into his communicator. "The signal jammers will stop the HK's communications for a while. It is time." Jeella shuddered with excitement.

Alpha and Delta teams were kill squads out to eliminate any Virtuous units on the roofs of Paradise. It was the first phase of Jeela's ultimate plan to fulfil the needs of the Forlorn. The afternoon sun was scorching. Jeella's bald head had trouble coping with the heat, so he donned a beanie – a weird beanie with little cartoons drawn upon it. He put on his goggles as well.

"What's next on your plan?" asked Rizal.

"Don't worry. Everything is under control. You will see."

Rizal received reports about clashes around Paradise. However, they were being taken out without raising any suspicion. The jammers were working. Eventually, the roofs of Paradise were free from the hold of the Virtuous.

"Jeella, all units report an all clear," said Rizal.

"Marvellous! Call your best sharpshooter out now."

"Why? You still haven't told me—"

"I *said* order your best sharpshooter to come here *now*."

"Dana. Get up here. Bring your rifle as well," said Rizal, hesitantly, into his communicator.

Climbing up the stairs, a woman in black combat jacket and jungle fatigues carried a heavy duffel bag with no effort at all. Her stance and the way she carried herself displayed experience and training that were on par with the best. She was Rizal's most trusted guard, and she never questioned orders, a trait Jeella appreciated greatly.

"Dana, Dana, Dana! Welcome!" cried Jeella. "I have heard many great things about you, and I love your work. The way your shots crack open a skull like a fruit makes me tingle with delight. I am fortunate to have a chance to watch you work today."

Dana ignored Jeella and proceeded to salute Rizal. She responded only to people she had trained or operated with. Rizal and Dana shared a bond; they had operated together before as part of the Black Guards. Their bond had been forged through trial by fire, and it was a bond that could never easily be severed, except through careless intentions of betrayal. Dana unpacked her bag and swiftly began to assemble her rifle.

"So who are you targeting, Jeella?" asked Rizal.

"Someone of importance," declared Jeella with a wink.

Rizal understood the importance of strategic assassination. He thought of only two possible targets that would result in a significant impact. However, assassinations were always coupled with repercussions that could bite back. To kill those two would definitely bring more harm than good. They could be turned into martyrs.

"No, Jeella. No, no, no … You can't possibly think about targeting those two! In death, they will be even more influential. If you kill them now, the struggle of their people will turn into a conflict. You are talking about another Great War happening!"

"You're rather smart, but orders are orders."

"You've let the prisoners escape, and now this? You are risking a war! By the Heavenly Flower, this is—"

"Shut it! You are walking a thin line of betrayal. Be careful. Do you not want peace? A solid peace that could last for decades? I thought you had devoted your life to ensure Bumi does not fall into chaos again."

Rizal felt a chill through his spine. Jeella's dark, sadistic stare caused the hearts of those who opposed him to falter. Even Rizal could not comprehend the power Jeella held over him. He was a nightmare Rizal dreamt of in the middle of the night, waking to a cold sweat that drenched his bare body. Rizal knew it was wrong, but his courage faltered in the face of a monster. Rizal nodded to Dana, and Dana aimed through her high-powered scope. She lifted her thumb. Her target was in her sight.

Through the cobbled stone alleyways, Penn avoided the crowd. They cut straight towards the Prince's location. People were staring down at Penn through open windows with blank stares and hateful dread. A few insults were thrown at him. But celebrations distracted him and allowed him to have no care for the petty jealousy of those who disagreed with him. Not everyone in Paradise was enthusiastically celebrating the Hibiscus Party's victory march.

"There he is!" said Penn.

Penn's bodyguards cleared the way to the main road. All those in the area pushed and shoved their way to greet the new hero of Paradise. To Arla, it was a display of worship for a man who could be replaced by the people. She was especially irked by a woman who gave Penn her baby's forehead to kiss.

"Hey, Arla! Jas!" shouted Idris. "And Commander!"

"Idris! Good to see you are all right. Thank you for everything. This day would not have come without your contributions and sacrifice."

Idris saluted. "Thanks to you, Commander."

The Prince celebrated while Tae kept a close eye on his surroundings. He was sure the Prince and Penn's lives were in danger. Nobody had gotten in touch with any other Virtuous units on the roof. Livi had gone dark.

"Idris, we need to get everyone to safety," said Jasmine. "We can't get in touch with anybody."

"I agree. And, look, those who supports us are mostly residents from Kampung," said Idris. "We do not have the complete support of—"

"Wait ... that means," whispered Arla. "*Quick!* Get the Prince out of here!"

Just as Tae was about to drag the Prince away, a sudden impact pushed the Prince onto the ground. A high-velocity round had struck his neck, and the wound bled profusely. Everyone had been caught by surprise. After seeing the amount of blood, Arla cried out for medics. She knew that a day of celebration had turned into a day of panic.

"Prince! The Prince had been shot!" screamed Idris. "Someone get help! Get help!"

Jasmine stood in shock as she watched her old friend choke on his own blood as he stared blindly into the sky. "Jas! Get your father to safety now!" shouted Idris.

Jasmine made no move. Arla took her place and took Penn towards a flower shop for cover, pressing his head down as low as possible. Tae dragged Jasmine along. They could no longer see Idris and the Prince. People ran around wildly in all directions. A lethal stampede was brewing.

"Dammit! I'm going back out to help Idris," said Tae. He went out of the shop and burst through a panicking crowd. To his surprise, the crowd avoided the space where Idris and the Prince were. The Prince was still gasping in a pool of his own blood.

"Tae … we failed," murmured Idris. The bloodied palm of the Prince was on his face; the man was desperate to hold on to life. As the Prince breathed his last, as he said, "Sail the stardust …"

The Prince's palm slowly slid away from Idris. His lifeless body looked nothing like the man they had once known. His eyes remained wide open, struck by disbelief and regret. Idris wept softly.

"Come on, Idris. We need to get out of here. The guards are coming," said Tae.

Idris saw a row of guards in riot gear closing in upon them. They terrorized and threatened anybody in their path. Their gaze was set on the Prince's body. Shots were fired again. Idris and Tae ran for cover into the flower shop. "Fuck! They want to take his body away! Damm them! *Why?*" yelled Tae.

"They do not want us to make his grave into a hero's shrine. He wanted to eliminate a place we could rally. They had planned for a war. We are at war," replied Idris.

"Guys, we need to get out of here. They are coming for Penn as well," said Arla. "We need to use the back door."

"Let's go!" shouted Jasmine.

Penn was surrounded by his four loyal soldiers. They risked their lives to protect the commander. They needed him more than ever to continue the fight. "I have failed. I did not think this would happen," said Penn. "I did not think they would do this."

"Sir, you need to tell us what to do next. We cannot let them do what they want. We need to fight back! I mean, we have weapons, and we have been training to fight a real war," said Arla.

"You don't get it. What I – no, we – have fought for was to *avoid* armed conflict. The point of my plan was to never have armed conflict. What we have fought for has turned to nothing. I am not going to go through another Great War. No more."

As they ran through the back door and into sleazy back alleys, stomping boots chased after them. Arla held on to Tae as she noticed the doubt he had. They ran aimlessly with no direction in sight. They needed to get underground, but a blinding flash from a grenade sent everyone to the ground. Idris took the brunt of the blast, sustaining serious injuries to his legs and his chest. He had trouble getting back up until Arla put her arm around his side. Jasmine was with Penn. They were both fine except for the ringing in their ears. Tae had sustained a few shrapnel wounds, but he was still able to fight. As the first guard stormed around a corner, Tae engaged him in hand-to-hand combat. In a swift move or two, he managed to steal the guard's weapon and turn it against him. A burst of three rounds killed the guard, and Tae began to direct fire down the alley where a group of guards was trying to reach them. Tae's suppressing fire was fierce enough to hold them back.

"We're trapped. They have us," said Penn.

"Oh no, they haven't," said Arla as she picked up another grenade from the dead guard and threw it in the direction they'd come from. A few hollers of *"Grenade!"* followed by a thundering blast, assured the guards that the Virtuous were deadlier when pushed into a corner.

To the benefit of Penn and his soldiers, the situation was remedied when Virtuous soldiers around the city took up arms. Gun battles could be heard from afar, and explosions were frequent. It was lucky the guards who chased them had to engage a different group of Virtuous fighters.

"Looks like we have some help. Let's move!" ordered Arla.

Tae led the way forward with his rifle at the ready. With a few precise headshots, they were able to defeat several guards and push forward to link up with a few armed Virtuous fighters. "It's the commander!"

"Gents! We need to get the commander to safety. Can you escort him back to his hideout?"

The fighters nodded.

"Jas, we need to link up with whatever resistance forces there are around the city. This assault on us was carefully planned. They are targeting all known Virtuous operating bases. They are going to use this opportunity to slaughter us. Tae, follow the commander and make sure he gets to safety," said Arla.

Arla and Tae were looking at each other with concern. The whole day had turned to chaos in an instant. They did not have time to recover; neither did they have time to analyse and predict the Forlorn's strategy. Most of all, Tae did not have time to say he loved her.

"Arla, I need to say something," muttered Tae. Arla gave him a kiss on his cheek and pushed him away. It was a silent call for him to keep going and never look back. Their moment of reunion would happen again, they believed. In their tradition, the mission always came first. Tae passed his rifle to Arla. "You need it more than I do now." And off he ran.

Idris was losing blood. Jasmine made a makeshift bandage out of her shirt and tied it as best she could on Idris's wounds. "Go, Jas. I will stay with him. Someone needs to link up with those who are fighting. They need to be organized. Let them know their commander is still alive."

"All right, Arla. Just get to safety. This son of a bitch still owes me a drink!"

"Come on, Jas. That was not the deal. It was you who owes me a drink," said Idris, coughing.

Jasmine sighed and gave him a reassuring smile before she ran off towards the sound of gunfire. With Idris's arm across Arla's shoulder, both of them stood up and walked off into the direction Tae had gone.

"Come on, Idris. We need to get you underground as well."

"Never thought I would get hit. Never had I thought I would get hit like this …"

"Shut up, you whiny little bitch. After this, you owe me a drink."

"Two drinks? I can't afford that. Maybe you and Jas would consider another alternative?" uttered Idris as his breathing became heavier. "How about a nice little bath together?"

"Hah! You wish!"

"The proposal is still on the table …" He coughed again.

"All right, tough guy. It's been a rough day. Let's get you patched up."

As they struggled along the path, they heard a rough burst of gunfire in the close distance. They were cautious and stuck to the walls as closely as possible. Arla placed Idris down against a wall. Silently, she made sure the path was clear. As she turned around a corner next to the green flashing sign of a grocery store, Arla saw a soldier lying on the ground bleeding, his hands clutching his chest. He was all alone; he was her friend.

"Arla … Arla …"

"Tae. Oh, Tae … No! No, no! Not now. Not now!"

Tae had been shot multiple times in his chest. His wounds were horrifying. Arla did not know what to do. She had lost Bell, and she was not ready to lose Tae. Her knees turned weak, and she fell next to Tae, holding on to his bloodied hands.

"Tae, please don't die. Please don't die. Don't you leave me! Don't you dare leave me!"

Idris heard Arla's screams. He gathered his strength and endured the pain as he went to them, but nothing had prepared him for the heartbreak of seeing Arla clutching Tae's body to keep him warm. Tae's blood was on her body, as the Prince's blood was on his. Idris choked on his own tears.

"Oh, Heavenly Flower, if you hear this, please don't take him away from me! Please don't take Tae away from me. Not when you have taken Bell away as well!"

The evening closed upon them.

"Betrayal … they took Penn …" whispered Tae. Arla's ear was next to his lips; his voice was low and soft.

"Shhh. It's all right, Tae. Don't say anything. Save your energy. I will go get help. I will go get help—"

"Arla … I lov—"

Without finishing, Tae slumped into a fallen dark night. His eyes were as wide as the moon; he was dead. Arla knew what he had been going to say, but she had wanted to hear it in full, spoken in his breath. Her wishes made the loss of Tae unbearable. She lay next to him, holding on to his hands as she used to when they danced like mad lovers, spreading their hearts across the Southern Lands. She kissed his cold lips, but never was it enough to bring back the kisses they had shared. Arla cried; she cried because he left without saying goodbye. She dreaded the thought that she might not have loved him enough. Theirs was an unresolved love, which left another shadow of regret in her attic. She prayed for the fortune of seeing one another again.

"Arla," said Idris. "He was my friend as well. We cannot … *Shit!*"

Incoming fire came in hot as the guards stormed across the other end of the road. They were no longer under the guise of riot control; they were killing anything in sight. All of Paradise was under lockdown. Idris had no choice but to drag Arla away. All avenues in and out of the underground were blocked. A huge operation had been launched in Kampung, and Arla and Idris had no choice but to find shelter in the jungle. They evaded capture as best as they could with help from a few Virtuous resistance fighters along the way. Idris's wounds took a toll on his strength. Arla had to carry him on her back.

"I guess I have lost a lot of weight," said Idris in a low voice.

"You? You're still as heavy as a log," replied Arla with a hesitant tone. She was terrified of losing Idris as well. Their only option was to hide in the jungle. However, with no access to medical equipment, hiding out in the jungle would seal the fate of Idris. If that happened, Arla worried she would not have the will to keep fighting. It was a cruel world; the jungle would be the best place to end it.

Under the roots and foliage of hundred-year-old trees, Idris and Arla held out as long as they could. Arla scavenged for food while Idris's wounds began to fester. Pieces of shrapnel were still embedded in his flesh. Symptoms of infection had begun to show. Idris had trouble staying awake. He slipped into unconsciousness often, while his temperature burned high. Arla made do with a cold wet shirt on his forehead. She tried to make him feel as comfortable as she could. Most of the time, Arla tried to contact the Virtuous for help. The signal, however, remained jammed.

On the third night, their hideout was no longer safe. Roaming combat patrols searched the jungles for pockets of survivors. They heard screams from afar. Their situation was similar to situations in some of the stories about the Great War the Prince and Deeza had told before. Arla could only imagine the horrors of those who were found. Within a minute, she could hear voices. Her heart raced as she carried Idris away. Step by step, she heard twigs and branches break on the ground not far from her.

Unfortunately, the guard who led the patrol was Dana, Rizal's best sniper. She was an excellent tracker as well. With countless bloody bandages littered in their hideout, Dana knew they were close. She gave chase.

"This is it, isn't it? I can hear them," murmured Idris.

Arla breathed heavily as she traversed the complicated terrain of the jungle. She tripped and fell many times, giving Dana the opportunity to tighten the noose around their necks.

"We can make it! We can make it," said Arla as she tried to calm Idris. But Dana's bullet found its target in Arla's leg. Arla rolled into the dirt, grimacing in pain. But she held her voice in check. She crawled on her belly like a desperate pig towards cover, pulling Idris close. She painted her face in mud and cowered stealthily under the cover of the shadows.

"Take the rifle, Arla. You need to fight. Stay low and remember your training."

Arla prepared her rifle and gently checked the amount of ammunition left. She cocked it, and she crept to a better firing position behind a huge tree branch. She was ready for an ambush, but the unexpected loud crunch of a twig caused Dana and her two patrolmen to raise their guns and spray rounds in Arla's direction. With her injury, she clumsily dodged and crawled backward into the cover of a huge tree. Bullets splintered trees all around them. Death had found her, determined to take her. Arla waited for their guns to run dry. All she had to do was to stay calm and wait.

They were reloading. The drop of their magazines had a distinctive sound. In a split second, Arla ran from cover to cover, using the shadows. They were aware of her presence, as she planted doubt in their will. Her adrenaline burst through the roof. It was a gamble with Death, and she was pushing to see how far her fortune would take her. Her addiction to cheating Death was by far her worst sin, with wrath coming in a close second. Dana barked orders to flank Arla's position. However, confusion over Arla's the exact location forced each enemy soldier to separate from the group. They stepped into Arla's jaws, and she played them like a puppeteer. She ran deeper into the jungle, tempting them to follow. She wanted to take the danger away from Idris. Arla later stalked her first victim.

Arla removed her boots and placed them next to the hollow trunk of a dead tree. Silence was her friend. Every step the enemy took, she doubled hers, tiptoeing to her first victim's back with a blade in her right hand. Her mind turned blank as she came in for the kill. Her left hand slithered to his mouth to muffle his screams of desperation while her right pierced her knife into his lungs with brutal accuracy, punching a hole causing a slow, excruciating suffocation. The tremble of his heartbeats became slower as the blood drowned him. However, his trigger finger had found the willpower to pull. It was his last moment of resistance. The crackle of gunfire alerted Dana and the other soldier to his dilemma. Arla retrieved extra magazines from her victim's combat pouch and lay prone. They were firing in Arla's direction, and she stayed as low as possible. She crawled as rounds whizzed by inches above her head, smashing anything that stood in their way. She changed to a fresh magazine and cocked her rifle, making sure everything was tightly secured. Rounds peppered all over, but fortunately, none of them had found Arla yet. She crawled over a dirt mound to find a better firing position. Darkness was her advantage, as Dana could not pinpoint her exact location. Applying marksman's principles, Arla breathed slowly and aligned her sights. She fired two shots. They did not hit the target, and she adjusted her firing line. She released two more rounds, and her target fell. Dana panicked and started retreating. Arla fired in short bursts, conserving her ammunition and maintaining recoil control. She stayed focused and maintained superiority. She took the fight to Dana and ran from cover to cover, releasing a few rounds every few seconds to suppress Dana. In the end, Dana took a hit through her chest.

As Arla walked over to Dana, her mind began to clog up with bloody rage. Thinking how close she was to dying made her crave revenge. Even in death, Arla's foes would know no peace. She took her blade and slowly slit open Dana's neck. Dana's eyes turned wide open, just as Tae's had been. It was a gruesome satisfaction for Arla. It felt good, and it kept Arla under control. Nobody said war was pretty. Thus she buried her judgements deep into a sullied earth. Arla ran back to Idris.

As she traced her steps back to Idris, Arla saw a man well dressed in a red suit standing over Idris. He had long, curly, dark hair. He spooked Arla, and she screamed, "Get away from him!"

The red man raised his hands and stepped back a few feet. He was wearing sunglasses, and the lenses were coated in silvery chrome. His wide smile showed his yellow-stained teeth. Typically, Arla would have trouble identifying these features in the dark, but it was probably due to sheer coincidence that he stood below the ray of a gentle moonbeam, like an entertainer illuminated by the grace of a stage light.

"Hello, Arla!"

"Who the fuck are you?" demanded Arla. She trailed the edges of tree roots, keeping the sights of her gun trained on the red man. Arriving at Idris's side, she checked his pulse. Idris was still alive.

"You know, if he does not get to a healer soon, he will die."

Arla still kept her sights upon the red man. "Who. Are. You?"

"My apologies," said the red man gaily, as he bowed. "I am known by many names. My names cover the sky, the sands, and the city. But my real friends remember me by my true name. I am Hamzees. Mazy Hamzees."

It took Arla a few moments to recall why that name was familiar. The red man felt the awkwardness. "I'm not what you pictured me to be?"

"No, not really. But what are you doing? Why are you here?"

"I'm here to give you a hand. Get it? Haha! Oh no, it was not really a joke. Sorry. But I am here to help."

Arla was doubtful of his identity. She was suspicious of the conditions that had caused his appearance. However, she questioned herself as to why a man with a red suit would be standing in the middle of a jungle at the start of war.

"Do you hear that, Arla? It's the sound of more guards coming to find you. I am offering you a choice, and it seems to be an obvious one. Do you want to die or do you want to survive?"

Arla looked at Idris. His face had turned pale, and she could lose another friend by making the wrong decision. Without hesitation, Arla carried Idris on her back and followed the red man.

"Don't worry, Arla. As long as you are following me, I will guarantee you my full protection."

"Where are we going?"

"To my airship, of course! It's time to sail!"

As they stepped into the hull of the *Hibiscus Airship*, Arla and Idris stepped into the surreal and unbelievable. Nobody could really comprehend the dreamlike sequence only Arla and Idris were known to experience. It was only through their memories of what they saw in the airship that this tale could be told.

The Navigator was truly a wisp of the imagination that could only be grasped by the innocence of narratives.

Chapter 15

❖━━❖━━❖

What Idris Saw on the Hibiscus Airship

He remembered the hibiscus tunnel. On one rainy day he had led a young girl to safety through that tunnel away from the guards. He had been reckless, making old hearts wonder why youth was wasted on the young. When he met Arla the first time, she was the same as he in every way; it wasn't common to meet someone who was his age, and this had opened the possibilities of sharing similar ideals and perhaps mutual love. Never had he thought that a first and sudden encounter might lead them into a whirlwind journey. Idris was his name.

A man with a scar on his right cheek had one day announced he had no intentions of degrading anybody who felt ill towards decisions of the past. All had done their best, as he had. They were the courageous individuals who had just advanced into the fire of their short and uninspiring lives, trying to leave their world as great as before. They were idealistic and stupid. He laughed at himself, pondering upon the other opportunities in life he could have chosen. But as he sat under a forlorn tree attempting to search for solace and redemption in his past, he knew with great fortitude that he would not change anything. And so he wrote, hoping the struggles of a lost generation would be passed on to the next. He apologized, and he questioned: when or where does a person's life begin? It was a mysterious query few souls could ask on their deathbeds, but many souls in the middle of everything knew it all began with a parent's love forged from the rose petals of autumn.

Dara had played a part in Arla's life, and what he did for her would affect Arla in so many ways. It was the same for Idris. His family had been his anchor as he journeyed through the waves of struggle in Paradise. They had died the way all orphans knew. He grew hatred and vengeance in his heart, almost burning away the love he'd once had. Under that forlorn tree, he sat, salvaging whatever burned shards of a long-lost love that remained. Old age might have blunted his words and memory, but his old and experienced imagination embellished his dreams with a dramatic touch. There was a certain guarantee, however, that his stories would remain true to their intentions and beliefs. There was no other way to immortalise creatures with mortal expiration. Then he remembered. His life had begun on that airship – the airship on which he and Arla had stepped to the other side.

Where should I start? How long has it been? Years have passed since the day I woke to the rumbling hum of the red airship's engines. I was in a machine, a machine that had healed my wounds, and I felt new again. The sand-brown walls and the metallic grating on the floor were similar to the interior attributes of other airships I had flown. I was alone as I sat myself up from the medical pod on which I lay. I only remembered myself passing a rifle to Arla in the jungle. Yes, I remembered. We were supposed to be dead.

The hull door creaked open. A man in a simple white monkish robe walked in smiling. He was the red man; he was Mazy. He asked me questions about what healers were capable of. He was a friendly man, but rather eccentric. I regained my energy, and I felt an unusual vigour stirring within me. I gave my thanks, and he smiled. He told me the medical pod was part of his design. He and a bunch of other healers had worked together to create an engineering marvel. Mazy passed me a glass of water, and I felt its coldness wake up my senses. I was glad to be awake and alive. I stood up and started to walk about slowly. He examined me, making sure the healing had gone well. He laughed as he lauded my persistence. Every time we spoke, he never ceased to call me "friend". Every step he made, he had a little bounce in his feet. Rather peculiar.

My stomach growled. The hunger was unbearable. In the canteen, Arla sat with plates of food. The fragrance of fresh sweet rice stirred me up. I greeted and hugged Arla before I dug my greedy hands into my feast. Arla and I talked, trying to catch up for lost time. She told me war raged, and Mazy had had no other choice but to leave the confines of our world. I turned mad and insisted we return when I heard we had left Jas and Mae back on Bumi. Arla explained it would be too risky to look for them. We were to wait until the situation had calmed before we returned. So, wherever we were, we were far away from home. I still felt guilty about leaving someone behind. It tore me apart.

Mazy and Arla led the way after my meal. We walked through the confines of the airship. It was my first glimpse of what it felt like to be travelling on such a craft. There were various tubes intertwined in an organized method. Gushes of steam sputtered around machines that kept it running. The entire airship seemed to be automated, for I had seen no crew members. It wasn't what I had expected, but it definitely had a life of its own.

We stood at the entrance to the airship's bridge. I had waited my whole life for that moment, and it seemed somewhere in my own life I had forgotten how much I wanted it. I was the happiest boy the world had ever known. When the doors swung open, my world changed into the unbelievable. You would love it.

It was a grand bridge. It reminded me of the ones I had sailed before – gold carvings of ancient nagas and hornbills reminded me of the old grand halls of Kampung. The only exceptions were the countless monitors that exhibited various data in graphs and charts. There was nobody else but the presence of three souls standing next to the ship's wheel. I stared up front in amazement when I saw colours that looked like dots of paint in the dark. They were stars, swimming inside wavy pools of colourful milk. I thought we were flying upwards into the sky, but Arla laughed. She said we had already left the sky and right there, as she looked at me with her starry eyes, she welcomed me to the Universe.

Mazy explained as much as he could about the endless possibilities hidden within the Universe. He mentioned that the airship depended strongly upon its sails, which absorbed the power of the sun. That power — which was the Ketuhanan — allowed the airship to escape and sail further into the unknown. Arla grabbed my arm and pulled me towards an airtight door. She turned wheel to unlock it. Mazy gave his permission, and we walked out onto the deck, allowing the wind to blow through our hair. Feeling the strength of the airship was an experience. Yes, it felt exactly the way you might think. There were simply no words capable of describing the intense will the ship had to push forward. There was nothing ahead, and there was no destination set. As the Prince would say: sail the stardust.

On the deck, Arla spoke to me about the war that was brewing back home. She missed Jas and Mae, and she could no longer go back for Tae and Bell. She hugged me, and we laughed. There was something she wanted to do, so we ran towards the lower decks of the airship. The lower decks had bunk beds meant to house at least twenty men, but only one was occupied. She told me of a secret deck from where we could see the stardust. We went down a few more levels. There, hundreds of crates were aligned and arranged. At the lowest point, Arla opened a hatch onto a small, fragile stairway. Underneath it was the darkness of the Universe dotted with starlight. No matter where I turned, the Universe was everywhere. I held on to the railings as tightly as I could.

She led the way, and I followed. It was the first time I felt afraid of falling down. It seemed to be an endless drop, and I could not tell which was up and which was down. It was disorienting until I accepted the fact the airship was my anchor.

At the end of the stairway, Arla radioed Mazy, and we felt the monstrous weight of the airship shift into another direction. A wisp of colourful clouds emerged through the ether. As we sailed through them, I felt sprinkles of moisture touch the tip of my nose. Through the clouds, I saw a huge star flying through the Universe. It left behind it a trail of blue-white dusty light like a tail. We were close, and we flew right into it. It was bizarre and weird, and I felt it with my hands as I reached out. It was the same light as the twinkling fireflies back in Kampung. We were sailing the stardust.

Through the radio, Mazy told us stories. He explained that we were flying through the spirits of mythical creatures who once ruled the worlds of the Universe. By the fate of carelessness, they had become extinct, and their spirits now forever ran free with the stars. I did not see anything, but my friend Arla saw everything. I had never seen eyes any bigger than hers.

Mazy informed us that he had a few stops to make in different worlds. That piqued my interest to incredible heights! We were to visit other worlds different from ours! We were ecstatic, and that night we were sleepless. We talked and talked about what we might see and what adventures were to be had. It was also the first time I had heard Arla talk about her father and the stories he had told her. She said she was now lying down on the same bunk he had slept on. Every time I turned my head to see her, she was staring up at her father's initials, which he had carved next to the bunk. She had left her own next to his.

As we arrived at the first world on our itinerary, we basked in the glory of a hero's return. The aliens – at least we thought of them that way – looked exactly like us, with only a few unimportant differences. They knew about the airship, and we did not hide ourselves. It seemed it was only the inhabitants of our own world who were ignorant on the existence of others. They welcomed us, and we celebrated. Their houses were made of mossy stones, and their world was covered in nothing but the open plains of yellow wheat fields. Arla and I had our jobs to take care of. If we were to stay on the airship, we were to work for Mazy. We had agreed, and we complied. Based upon the ship's manifest, Arla and I unloaded the necessary crates. In the night, we partied to exotic music and refreshed ourselves with tea and biscuits. We met a few men and women who had originally hailed from Paradise: they asked for news of back home. They did not like what they heard, but it did not dampen their mood. They used to be part of a crew on the Hibiscus Airship, *until they decided to stay back. It felt better they thought, but mostly they had started a new life with a family because the prospect for opportunities were abundant. On that first world we visited, only the rose flower grew, bright and deep red in colour.*

It was the same for all the other worlds we visited. Their cultures varied, and each was as interesting as the next. We learned many things and explored many exotic locations we had never thought existed. We climbed the highest mountains and swam in the deepest seas. We trekked through the snowiest lands to the driest of lands. We faced hostile pirates who did not hesitate to try to steal our goods, and we fought courageously to defend the helpless innocent. And Arla always kept a petal of the flower that grew on the land of each world we visited. If I remember correctly, I still have Arla's collection of the various trinkets she collected. You can take a look later if you want to.

When we were flying through the Universe, Arla and I mostly talked. Mazy joined us occasionally, but he mostly kept to himself in the bridge. It was not an unfriendly gesture; it was a yearning to maintain solitude. When we told him one day about what happened to the Prince, Mazy locked himself in the bridge for a fair amount of time. Arla believed we all mourned the loss of a friend in different ways. That was when we realized we hadn't taken the time to mourn the loss of our friends. We were on the deck when Arla really broke down. She wept hard – as much as her chest could bear. It reminded me of a time when I'd found her in that tub trying to kill herself. She laid bare her emotions and she mourned with the heavy burden of loss. I sat next to her and waited. She needed a friend, and I was there. She cried until her burden left – until we both realized there was so much more to life than just surviving it.

During my time on the airship, I noticed that Mazy had the qualities of a cold man – not the cold touch one feels on the skin, but a cold persona that stemmed from his heart. There were moments when he could not really express the right emotion for a given situation. When Arla and I were on the deck, pouring our hearts to the Universe, Mazy displayed a blank demeanour that seemed to not compute. I ignored it, and I made no judgement. According to the Prince, Mazy had seen many terrible deeds in his life. Arla and I were fortunate to have our lives still intact.

One fateful day, the airship landed upon a world where the beautiful white flower grows. It was pale, and its petals were smooth. The moment we stepped onto the land, we smelled the most fragrant scent one could imagine. It reminded me a little of my dear friend, Jas. And my memory served me well, for the flower that grew was called Jasmine.

It was a huge world – bigger than ours. Its lands were covered with snow-capped mountains and green, lush valleys. Melted snow flowed down through the mountain's crevices to form mighty rivers in the valley. Along those rivers, life flourished and villages prospered. The people who lived there had the same wilful eyes as Jas. Mazy confirmed my suspicions. We were to visit Jas's mother.

Jas's family home was located on the peak of a lonely mountain. It was the toughest climb Arla and I had ever had to embark upon. It was almost impossible to conceive the amount of energy a woman needed to climb back down to get supplies. Mazy said nothing much, while Arla and I did not pursue the issue any further. Whatever questions we had, we saved for Jas's mother. As we finally reached the peak, the winds howled, and the winter breeze stroked us hard right down to our bones. To live in a place like that, Jas's mother must have been crazy.

From under the fog of winter, a small wooden hut emerged. Mazy opened the decrepit door. The lack of light was testament to the years of abandonment it had endured. The hut contained nothing but cobwebs and spiders. Mazy placed his pack next to the fireplace and began to build a fire. Arla and I huddled together, and we kept each other warm. As the fire burned, Mazy sat and told us a story about Jas as he passed around a bag of biscuits.

Jas's mother had once been a farm girl in her world, working in farms every single day to provide the necessary sustenance her family needed. But then came a time when war broke out. It was a war based on faith.

Communities separated, each believing its own "creator" was far superior to the rest. Jas's world fell into chaos. Even in that hut, raging battles developed over differing regions. Mazy tried to stop that war just as he'd tried to stop the war back on Bumi. But it was in Jas's world that he came to realize that violence will never be tamed by violence. The airship's weapon existed only to further divide a gap. Mazy told us that Dara and Penn had been part of his crew during that skirmish. They were young men then. They were loyal, and they were idealistic. The skirmish changed both of them.

At the funeral of Jas's mother, Dara and Penn had stood staring at her frozen grave. Dara turned fearful of committing himself to another pointless cause. Penn, who had lost the woman he loved to the war, carried his baby daughter into the airship, vowing to make Bumi a better place. Dara and Penn grew apart. Jas's world did not see any intervention from the airship anymore.

On every world the airship visited, people greeted it with fear or with joy. The airship was a monster, but also a blessing, and Mazy was conflicted. He still could not find a way to truly save Bumi. From what he understood, he was worried his airship would one day be used to rule the Universe. He was worried about adding an ill effect to an already fragile reality.

In that hut, we spent a night. I was sound asleep until I heard the wind stop wailing. The winter night had turned serene. Through the window, the winter moon shone its dreamy glow upon my face, and in its glory, I saw Arla standing next to the window. She said she had seen it. With graceful haste, she stepped through the door under the cover of her duvet. I followed.

We heard the white wolves howl from the valley below. It was a lullaby sung to sleepy heads as a reminder that their world still breathed. There was a tale told by the elders of the land. If the white wolves disappeared, the world would soon follow their fate. The spirit of white wolves was forever intertwined with the roots of the land. They were guardians, and the world was their home. Arla told me she had seen Bumi's spirit – the tiger from the Pasir Lands. Arla said it had been too far away to be seen clearly, and she believed it might have been the last. She said it had lonely eyes.

We walked on the snow, leaving behind our footprints as we went along. It seemed we were making a mess, but a beautiful mess it was. Arla held my hand as we stood in front of a gravestone. The name on it had been worn down by the wind and weather; barely a trace of the inscription was left behind: "… loving mother and soul mate". We were silent. Jas would have wanted to be there with us. She had never known her mother well, and there she was – her mother had existed. Arla crouched and touched her tombstone, saying nothing but a silent prayer. Next to her tombstone grew a lonely Jasmine flower. Arla plucked a petal and placed it in her pocket. She wanted to show it to Jas when we got back.

The next morning, we left Jas's world. We never knew why Mazy had brought us there. He had been rather quiet. I somehow felt the hut had once held something happy for Mazy. Although we had seen the hut as a terribly forsaken place, someone else may have seen it as a place that housed the best of memories. Mazy never told me what it was, or the reason he had gone back. I had my own theory, but the more I guessed, the sadder I felt about my ideas. Arla and I … we just let it go.

Back on the airship, Mazy returned to his usual self. His eccentricity returned, and his occasional joviality along with it. Arla and I had lost track of time. We no longer knew when we were or where were we. We did our part to see the Universe, and there was still so much to see. We felt hope, knowing we were not alone. I saw the airship as a harbinger of our liberation. With the airship, Bumi would understand. Once they had seen the airship and the places it could go, we would no longer be trapped in an unproductive cycle. We would live with passion once again. And, maybe, we could stop fighting each other.

I was on the storage deck cleaning up floors. Arla found me and asked for a game of checkers. She had finished her chores, so we talked again, and we laughed. I had never realized how much I missed smiling. And I had never realized how much I had missed Setia. I told Arla about my life. She was the first to actually listen to everything – how I lost my family and how I grew up. Our stories were similar. Since that day in the tunnel,

I never thought our friendship could grow the way it did. We loved each other, and we shared a bond. We laughed and laughed until our echoes rung throughout the airship. I vowed to return to Setia and marry her, and maybe have a kid or two. I was young … such innocent dreams. The airship was to me … well, interestingly, the airship was not really something magical. It had been magical at the beginning, when young minds were innocent. As one travelled with it long enough, it became something dreamily familiar. The element of magic disappeared, and it became like someone you knew. It became a friend, and living with it, one found oneself. To say that it had a life of its own was probably magical, as it hummed and drummed while its gears turned. What I saw on the airship was adventure, and on the storage deck, what I saw was my dear friend, Arla.

There was no one living on the last world we visited. The edge of a huge white salt land met the sea. Mountains covered the horizon where carvings of stone giants gazed upon strangers. Arla walked along the edge of the sea, the water touching gently on her feet. She had probably made the first ripple in its enormity. The ripple dispersed far away to send a message.

In that world, Arla and I confronted Mazy about the reasons for the journey we had taken. It had been surreal. But as we had been travelling, our world had come closer to death. Mazy kicked the ground and did a little jig. We knew he was angry, but it did not bother us much, as we too were angry. The most interesting people were angry. He danced with all his heart until he stopped to catch his breath. We sat on the ground to enjoy the show. As he danced, he sang at the top of his lungs. It was a song about sunshine and the shadows it created. He mentioned it had been sung by a songstress of his kaum. Finally he stopped and put his head back as he looked up into the sky. He just wanted to keep flying. It did not matter what was real and what was not; every story had its truths. He wanted to change things, but in that empty world, he realized it was not up to him. We asked whose responsibility it was, and he pointed to us. The adventure was to guide us.

As we floated back through the Universe on a course towards home, Mazy prepared tea for us. He thanked us for accompanying him on the journey. Many others before us had gone through that same journey, and the outcome had been the same. Some left Bumi and lived in other worlds, while some decided to stay at home and change it. Most of those who returned had forgotten about their journey and had been corrupted by society's dull imagination. They grew up living idly. The airship was remembered only as a dream children told. Adults never talked about dreams; they always talked about "reality".

I drank my tea, and we sat quietly. It was the end of our brief adventure, and in that brief moment, we were endless. We were free from the shackles of our world; we were full. But the melancholy of ending a journey as good as that one was painful. Arla and I were afraid we would never again experience something as great. Would we be drowned by a curse of emptiness? Would we be paralyzed, hoping to touch the airship once again? Mazy noticed the look in our eyes. He had seen the same look in the eyes of those who had travelled before us. He asked us seriously and wondered: Did we really want to go back?

Chapter 16

When They Returned

Arla and Idris were home. The *Hibiscus Airship* had landed in the Pasir Lands, within the vicinity of the Southern Lands. A few had noticed the presence of an unknown airship. Air raid sirens had blared for a battle about to ignite.

"How are we going to explain this?" asked Idris. "I hope they don't bomb us first or something like that. Questions first?"

"Mmm … not much has changed since I left," said Mazy. "It's a little rundown, but still has its charm I see." He carefully took out his sunglass and put them on. Arla smiled.

"I seriously hope both of you made the right choice in coming back here," muttered Mazy.

The trio walked from the airship towards the first Virtuous guard post. They were halted, and the lookout had his gun sights marked upon them. The suspicious strangers raised their hands, called out their names, and said who they were. Tension rose when nobody recognized them. Though the costumes they wore were vaguely similar to the local form of dress, Arla, Idris, and Mazy looked as if they were from another world.

Two Virtuous soldiers came out of their bunker and proceeded to cautiously check these peaceful intruders. They were dumfounded at the sight of three eccentric individuals smiling and grinning.

"Halo, we're with the Virtuous. I'm Idris. I used to be a captain in your ranks. Is it possible that we could meet your commander?"

Without saying a word, the guard punched Idris in the groin. Arla and Mazy immediately raised their hands up. "We just want to see your commander!" said Arla. "We are Virtuous soldiers as well!"

"Well except for me ..." whispered Mazy.

"Shhhh!" replied Arla.

With hoods covering their heads so they couldn't see, and their hands tied behind their heads, the trio was marched in single file towards an unknown location. Idris continued to groan in pain. They heard gossip being thrown around as the Southern people lined up to witness their march. Equal comments of flattery and criticism were hurled about. But none was as offensive as one remark that described Idris as limping like a newly circumcised monkey.

Arla was taken to a holding cell. A dry draught emerged from a rat-sized hole. The air coming through stunk and made the whole cell stuffy. To anyone who was claustrophobic, it was probably the worst place to be. Arla was not amused. She yelled for the attention of the soldiers who guarded her, asking them for water and food. She also screamed derogatory insults to stir the rookies' emotions. This gave Arla a fun distraction. She managed to convince some of them to give her water, although she was unclear of its origins. With it, Arla was able to pull through.

On her third day of confinement, with only a meagre measure of bread for food, Arla was taken to an empty room for interrogation. She noticed a contraption that looked like an uncomfortable bed. It was an interrogator's wet dream. The soldiers placed Arla's bare back on to the chilly bed. Arla squirmed as she tried her best to confine her irritation.

A female soldier wearing a green leather jacket started by asking obvious questions. Arla responded to every question with a simple one-word answer that would have annoyed the friendliest of interrogators.

"I just want to see your commander," said Arla as interrogation went longer than it deserved. Green-leather-jacket soldiers always seemed to be oblivious to the art of making people talk. Arla took advantage and controlled the pace of negotiations.

"I never thought I would see you again," said a familiar voice from a corner of the room. She no longer had that wild hair Arla had come to know. The eyes of the woman in black military fatigues were drowning in exhaustion. Although her face had assumed the façade of an elderly woman, her features remained consistent enough for Arla to recognize her. It was Jasmine. The spirit of her old friend that Arla remembered, however, had been misshapen and now existed as desolate rags of old age.

"I cannot believe it," said Jasmine. "You and Idris. Where did you go?" said Jasmine. "I thought you were all dead."

"Jas ... Jas ... I ... You poor thing. Look at you," Arla said softly. A tear slid down Arla's cheek. She felt the numbness of abandonment pour out with Jasmine's words. Arla had no words that could ease her guilt.

"It's all right, Arla. I just wish you had taken me along as well. I heard ... you've seen my mother?"

"We did," said Arla, but she choked on her speech.

"You don't have to say anything. Idris told me about Mazy and the adventures you had. His eyes held the same emotion yours hold. That guilt—"

"I'm sorry, Jas. We were trapped in the jungle. If it wasn't for Mazy, we would have been dead."

Jasmine lifted her arms, and instinctively her soldiers left the room. Jasmine tied her hair unto a ponytail and raised her sleeves up to her arms. Arla was still restrained upon the bed.

"Idris and Mazy, are they all right?"

"Yes, of course they are. I had a long chat with Idris. We caught up on many things. My mother was the highlight. He told me about it with so much life, I actually felt she was still alive next to me. I felt I belonged somewhere. After all these years, it was weird to find out that I am not from this world."

"But you are from this world. You are the daughter of both worlds. You are proof that other worlds exist, and you are an example of the belief that we can exist together."

"Then tell me, Arla. Why do I feel as if this world I have been fighting for has forsaken me in everything? Why do I feel I do not belong? Why should I fight for it? I should … just go home."

"Your father, Jas. You are still fighting because of your father."

"Hahaha! Don't you know? He is dead!" shouted Jasmine. "He was executed. I was too late. His ashes were never returned. And here I still fight on. Why? I'm tired, Arla. I am so tired."

Jasmine walked over to Arla's side and gently rested her head on Arla's shoulder. Jasmine quietly wept while all Arla could do was to comfort her the best she could.

"I am sorry, Jas. I did not know. I am really sorry. But we can make this right together again. We can make this right. We can go back to where we were. Maybe we should leave this world together and let it be. We don't owe it anything."

Jasmine removed herself from Arla's embrace and gave Arla a long-overdue hug. Arla felt as if they were friends again. She felt a long-expired bond had been reformed and all was well. Forgiveness was the sweetest redemption a person could give.

"I'm glad you are still alive, Arla. Everything will be the same again. I'm glad."

"Do not worry, Jas. We will take care of you," Arla whispered as she kissed Jasmine on her forehead. It was the reassurance that Jasmine had sought for a long while. "Jas, let's reunite with the others. There is so much we need to talk about. How is Mae? Is she with Idris now?"

Jasmine did not answer. They walked arm in arm as Jasmine dragged Arla out of the interrogation chamber and into a locker room where Arla dressed properly in new clothes. Jasmine knew it would be bad news to mention Mae, and she did not want to cause any more unnecessary hurt. Jasmine thought it was best for Arla to figure out Mae's story herself.

When Arla was ready, they walked along a corridor. When they reached a door through which Arla could hear Idris and Mazy speaking, Jasmine turned to Arla and stared at her. "Mae is dead. She killed herself … for Tae."

Arla felt another surge of guilt shoot through her skin. It was another punishment she had to endure. Jasmine wanted Arla to feel it. With her steely eyes, Jasmine wanted Arla to understand Mae's death was her doing. It was her responsibility; it was her treachery. And in Arla's heart, she admitted her fault.

Mae's death was her burden to carry, and the dead give no forgiveness.

"She found her brother's body," said Jasmine. "It had been left to rot on the streets. She carried him back home and I helped. I attended Tae's funeral by the lake. Too many good men had died that day. And we thought both of you had died as well. You can't imagine the sorrow and hopelessness we felt."

Mae's love for her brother had been strong. Mae had always stood on the sidelines as she watched her younger brother grow up to be a man. She saw him grow in strength and in mind. The moment he found another woman to share his love with, Mae knew he was ready to leave her to live his own life. Mae's heart broke when she knew her little brother would no longer follow in her footsteps. Her long faithful companion through the up and downs of her life would no longer be there. She celebrated with jubilation, but the strings of her heart tore silently. Tae noticed that, and they had a talk – by the same lake where he was later cremated – about how they would always be together no matter the changes of time. Tae vowed to take care of Mae as he always had. When Mae saw his lifeless body resting on the streets alone, her final heartstring broke. She said a final farewell at the lake and the waters claimed his ashes. With no friends besides Jasmine, Mae on one lonely night had strapped herself with explosives. She stood alone in front of the guards' headquarters, and she rushed in. Paradise went up in flames that night. It inspired many among the Virtuous to die rather than surrender. Mae became a divine hero, her story passed on as a tale of courage.

Arla was next to Jasmine on the platform where Arla had first met Penn. Idris and Mazy had brought the airship closer to the Virtuous base of operations where countless soldiers stood in awe. They could not believe the stories they heard were true. Whispers swam through the ranks as they wondered about the intentions of the man who rode in it – the man they knew as the Navigator. Mazy was a mystery to them. They saw him as a god, but also as a ghost that manifested itself in flesh and blood. Their perception of reality had been temporarily warped into fantasy as they dreamt about whether Mazy measured up to the stories told. Mazy was a legend, an ethereal force with a mysterious power that held sway in the mind of mortals. He himself did not realize it, but Mazy stood on the same pedestal as the Heavenly Flower herself.

"I feel the same, Jas," said Arla. "So much has changed, and I still have not grieved enough. There is so much hate. So much death. If you want, we can leave this place together. Mazy said the decision was ours. This will be his last trip here. He will never return again."

"Why now? Why did he show up in the jungle to save you and Idris?"

"I'm not sure. But he saved us. We are back here to take you along with us. Let's move to another world, Jas. Let's leave everything behind."

"It's not simple, Arla. I want revenge. I want to kill the ones who are responsible for my father's death. I want to at least be certain they die."

"I understand, Jas. But this anger of yours will not give you the answer you need. Just let it be and leave. We have disturbed the fate of this world long enough. Maybe it's time to just let it go."

"That's what a coward would say. Listen to yourself, Arla. Have you forgotten the principals of the Hibiscus Party? They were based on the words of the Navigator himself. Are you saying it was all for nothing?"

"I'm not saying anything, Jas. On my journey on the *Hibiscus Airship*, I saw something different with my own eyes. Mazy did not say much. He let us see and let us develop our own thoughts. I believe he took us on a journey to tell us there's another way. There's another way we can live."

"Such dreams! I do not have that luxury. Every day is a fight for survival. Just across the horizon lies an armada of dragons ready to attack. We repelled a few assaults, but the next one will be the last. I have suffered too many casualties, and our food supplies are running low. The Southern Lands depend on the Gardens in Paradise for food. With their sanctions, we lost the will to fight. But no matter what, I will not abandon my men. Not like you …"

It was desperate. Arla had walked through the Southern Lands and noticed the countless injured men and women lying restlessly on the ground. The dead were stacked in piles, ready for the coroner, who would light them on fire. As they burned, their ashes were carried away in the embrace of the wind. Mourning mothers, sisters, and widows gathered around the bonfires, wailing as they wished to follow their loved ones to a place they could not go. Young boys and girls carried guns that were bigger than themselves, standing next to each other looking into oblivion. They held their guns tightly to their chests. When Arla walked among them, they saw her as the dark angel they had prayed for.

"Can you stop it? Surrender?" asked Arla

"Surrender? Did you hear what you just said? Seriously, what did that weird guy do to you on his airship?"

"Your soldiers can barely fight! Do you want to see them die for nothing?"

Jasmine delivered a swift hard slap that sent Arla flying onto the floor with her hand on her cheek. Jasmine stood on top of her, tormented by the fate of revenge.

"Arla, they did not die for nothing! They died for the Hibiscus Party! They died for Bumi! That airship! That airship was the thing that started it all. And you want to give up? Even after they killed our friends? You want to just give up? When the Forlorn are still out there?"

"You can choose to surrender, Jas. Before the innocent gets killed—"

"I can't, Arla. I can't! We started it. We will finish it. I will not abandon them."

"We fucked up, Jas. The only way is to leave this place and let it heal itself."

"You've changed, Arla. You have turned into a coward."

It was the break of dawn. A young sun rose from the horizon, where the Pasir Lands lay. An armada of Forlorn warships had lined up in preparation for the final assault. Black dotted lines filled the skies like flies homing in on a corpse. Jasmine stood by her men, making sure they knew she was there with them to the end. "Check your ammunition," she told them. "Make sure your rifles are set. Kiss your family goodbye. This will be our last stand! Do not meet them on the field. Let them come to us in our lands. Remember you have done your best! You are the Hibiscus! Let this be our finest glory."

The thunderous wrath of the Forlorn came in waves of bombardment. The ground shook as explosive shells broke the Virtuous defensive line in an instant. Panic surged through its ranks as soldiers and officers ran in all directions with no purpose. Only the loyal and the determined stood with Jasmine. As the behemoths of destruction came hovering above them, hundreds of Black Guards parachuted down among them for the final extermination. Every nook and cranny of the Southern Land was fought over to the bitter end. Every son and daughter unhesitatingly sacrificed his or her life for an idea preached by his or her father.

Room by room, door by door, Jasmine had managed to regain certain sectors of the Southern Lands back from the Forlorn. She prayed for her last stand to be mindlessly glorious. If she died, she would take the entire Southern Lands industrial complex with her. She would scorch the earth completely, turning it into another barren wasteland. The last fragments of the Virtuous resistance had gathered in a warehouse. Heroism had taken over their minds, and a glorious and honourable suicide was their wish.

Jas's faithful right-hand man cried to the survivors, "To the call of the trumpets shall we heed! Run and charge down the valley of Death, for the first Virtuous brigade will stand against their tide of victory!"

With the cheer of the Virtuous, Jas led a charge out from the warehouse and into the open. As the blinding glare of the sun distorted her sight, a huge flash of flame burst out from one of the Forlorn airships. It had taken a hit from an unknown attacker. It had sustained serious damage, causing it to gently crash into the ground. The other Forlorn captains were alerted to a new threat and refocused their weapons. And, like flies, the ships dropped from the skies one at a time. Jasmine's saviour came in the form of a menacing red airship. It was huge, and its cannons were terrifying. Nothing stood in its way, and nothing caused a dent in its hull. In a few short minutes, the greatest battle known to Bumi had ended with severe casualties on both sides. The red menace was the only airship left flying. Jasmine and her soldiers stood in awe of a monstrous god.

The red airship landed among a desecrated heap of its fallen foes. Its sheer monstrosity struck fear and gladness in Jasmine's spirit. She could not believe she had survived.

From underneath the airship, Arla ran out shouting for Jasmine. Idris followed. Jasmine's wide eyes had doubtfully accepted the mass spectacle of ashes and red.

"Jas! Are you all right? We thought we were too late!" said Arla. She was carrying a rifle, poised to fight.

"Arla … Idris … What happened?"

With open arms, Arla and Idris engulfed Jasmine in a warm embrace, although her demeanour was cold. Mazy was on the deck gawking at three close companions. His face was blank and lifeless. Jasmine sensed his disquiet. As she gazed from below, his cruel imposing stature shadowed his battlefield with an iron fist. Jasmine felt his arms shake. The call of danger and death fuelled his capacity for excitement. Jasmine recognized his addiction, and he knew she did.

Jasmine and her most trusted captains were invited to board the airship. They gawped at its innocent, unfamiliar interior, questioning how a machine of such fearful power could appear to have such a modest temperament. Mazy wore his rainbow-coloured dress. His eyes were hidden behind round shades. He was mellow, and his manner was enthusiastic as he gave Jasmine a long hug.

"Jasmine, Jasmine, Jasmine!" said Mazy in a peculiar voice. Arla and Idris took no notice. "Such courage you've shown in battle! Look at how much you have grown since I last saw you as a little babe!"

"Thank you."

"Your father would be proud. I always was fond of him, and your mother as well. They were such wonderful people. I apologize for not taking a chance to visit you as much as I should. I am a bit shy. But no matter! We are back together again!"

Jasmine was tired. She did not care about her past. She was angry, and she wanted to finish the fight. She saw no other way to end the war peacefully. Her corrupted anger presented her an opportunity to bring her dreams of revenge to reality.

"Mazy, I am glad as well. I forgive you for not helping my father and me bring back Bumi on its feet, and I forgive your complete selfish intention to let the Forlorn take over."

Mazy sighed. "I have tried my best, Jasmine. I tried to save the world, but the world did not need saving. I realized there was one thing the Prince and I could not fight. It was like fighting a ghost. No matter what we did, no matter how hard we fought, we could not help but realize that we were turning into the power we fought against."

Jasmine walked towards the airship's wheel and held onto it, caressing the old mahogany wood it was made from. She felt a familiarity with it. "What was that ghost?"

"Greed, my dear. The Prince and I tried to bring out the best of society. But the more we held on to that hope, the harder it was to grasp. It wasn't long before someone we trusted took advantage and betrayed us. I won't forget that face – that child we thought could take over from us."

"Who was it?" asked Jasmine.

"Allorn – the guy you know as the face of the Forlorn. He started it. He thought it was better to govern the world through control. It wasn't with an iron fist, but it was something subtler. He was a genius. I give him that."

"How did he do it?"

"Usually, the best way to control how people act, think, and feel is to give them what they want – hope, salvation, and freedom. Although, in his case, these concepts were never real. A false sense of security was all it took to plant a seed of control within the minds of the people. Time took care of the rest."

"So he did it without the people even realizing it. Like a ghost."

"Yes, very much so," Mazy said. "We tried to stop him, but he grew stronger until I became a villain in a cautionary tale – a monster out to get children."

"But with your airship you could have taken Bumi back!"

"I have to admit, Jasmine, that the tale had some truth in it. I built this airship to travel to worlds beyond ours. But as a monster, I gave it weapons. I have used it before, and that use resulted in the Pasir Lands. An entire population was wiped out in a blink of an eye. Those who supported me and my plans turned away in an instant. I vowed never to return."

"Only you did return."

Mazy smiled and adjusted his round shades. "I travelled to different worlds. Those who were part of my crew and those who would not stand with the Forlorn left with me. As the years went by, most of my crew decided to stay on other worlds for opportunities they never had on Bumi. In the end, I was left alone. Penn and Dara were among the few on Bumi who wanted to make a difference. They wanted to bring meaning to their lives and the lives of others. I taught them as much as I knew. They were clever and determined. I've never had greater students or more loyal friends."

"And now, they are dead," said Jasmine. "Because of you, they are dead. They are dead because they followed an idea! A stupid idea about our world could change through senseless violence!"

"You've got it wrong, Jas. I never taught them that. I taught them about other worlds, other cultures, and how we could peacefully coexist. Through innovation and exploration, we can understand how we could live together! I have never shown them violence or religion. I have shown them what their minds are capable of achieving. I have shown them the limitless powers of imagination and reason. Through that, the understanding of our spirit could burn like wildfire. I hoped that, if I sent them back to Bumi, they could pass on the torch to you – both of you. I believed it was the only way to fight back against our wicked nature."

"You don't have the right to justify your actions. They are dead! People are dead! They died believing in your ideals."

"I am guilty of it. You cannot imagine the weight of the burden I carry. I tried to stop the killing … the senseless killing. Penn and Dara did what they needed to do. Their actions were of their own, and they tried to achieve their goals peacefully," said Mazy with a sigh. "I am old now. My bones ache in many different places. I am tired, Jas."

"So am I. I just want everything to end," Jasmine said, nodding in agreement.

Arla felt for Jasmine in many ways. When Arla and Idris had sailed away on the airship, they had seen it as a peaceful vessel that spread a message of harmony. But Jasmine had grown up. She had grown into a spiteful adult who saw the airship as an instrument of war. Arla and Idris deeply wished she had gone with them.

Jasmine walked over next to Mazy and gave him a hug. She felt the thin frame of his body under his clothes. He was feeble, and his heartbeats were weak. Mazy was really living his last. Thus, trying to end his misery, Jasmine took out her knife and stabbed it through his chest. He held onto her back, feeling the pain surged through his nerves. Arla screamed, and Idris ran to them.

"The world will be a better place without the old interfering any longer," whispered Jasmine into Mazy's ear. He smiled as a stream of tears flowed down his cheeks and he slumped to the ground, his blood drenching his rainbow-coloured garments. For a long while he sighed. Finally he was able to greet his friends and family members beyond worlds and the stars.

Idris tried to save Mazy, but realized it was too late. With Mazy cuddled in Idris's arms, the world seemed to spin on a weird axis that Arla could not understand. Mazy had been an important relic who had given them hope for saving what was left. Her mind drowned in utter hopelessness, and her colours melted away. With weapons raised, Jasmine and her captains took over the airship, leaving Idris and Arla to decide if they wanted to be hostages or willing accomplices.

"Please, let us put his body to rest," said Idris reluctantly. "Just let us do that, and we will help you."

In the Navigator's chamber, Arla and Idris removed Mazy's bloody clothes. They bathed him and dressed him in his favourite red suit. They placed him on his regal bed. The window gently let in the afternoon light, illuminating him like a saint who had finally found peace. They surrounded him with various trinkets he had collected through his travels, and gave him a silent farewell speech.

"She did not have to kill him. She did not have to," said Arla.

"She has changed, Arla. Everybody in this world changes. Do not think this is your fault."

"It was my fault. I trusted her and I invited her on board."

"Listen, Arla. There are so many things we cannot change. What matters now is that we save what we can for the future. Jas is going to use this airship, and she will definitely not use it for peaceful means.

Whatever happens, we need to delay her from using it as a weapon. If all else fails, we need to destroy this airship."

"Wait – what? Are you insane?"

"Mazy and I talked about this when you were with Jasmine. He told me that, if anything were to happen to him, I should destroy the airship. It is too dangerous to be in the hands of the Forlorn or the Party. He gave me this as well." Idris retrieved a small drive from his pocket. It had the Hibiscus flower printed on it. It glowed in a radiant colour of green. "This, Arla, contains every bit of knowledge Mazy ever gathered. If we are needed to rebuild this world, this will help us."

"But it won't come to that, will it? Having to rebuild Bumi?"

"I don't know, Arla. I hope not," said Idris. "But, anyway, when the time is right, I need you to create a diversion. I will run off to set the airship to self-destruct. Do you still remember how to control the airship?"

"Yes … yes. I still remember. Mazy taught me well."

"Good. When we head back into the bridge, you take the wheel. All right?"

Arla agreed. Idris gave Arla a warm embrace and kissed her on her forehead. They looked into each other's eyes and remembered how far they had come together as friends. They knew an end was coming, but it was the journey they'd shared that made it hard for them to leave each other.

Under the orders of their new captain, Arla flew the airship directly over Paradise. The Forlorn military airships had tried their best to halt the red airship's advance, but to no avail. They had been crushed in its immense power. Jasmine's comrades cheered on. Arla noticed a dangerous smirk on Jasmine's face as she stared forward at the objective of revenge. For a long time, she finally felt an exhilarating intensity of having nothing standing in her way. Her arrogance grew by the distance.

Paradise was in a state of panic. Civilians ran on the streets trying to get away from the shadowy grasp of the airship by running into the

Pasir Lands. Priestesses from the Temple preached and prayed as the day of reckoning had arrived. Lady Malla rallied her people to sacrifice their lives for the defence of the city. If they died, the Heavenly Flower would grant them their wishes. With her call, many had stayed back to make a stand.

"If they are eager to meet their Goddess, I shall grant them their wish," said Jasmine.

With an order, one of her captains launched an intense barrage of exploding shells down onto the streets. People were blown to pieces, and their blood flooded the drains. Lady Malla survived the first onslaught, but her legs had been crushed. She was alone, covered in the blood of innocents. She crawled, but the stumps of her legs bled profusely. She turned to stare up into the sky, and nothing looked back. With eyes wide, she died alone.

The sheer intensity of destruction caused Mr Allorn to offer his surrender on the roof of his building. With a megaphone, he worshiped the red airship's brutality and cruelty. But Jasmine had no intention of surrendering. With the power she had at her fingertips, she wanted to end everything. She wanted to take everything along with her in a glorious blaze of mutual destruction.

"Ma'am? The Forlorn want to surrender. We have won! We did it!" said one of her captains. "Ma'am?"

"Arla, set the main gun to this coordinate, please."

"But, Jas, that would destroy the entire city."

The captains were struck with disbelieve. When they realized that insanity had consumed their commander, Jasmine took out her pistol and shot them dead. They never stood a chance.

"Thank you both for being here with me."

"Jas, what are you doing? This is insane!" shouted Idris.

"The Forlorn have given up!" said Arla. "Do not cause any more unnecessary deaths!"

But Jasmine's determination was set. She pulled her gun out and threatened Arla. "Do it! Set the guns to these coordinates!"

"Jas! The blue beam! Do you remember? The one I told you about? It will turn Paradise into a desert. The world will die!"

As Jasmine was about to pull the trigger, the voice of Mr Rizal on the radio caught her attention. "Look down below, Jasmine," he said. Jasmine looked through a monitor and saw Rizal and another man standing next to a hooded man who was on his knees. Jasmine paused to answer his call.

"Here! Is this what you want? Is this why you have come here? For revenge?" screamed Rizal. Rizal removed the hood from the kneeling man and revealed Penn. He was still alive and healthy. Jasmine stared with disbelieve while her father stared back up, smiling.

Jasmine lowered the ladder and ordered Rizal to bring Penn up into the airship. They would conduct further negotiations on the deck. Jasmine's insanity calmed. Arla stayed on the wheel while Idris and Jasmine went to meet their guests.

"Nice ship. I never thought it was real. To see it is awe inspiring," said a man wearing aviator shades. His beanie covered his pale, bald head.

"Who is this? I said only you and Penn," demanded Jasmine.

"This is Jeella. He will be our negotiator," said Rizal. "As you wished, here is your father."

Penn walked over and kissed his daughter on her cheeks. He was proud of her accomplishments and the courage she had shown. His eyes beamed with delight. "My daughter, look at how much you have grown."

"I've missed you. I thought you were dead," whispered Jasmine.

"Don't worry now. We are back together. Idris, my good man! You are still alive I see!"

"Yes, Penn. I am alive."

"You don't seem happy to see me. Why is that?"

"No, I am glad, Penn. We have seen too much. We are just tired. You, however, seem as if you have just awakened from a nice nap."

Penn shook his head and smiled as he placed his arms around his daughter. Jasmine cuddled into his safe embrace. "Come! Let's continue this discussion on the bridge, shall we?" said Jeella, pointing the way.

"I thought we were to discuss our plans on the deck?" said Idris.

"Come now," said Penn. "I really want to see the cockpit of the famed *Hibiscus Airship*. It's every child's dream to see it!"

With his sheer size, Rizal pushed Idris away and led the way. As they entered, they saw Arla at the helm focused on maintaining the airship's altitude.

"Is that the Navigator?" asked Rizal.

"Yes, she is," replied Idris.

"Where is Mazy?" asked Penn. Jasmine still held on to Penn. She was trying to return to being the innocent girl she had been years ago.

"He is dead," said Arla. "Your daughter killed him. His chamber is his tomb."

Penn's face paled as he showed remorse as a brokenhearted friend. He walked off to Mazy's chamber to pay his last respects. Jeella sauntered about, checking the dials and gauges of the airship. Rizal stood in a corner keeping an eye fixed upon Idris.

"So, you are the new Navigator? You are beautiful. Mazy chose right, didn't he?" said Jeella. He walked closer to Arla. "Is it just me, or have I met you before? What is your name?"

The scent of his breath sent a familiar chill down her spine. A painful sensation she had felt before came back to jolt her senses. She remembered the abuse she had experienced a long time ago – a monster with creeping fingers crawling on her body. Arla started to shake, and her vision darkened. Jeella gently placed his hands on her waist and whispered in her ear, "What is your name, love?"

"*Hey!* Get away from her, you disgusting shit!" shouted Idris. "Do not touch her!"

"I remember this smell," said Jeella, not paying attention. "Your smooth skin – it reminds me of a little girl I once knew. She was amazing. I cannot say much about her parents though. Sad really. I told those kids to not kill them – just to threaten them. But they got ahead of themselves. Too drunk to know what's right. But, hey! At least that little girl's parents won't be trouble no more."

"Arla, what is he saying?" asked Idris.

Her name – Arla – floated around the airship confirming to Jeella that his instincts were right. His longing for pleasures of the flesh sent a prickle of desire to his skin. His expression lighted up with delight, like a pig presented with fresh food. "I knew it! You are Arla Hibby. My, my, my, look at how much you have grown. Much better!"

"I said, don't touch her!"

Idris came at Jeella hard and punched him, pulling him away from Arla. She was paralysed at the helm, afraid to move. Jeella parried a few more attacks by Idris until Rizal came in and choked Idris into submission. Idris struggled pointlessly under Rizal's arms. Jeella laughed out.

"Enough! What is this? Jeella, enough of your ridiculous antics!" ordered Penn. "Leave Arla alone."

Idris stopped moving and realized the truth that had struck him hard. It was hard to swallow at the beginning, but he pieced everything together until he recognized the possibility that Penn was working with the Forlorn – or worse yet, he was the Forlorn.

"I'm sorry, Idris. Do pardon Jeella's rudeness. He can get a little out of control you see."

"Where is Jasmine?"

"Oh, she is in the chamber with Mazy. She and I had a little talk, you see, and right now she is making up her mind," said Penn.

"Making up her mind about what?"

"To stand by her father's side as usual or to give in to the fate of those who have been betrayed."

Idris struggled again. His anger fumed until Rizal had to knock him into the ground. Idris felt himself drift close to losing consciousness. Arla shivered.

"I am really sorry it had to come to this, Arla. It was necessary," said Penn. He walked in front of Arla and stared deep into her eyes, finally confronting a truth he so desperately needed to tell.

"I am sorry I lied to you. But it was a necessary lie for my plans to work. Our world is dying, Arla. Our world does not contain the unlimited resources we make ourselves think it does. Our population grows. We breed and feed like drunken parasites. Look down there! Look at how they run around with no point in sight. They keep breeding continuously and selfishly, and the excess population sucks the life out of this world. The more they produce, the more they destroy. My solution – or the Forlorn's solution – is control. It is the only way. We needed to control their lives. We need to control the population growth of our world. To start anew, we needed a war to exterminate the excess population."

"Did ... you ... kill ... my ... family?" Arla questioned. Penn ignored her.

"Mazy told me his story once," said Penn, "about how he met the Prince. It was a bleak and tragic era they lived in. But his story had a hidden truth – a truth about how the world's ills stemmed from us and from the lack of love we have for our world, which has consumed our world and left it as a rocky existence. Extermination was the only way."

"What are you talking about, Penn! This airship was the answer! We could have taken people to other worlds and let them live there in peace!" Idris emphasized.

"I would expect you to realize something important, Idris – you know, from the travels you enjoyed with Mazy. Do you remember Jasmine's world? What did you think happened over there? We came in, and we disrupted their way of life, thinking we could make things better for them. We showed them our ways, and they wanted more. They completely disregarded their own culture and ideals. They wanted an airship for themselves until they, too, killed each other for power. We colonized them in their minds. Without realizing it, we affected the fate of another world through our hands. How arrogant were we? We fucked up ourselves, and then we fucked others? And here we dare stand thinking we can live in another world without colonizing it to our own selfish greed. It wasn't a solution, and I strongly believed we should let other worlds decide upon their own fates. Dara and I saw this, and we left the airship. But it was only I who sought to find the best solution to our problem. And after years of searching, and finally meeting Mr Allorn, I believed this was the only way to make sure our world had a future."

"There is a better way," said Idris, as he winced at the pain of Rizal's weight on him.

"Still thinking about yourself, aren't you?" asked Penn. "You think colonization is better as long as you survive? So arrogant! Please let me tell you this: other worlds were having the same problems we were, and naturally they all turned to war. Their wars drained them, and their situations were hopeless. At least in our world, I tried to make deaths more meaningful! At least the Forlorn attempted to make death desirable and not pointless the way Mazy and the Prince had to fight. They fought to give up, while we fought to become heroes and to be blessed with the grace of the Heavenly Flower. Isn't that a better death than the rest?"

"You sick fuck! Tell that to those you had killed!"

"They are dead, Idris. Probably in a few seconds before their world turned black, they might have realized the truth. I sleep at night knowing their sacrifice has bought time for us to keep living."

"So you chose who died and who lived? You bloody shit!"

"I take no pleasure in it, Idris. I created the Hibiscus Party as an avenue to recruit people who had nowhere to go and nobody to care for them. I recruited people who did not have people who would miss them when they died. They were easily moulded to execute orders flawlessly. It's amazing how a purpose can inspire an individual to do extreme things – even giving up their lives."

Idris was speechless. Arla remained where she was, hoping not to catch a glimpse of her monster.

"We calculated the right percentage we needed to exterminate as the Hibiscus Party grew," continued Penn. "The percentage needed was higher than what the Party could afford; therefore, we needed to encompass those who were not in the Party. We needed a politically justifiable war. That's where Lady Malla fitted in with the Heavenly

Flower. There is nothing more powerful than the power of religion. With her followers and a constant influx of new believers, we had the necessary percentages to launch a great Red Flower Revolution. Everything was going according to plan until the *Hibiscus Airship* came into the equation. We had exceeded our quota. You, my friends, are now killing unnecessarily. I need to stop you. I am here now."

Idris was in despair as he finally accepted the lie he had been living. He realized he had wasted the love he had with Setia for a path not of his choosing. He was a puppet, and he had played well to the desires of a puppeteer and a grand audience of the fortunate. Jasmine sauntered onto the bridge. She had made her decision.

"Father, I am ready."

"My dear, I am glad to hear it. Is that what I think it is?"

"Yes, it's the petal of a white flower. Arla gave it to me. It was the flower next to my mother's grave."

Penn embraced Jasmine. "You look so much like her – so beautiful. I miss her so much."

"Thank you, Father. Thank you for everything."

Jasmine stood in front of Arla and held on to her hands. She looked deep into Arla's eyes, and Arla looked back. "Do not be afraid, Arla. This was meant to be. You are the Navigator now. You need to lead the world into a better future."

"My dear, what are you saying?" asked Penn.

Jasmine gave Arla an innocent, playful smile just like the smiles she'd given when she was young. Arla felt a calm surge through her stormy heart as she finally had her bearings straight. She remembered her friends who had given her a chance to live: Tae, Mae, the Prince, Deeza, and, of course, Bell. Their willing sacrifice had given Arla a chance at a life worth living. Theirs was a different sacrifice compared to the sacrifices made for Penn's ambitions. Their bond was forged through a journey of self-sacrifice and love; it was a compassionate martyrdom. With the memory of her friends, Arla turned the wheel to the direction of the Forlorn. Everyone fell and tumbled. Idris rose and ran to begin the necessary self-destruct sequence in the engine room. Rizal ran after him.

In the engine room, Idris, struggling to stay on his feet, began to adjust the correct valves that would produce the right pressure to exploit his plan. He felt the airship crash into buildings. The impact was strong enough to knock down a few steam pipes, causing white steam to fill the room. Idris heard footsteps. Rizal had arrived.

"You are like Tae," shouted Rizal. "I admired his fighting spirit. I really regretted his death. He did not deserve to be betrayed. He would have made an excellent guard. He would have protected Bumi from anything!"

"He did protect it!" Idris replied.

From behind the concealment of white steam, Idris charged with a broken pipe. It caught Rizal by surprise as Idris's makeshift weapon managed to pierce his abdomen. Idris kept stabbing Rizal until his back was up against the wall. Idris was fighting a cornered beast. Rizal was in a craze, trying desperately to grab hold of his foe. As another crash happened, the airship tilted on its side. Idris was thrown like rag doll amidst falling debris. Rizal had the terrible fortune of having the generator fall on him. It crushed his torso, but he was still alive.

Idris was in a daze, and his body ached in many places. He got up and staggered carelessly among fallen debris. He climbed up on what used to be the deck of the engine room. He wanted to see if the engine was still capable of self-destruction. He was lucky. The engine purred to life again and finished its self-destruct sequence. Within five minutes, the airship would burn in flames, leaving nothing that could be scavenged to build another *Hibiscus Airship*.

"Please …" Rizal begged, coughing. "Don't leave me …" Rizal coughed up more blood. He was the toughest man Idris had ever seen. To still be alive with half of his body crushed was testament to the challenges faced by Tae when he fought Rizal. Idris nodded to him in respect, but left him alone to either bleed out or burn. As the minute hand struck, Rizal's screams could be heard from the depths of hell.

Idris tried to get back onto the bridge, but his path was blocked by debris too heavy to shift by himself. He decided to approach the bridge through the deck, but the awkward orientation of the airship gave him no easy access. Idris crawled through metal struts and wooden beams to escape the airship. As he tried running back in through the other side, but an explosion threw him backwards onto a green lawn. The concussion he suffered made it tough for him to stand back up. He was helpless as he watched the fire consume the airship from tail to bridge.

Idris hoped the others were still alive.

"Jasmine! Jasmine! Where are you? Are you all right?" hollered Penn as he struggled to free his leg from the weight of a metal strut. "That crazy woman! Jasmine! Where are you?"

The fire had claimed the Navigator's chamber. The temperature rose, and Arla sluggishly regained consciousness. She felt the weight of the explosion on her body. Through her blurry vision, she could see the damage the airship had suffered. She was glad Idris had succeeded. Arla gently stood up on her two feet to find her left arm broken. She created a temporary sling using the clothes of Jasmine's dead men. She looked for Jasmine, but she was nowhere to be seen. Thick black smoke slowly encroached upon the bridge, giving Arla little time to find her friend. She too shouted out loud, "Jas! Where are you!"

"Arla! Arla! I need help! Please, I need your help!" replied Penn in return. "We can help each other to find Jasmine! Please, I need to save my daughter!"

With a heart heavy with a guilt, Arla followed his voice. In a corner, next to the raging fire, lay Penn, injured and pinned to the ground. Arla immediately tried to remove the strut from his legs, but the sheer weight of the metal was too much for Arla. "This is too heavy. I cannot lift this," said Arla.

"Keep trying! We can do this! Let's lift it up together."

They tried again and again. They managed to move the strut a little, but they realized that moving it could cause even more debris to fall on them. Arla started to choke on the thick smoke. They could hardly breathe. With every bit of energy they extended, their reactions became sluggish. It wasn't long before they both would pass out. Arla seriously considered leaving Penn behind. "Penn, it is hopeless. I cannot lift it up."

"You are not going to abandon me you hear! Chop it off!"

"What? What did you say?"

"I said chop my leg off! Fucking chop it off!"

"With what? There is nothing sharp!"

"Anything, dammit! Jasmine! Where are you?"

Through the smoke, a hand emerged to touch Arla's shoulder. Arla was relieved to find it was Jasmine.

"My dear! Thank goodness you are safe!"

"Arla! Help me lift!" ordered Jasmine, whose face was covered by a water-drenched cloth.

As they lifted, the strut moved. The wooden ceiling of the airship came crashing down upon Penn's rescuers. Penn was further trapped within a heap of debris; the pain he felt was unbearable. All hope for Penn was lost.

"Just go! Both of you, just go. Get out of here."

"No, Father! We can still save you!"

"No, don't! The fire is already here. I can feel it. Go before it gets worse! Arla! Drag her away, please," said Penn.

Without hesitating, Arla pulled Jasmine away from Penn. Jasmine screamed as she slowly lost sight of her father within the black smoke. Through the confines of corridors, Jasmine heard her father's faint whisper. The black smoke might have gotten to him first, thought Arla. It was a better way to go.

Jasmine and Arla helped carried each other as they looked for a way out of the burning airship. As they stepped upon green grass, the taste of fresh air was delicious. Breathing had never been so wonderful as they regained their composure and focus. Jasmine said nothing. She lay down upon the grassy lawn watching the airship turn into a flaming tomb for men she used to know.

"There he is! I can't believe it! He made it out!" said Arla as she ran over towards Idris. He was unconscious, and Arla immediately gave him the kiss of life. Idris woke up to the violent pumping she was administering to his chest, causing him to choke and beg for mercy.

"Stop it! I'm awake!" Idris said. He was glad Jasmine and Arla were safe. They were the only friends he had left. Arla laughed.

"Jasmine! Come on over here!" Arla hollered.

Jasmine was recovering on the ground, her hands shielding her face from the glare of the sun. But someone's shadow suddenly emerged to block out her sun. He was breathing heavily, and his lungs wheezed. Jasmine at first thought that, by some miracle, her father had survived. But from the way he stood and the way he longed, she knew it was not Penn.

"Enjoying the view I see," said Jeella shallowly.

Realizing the danger was not over, Jasmine rolled over to her side as fast as she could. But Jeella had anticipated her strategy. The bottom of his boot found a spot on Jasmine's torso that would do nothing but cause pain. He kicked repeatedly. She choked in pain as his attack pinned her to the ground. She managed to block a few blows, but his sheer anger destroyed her stamina, and she was unable to defend herself. With a good stomp on her head, Jeella crushed her into a lifeless body.

"Jasmine!" shouted Arla. She stormed forward as fast as she could, trying to tackle Jeella, but before she could reach him, Jeella smiled and ran away. Arla stopped at Jasmine and saw blood coming from her mouth. Bruises covered her face in a gory mess. Idris gave chase, and with a determination to finally defeat her monster, Arla wasn't far behind.

Jeella ran away like a maniac, pushing and shoving anybody who stood in his way. He shoved innocent bystanders into the path of his pursuers to delay them as much as he could. After a short distance, Jeella ran into Arla's school. Students and teachers who were gathered at the gate witnessed the grand scale of destruction the airship had left in its wake. They had been ordered to evacuate. It was a perfect place for Jeella to escape to.

Idris and Arla charged through the main entrance. Nostalgic memories of the bad and the good filled Arla with conflicting emotions. She noticed nothing much had changed in the place where she'd grown up. She knew the place like the back of her hand, giving her an advantage as she and Idris went on a hunt for a monster. Idris opened a janitor's closet and picked up duct tape and two brooms. Arla broke a nearby window and collected the sharpest glass shards she could find. With ingenuity, Idris taped the shards to the broom handles to create a makeshift spear for each of them. They were armed, and they were ready.

"Stay together," Arla whispered. Idris nodded.

Arla's school had turned silent as a grave. There were a few little stragglers left behind, each in a rush to get out. They cared nothing for a man and a woman carrying broomsticks in the hallway.

"Where is he?" asked Idris.

A scream came from the end of a corridor where Jeella made a disturbing appearance. He laughed profusely with his yellow teeth flashing. He carried a small, innocent, young girl, his slimy hands covering her mouth. Idris and Arla gave chase until they cornered him in front of a bathroom.

"Don't come close, or I will break her neck," said Jeella. "Do you remember, Arla? Do you remember when my hands crept to your neck like I'm doing to this little girl? I tasted what you felt! I taste the same with this girl."

"Let her go!" replied Idris.

Arla and Idris froze in place. Jeella was too unpredictable, especially if it involved the life of an innocent young girl.

"It's going to be all right. Just look at me," said Idris to the little girl. She was crying softly.

"Oh! She really reminds me of you, Arla! Look at the way her tears flow. So similar ... especially her skin. So smooth. Do you remember?"

Arla dropped her spear and walked up closely to Jeella. "Yes, I remember your cold, merciless touch that defiled me and scarred my mind."

"Mmm? Keep your distance, Arla. We don't want to have the blood of a little girl on your hands now, do we?"

She maintained a distance and walked around Jeella. "I remember that night when my parents were killed in cold blood. I remember you the most," said Arla. "I did not know about fear and insanity until that night. I was so scared, my fear crippled my capacity to live another day. That was my fear of a monster – a monster like you." She stopped and faced Jeella. "But like any other monster, you can be defeated. It took a long time, and it took a long journey, but now I finally know I can stand against you. For too long you have haunted my mind and my soul. My friends – my friends who have lived with me – they have helped me stand against you. I owe everything to them."

Jeella sensed a change in Arla. He now held no sway over her. The crippling fear that had once rooted Arla to his control no longer dominated her state of mind. His chain of slavery had been broken. Arla gave the girl a gentle smile. "All monsters can be defeated," she told the child. "You have family to help."

With an act of courage, the little girl bit Jeella's hand with all her might. Jeella let out a shriek that sunk Idris's heart in an instant. He had never felt the kind of dark abyss a man like Jeella could impose on another. He finally understood the bravery Arla had demonstrated as she lived every day with her memories. Idris was proud of his friend. She had changed since the day he had met her a long time ago.

Blood flowed from Jeella's hand as he lost his grip on the girl. Arla took a chance. She attacked and pulled the girl away from his grasp. Jeella skittered into a corner of the room and escaped.

"Idris! Take the girl to safety!"

Without hesitation, Idris left with the bloodstained little girl. He passed the girl to a teacher who waited outside. The blood on the girl shocked the teacher, but the little girl managed to convince her teacher that Idris was her saviour. The teacher promised to get help as soon as possible. But time had been wasted, and he realized his mistake. She shouldn't have let Arla deal with Jeella alone. Swiftly, Idris ran back to find her.

The hallways were drenched in the evening sun's deep orange glow, casting shadows of pillars on the floor. Idris followed a trail of bloodstains on the floor. He detected signs of a few scuffles in areas where the droplets were disturbed. He could not tell if the blood he found was from Jeella or Arla. He knew no man could still be standing on two feet with that much blood lost. Arla had most probably been injured as well. His thoughts for her safety were further complicated by the fact he had completely forgotten about her broken arm. She was not fit to fight a madman. Idris deeply regretted his mistake. He should not have left Arla to fight her monster alone. It was a mistake that could mean the end of Arla.

The blood trail led Idris towards a garden where he saw two silhouettes standing underneath an oak tree not too far from where he stood. They were struggling in a fight with each other, and one fell over the other. Idris could not tell which was which, so he ran as fast as he could. It wasn't far, but his mind played tricks on him. As eager as he was, time and distance seemed slow and far. It felt like a dream to Idris. His heart raced as he noticed they had stopped. They were now standing still, facing each other closely.

"Arla!" shouted Idris.

When he got close to them, Idris saw that Arla had pierced Jeella with a broken stick. She twisted her weapon in different directions, relishing in a pain Jeella suffered. The physical pain Arla exerted was no comparison to the emotional trauma she'd had to endure over the years. To Arla, it was a satisfying craving she had sought a long time. It was a revenge that calmed her anger and her spirit. In his final breath, Jeella felt fear, and he passed on to an unknown. Arla let go of Jeella, and he tumbled to the ground at her feet. She was the last person he saw.

"You did it! I can't believe it, you did—"

Before she could celebrate, Arla stumbled a few steps backwards and collapsed against the bark of the oak tree. She sat down, gently holding on to a glass shard that was embedded in her torso. She was covered in her own blood. Her broken arm lay slumped at her side while the other kept her wound from further bleeding. Idris removed his shirt and immediately applied first aid the best he could. Arla turned weak, and her lips mumbled his name as she thanked him for everything.

"No, Arla. It's not your time yet, you hear? You are going to make it."

"I was careless," she whispered, and she coughed. "I'm losing blood. I don't think I am going to make it."

"You will, dammit! Just keep talking to me!"

Tears welled up in Idris's eyes. The sun on the horizon shone upon them.

"What a view," said Arla. "Bell and I used to have our lunch here together. It was my favourite thing to do. I can't believe I ended up here. What a fitting end ..."

"Hey, hey! Wake up! Keep talking to me. Don't you go to sleep. Do not leave me alone!"

"Idris ... thank you. You saved me ... I was glad I met you that day when we climbed into that tunnel."

"And I am going to save you again, you hear? Keep talking! Oh no ... no ... Help! Anybody there? Help!"

"It's all right ... come closer."

A gust of evening wind carried the scent of a longing. Idris moved close to her lips thinking she wanted to say something. With a quick peck, Arla gave him a kiss on his cheek.

"Arla?"

The silence under the oak tree was suddenly deafening. Idris's faded scream filled Paradise. Come twilight, Idris's world faded into black.

Chapter 17

Last Farewell

Arla was fortunate to have survived her encounter with Jeella. Help had come not a moment too soon, and she was stabilized in the Healing Chamber of Paradise. It was also fortunate that Idris had the blood type Arla needed. Idris volunteered to share his blood the moment he got word of his compatibility. Arla went into a coma for a period of six months. Jasmine recovered next to Arla, recuperating from her injuries, and adapting to her new way of life because she had been partially paralysed. She had to depend on a wheel chair most of the time, but she barely left Arla's side until she woke. They were then inseparable. Even in old age, their conversations were playfully youthful.

Bumi was at the dawn of a golden age. The Forlorn had eventually crumbled after the Red Flower Revolution. Mr Allorn had managed to survive; however, without Penn's leadership, the Forlorn was plagued by infighting. The elite and the wealthy relied heavily upon their laurels to provide their sustenance. They never understood the creative hard work that must be invested to maintain a stable community. They depended on commoners to work while they consumed relentlessly to support their own lazy lifestyle. Years of Forlorn control had helped the elite get what they wanted without moving their muscles bit. The commoners, devoid of the privileges the elites had, soon were bound by ineptitude, as were those who controlled them. Paradisians scavenged and degraded themselves to their lesser instincts. Iron horses that once galloped on the streets were nothing more than crumbled scrap. Those remaining few who were hardened by the beatings of stubbornness in their hearts kept Paradise from melting into chaos, and Paradise endured.

With the knowledge preserved by Mazy, Arla and Idris went on to build a community from the ruins of Kampung. It was a community for those who were weary of the Forlorn regime. Grand architectural marvels were rebuilt, and its history was preserved. The community strove as more joined in the work. People from underground believed in grander ideals and dreams. They strove to live and ensure that a better world was passed on to the next generation. It was a community in which knowledge and education were pinnacles of accomplishment, and hope derived from witnessing bliss in the eyes of others rather than through a selfish faith of an afterlife. Their community operated on its own, and its existence remained a concealed entity, like a word of fiction.

With the end of the Forlorn's military might, the seeds of Arla and Idris's plan to rebuild came to fruition. Jasmine, even though she had been partially paralysed on the last day of the Red Flower Revolution, led a council that governed with a new administration for the people. Through covert approaches and dealings, Arla and Idris managed to convince engineers, healers, and agriculturists to defect from their old government to join their banner. The Gardens had stopped producing food at an optimal level, while infrastructure had become degraded; some had even collapsed. Realizing tragedy was afoot, loyal Forlorn subjects had clung on harder to a dissipating mist, passing responsibility and blame like wild dogs barking into a non-existent night. Only in a matter of time, the old government fell, and the new world grew. As Paradise's corrupt union collapsed, and a new age of prosperity and influence took its place. It was a cycle of rebirth.

Arla and Jasmine formulated foreign policies to deal with other worlds that were part of the Universe. Trade agreements were established, and a set of controls towards cultural intervention was drafted, maintaining respect for the differences among the different worlds. With the cooperation of other worlds, peaceful technology and knowledge were shared and expanded upon. The future was bright, and the Universe had turned into one. Fleets of airships dominated the empty and dangerous domain of space. It was a treacherous domain fit only for those who were adventurous and curious – people who craved a freedom not many possessed.

Idris dedicated his life to preserving the real history of Bumi. His policies for education were profound and not confined to the demands of society. He designed education to fit in the idea of self-learning. It was a system meant to inspire young minds to learn for themselves even after they graduated. Children were taught the most fundamental elements of life, and the meaning towards achieving happiness. As he usually mentioned, "The journey is all that matters. Wonderful relationships are the treasures you see at the end."

But they knew that time was an independent factor that kept everything under a constant cycle of change. Their bond built through countless years of hardship would soon be broken to the natural limitations of physical cessation. The obsession to search for a fountain of youth would bring disappointment when people comprehended that immortality worked in a unique way. A person's physical form might be destroyed and take its place among the stars, but individuals actually live on forever as those who were still grounded by gravity remembered their names and their lives. It was one of those ethereal awareness that made people feel as if a delicate force was floating between gigantic waves of high seas. We are within ourselves, and at the same time, we explode like Roman candles as we express the hidden power of our noumenon.

Jasmine was the first from the era of the Red Flower Revolution to pass on. She gave a speech at the newly upgraded Gardens during a Harvest Festival. She enjoyed watching young adults dance away with their partners. Idris and Setia sat next to her, clapping and cheering. Late in the night, without anyone noticing, Jasmine slipped into a nap from which she never woke. She passed away as an old woman. She never found someone to love and spend the rest of her life with, but she had been content with the love Arla and Idris showed to her every single day while she lived. Her body was cremated in the underground lake of Kampung. Her name and a statue would stand forever facing the waters of the lake, guiding heroes back to shore and into the heavens. Arla didn't attend her funeral. She kept to herself, as she felt her old bones creak a whispered portent that her own end was near. She waited eagerly to join the spirits of the Universe.

Death is a secretive phantom, a woman who enters, her arrival unannounced. Her beauty demands the respect of all, even though her beauty is unseen. When Death visits, she kisses like a long lost lover who returns to reclaim one's heart. Nobody has ever rejected her temptations to the other side. Death visited Arla on one fine afternoon when she was standing upon a stool to reach a picture. With her deteriorated physical strength, Arla fell down hard on the floor. She spent her last few days going through pictures of years gone by. It was said that, on her deathbed, she held on to memories. In her will, she declared she was to be cremated and buried under the oak tree where she and Bell had shared their love.

Idris was the last hero left from the era of the Red Flower Revolution. He too, was not going to live forever. Hence, it was in my interest to meet him before the tragedy of old age took him forever. I was indebted to him. I thought it was best to listen his words before Death's seduction took him.

We were walking upon the streets of Paradise. He told me stories of places where the most important milestones in his life happened. He was jovial and interesting; there was not a moment in which he had to pause. He was a man who had led a life he was proud of. Nothing stood in his way but the decay of age. Upon reflection, he was also a man of contemplation. Sometimes we walked without saying a word. The best moment to know a man is when he is at his most silent.

Setia was still as beautiful as she had been when they were young, adding her smiles to the stories of her life with Idris. All of their family shared the same passionate eyes many had come to know. Idris's humbling speech and his encouraging motivation spurred his students on to a better wonderment in the rainbows. I was one of them, and the most concerned. I never knew of a world before mine. It seemed we were two strangers walking upon a different frame of existence. But the seed he had planted was the flower I saw.

"I can't believe that all happened. It's amazing," I said.

"Yes, boy. It seemed amazing to me as well. Same perspective I believe."

"Did you ever have any regrets?" I asked as I chewed upon a biscuit we shared.

"Never. The joy, the grief, the anger, and the pain – I would not trade them for anything else. But sometimes I wish I had a chance to relive it all over again."

I gave him the last piece of the biscuit. "Here … it's the last bite." He kindly rejected. We walked for a few more steps until we reached a café where we could buy coffee. The interview with him had already ended, and I just wanted to hang around to get to know him better. He was not the way I had expected him to be. Even though he was a hero and all, not many people recognized him as they carried out their daily lives. He was like a character among many other stories that were told in Paradise. Idris's name still was whispered in the night, but the true nature of Idris had faded into a wisp of fantasy. He had turned into a figment of everyone's imagination, larger than life.

"Did you know that Arla was raised in that old orphanage that used to be over there?" he said, pointing on to an old decrepit building designated for demolition. "When I was in the Hibiscus Party, I was ordered by Penn to keep a close eye on her."

"You know, I always wondered. Why did Penn want you to rescue her?"

"I don't really know. I never did ask him about it. It could be because he loved Arla as his own daughter. Maybe it was because the guilt he carried for killing his best friend, her father. I'm not really sure."

"During that incident on the airship, when you realized Penn was actually working for the Forlorn, you must've known what he was up to."

"All I can say is that he was not a bad man. He was an individual who fought for what was right. The Navigator had influenced our minds in many ways, and each of us would end up with a different story to tell. I cannot tell you exactly what really happened. But I can tell you the version that I believe is true."

Idris and I walked down the street, passing by the old abandoned orphanage. He breathed a sigh as he took a sip of his coffee.

"Well, what version is that? Why did he want Arla?"

"He knew Arla was the key to finding the *Hibiscus Airship* and Mazy. He wanted to use Arla to destroy the airship before the Forlorn could use it for power," he said, stuffing his fingers into his jacket pockets. "There was a promise between Dara and Mazy. If Arla was found to be a special child with a curious mind, Mazy would come back to take Arla so she could learn all about the airship. Penn knew about this and wanted Dara to help him bait Mazy to reveal himself. But Dara refused."

"So he had Dara killed?"

"No, that wasn't what he wanted. He was working with the Forlorn, but he was also working against it. He was desperate to reach the airship first. He told Mr Allorn that Dara had been the guy who knew where Mazy was. He innocently thought that, once the information had been 'extracted', he would get to the airship first. But Mr Allorn hired a monster. Jeella went overboard intentionally. The criminals Jeella hired were out of control, and Jeella did not even care. Penn vowed to avenge the death of his friend. He was guilty for a deed he regretted very much. He hoped that, by bringing Arla into the Party, he could at least redeem himself and have the adventure she had been denied."

"But the Party was a lie, wasn't it? Why would he want to initiate Arla into the Party if it was to redeem himself?"

"The Party may have been part of an elaborate plan for mass extermination, but it was how he ran it that gave hope to its members. He was still *the* Penn that Dara had known. I am not condoning the vile acts he committed; neither am I forgiving him. There was still a good man in him. Nobody could be a good man for long when an act of violence tore a family apart. He saw the airship as a monster, and as a good man, he acted to slay it for the betterment of our world."

"But what he did – that was evil."

"Say what you may. He is dead. The dead will never speak again. Whatever his plan or motivations were, we will never hear about it in his voice again."

We had passed through Arla's old school and walked the plains of green grass towards a solitary oak that stood on a small hill. On the summit of the hill, we saw the *Hibiscus Airship* lying in ruins not far off. It had been turned into a memorial to mark a brief war that had once raged. In its wake, the skyline of a thriving and blooming city emerged from the ashes.

"Beautiful, isn't it?" I said. "It's all because of Arla, Jasmine, and you. I could not imagine what would have happened to Bumi without you."

"It was not just us. Tae, Mae, the Prince, and the brave souls who gave their lives for a future – willingly or not – also deserve recognition. They gave us a chance to survive another day. They are the unsung heroes."

I kept silent. I enjoyed the view as the rising sun emerged over the horizon. The calm morning breeze gently shook the leaves on the oak tree. Old, ageing leaves that had hung on for too long gently fell from its branches, landing softly on the green grass. Idris and I were fortunate to be graced by the dance of the falling leaves. We sat there until the heat from the sun was too much to bear. Idris touched the bark of the oak and whispered a few words I could not hear. We walked down the hill and back to his home.

"What did you say?" I asked as I opened the front door of his apartment. He had the most humble abode I had ever known. Trinkets filled his home, each one representing a memory from his life. Setia was in the kitchen cleaning up the dishes. She greeted us with the abundant cheer I had come to love. Even though I was usually there for only a short visit, she always wanted to cook something for me. I did not mind; I had loved her cooking since I was a little child.

"Hmm?"

"I said, what did you whisper to the oak tree?"

"Only she would know …"

I felt terrible allowing myself to pry into the personal affairs of Idris. All these years, the bond between Arla and Idris had been filled with wonder. They loved each other, but not as lovers do. Their love for each other was a testament to a beautiful friendship. They were soul mates whose fates were intertwined with the threads of a great journey. We had a light meal at the dining table, coupled with nice tea. It did not take long before Idris requested that we leave him alone in his bedroom.

Under the dim lighting of a table lamp, I wrote furiously, putting on paper the first notes I would use in writing my book. I experienced a fierce wave of inspiration. My words danced with furious love over an empty white plane, and I prayed my words would interweave my fate with the past. The embellishment of life with words demonstrates a conviction of what a wonderful world we live in.

I continued writing into the night, until finally I needed to leave. The stars had emerged in the company of the moon. I knocked upon

Idris's door, entered his room, and walked to his side. He was just waking after a long nap, and he was a little delirious in my presence.

"I will be leaving now," I said. "It's night, and I will be working tomorrow."

His eyes were open, staring at an empty ceiling. His was lethargic and not quite awake. "I see it," he said. "Look at the beautiful colours. I am sailing the stardust ..."

I looked up, but I saw nothing but the plain, normal ceiling. He woke. "Ah, yes, my dear boy. Thank you for visiting. You need to work tomorrow? Do not let me hold you. Thank you again – for everything."

It was the first time I had seen him weak and his eyes old. He had raised me up well, and I saw him as a hero. A child imagines that the heroes he or she grows up with must have the power of immortality – they will never grow old. But it was a selfish fantasy that tricks our minds from expecting the inevitable. As I hugged him and said my last farewell, I felt deep regret I had not allowed myself to understand that everyone ages, and Death was knocking. Maybe if I had seen it sooner, I would have cherished the moments we had much more. I was not sure what made me believe it, but I knew that was the last time I would feel his embrace.

In the night, he drifted against the waves of stardust, guided ceaselessly into the arms of the Universe. It was the grandest farewell a living being could ever receive.

A journey well lived ...

Printed in the United States
By Bookmasters